SKORZENY

Dancing with the Devil

A NOVEL

HUGO N. GERSTL

SKORZENY

Dancing with the Devil

A NOVEL

HUGO N. GERSTL

PANGÆA
PUBLISHING GROUP

SKORZENY: *Dancing with the Devil*

ISBN 978-1-950134-12-0
Pangæa Publishing Group
www.PangaeaPublishing.com

Editor: Pnina Ophir
Proofreading: Dory Morik
Special advisor: David Shomron

Cover images:
Creative Commons "Otto Skorzeny,"
Bundesarchiv, Bild 101III-Alber-183-25,
© Alber, Kurt, licensed under CC-BY-SA 3.0 DE

Red abstract light smoke background © Uldis Bindris / Dreamstime

Cover design and typesetting by
DesignPeaks@gmail.com

For information contact:

PANGÆA PUBLISHING GROUP
25579 Carmel Knolls Drive
Carmel, CA 93923
Telephone: 831-624-3508/831-649-0668
Fax: 831-649-8007
Email: info@pangaeapublishing.com

To

Mark & Bev Fienberg and
Kathy Turkell, Peter Evans and Greg Cohen
who never thought they'd end up as Dedicatees

To Colleen Miller

*

And, as always
FOR MY LORRAINE

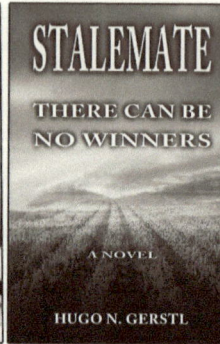

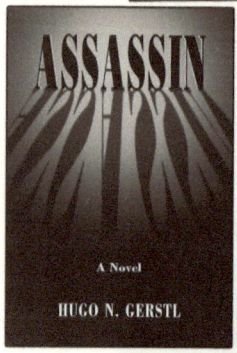
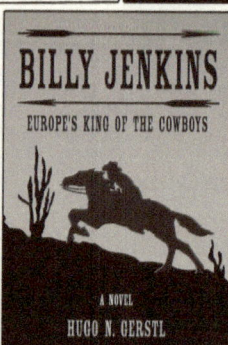

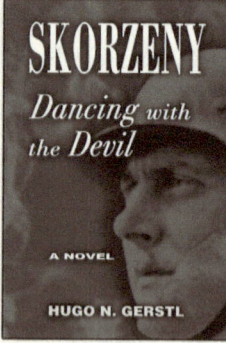

Prologue – April 1962

The man with the large, jagged scar on the left side of his face had been seated at his favorite table in *Horcher's Restaurant-Bar* for ten minutes, when a patrician-looking woman, conspicuously younger, joined him. He stood and held her chair out for her as she sat, and nodded familiarly at the headwaiter. Moments later, another waiter brought them cocktails.

They'd been sitting at the table, casually conversing, when the bartender approached them, accompanied by a strikingly pretty woman in her late 20s, and her escort, a well-dressed man of about forty. The two newcomers were somewhat younger than the first couple.

"Herr und Frau Skorzeny," the bartender said. "Permit me to introduce you to two of your countrymen who are in Madrid for a brief visit. They seem to have had a most unfortunate incident. They were robbed at gunpoint a few minutes ago. Someone told them this place was a haven for Germans."

"I'm so sorry," the first man, who was quite tall and ruggedly handsome in spite of the scar, said sympathetically. "Perhaps you might join us for a drink to calm your nerves. Waiter?" he called, "Drinks for our new friends."

"Thank you," the other man said, after he'd ordered for himself and his companion. "I am Hans-Dieter Dielmann. This is my fiancée Anke."

"Otto Skorzeny," the taller man said, shaking the other's hand. "My wife, Ilse. You are not originally from Germany?"

"*Wien,*" Dielmann replied. "But how did you guess?"

7

"I recognize the lilt. I was born in Vienna. One never loses that accent."

"*Grüss Gott*!" The four of them held their drinks aloft and clinked glasses.

For the next half hour, the two couples engaged in animated conversation. It became clear that each found the other's companion to be more than a little bit seductive. There were more drinks, then somewhat flamboyant flirting, and soon Skorzeny's wife invited the young couple, who had lost everything — money, passports and luggage — to stay the night at their sumptuous villa. There was something irresistible about the newcomers. A sense of sexual promise between the two couples was in the air.

After the four entered the house, at a crucial moment when the playful flirting reached the point where it seemed time to pair off, Skorzeny, the charming host, pulled a gun on the young couple. "I know who you are, and I know why you're here. You're Mossad, and you've come to kill me."

The young couple did not flinch. The man said: "You are half-right. We are from Mossad, but if we had come to kill you, you would have been dead weeks ago."

"Or maybe," Skorzeny said, "I would rather just kill you."

Anke spoke up. "If you kill us, the ones who come next won't bother to have a drink with you. You won't even see their faces before they blow out your brains. We want you to help us."

After a long minute that felt like an hour, Skorzeny did not lower his gun, but he asked, "What kind of help?"

"Israel needs information. We'll pay you handsomely."

"Money doesn't interest me. I have quite enough, thank you."

"Name something you want, then."

"I need Wiesenthal to remove my name from his list."

"Okay," he said, "that will be done. We'll take care of that."

Skorzeny finally lowered his weapon, and the two men shook hands.

PART ONE

1

In my life, I've been called everything from the most dangerous man in Europe to Hitler's favorite soldier; from daring hero to archvillain; and from ultimate opportunist to the devil's right-hand man. I've saved hundreds of articles from newspapers and magazines spanning the globe, mostly sent by friends, which attribute the most fantastic, vile, and perplexing actions and plans to me. So many people, friends and enemies alike, have started or spread rumors and defamations, and an equal number have overexaggerated my so-called "heroics" until the line between truth and supposition has become irretrievably blurred. What good would I accomplish by denying the charges against me? People will believe what they want to believe, just as they always have.

Yet, I am not the only one affected. I think of the comrades at whose side I fought, of the brave soldiers I commanded who died in the maelstrom of war, whether on the field of honor or lost forever on the steppes, in the forests, or in the prison camps of Soviet Russia. No matter what is now said, I believe those on both sides of the cataclysmic events of my lifetime never personally fought unfairly, even though they were involved in a dirty war the likes of which mankind had never before experienced.

In spite of everything that has happened in my life, I firmly believe there is military honor and that it will continue to exist as long as there are soldiers, or until one-half of our planet has destroyed the other half. Is it ever possible to learn from the past?

This book is not intended as a denial, nor as justification for what I said, witnessed, and did. Nor can I, nor do I, claim any sort of moral high ground, either in my personal or in my professional life. It is, quite simply, a story told by a witness to recent history, one who has had time to reflect on events and people, on conditions and plans; a witness whose chief characteristic was to be a patriotic German who was born in Vienna, the Imperial Capital of Austria-Hungary, in 1908.

I'm told that of all five senses the most powerful and the last to go is that of smell. Indeed, I can still recall the smells of my childhood and my youth, *Würstl* in the *Prater*, Vienna's great amusement park, or in the street fairs outside City Hall, sizzling, greasy, salty-sweet. Cotton candy. *Kaffee mit schlagober*, strong, rich coffee with gobs of whipped cream which, to this day, cause me to remember the afternoons my father took me to the Sacher Hotel. The yeasty savor of *Sacher torte*, the sweetest-smelling pastry in the world. The vanilla-egg aroma of *Salzburger Nockerl* or *Palatschinken*, thin, doughy crepes filled with apricot or plum jam and topped with powdered sugar.

The rich, comforting smell of old leather chairs which had felt the brush of saddle soap for generations. The pungent, acrid smell of death and cordite on the fields of battle. The breath of young girls with whom I stole a kiss in a dark corner. And the most mesmerizing aroma on Earth, a woman's own scent just before or after she's made love.

When I was 18, I decided to follow my father and my older brother Alfred into engineering. I entered Vienna Technical College engineering school in 1926, where I found myself one of youngest in my classes.

Most students, war veterans who wanted to complete their studies, were much older. Although these battle-hardened former soldiers, who'd seen more than their share of misery and death, commanded my respect, I hungered for things I'd not yet experienced: physical fulfillment of two sorts.

I had by then attained my six-foot-four-inch height and had hardened my body through a regimen of competitive sports and a Spartan diet. I felt gratified when several fraternities sought me out. The most attractive, the *Marcomannia Dueling Society*, followed the tradition that revolved around student duels. These brotherhoods had been famous in Germany and Austria since the Revolution of 1848. The *akademisches fechten,* on the dueling floor with long, doubled-edged swords, was a way of life.

Shortly after I joined *Marcomannia*, I attended my first *mensur*, which took place one evening in the basement of our fraternity house. The room was quite large, 40 by 45 feet. Members of both competing fraternity houses, our *Marcommania* and the *Teutonia*, whose house was three blocks away, crowded around a large mat that had been placed in the center of the room. An overwhelming pungency pierced the air, a combination of male sweat, unwashed bodies, nervousness, determination, and not a little fear.

From different corners, two men approached the referee, who stood quietly in the center of the room. Each wore similar padding covered by chain mail to protect the body, fencing arm, fencing hand, and throat; steel-mesh goggles covered the eyes. I heard the referee speak clearly, words he'd undoubtedly uttered more than a hundred times.

"Gentlemen, *Mensur's* neither a duel in the traditional sense, nor a sport. No one 'wins,' no one 'loses.' The fighters stand their ground at a fixed distance throughout the duel. Each of you fences at arm's length. The goal is not to move but to stand in one place, while attempting to hit the unprotected areas of your opponent's face and head. You are not allowed to flinch or dodge. Your goals are twofold: you try to inflict injury to your opponent; and if you are struck, you endure your *Schmiss* – your wound – in the heroic spirit of a German warrior."

Two older gentlemen approached the center of the mat. "These medical practitioners, Doctors Schneider and Weissbrodt, will be in immediate attendance to ensure that no *serious* harm comes to you. Whichever of you suffers the *Schmiss* will be properly stitched. Like me, either one of them can stop the fight at any time."

"Are you sure you can take this, Otto?" Clement DesRoches, one of my fraternity brothers, asked. "The first few times I saw a *mensur* were pretty nauseating. I've seen some vicious scars." I noticed that Clement himself bore a jagged scar on the left side of his face, running from just below his ear to his lower cheek. "Some of those 'doctors' are quacks, but most are legitimate. Sometimes they're encouraged to do a poor job of sewing the scars back up, so they look even more gruesome than they are."

At that moment, I heard encouraging shouts as the referee blew a whistle and the two combatants started hacking away at one another. There was little finesse and virtually no grace as the young men seemed fully intent on killing one another. As I watched, I deduced there were three movements, the feint, or false attack, the swing of the sword in a slashing manner, or the stab. Each man issued a low growl from time to time to distract the other's attention.

After what seemed like only a couple of moments, but may have been more, I heard a loud voice shout "*Ergebnis! Score!*" followed by a shocked scream. The room exploded in a cacophony of sound.

"*Halt!*" shouted the judge, blowing his whistle sharply three times.

"*Schmiss! Schmiss! Schmiss! Schmiss!*" echoed through the room, the shouts coming from our side as the *Marcomannia* brotherhood ecstatically gave voice to their great victory.

"*Betrügen! Betrügen! Betrügen!* (*Cheat! Cheat!*)" came a return roar from *Teutonia*, but I noticed it was shouted more in resignation than in passion.

The vanquished man lay face up on the mat, trying not to scream as his brothers poured red wine into his fresh wound, which already displayed blood and gore and gave off a sickening sweet stench. I felt blood rush from my head to my stomach and back again, and knew with a certainty that I would faint unless someone relieved me very soon. Thank God, Clement, who was nearby, pressed a cold, wet rag against the back of my neck and passed a vial of ammonia under my nose.

As he propped me up and walked me to the far end of the room, I wondered how – or if – I would survive my own first *mensur*.

In the *Marcomannia* we wore white caps, black bands, and our chests were trimmed with white and gold. Every year on the first Sunday in September the student groups joined with the masses of people at Heroes' Square to officially demonstrate for union with Germany under the black, white, and red flag. This was the only political demonstration in which I regularly participated from 1924 to 1934. On the other hand, I played a great deal of sports: soccer, track and field, skiing, kayaking on our beautiful Danube, and sailing on our Alpine lakes.

I will always be an *Echte Wienerer*, a real Viennese, at heart. To this day, there is nothing more distinctly Viennese than the *kaffeehaus*. On September 5, 1926, my three closest friends, Heinz Rogge, Baldur Schnacke, Clement DesRoches, and I left the German Union demonstration at 4:00 in the afternoon. We were all in a celebratory mood since the day before the League of Nations had voted unanimously to extend an invitation to Germany to join.

By the time we reached the *Innere Stadt*, it was drizzling and Austria's once-Imperial capital, wore a moist, gray cloak. The soothing *whoosh-whoosh* of the windshield wipers combined with the wet cobblestone streets, and the glorious spire of St. Stephen's Cathedral. Vienna's magnificent buildings, monuments, and parks, which lined the *Ringstrasse,* never ceased to enchant me.

Although Austria was feeling the pinch of the punitive Versailles Treaty, it was not as bad here as in Germany, but since Austrians were German at heart, we could not help but lament over the down-spiral of life in our neighbor to the northwest. But Vienna? Better a splintery park bench in Vienna than a mansion in any other city in the world.

After we'd parked Heinz's car in a side street off the Ring, the four of us walked three blocks to Café *Weissenhof,* our favorite coffee house. As I entered the L-shaped place, I glanced around the high-ceilinged oak and teakwood-paneled main room with its chandeliers and comfortable booths. The pendulum on the large clock on a nearby wall swung gently, hypnotically from one side to the other.

"Just like last time, it's ten minutes behind," Clement DesRoches said, glancing at his wristwatch. "It's 4:45. The *Tageblatt* will be delivered in twenty minutes. Meanwhile, I'll read the London *Times* to see what they have to say about the League of Nations vote." He got up, walked down the bay to a rack near the front door, and took out a freshly pressed copy of the English newspaper which had been inserted through a slotted stick, then fitted inside a rattan frame.

When Clement returned, Josef, a swarthy, middle-aged waiter, who'd often attended us before, and who always looked as if he needed a shave, approached our booth. "The usual, my respected near-Herr Doktor-Engineers?" he asked solicitously, knowing each of our preferences for Viennese coffee with whipped cream.

"Thank you, yes," I responded.

Within moments, Josef returned bearing four cups of coffee and eight glasses of water on a large tray, which he set in front of us.

Baldur remarked, "One reason I love Vienna so much is that every waiter in every coffee house in the city seems cut from the same mold: they suck up to you, but they're always so very formal. They invariably wear white jackets, heavily starched shirts, and silk ties. They always address you as 'Herr Doktor' or 'Herr Professor,' no matter your station."

"Even better," Heinz said, "for the price of a cup of coffee, you can read newspapers in a dozen languages from all over the world for hours on end, and no one will ever ask you to order anything else."

Since we'd frequented several cafés in the *innere stadt*, we had learned to differentiate who patronized each: the *Cafe Freyung*, where medical students discussed everything from the dissection of a cadaver to Freud's latest works on psychotherapy; the *Vindobona*, where philatelists traded stamps from all over the world; the *Herrenhof,* where we'd watched chess games that never seemed to end; the *Schubert,* where every musician in town traded gossip; and the *Pucher,* where all the deals were made.

After half an hour of convivial talk, I spoke what had been on my mind for days. "Guys …" I began."

"You don't have to say it, Otto," Clement replied. "Your first *mensur* is coming up next Thursday and you're scared witless."

"Well, uh … sort of."

"Not 'sort of' my friend," Baldur said. "We've all been through it: the runs, the dry heaves, the anticipation of horrible pain."

"Hey, Otto, don't be ashamed. You're only showing you're as human as the rest of us." This from Heinz Rogge.

"You don't have to go through with it," DesRoches said, not unkindly. "A surprisingly large number drop out. There's no dishonor in that."

"Clement, you have the ugliest scar I've seen," I said. "Truthfully, how bad was it?"

"Making love to a woman's a helluva lot more fun," he said to raucous laughter and some embarrassing asides.

"DesRoches, tell the truth. You never got so much as a French kiss when you didn't have that scar, but since they now see you as the big brave warrior with the manly mark of the *mensur*, you've seen more arse than a toilet seat."

I didn't know what to say to that. I'd been with one or two girls before my initiation into the *Marcomannia*. I emphasize the word "girls," because I have since found there is a vast difference between an experienced woman who's learned to enjoy the greatest connection a man and a woman can have, and an innocent virgin, who might be the most fetchingly beautiful creature in sight, but who's too frightened and timid to be anything but a disaster in the kip. I've been told the Mohammedans imagine paradise as a place where each man gets 76 virgins. If that's so, I think I'll pass on the Mohammedan vision of such a place.

"How much does it hurt when it happens?" I persisted.

"The moment it happened to me, I'd never felt such intense pain in my life. But I kept repeating, 'This too shall pass, this too shall pass.' That kept me from fainting dead away. Two days later, maybe three, I could hardly bear to look in the mirror when I saw how grotesque I looked, but the pain seemed to fade away very quickly. When the swelling went down … well, what you see is what you get."

"Not pretty," I said.

"Maybe not if you're an Englishman or an American," Schnacke replied, "but every culture sees beauty in a different light. The *schvartze* Africans put longer and longer sticks in their mouths, to stretch their lips two feet out from their faces. The Red *Indianer* in America paint their faces or carve them up like totem poles. You can ask everyone at the *Marcomannia* house. When a sweet *mädchen* or even a married *frau* sees a man with a scar, it's like catnip to them."

We continued our discussions for several evenings thereafter. I won't say I was eagerly looking forward to the disfigurement I was told would follow my first *mensur* fights, but I was determined that if my comrades could survive such baptism, so could I.

In all, I fought 14 such duels. Looking back, I am not the least bit ashamed of my dueling scars which, as so many later photographs showed, were unusually long, deep, and wretchedly jagged. In my opinion, the dueling floor taught me courage, coolness, and strength of will. Although I can still feel the searing fire of the first time the sword's edge ripped my skin from my skull to my throat in a wide, yawning chasm of blood and gore, Clement DesRoches, who died all too young in a useless demonstration against the Dollfuss government, was right: the momentary anguish of the trauma was quickly erased by what happened thereafter.

2

Any man who thinks all women are the same – "in the dark all cats are gray" – simply knows nothing about women. The ability to beguile, tantalize, bedazzle, and cause a man to resort to murderous violence or reduce him to beggary is by no means limited to the young, the beautiful, the voluptuous, or those movie sirens who command a fortune and an army of lusting lovers on the world's movie screens.

Like any man, or for that matter like any woman alive, in my lifetime I have witnessed tall, strong, incredibly handsome men hanging onto dowdy, fat, often repulsive-looking harridans as though they were the Holy Grail. I've seen an equal number of women who could command a king's ransom falling at the feet or into the arms of bald, paunchy habitués of dens of iniquity, who cheat almost nightly on these beauties, or spend what nights they are not cavorting with strange conquests drinking themselves into oblivion in the lowest and most loathsome bars.

Regardless of what one might hear from others, the love of a lifetime, or the lust of a lifetime, call it what you will, survives a happy marriage, indeed well into one's old age, and is forever burned into one's memory.

Shortly after my twentieth birthday, in September of 1928, I started my third year of engineering school. As my *Marcomannia* brothers had foretold, the large scabrous scar on the left side of my face was a woman magnet. There'd been a few casual encounters since my introduction into the *mensur*, but nothing so memorable as to upend my life.

Rolf Hollander, a fellow my own age, transferred into my third-year class. While he was not intrigued by dueling or fraternity life, he was a decent chap and bright enough that we soon became part of the same small study group. He lived in Vienna, as most of the engineering students did. Frequently group members would visit one another's homes or go out together on weekends to study, drink, or discuss matters that occupied the minds of most young men and, I suppose, most young women as well.

Rolf lived in the Alsergrund District, the Ninth *Bezirk*, a few miles northwest of my parents' home. By that time, my brother Alfred had married and gone off to work with a large architectural firm. My newly-acquired acquaintance had a younger brother and two younger sisters. His father Friedrich was a well-reputed *Rechtsanwalt*, a lawyer whose offices were on the first floor of the family residence, but who, because of his popularity, frequently traveled the length and breadth of Austria. On any given date, he might be in Innsbruck, Klagenfurt, Lienz, Salzburg, cities in Germany or the newly independent state of Hungary.

While Rolf's mother, Lisbeth, a small, slender, dark-haired woman, was by no means unattractive, one would hardly think of her of an object of sexual desire. She dressed in the modern fashion of the day, a reasonably pretty, well-preserved 38-year-old mother of four nearly adult children. She exerted no particular attraction for me, nor, for that matter, did she seem attracted to me except as one would look at a son's friend.

As the school year progressed, the Hollanders invited me on one or two holidays in Semmering or, during the chill of winter, Velden-am-Wörthersee in the Carinthian Lake District, the warmest part of Austria. My parents, in turn, invited Rolf and me to visit them in the Salzkammergut, where they owned a small apartment in Hallstatt, which even to this day I believe is the loveliest spot on God's earth.

By the summer of 1929, economic conditions had worsened significantly and there was fear of a worldwide financial meltdown. Still, life went on and the Viennese seemed to live for the day. Men and women took to bathing at the popular public plunges of Krapfenwaldbad, Gänsehäufel, and Kongressbad, where I was intrigued by the shockingly daring one-piece swimsuits that young women wore that season, swimsuits that only a decade before would have led to arrests for indecency. But that summer the "flapper" look of "Dixie Dugan" styles imported from America, and the even more risqué attire from notoriously loose-moraled France, had come to Austria.

During the school break in July, the Hollanders told me of their summer plans. The *paterfamilias*, Friedrich, would be teaching a Continuing Education course in Salzburg, followed by a week-long round of negotiations in Munich. Rolf's younger brother, who'd be starting University in September, planned to attend a week-long orientation program in Linz. His two sisters had enrolled in a youth summer camp in Velden-am-Wörthersee in the south.

Rolf told me he'd be going to Venice to visit a young lady whom he'd met in Klagenfurt. "And no, Otto, you are *not* invited" he remarked with a barely concealed grin. "I'm going to find out if what they say about the Latin ladies from south of the border is true. But that does leave a bit of a problem."

"What's that?" I asked.

"With everyone gone, Mama will be home alone for ten days, packing and getting ready for the family to take the train to *Karlovy Vary* for our annual trip to the spa when everyone returns to *Wien*. I hate to think of her being left alone in our house to fend for herself, even though we've got neighbors to help her in case of an emergency."

"Any reason she couldn't just go with your father?"

"Papa's got so much to do all day, she'd be even more alone and bored in a strange town where she doesn't know anyone. I was wondering if you wouldn't mind calling her on the telephone once or twice during the week, maybe even come over to visit, just to make sure everything's all right? After all, you're the closest thing to a third son and I'm sure she'd appreciate it."

"That doesn't sound so difficult," I replied lightly. "Summer's not dueling season, so my plate is hardly full. You'll be leaving when?"

"Papa's leaving Friday. The rest of us are leaving over the weekend. We'll be back Monday week. You're sure it's not a bother?"

"Of course it is," I said loftily, placing my hand on my chest and doing my best to give a woeful look. "But somehow I'll manage to do my duty for God, country, and my friends."

On Tuesday of the following week, I telephoned and spoke briefly with Frau Hollander. "I'm just checking in to make sure everything's all right," I said.

"What a good son you are," she answered. "There are moments when the house feels so empty, but for the most part I enjoy the peace and quiet with five less people around every hour of the day. As a matter of fact, I feel I'm having a brief holiday myself."

"Well, I'll not disturb your holiday," I said. "As long as I know you're safe and sound."

The next day, Wednesday, I had absolutely nothing planned. Early in the afternoon, I thought I'd surprise Frau Hollander with a brief visit. As was customary in Vienna, I stopped by a kiosk and purchased a small bouquet of summer flowers as a token gift.

When I got to the Hollander residence, I pushed the bell at the ground floor entrance. There was no answer, but Rolf had taught me the passcode months ago and he'd given me his key to the second floor living area, so I thought I'd check the apartment to make sure everything was in order, leave the flowers and a small note, and depart shortly thereafter, before the lady of the house returned.

As I entered the living quarters, it was far quieter than it had been during any of my past visits. Suddenly, I heard what sounded like a soft moaning coming from the direction of Rolf's parents' bedroom. I stood transfixed for a few moments. The moaning became louder and faster.

A mass of confusing, conflicting thoughts went through my head. Could the mother of one of my closest friends be having a clandestine affair? Or worse, could she have been taken by a sudden illness or have suffered an attack from an intruder?

"Frau Hollander?" I called out, not in a particularly loud voice. The last thing I wanted to do was embarrass her or cause her panic, but I did want her to know that immediate help was available if she needed it. The moaning ceased in mid-breath. "Frau Hollander? Frau Lisbeth?" I called out again.

"*Wer ist das*? Who's there?" came a tremulous voice from the bedroom.

"Otto," I responded. "Are you all right? Do you need help?"

"Otto Skorzeny?"

"Yes."

"I'm fine," her voice came from the bedroom. "I went swimming this morning. After I got home, I felt exhausted, so I was just taking a nap. I must have been dreaming. I'll be out in just a few moments. You know where everything is. Perhaps you could make us some coffee or tea?"

"Certainly. Take your time." I was relieved to find that none of my suspicions or fears were true. I started boiling a pot of water for the tea and searched the cupboard for some Maria biscuits, which I knew was an afternoon favorite in the Hollander family.

"Otto?" my friend's mother called from the rear area of the house. "I'd really appreciate if you could help me move a few books into the living room. I've been trying to get Friedrich and Rolf to move them for weeks. I thought as long as you're here … We can take tea as soon as I get them out to the front of the house."

"That shouldn't take much time at all," I replied, turning off the fire under the tea. I'd passed Rolf's parents' bedroom many times, but the door had always been closed. When I came within a few feet, I noticed the door was open. A strong, pungent, but not unpleasant scent came from within the room. "In here," she called from the bedroom. I walked in not knowing what to expect.

I felt a sudden shock such as I'd never experienced before.

Frau Lisbeth Hollander was wearing a bathing suit that made those I had seen at the pool look as modest as a nun's habit. She was by no means possessed of voluptuous curves, but the top of her outfit left very little to the imagination. As she slowly, tantalizingly pulled the top of her swimsuit down, I found myself gasping at the beauty of her small, perfectly formed, cone-shaped breasts, their hard nipples protruding. I was thunderstruck.

Frau Lisbeth Hollander, *Rechtanwalt's* wife, mother of four, by no means in the first blush of youth, gave me a look the likes of which I'd never seen, before or since. It didn't matter whether she was the *hausfrau* or the consummate siren. She could have been any of those things, or all of them, or none of them, and it would not have made a shred of difference.

I approached the bed stiffly, almost in a trance, pulled by invisible strings.

"Would you like to see the rest of me?"

All I could do was nod dumbly.

"Touch me, then," she said. "Wherever you want." I reached out hesitantly. Lisbeth grasped my wrists firmly.

"Ah, such lovely, strong hands," she breathed. "I can feel them on me already." She tugged at my right hand until it touched her left breast. She may have been small, but never had I felt anything remotely as soft, yielding, and sensual. Moments later, I cupped both of her breasts in my hand. How different she felt from the other girls with whom I'd been, girls who'd each been better endowed. I felt an overwhelming sense of tenderness coupled with raw animal lust.

As I squeezed her, alternately softly, then rougher, she uttered the same moaning sound I'd heard when I'd first entered the apartment. The scent I'd inhaled when I'd come into the room was noticeably stronger.

"You said you were asleep and dreaming," I ventured. "I heard …"

"I know what you heard," she murmured. "I was neither asleep nor dreaming. I heard you come in and I thought …"

"What did you think?"

"How exciting it was to be doing what I was doing, knowing that a handsome young man was so close by. And how badly I needed this…"

Her body stiffened, then spasmed. Without another word, she pulled the rest of her bathing suit down until she lay totally nude, her tiny figure as beautiful and perfectly formed as the statues of Venus di Milo I'd seen in the *Kunsthistoriches Museum*. Her eyes closed. I need not even have been there. She started stroking and pulling at her womanhood, slowly and gently, then faster. While she was gasping, I simply stared, transfixed by what I was witnessing.

I reached down and started stroking and rubbing where her hand had been a moment before. Her spasms became stronger, her movements stiff and involuntary. I feared she might break apart from her ever-increasing jerkiness, but she just kept moaning and gasping. A sudden hot, slippery fluid gushed into my hand. Moments later, she shrieked. Her body shuddered and collapsed. Her face and breasts were splotched with red, and her breathing came in harsh rasps.

"Oh … my … God!" she finally moaned between ragged breaths. "Oh … my …God!"

We both lay silent for a short time. Lisbeth breathed slowly and softly, as if in a gentle sleep. I glanced at her body, feeling myself growing larger and harder than I ever remembered. But with her sleeping, there was little I could do except touch myself.

I closed my eyes for what seemed like only a few seconds before I felt her warm, moist lips encircle my member. She alternately licked me gently, tantalizingly, bit me softly, then sucked with gentle force. I could not stop myself … did not want to stop myself … and when I came it was as though a thunderstorm had ripped my body apart, such was the intensity of the release I felt.

Afterward, we both dozed for some time. When we awoke, more or less simultaneously, the shadows were lengthening at her bedroom windows. The musky smell of our lovemaking was intense and permeated the room as we looked deeply, lustfully into one another's eyes, fully knowing what was to come and what we were about to do.

Just as I reached for her, she said, "Wait, my dear."

"Don't you want it?" I asked, somewhat petulantly.

"As much as you, as you found out a little while ago." She put on a pair of black lace panties and started to pat herself dry. "But what I *don't* want is to get in the family way."

"Schwanger?"

"That's right, darling. The last thing I need is another baby. When you get to be my age – don't look at me that way – four is certainly enough. Not to mention Friedrich would not be pleased."

"So that's *it* for tonight?"

"I didn't say that at all. There's a pharmacy within a few blocks of here. I'm sure it's not closed yet. While you're out on your shopping errand, I think I'll shower so I'll be all clean, sweet-smelling, and ready for more love when you return."

Soon I was on my way. Within half an hour I'd returned to the building ready for an entire night of promised delights. I'd just come to the door of the apartment and taken out my key when Lisbeth pulled the door open.

"Otto," she said delightedly, in what was certainly a louder voice than it needed to be. "What a nice surprise! It seems *two* of my 'boys' have come to visit their old mom. Rolf, I'm so glad you decided to come home early. Otto called just a few moments after you returned. I suggested he might like to come over and we could all spend a wonderful evening together listening to you regale us with your tales from the South."

Quickly recovering from my shock, I said, "This calls for a celebration. I suggest we go to a nearby *Wursthaus*, since I can't afford much more on student's budget."

"Not necessary," Lisbeth said. I noticed she was wearing a modest, loose-fitting dress. "I can warm up a quick meal here. What news to report from Italy?"

"Venice is truly one of the loveliest cities in the world," Rolf began, entirely oblivious to what had gone on in the apartment scarcely an hour ago.

"And …?" I prompted.

"And … nothing," he said. "When I got there, Maria *and her two girlfriends* met me at the station. "Not at all what I'd expected. Did you miss me, mom?"

"Of course, darling. I finally managed to move the books I've been asking you and Papa to carry to the living room for months. When I was done I took a long, leisurely nap and a hot bath." She glanced in my direction. "Ah, the rigors of being a lonely matron," she sighed. "Otto relieved my boredom by telephoning me a couple of times to make sure I was alright."

"Thanks for that, Otto," Rolf replied. "There's a good, loyal friend."

"It was not the hardest thing I'd ever managed," I said. "After all, what are friends for?" After another hour or so, I excused myself.

"Aha, no doubt a lovely young fräulein is awaiting you?" Lisbeth ventured.

I smiled a wolfish smile at them both. "Ask me no questions and I'll tell you no lies. I'm glad you're safely home, Rolf. I guess I won't see you again until after the family returns from the Spa."

"I suppose not," Lisbeth said, "but I can't send you home without a sweet." She disappeared into the back of the apartment and emerged with a small pastry box which she handed to me at the door. "Now don't open it until you leave," she said. "The last thing I need is to find pastry crumbs on my floor."

I left in a mood which combined crushed expectations, sharp sensual memories of what had happened earlier that afternoon, and relief that Rolf had not appeared half an hour before he did. The packet of condoms in my pants pocket reminded me of how much more there could have been, but one doesn't always get everything one wants in this life precisely when he wants it.

When I got back to my room, I felt I'd like something sweet to eat before I retired. Lisbeth had thoughtfully given me a pastry box. Undoubtedly she knew that a young man could hardly say no to a light, flaky nibble at the end of the day.

But when I opened the box, it was hardly what I would have expected. A black bra, a still moist pair of panties bearing Lisbeth's scent. And a handwritten note: "11 tomorrow at Schickelgasse 24/3, 7ᵗʰ Bezirk. Be <u>prepared</u> to <u>come</u>. L-."

Three- and four-story apartment houses lined narrow Schickelgasse on each side. Number 24 was inconspicuous, indistinguishable from the rest of the buildings. The street was relatively empty at that time of the morning, since it was a workday. A terrier dog walked by, lifted his leg and left a drop or two on a hydrant, sniffed at a nearby garbage can, and disappeared up the street. Dressed as I was in ordinary work clothes, except for my height and the noticeable scar on my left cheek, I was as much a part of the street scene as the dog and the apartment houses.

I sensed her presence before I actually saw her enter the street and walk determinedly toward 24. This morning, she wore a skirt cut below her knees, white blouse, and a dark blue jacket. Her hair was pulled back in a bun. She looked like a businesswoman or a tourist, not unusual for Neubau, which was a five-minute walk to the center of town.

"How did you find this place?" I asked.

"We bought the apartment early on," she replied. "Friedrich needed a place where his clients could stay overnight. Later, we rented it out. Right now, the tenants are on holiday and we told them we'd stop in and check the place before we went to Czechoslovakia."

"Where's Rolf this morning?"

"Went to the Prater with some friends. Friedrich called earlier this morning and told me negotiations are going well. His schedule is still the same, back Sunday or Monday. *Alles in ordnung.* Everything seems to be perfectly normal. I told him I'd come here today a little after eleven. Which," she smiled mischievously, "is exactly what I intend to do."

I shivered in anticipation of what we both knew would happen, despite the warm, late-summer day. "Would you like to stop at a *konditorei*?" I asked.

"Didn't you have enough pastry last night?"

"I hardly slept a wink after I opened the box."

"Some kind of aroma?"

"Uh-huh."

"I hope they didn't deprive you of *all* your sleep," she said, slipping her arm through mine. "Or all your strength."

"Lisbeth, I couldn't help but think of you all night."

"Not of other girls?" she smiled, teasingly.

"How could I … after you?"

"Such scandalous talk about an older woman."

"You could be *fifty* years my senior and it wouldn't make any difference."

"Mmmmm," she said, trembling slightly. "I wonder if you'll feel that way a year from now, let alone fifty. Perhaps we should check out Apartment 3 to make sure it's clean and tidy."

Words were a burden, and we didn't speak again until we'd climbed the stairs and entered the place. No sooner had we closed the front door than we were locked in a tight embrace, kissing hungrily, our tongues searching out one another's. Lisbeth ground her pelvis again me and her soft moaning started where it had left off yesterday. My hand slipped inside her blouse. She wore no bra and didn't need one. Her nipples were taut and hard, begging to be stroked. I was quick to respond to their call.

I picked her up easily. She ceased her moaning long enough to point out the nearest bedroom, where we found a large matrimonial bed. No sooner had I carried her there and laid her on the bed than I removed her jacket, unbuttoned her blouse, and started sucking and nibbling at her breasts. She reached down and tugged at my belt, urging me by her movements to remove my clothing as well.

I pulled at her panties, sliding them down her lovely legs as she arched her back. I buried my head between her legs. Her body jerked as my tongue made contact. Her moans turned to gasps as her spasms came faster and faster. Suddenly she drew in her breath as if she were choking. In the next instant she simultaneously screamed, her body let loose a flood of viscous fluid, and she collapsed in ecstasy, panting as though she'd never stop.

By that time, my own passion was at its zenith and I could wait no longer.

"The rubber," she rasped. "I don't want …"

I tore at the latex and was almost unable to get it on fast enough before I slipped into her tight, wet cavity. She must have spent years training the muscles inside her to drive a man insane with desire. Somehow she managed to lie with her arms at her side while squeezing me from inside her lovely body. She rose to meet my every thrust and backed away as I pulled back, heightening the impact of what we were doing. It could not have taken more than a few seconds when I felt myself climbing the final hill before …

As I moved in and out of her faster and faster, Lisbeth suddenly grabbed my hard-on with her hand and squeezed hard. The shock of what she was doing stopped me immediately, just before I started to come.

"Slower, darling," she whispered. "It will be better for both of us."

She proceeded to tease and tantalize me with her hands and her lips until I was beyond ready. I entered her again and this time there was absolutely no way I could stop. When we came together, the explosion rocked us both. What happened at that moment was beyond anything

I'd experienced in my life. It was then I truly realized it was the woman rather than man who had the greater power to control the lovemaking.

"Lisbeth ..." I stammered through a fog.

"Sshhh, darling, sleep for awhile."

Before we separated from one another in late afternoon and had gone our separate ways, we'd made love twice more, each better than the last. I was filled with conflicted emotions, guilt, spent lust, betrayal ... but the one that overwhelmed all others was that I could never let her go.

During the next few years Lisbeth and I shared our mutual delight with one another at carefully, cautiously selected times and places. Thankfully, no one to my knowledge ever found out about us. She continued to be the most thrilling sexual partner I'd ever had. I remember her lovingly and gratefully, even to this day. There are still times when I ask myself, "What if ...?" But that question was never answered.

3

"Herr Skorzeny?"

"Herr Schreiber," I responded. "I'm privileged you gave me this opportunity to meet with you."

"The Hollanders spoke highly of you. I respect Friedrich's judgment. I assure you that Frau Hollander is far brighter than most women in Vienna. Indeed, although you'd never think so now, Lisbeth Rausch was one of Vienna's great beauties in her day. I see from your resume that your father Anton was also an engineer and your brother Alfred the same."

"Correct, sir."

"You've heard of *Schreiber Gerüst?*"

"You're into scaffolding in a very large way, Herr Schreiber."

"You flatter me, Mister Skorzeny. Our company has managed to hang on, even in light of the economic crisis that struck Austria after the American stock market crash." He sighed. "God knows how long, though. Who'd ever have thought that thirteen years after the Great War ended the proud remnant of what was once the greatest Empire in Europe would be reduced to begging loans from anyone trusting enough or greedy enough to even look our way?"

"They say things are worse in Germany. People take a wheelbarrow full of money to the bakery simply to buy a loaf of bread. If I may be

35

so bold as to ask, Herr Schreiber, how come you're even considering hiring me? When I graduated two months ago, I was told, 'Otto, this is 1931. They're laying off engineers left and right. What makes you think anyone would be looking to hire a newly minted fellow like you? You'd have better luck applying as a waiter.' You're the first one who's granted me an interview."

"Well, one thing's for sure, Herr Skorzeny. It's not because of your beautiful face." The older man, nearly a foot shorter than me with a small potbelly and an obvious toupee replied, chuckling. "A rather pronounced *schmiss*, I take it?"

"That's right."

"Would I be making a naïve guess if I suggested you favor reunification with Germany?"

"I've never hidden that, Herr Schreiber. Many of our countrymen who haven't turned their eyes toward Moscow share my feeling. Both countries share the same Germanic people."

My prospective employer bade me sit down in one of two comfortable leather chairs across from him. He pressed a button on his desk. Shortly, a functionary appeared bearing a tray with two china cups and saucers, a pot of coffee, and an assortment of croissants.

"What do you feel about the National Socialist Party?" he asked bluntly.

"I'm not sure my countrymen want such a fundamental revolution as the Nazis talk about, but their views of united German-Austrian people appeal to me. If that means I've just failed my candidacy to work with *Schreber Gerüst*, I'll excuse myself now."

"No, you may remain seated, young man. Although I myself am apolitical, I've never denied anyone the right to speak his piece or to express the courage of his convictions. You're aware we have a lot of Socialist-Marxists and Communists on our payroll?"

"I'm not surprised. That's common in the building trades. I'm not so inflexible to believe my way is the only way. I try to get along with everyone as best I can."

"We don't pay high wages."

"Any wages are better than none, Herr Schreiber. It's high time I stopped depending on the Hollanders, my parents, or handouts. All I ask is an opportunity to prove myself."

"Ach, so many young men say that, Herr Skorzeny. I'll tell you what. Hoffritz, the huge general contractor, has an important bid opening in a week. We're one of their prime subcontractors. If they're successful, we're looking at a year's worth of work, maybe even more. Our key construction superintendent, Greiff, will need at least three project managers. Hopefully, this could be the opportunity you've asked for…"

†

"I'm so proud of you, darling boy! A year ago, you were pounding the pavements, knocking on any door you could find. Now you're a junior partner!"

"Lisbeth, not even the promotion could be better than what we just did," I said, gently nibbling at her breasts.

Our relationship had reached the point where I enjoyed her intelligence and her penetrating worldview *almost* as much as the other. Georg Schreiber had been right when he'd said she was one of the brightest women in Vienna. Indeed, although she never paraded that aspect of her personality, she was one of the brightest human beings I'd ever met.

She continued, "Otto, I know you're a confirmed member of the Austrian Nazi Party. I don't fault you for that, but you know how unstable Austria is today." I did indeed. The Marxist *Schutzbund* on the left and the *Heimwehr* on the right had been battling it out in the streets, each strutting around with their funny little uniforms, while NSDAP simply watched and got stronger each day. The Christian-Democratic government was failing.

"You're not telling me something I don't know, Lisbeth."

"Last night Friedrich told me in confidence that the Christian Socialists lost their greater German allies in parliament. Today, while you and I were otherwise engaged, it's quite possible that the Social Democrats called for dissolution of the National Council. Friedrich believes if that happens, Dr. Renner will step down as chancellor. The rumor is that President Miklas will offer the job to Dollfuss."

"Millimetternich?" I said using the nickname given to him by several wags in the newspapers. The comically tiny Dollfuss, who stood only 4-feet 11-inches tall, had been the butt of coffeehouse jokes in Vienna all his life. One could order a "Dollfuss" cup of coffee, meaning the smallest cup. In contrast to his own diminutive stature, his personal assistant and secretary, Eduard Hedvicek, was a very large man, 6-foot 7-inches tall. "But Dollfuss has only had a year in the federal government."

"That doesn't really matter," my lover said. "Who'd even want the job of chancellor?"

Nevertheless, that's precisely what happened. When he was offered the job, Dollfuss at first declined, then accepted. He was sworn in on May 20, 1932, as head of a coalition government between the Christian-Social Party, the *Landbund*, a right-wing agrarian party, and the parliamentary wing of the extreme nationalist *Heimwehr*. With the economy failing more and more quickly, Dollfuss had no option but to go the League of Nations for a bailout.

The terms of the loan of $45 million from the League were stiff: Austria had to agree not to enter a customs union with Germany for twenty years. Since by that time I was a staunch NSDAP member, I was furious at what I felt was a betrayal of our German heritage.

I watched helplessly as things went from bad to worse. In March 1933, Karl Renner, the Social Democratic president of the National Council, resigned. Two vice presidents belonging to other parties, resigned as well. Without a president, parliament could not conclude its session. Dollfuss asked President Miklas to adjourn Parliament indefinitely. When the National Council wanted to reconvene, days after the resignation of the three presidents, Dollfuss' police force barred the entrance to the parliament building. With a stroke of his pen and the aid of law enforcement officers, the Chancellor effectively eliminated democracy in Austria. From that point forward, he governed as dictator by emergency decree with absolute power.

The meeting convened on the evening of May 20, 1933, one year to the day since Engelbert Dollfuss had replaced Karl Renner as Austria's chancellor. Twelve of us assembled in a cottage in Donaustadt, southeast of Vienna. Besides myself, there were three other members of the National Socialist Party, four representatives of the Communists, and four former Social Democratic members of Parliament. The three elements represented the "outs." Agents of the right-wing *Heimwehr*, which supported the Dollfuss government, had been excluded from the meeting.

Even though the Communists and the NSDAP were bitterly at odds against each other politically and philosophically, we'd been in direct contact with one another for several weeks. The political fiction of democracy in Austria, such as it was, appeared to be coming to an end.

The meeting started on a tense note as Radicki, one of the Communists, said, "This whole thing started when Hitler acceded to the chancellorship in Germany at the beginning of this year. Dollfuss feels Germany breathing down Austria's neck and needs to find any way he can to stop it."

"Not quite correct," I responded in what I hoped was a civil tone. "Our polls indicate that the Austrian National Socialists could gain a significant minority in future elections if honest elections were held today. Seventy-five percent of the Tyrol would vote NSDAP."

"But our followers command the east ..." This from a second Communist sympathizer.

"I'm not for a moment disputing that Moscow's influence in Austria has increased dramatically," I responded. "Whether we agree or disagree is irrelevant. As much as we may publicly despise one another, we *need* each other to keep balance and democracy alive. Even if neither NSDAP nor the Communists ever marshal enough votes to gain control of Parliament, when one or the other of us becomes part of a coalition, we at least get a piece of the pie instead of starving."

"Herr Skorzeny is right," a Social Democrat piped up. "But what happens if the midget does what he sets out to do? He's got the *Heimwehr* and his police guards."

"We've got the *Schutzbund* ..."

"Yes," another NSDAP member said. "That means the *Heimwehr* and Dollfuss can pick the Communists off, further fracturing the delicate balance we've tried to achieve."

A tall, cadaverous-looking graybeard, whom I recognized as having been a senior Social Democratic member of the Assembly, sucked on his pipe and ruminated, "An eye for an eye makes the whole world blind. My friends, I'll wager that Chancellor Dollfuss intends to outlaw the Nazis and the Communists in one stroke of a pen. Then he gets to pick and choose which party will be in power by simple majority."

A younger, red-headed man said bitterly, "What difference would that make? He's already shut down the National Assembly and blocked the members from entering the Chamber."

"Perhaps," I suggested, "an apt analogy is, 'If we don't hang together, we'll sure as hell all hang separately.' What if we were to outmaneuver Dollfuss by putting aside our differences for however long it takes to reestablish democracy as we know it and immediately announce the formation of a united front?"

"An interesting idea," the graybeard responded. "But under what banner?"

"Let's give that some thought," the first Communist speaker said. "I propose we meet back here in two weeks, after we've met with the senior authorities in our respective movements, and work on a strategy."

"And I suggest," the red-headed man, who I estimated at being my age, 25, said hotly, "that will be too late! Mark my words, we will see the beginning of the end of Austria as we know it!"

"Now, Hjalmar," the man sitting next to him said placatingly, "how much can change in a few weeks?"

"Everything!" the red-headed man said, and stomped out the door angrily.

Hjalmar proved to be tragically prescient. On May 26, 1933, Dollfuss outlawed the NSDAP. On June 19, 1933, he banned the Communists. Those were his first major mistakes.

Next, taking a page from what had come out of our clandestine meeting a few months before, our chancellor set up a dictatorship with his new party, the *Vaterländische Front*, which had the support of the *Heimwehr*. To bolster his foreign position and prevent Austria from uniting with Nazi Germany, Dollfuss met the Italian dictator, Benito Mussolini at Riccione in Northern Italy in August 1933. The *Duce* guaranteed Austrian independence at the cost of abolishing all political parties and revising the Austrian constitution along Fascist lines. At Mussolini's prompting, Dollfuss quarreled with the organizations of the left and harassed the Marxists and the workers.

Clement, Baldur, and Reineke, three members of my old dueling fraternity, *Marcommania*, started back toward my car after a convivial afternoon in Café *Weissenhof.*

At 7:00 that evening, we were nibbling on sweet pastries we'd just purchased when I heard whistling sounds, followed by a series of concussive explosions. Moments later, four armored trucks roared into *Rathaus Square.*

"What the h---?" Baldur exclaimed. His voice was drowned out as three more armored trucks, sirens blaring, drove into *Rathaus Square* from the opposite direction. Moments later, the trucks opened fire on the crowd. I heard what I swear was the noise of bombs exploding and saw a man run into the square shouting, "They've set up blockades on the *Ringstrasse!"*

"The church! The church!" a woman screamed. "It's been hit!"

Things had just started to quiet down when two more armored vehicles escorted by five police cruisers opened fire on the square from a third direction, killing and injuring numerous innocent civilians who'd done nothing but come to watch the demonstration.

"Stephansdom!" I shouted to everyone within hearing. "The police will never attack it!

My comrades and I managed to organize a hundred locals who'd not been hit. The able-bodied were just starting to stream toward the Cathedral when a fourth wave, five more armored vehicles, rained further death and destruction on the First *Bezirk.*

"Clement!" Baldur screamed, rushing toward our fraternity brother.

I ran to my fatally injured friend's side. "Clement -?" Then I saw the gaping hole from his neck to his stomach. What had been his intestines were already starting to spill out. Clement DesRoches, unable to breathe, drowned in his own blood.

I howled in agony and frustration, but my voice was cut off by the Blam-Blam of gunfire and I was knocked to the ground as a crowd literally ran over me. I barely heard a stranger's muffled "I'm hit! I'm hit! Oh, Christ! Mama! Mama!" before a truck that had been accidentally subjected to gunfire rolled over on him.

As I felt myself start to go in and out of consciousness, the screams grew fewer and turned to desperate moans as more perished in this senseless travesty that the government-run newspaper loyally reported as a courageous police action to restore order when anarchy threatened the capital. Within two days, the government claimed the destruction had been caused by Communist and Nazi rioters gone out of control, and thanks to the brave efforts of the *Vaterländische Front's* law enforcement officers, only twelve people had died.

In truth, more than 400 were killed and 2,000 injured in riots that erupted in Vienna, Linz, and Graz in February 1934. Chancellor Dollfuss used the riots as an excuse to ban the Social Democratic Party organization, thus removing Austria's most strongly anti-Nazi force from the scene. The stage was set for the beginning of the end of an independent Austria.

4

By the end of February 1934, I realized that my long-term relationship with Lisbeth Hollander would never lead to anything more that hidden trysts, and that she had no intention of leaving *Rechtsanwalt* Hollander. Our loving friendship had matured into less loving and more friendship. Although Lisbeth was still an incredibly erotic woman, she was now in her mid-forties and I, at twenty-six, was still unmarried.

I'd remained friends with Rolf, albeit we were not as close as before, since he'd aligned himself strongly with the pro-Dollfuss faction while my loyalties vacillated between the Nazis and the Communist sympathizers.

Matters came to a painful head one afternoon, after Lisbeth and I had enjoyed one of our increasingly rare, but even more ecstatically delicious, bouts of lovemaking. After we'd showered together, I gazed with never-ending amazement at her incredibly beautiful, sensual body as she dressed herself. She looked over at me tenderly and matter-of-factly said, "Otto, darling boy, I think the time has come for you to find a suitable wife."

"I could never …!" I started to protest.

"Sssh," she said, putting her fingers gently to my lips. "I'll never stop loving you. You know that. But it's time. Indeed, when I was your age, I'd already had two children and a third on the way. You should be thinking in that direction, my sweet."

"But," I said miserably, "does that mean …?"

"We don't need to answer that question right now. No matter what happens, we will always love each other."

I'd first met Herr Schreiber's younger daughter, Margareta, then a coltish teenager of sixteen, in 1931, when I'd come to work for her father. Since I was not only a mature twenty-three, but seriously involved with an exquisite woman eighteen years my senior, I took little notice of "Gretl" at that time.

But after my talk with Lisbeth, I'd taken a "second look" at the now 19-year-old Gretl Schreiber, and realized it would not hurt my career to set up a favorable marriage with the owner's daughter. Besides, Margareta had matured into an attractive young woman. I started paying serious court to her. In April 1934, Gretl and her father approved my proposal of marriage. We tied the knot at the end of the following month.

At the beginning of June, Gretl and I set out for our Italian honeymoon on a motorcycle and sidecar. For the next three months we visited Venice, Ravenna, Bologna, Pisa, Florence, Rome, and the Apennine region of the Abruzzo. Both of us were captivated by ninety-five-hundred-foot-high Gran Sasso, the highest peak in the Appenines. We ascended the massif by funicular, the only way to get to the Alpine meadow just below the summit, where we spent two magnificent nights at the Imperatore Hotel. Little was I to know the decisive role that highland aerie would play in my life several years later.

From Gran Sasso, we descended into *Firenze*, the very heart of Tuscany. As an engineer, and having been exposed to a degree of cultural sophistication, thanks to my association with the Hollanders and others in their circle, I suggested to my bride that we check in to our quarters on the Via Faenza and immediately thereafter attend the *Accademia* to see the incomparable *David* and the Uffizi, one of the premier galleries in the world. I was somewhat disappointed when Gretl professed she'd never heard of either of these places. I suggested she might be exhausted from our day-long ride and she might want to relax until dinner. For my part, I said I'd stop by the nearest kiosk to catch up on the news and return within half an hour.

When I got to the newsstand, I found *La Nazione* had just been delivered and the attendant was selling papers as quickly as he could hand them out. It took me only a moment to see what the excitement was all about as I read the headline in huge, boldface type posted above the newsstand.

ASSASSINIO! DOLLFUSS COLPO MORTALE!

As soon as I returned to our room, copy of the paper in hand, I outlined to Gretl what the newspaper reported. Although the details were sketchy, it appeared that two days before, on July 25, 1934, a group of conspirators forced their way into the *Bundeshaus*, with the avowed purpose of compelling Chancellor Dollfuss to resign. The *putchists'* plot had gone horribly awry. One of my NSDAP associates, Otto Planetta, swore he'd fired only one shot on the floor in front of the chancellor, but investigators found *two* bullets lodged in Dollfuss' spine. The autopsy on the assassinated leader's body was done with undue haste. Many thought it was a cover-up. The *putchists*, after having been assured that they would be taken safe and sound to the Bavarian frontier, surrendered their weapons and were immediately arrested.

While my feelings concerning the event were mixed, my overwhelming emotion was relief that I had not been anywhere near

Vienna at the time of the assassination. My sympathies were well, if not widely, known. Since there was nothing I could do about the event, Gretl and I remained in Florence for three days before we continued on to Rome. Within two days after we arrived, I heard Benito Mussolini speak from the balcony of the old Austrian embassy. My feelings for Italy had been favorable from the moment Gretl and I crossed the Austro-Italian frontier. By the time I reached Rome my prejudices against Italy had totally disappeared.

These feelings occurred again and again on my trips to the various nations of Europe. I concluded that Europeans constitute one big family and we could easily get along with everyone as long as we respected one another while guarding what makes each of us special.

Scarcely had I returned from Italy when I found myself in the middle of a political uproar which had seized Styria, Carinthia, and the Tyrol after the radio announced that the *putsch* had been successful and that Dr. von Rintelen, the Austrian ambassador to Rome, had been asked to form a new government. It turned out to be a false rumor. von Rintelen, who had walked into the trap, chose to commit suicide.

Although many of my fellow National Socialists escaped to Germany, within two months thousands of our other comrades and a majority of the Marxists found themselves in concentration camps at Wöllersdorf and Messendorf near Graz. More than two-hundred conspirators were brought before a court-martial immediately. Of the sixty sentenced to death, President Miklas reduced the sentences to life at hard labor for all but seven National Socialist leaders and two members of the *Schutzbund*, who were hanged. When Dollfuss's successor, Chancellor Kurt Schuschnigg, declared an amnesty two years later, 15,583 political prisoners were released.

Although my country was spiraling down into near-anarchy, I did not participate in the political drama unfolding before my eyes. I had taken on much more of a leadership role in *Schreiber Gerüst*, which was just as well, for even Herr Schreiber became aware that as he was aging, I had become vital to the continued success of his operation. I never knew whether my ultimate superior ever found out that although Gretl was a pretty girl who gave what she could to the marriage, she was by no means Lisbeth. From time to time I continued to avail myself of Frau Hollander's companionship and the fulfillment she provided.

Today "historians" almost universally condemn the so-called "rape of Austria" by the aggressive German Reich. They replay *ad nauseam* the tearful departure of Chancellor Kurt Schuschnigg, buttressing his claim that he had no choice but to surrender independent Austria to the beast next door. The popular story holds that Austrians, those sweet, lovable people who all cavort in *dirndls* and *lederhosen* and jump happily around in *schuplattler* dances where they slap their Alpine shoes, were crushed, demoralized, and enslaved by the Third Reich.

The real story had far more shades of gray and was far more complex. I know because I was there as an eyewitness to the real history.

Kurt Schuschnigg replaced Dollfuss four days after the assassination. While his tenure in office was marked by policies slightly milder than that of his predecessor, he ruled mostly by decree. That is not to say our new chancellor had an easy job. He faced the management of a near-bankrupt economy; he had to maintain law and order in a country which was forbidden by the terms of the 1919 Treaty of Saint-Germain to maintain an army in excess of 30,000 men. At the same time, he had to cope with armed paramilitary forces in Austria, which owed their allegiance not to the state but to various rival political parties. He also had to be mindful of the growing strength of the Austrian Nazis, who supported Adolf Hitler's ambitions to absorb Austria into Nazi Germany.

Schuschnigg's overriding political concern, however, was to preserve Austria's independence within the borders imposed on it by the terms of the Treaty of Saint-Germain, and at that his government ultimately failed.

On July 11, 1936, the Chancellor officially admitted that "Austria is fundamentally a German state." Nevertheless, he was against union with Germany, describing Austria as "a better German state." While he mobilized his police to suppress everyone who expressed views which were friendly toward Germany, he also signed an Austro-German Agreement which allowed the release of imprisoned July Putsch insurgents and the inclusion of Nazi sympathizers in the Austrian cabinet.

In 1935, I joined the German Gymnastics League, a sports association of sixty-thousand which desired unification with Germany. By 1936, we'd organized into quasi-military platoons. Concurrently, Moscow gave its Marxist leaders specific instructions to band with the outlawed Social Democrats in fielding a people's front, something I'd suggested at our clandestine meeting two years before.

Meanwhile, Gretl and I separated, thank God before any children were conceived, and quietly divorced in mid-1937. Although Georg Schreiber was aware that our marital ship had hit the rocks and run aground several months before, he was a decent, by no means vindictive man. Concurrent with the ending of my marriage to Gretl, Herr Schreiber and I dissolved our partnership. Although he paid me a generous settlement for my share of *Schreiber Gerüst*, which would enable me to stay afloat for a couple of years, I found myself unemployed as Austria entered 1938 in an increasingly desperate state.

With time on my hands and reasonably well-heeled, I cast about and found an interesting, if minor, role in city politics. I became much more active in National Socialist activities at the beginning of 1938. I willingly volunteered and shouldered thankless jobs. NSDAP extended me a degree of nominal power while they continued to sap my time and energies. In January, I was promoted to 8ᵗʰ *Bezirk* District Representative. For the most part, that meant attending meetings on Wednesday or Thursday evenings and eating würstl and drinking beer, courtesy of the Party.

Our board was aware that von Papen had arranged for Chancellor Schuschnigg to meet with Hitler at the Führer's Berchtesgaden aerie. I was told by an inside source that "Hitler carved Schuschnigg a new arsehole" at the meeting. While I had no idea how truthful that statement may or may not have been, within a few days of the chancellor's return he named Arthur Seyss-Inquart Minister of the Interior, with full control of the police. I knew Arthur as a brilliant lawyer and a Catholic who, like most Austrians, favored union with Germany. I also knew that at no time did he ever belong to the National Socialist Party.

At the same time, he appointed Seyss-Inquart, Schuschnigg made extraordinary efforts to reach an agreement with the leftists. In light of Moscow's pressure, Dr. Schuschnigg embarked on a course of action which I'm sure he believed would salvage and preserve Austria's independence.

†

"**PLEBISCITE!**" screamed the evening edition of the *Krone*, Vienna's largest newspaper as the sun set on Wednesday, March 9, 1938. Everywhere I walked that evening, I saw and heard crowds of people talking, some anxious, some jubilant, most bewildered about what our chancellor had done. He'd announced that four days hence, on Sunday, March 13, there would be plebiscite – a direct question to be put to all of Austria: *Are you in favor of, or against, a free, German, independent, social, Christian and united Austria? Ja oder Nein?*

As a loyal NSDAP member, but also as someone who was quickly becoming more than adept at how the politics of my homeland operated, I was surprised and cynical over what Schuschnigg proposed. The problems with his proposal were obvious. First, the balloting was to be completely open and public – no secret ballot. Since the last vote for the National Assembly had taken place in 1929, there were no accurate voting lists. We were told that none were necessary. The *Vaterländische Front*, the only organization dealing with the plebiscite, would take care of everything.

Those who were employed were required to vote at their workplace. Every citizen over the age of 25 could vote: they needed only to show the family register, a rent, gas, or light receipt, a bank book, and an identity card issued by the *Vaterländische Front* or the *Landbund*. If the voting proctor knew you, you didn't even need personal identification papers. The polling stations only had YES ballots. Those who wished to vote NO had to bring a ballot marked NO with them and ask the official election overseer for an official envelope in which to place it!

"That's insane," I said to one of my friends on the Board. "It would be easy for fifty transients to give Schuschnigg several thousand votes if they began their route through the various polling stations early in the morning."

"No kidding," my associate, Rudy Schuster, said. "Meanwhile, the Austrian radio and the government press remind everyone in no uncertain terms that every citizen who votes NO is guilty of high treason – a traitor to the State."

On the evening of March 10, I took up my nightly vigil outside the chancellor's residence. The Party posted such "ears" everywhere in the First District. It was not difficult to learn a lot, since councilors, lawyers and politicians, who were *thought* to have inside information, traded mostly in unsupported rumors, while lowly clerks, bureaucrats, and janitors, who really *did* have inside information, talked in quiet, monosyllabic voices. I listened much more intently to what these faceless, nameless civil servants mumbled or murmured to one another.

"Schuschnigg's issued a mobilization order. The *Vaterländische Front* militias are ready for action."

"Yes, but I saw a few men I knew from the *Schutzbund* troops, the Marxists, wearing the camouflage light gray uniforms of the *Vaterländische Front.*"

My watch ended by nine o'clock, but since I lived nearby, and since my antennae had been alerted by the mention of two opposing militias, I was back at my post by eight the next morning. The scene I witnessed was straight out of the theater of the absurd. Troops paraded through the streets of Vienna, their fists raised in the Communist salute, followed by columns of trucks from the suburbs flying the red flag with the hammer and sickle. Workers raised their fists, sang the *Internationale,* and shouted, "Vote YES for freedom! Down with Hitler! Long live Moscow!" Meanwhile, aircraft bearing red-white-red Austrian flags dropped tons of leaflets exhorting the public, "Vote YES!"

I heard later that afternoon that about 1:00 p.m. Chancellor Schuschnigg had announced that the wording of the question was to be changed, but that Göring had telephoned him and demanded that the government step down. My Gymnastics League confederates told me that German troops were massed along the border.

By nightfall, the government announced mobilization of the workers' militias. Shortly thereafter, I received a call from one of the leaders of the German Gymnastics League telling me to get my defense platoon together. My League associates and I joined a huge crowd of people gathered in front of the chancellor's office, all of us anxiously sorting through various rumors.

Suddenly, at eight in the evening, Seyss-Inquart, speaking from a balcony abutting Heroes Square, called on everyone to be calm; that the police and the National Socialist security service would ensure the peace and order were maintained. As I looked around the huge square, I was amazed to see that a large number of people, including some of the police, had donned swastika arm bands. It seemed everyone had become good National Socialists once they learned that President Miklas had accepted Schuschnigg's resignation.

At first the president refused to name Seyss-Inquart as Schuschnigg's successor. Miklas was an honorable man, who had strong principles and fourteen children. What he didn't know was that two of them belonged to the underground SA. The end of Austria as an independent state began that night when we embarked on a torchlight parade through the streets of Vienna to the front of the chancellor's office. People cried, laughed, and hugged one another when we'd circled back to Heroes Square.

At 11:00 that night, I heard a sudden roar from the sea of humanity gathered below the balcony of the chancellery as the swastika flag was raised. Shouts of "Heil Hitler!" bombarded the square. Still, President Miklas stubbornly continued to search for a successor chancellor. By midnight the president had been forced to appoint Seyss-Inquart. The new chancellor immediately handed the president a list of new ministers.

When Seyss-Inquart finally appeared on the balcony and started to speak, I couldn't hear a word of what he said. Suddenly everything grew quiet, and we all joined in singing the German national anthem:

Deutschland, Deutschland über alles, über alles in der Welt ...

Germany, Germany above all else,
Above all else in the world,
If it always stands together
Fraternally in defense and defiance,
From the Meuse to the Neman,
From the Adige up to the Belt
Germany, Germany, above all else,
Above all else in the world!

I have since read that democratic principles were violated. But not a shadow of democracy had existed in Austria since the assassinated Chancellor Dollfuss had dissolved parliament in March 1933. After Dollfuss' tragic death, President Miklas named Schuschnigg chancellor without consulting the Austrian people.

After midnight, there was nothing left for us to do at Heroes Square, so my friends and I made our way to a side street behind the chancellor's office. We still wondered whether the rumors that Hitler had ordered German troops to march into Austria were true.

At that moment, a black limousine pulled out of a driveway into the street. As we stepped aside to let it pass, I heard a sharp voice. "Skorzeny! Do you have a car?" I recognized Bruno Weiss, president of our German Gymnastics League.

"Yes," I responded.

"Good. We need a man with a cool head and common sense. Did you see the big limousine that just pulled out? It's carrying President Miklas to Reisner Strasse, which is occupied by a unit of the guard battalion. We've just learned that an SA battalion has received orders to go to Reisner Strasse as well. The federal president is supposed to receive protection from the new government. We must avoid a confrontation between those two units at all costs. Do you understand?"

"Completely, Herr Weiss, but I have no authority..."

He interrupted me with a wave of his hand. "In the name of the new chancellor, I instruct you personally to go to Reisner Strasse and intervene to avoid any incident. Take some of your associates with you. I will inform the chancellor that I've given you this mission. I'll try to reach an agreement by telephone, but it would be better if you could be there. Telephone the chancellery as soon as you arrive. Now get going, Otto! The minutes are precious."

And they were. Luckily, I was able to recruit a dozen comrades on the spot. Some of us loaded into three cars, others jumped onto motorcycles, and off we roared into the night, straight through the crowd, which cleared a path for us. We arrived in front of the palace just as the president drove in. We stayed right behind him. I ordered that the large entrance gate be closed.

The president was just about to go up the stairs when we entered the large hall. A young guards lieutenant appeared at the second floor balcony and drew his pistol. The loud shouts of the guards soldiers and those of the president's entourage mingled. Frau Miklas appeared, completely distraught.

Then, out of nowhere, I shouted louder than the others: "*Quiet!*"

"Weapons ready to fire!" ordered the lieutenant.

We had neither weapons nor armbands. We had no idea if anyone would even listen. Twenty guards soldiers flanked the second-floor gallery. The president still stood on the staircase, looking at his wife without saying a word. I could hear a growing tumult from the street. The SA people, who'd jumped down from their trucks, were demanding that we open the gate. I prayed it would hold.

"Quiet, gentlemen!" I shouted again, "Herr President, please listen to me."

He turned and looked at me in surprise. "Who are you, sir, and what do you want?"

"I am engineer Skorzeny, Herr President. May I call the chancellor on the telephone?"

"Certainly, but tell me, what does all that noise outside mean?"

I knew what the noise meant, but I couldn't say it. The SA might be preparing to storm the palace, which would have resulted in a bloody firefight. Instead, I said, "Please excuse me a moment, Mister President. I will go and see at once."

With help from my Gymnastics League friends, we were finally able to calm everyone down. As President Miklas looked on, I called the chancellor's office. Dr. Seys-Inquart came on the line immediately. Fortunately, Bruno Weiss had taken the necessary steps. The new chancellor spoke with the president for a few minutes. Then, Miklas handed me the receiver.

"Congratulations, Engineer Skorzeny," Seyss-Inquart said. "Your conduct was exemplary. Now I ask that you assume command of the guards battalion detachment. Please make sure the guards maintain order inside the palace while the SA keeps order outside. Finally, I ask that you wait at the palace for further instructions."

"*Jawohl, Herr Chancellor!*" I said, snapping to attention, even to clicking my heels, which, under the circumstances, did not seem like something out of a Strauss operetta. "It is my privilege and my honor, Sir!"

For three days and nights I carried out my mission, to the apparent satisfaction of everyone, without incident. In the end, Chancellor Seyss-Inquart thanked me with a proud handshake and a comradely pat on the shoulder. I was still naïve. I believed I had entered active politics, not by chance, but through the large gate.

♦

I witnessed Hitler's triumphant entry into Vienna from a lofty vantage point, the palace balcony. I was ecstatic. We were welcoming one of our own. Whatever they might say about Hitler today, he had endured hunger in Vienna. There, before our eyes, he took his place among the greatest Austrians, Rudolf, Maximilian, Carl, Ferdinand, and Josef, all of whom had been German emperors. Hundreds of thousands of my compatriots joined me on the Ringstrasse that morning. It was magnificent, wonderful, with a sea of flags and flowers, endless applause, and bright, spirited military music. Then, we sensed a movement and curiosity in the crowd as the *SS-Leibstandarte Adolf Hitler*, the elite unit that guarded the Führer, arrived.

At that moment, I wanted, more than anything, excepting, of course, Lisbeth Hollander on the day I first beheld her incredible body, to become a member of that crack unit; to stand next to the great man himself, and to guard his very life.

I have never been able to explain where my countrymen got hold of the tens of thousands of flags anticipating the "rape of Austria," and how attitudes had completely changed overnight.

On March 10, Archbishop Cardinal Innitzer of Vienna had endorsed Schuschnigg's plebiscite, declaring, "As Austrian citizens, we are fighting for a free, independent Austria!" Slightly more than a week later, he turned his clerical collar and declared, "It is our duty as Germans to speak out in favor of the German Reich."

By the end of March 1938, the new government called for another plebiscite to take place on April 10th. This time it would truly be a free and secret vote. The question to be answered was, *"Are you in favor of a union of Austria with the Reich?"*

On April 3, 1938, Dr. Karl Renner, the socialist politician who had led Austria as its first chancellor when I was only ten years old, who would preside over the National Council until 1933, and who, oddly enough, would head Austria after the collapse of the Third Reich from 1945 until his death in 1950, proclaimed, "As a social democrat and as the representative of the right of self-determination of the nation, I will vote *JA!*" After the *Anschluss*, Dr. Renner lived in Goggnitz at the foot of the Semmering. Thanks to the pension granted to him, he survived World War II peacefully and unharmed. When the invading Red Army found Dr. Renner at the end of the War, they persuaded him to write a letter to Marshall Stalin in Moscow in which he stated,

> "The Red Army found me when it entered my home town, where I trustingly awaited the occupation with party comrades. For this I thank the Red Army and you, its glorious supreme commander."

During my life, I found that the solid, unwavering patriotism and resolve of the Austrian people against the powers of surrounding nations had about the same resistance and strength as a sheaf of wheat blowing in the wind. It will bend in whatever direction the wind blows, while maintaining that "Red-white-red until we're dead" (the colors of the Austrian flag) has a rather ambiguous meaning depending on who's in control.

A month before, when Schuschnigg announced the plebiscite for an independent Austria, he believed the plebiscite to maintain Austrian independence from Germany would pass by a substantial majority. On April 10, 1938, when the official count of the new Plebiscite was tallied, the vote was:

For the union of Austria with the German Reich:	4,284,295 votes
Against the union of Austria with the Reich:	9,852 votes
Spoiled ballots:	559

But at the end of the day, all was not sweetness and light between the two partners of the union. I have read about the United States after the War Between the States, when the victors brought "carpetbagger" politicians to rule the defeated Confederate States. So it turned out in Austria. Although the Reich produced many superb administrators, they were, unfortunately, not the ones they sent to govern what was now called Östmark. This was, in the end, only to add to the tragedy that befell my homeland.

5

―――

"Herr Skorzeny, I was not aware that you were as tall as me and that your *Schmiss* was just as ugly!" This was the opening salvo when I met the newly-appointed State Secretary for Public Security in the Seyss-Inquart cabinet. Ernst Kaltenbrunner and I felt an immediate kinship and our friendship was to last until his death.

"Twins we may or may not be, *Brigadeführer*," I answered, using his SS rank, which I knew he preferred to his status as a member of the Austrian cabinet, "but if you're saying neither of us will win a beauty contest, that is most likely an accurate assumption."

Kaltenbrunner laughed out loud and grabbed my arm in a brotherly half-embrace. "I appreciate what you did to save President Miklas' life," he continued. "I understand you received your pilot's license some months ago. Have you ever thought of applying for the Luftwaffe?"

"I tried a couple of months ago. Can you believe, they said I was too tall and too *old?*"

"At 31? You're a mere lad, Skorzeny, five years my junior."

"That may be true, *Brigadeführer,* but you and I as Austrians know we're a little more flexible than our German brothers with their *Alles in ordnung, alles in butter,* and all that."

"Otto," Kaltenbrunner said, addressing me for the first time by my Christian name, "I've been watching you more closely than you might imagine during the past several months. I consider myself a good judge of character and I like what I've seen. Forgive me, I seem to have forgotten my manners. Heinz," he addressed his adjutant, "could you bring us some *kaffee mit schlag* and some *Sachertorte?*"

Kaltenbrunner's assistant saluted, issued a sharp *Jawohl, Herr General!* and left my new friend's office.

"Have you ever thought of joining the *Schutzstaffel?*"

"The SS? Who hasn't? But how would I go about it?"

"I could speak to some people about that. Meanwhile, the war hasn't started yet. There are some friends I'd like you to meet. You never can tell what they might be able to do for your career. Ah, thank you, Heinz," the Brigadier General said as his assistant brought in Viennese coffee and pastries and arranged the china-and-silver plate setting for Kaltenbrunner and me to enjoy what turned out to be a most convivial and productive two hours.

At one point, I delicately broached the statement he had raised about a war having not started yet.

Kaltenbrunner airily deflected the question. "Did I say that? I must have misspoken, but as everyone knows, despite the Führer's best efforts at trying to secure peace through last September's Munich Pact, it was necessary for the Reich to assume a greater role in protecting Czecho-Slovakia's German minority a couple of months ago. Certain European nations are spreading defamatory lies about the motivation for our move, and … you never can tell what irrational and ill-motivated leaders like Stalin might do."

Friday, May 5, 1939. After the 4½-hour flight from Vienna, our three-engined, 17-passenger Junkers J-52 touched down at Hamburg's Fuhlsbüttel airport. *Brigadeführer* Kaltenbrunner had called ahead to ensure that we'd be picked up shortly after the plane landed and driven the 130 miles from the airport to *Stadt des KdF-Wagens*, Germany's newest town.

"Not Stuttgart?" I'd asked Kaltenbrunner when he was planning the journey.

"No," Kaltenbrunner had replied. "Doctor Porsche moved from Stuttgart to the new city last year. His son Ferry continues to manage the Porsche Works, but the old man's been tasked with developing the KDF-Wagen."

"The *Volkswagen*?"

"Uh-huh. The Führer wants to put one in the hands of every German citizen who can afford 990 Reichsmarks, $396 U.S., payable at the rate of 5 Marks a week. That's why he called for an entirely new urban center to build those cars as quickly and cheaply as possible."

"Who's financing this venture?"

"The government, with Schacht's help."

"I thought he'd fallen from grace," I said.

"He might not be in Hitler's inner circle but he's still president of the Reichsbank."

The airliner had taken off from Aspern Airfield in Donaustadt at eight that morning. By 4:30 that afternoon, our driver had dropped General Kaltenbrunner off in town, then proceeded to take me to a middle-class residence halfway up the hill to Wolfsburg Castle, the only building in the area than seemed more than ten years old.

I was greeted at the door by a short, dapper man who appeared to be in his early sixties. He held out his hand, grasped mine firmly, and said, "You are Otto Skorzeny, yes? An engineer? Your father must be as proud of you as I am of my Ferry! It's always a wonderful testament to a father when a son wants to follow in his footsteps. I am delighted to meet you … may I call you Otto?"

"Of course, Herr Doktor," I responded. While I kept my composure on the outside, I was overwhelmed to be in the presence of the legendary pinnacle of Austrian engineering himself, *Doktor Ingenieur Honoris Causa* Ferdinand Porsche.

"Ah, yes, 'Doktor,'" he mused. "You know of course that I never really earned any kind of university degree. They found fit to confer an *honorary* doctorate on me when I turned 41. But come, young man, there's no need for you to stand out in the cold like a cabbage. I've put by some reasonably good wine, or *schnapps* if you prefer. But it would not look good for the two of us to be seen 'bending the elbow' outdoors. Besides, we're blessed with the company of two others this evening, Ferry, and Dr. Hjalmar Schacht. You've heard of him?"

"The money man behind this project."

"You are quite direct, Herr Skorzeny," he replied, seeming not at all offended.

"We are both men of action, Dr. Porsche. Indirection ill becomes us."

"Well said, Herr Skorzeny. Let's adjourn to more comfortable quarters.

As we entered an informal living room, Dr. Schacht, dressed in a conservative dark gray business suit, rose, nodded stiffly, and resumed his seat on a sofa. Ferdinand Porsche *fils* came over and shook my hand with the same firm grip as his father. I warmed to him immediately as we moved to two easy chairs, leaving the two senior potentates to discuss "large" matters, though still within my range of hearing.

"So, Ferdinand," Schacht addressed the senior Porsche. "How go things in the new company town?"

"The *town* is certainly up and running, as you can plainly see."

"And production of the Volkswagen? How many have been delivered to customers?"

"None, Hjalmar."

"*None?*" The banker's eyebrows lifted. "*Warum nicht?*"

"Orders from above. Twenty days ago, we were told to convert to production facilities for the *Kübelwagen* and the *Schwimmwagen.*"

"Interesting," Schacht replied.

When I heard this, I casually remarked to Ferry, "So there may be substance to the rumors."

"Uh-huh. Our factories in Stuttgart are also converting from civilian vehicles, not only to amphibious vehicles but to tanks as well."

"Not your passion?"

"Absolutely not. Race cars, yes. I actually got hooked on them when I was ten years old, on Christmas Eve 1920. My parents fooled me when they gave me a miniature coach pulled by a goat. When they saw how downcast I looked, Papa raised his eyebrows and said, 'Not exciting enough for you, Ferry?' 'Well …' I replied, 'it's not exactly what I expected. I am ten, you know.'

"'Go on, Ferd, show him the real present,' Mama chided

"'Oh, all right,' Papa said in mock exasperation. 'Help me dig it out from under this pile of hay.' Little by little, my real gift appeared: a petrol-driven miniature car with a four-stroke, two-cylinder engine specially designed by my father. The following year, Dad let me drive a real race car, an Austro-Daimler Sascha, and from then on you couldn't hold me back."

"Where do you think the Führer's plans will lead?"

"Between you and me?" Ferry said standing up and motioning me to a far corner of the room. "Oblivion and the destruction of Germany," he said very quietly. "Frankly, I think his Jew-hating policies are just plain stupid. Dad's business partner and financial backer, Adolf Rosenberger was Jewish. Dad had to pretend Rosenberger was an 'employee' just to get him safely out of Germany. He was only able to do that because of Papa's 'good friend' Schacht."

"How did that come about?"

Ferry led me over to a sideboard, poured himself a light *hock* wine, and when I nodded, he poured me a glass as well. In a still-lower voice he said, "At first Schacht was extremely hostile to Germany's Jewish population. I remember hearing him speak in 1933, a couple of years after we'd moved to Stuttgart. He said, 'The Jews must realize that their influence in Germany has disappeared for all time.' A year later, when he thought it would be good for the Reich's finances, he arranged a deal with the World Zionist Organization, where German Jews could pay 15,000 Reich marks to emigrate to Palestine. From then until the end of last year, 175,000 Jews, including Doctor Rosenberger, reached Palestine under this agreement."

"So at the end he was not such a Jew-hater after all."

"Schacht didn't mind taking Jewish money. Despite saying that the Jewish influence was a plague on the Reich, he disagreed with what he called 'unlawful activities' against Jews. He pointed out that Jews had fought bravely in the German Army and deserved to be treated fairly. How do you feel about the Jews, Otto?"

"I've known good ones and bad ones. I really don't care one way or the other. The ones I knew in Vienna certainly didn't look like the caricatures in the *Völkischer Beobachter*."

We edged closer to the older men, eavesdropping on their conversation.

"A shame your Ferry is married," Schacht said. "That's not to say Dorothea's not a wonderful woman, but my friend's niece Emmi ..."

"Enough!" the senior Ferdinand snapped, but jovially. "Every time you see an eligible young bachelor, you say much the same thing. Otto," he called out. "Are you by any chance single?"

"Oh God!" Ferry moaned. "Here we go again with Emilie."

"Have you met her?"

"Once in Berlin. Actually, a very attractive woman in her late twenties. I think she was engaged but then broke it off. Old Uncle Hjalmar has set himself up as a matchmaker." He turned to Schacht and remarked, "Do you ever stop to think Emmi might stand a better chance if she were to find a man on her own?"

"Quiet, whelp!" the banker replied, showing that he might not be so stiff and stuffy after all. "Otto, are you or aren't you married?"

"Not," I answered.

"Surely you're not …?"

At my withering look, he stammered, "I … I didn't really mean that, of course, but a young man of your age?"

"I was married Herr Reichsbankpräsident. Five years, no children."

"Good. I mean … well … have you ever been to Berlin?"

"Never, Herr Schacht."

"Perhaps you might like to ride back to Berlin with me?"

My Vienna had been soft and alluring with the same roundness one associates with a beautiful woman. Berlin seemed a much more masculine city, square, bold, and arrogantly impressive. Wehrmacht soldiers strutted proudly on every major street, Unter den Linden, Friedrichstrasse, Kurfürstendamm, and, of course, through the Brandenburg Gate. The more I saw of Hitler's planned Welthauptstadt Germania, World Capital Germania, the differences between the two cities became even more pronounced in my mind. Vienna sought to express its graceful history and genteel, gemütlichkeit lifestyle, while Berlin sought to impress both citizen and tourist with its power, might, and stark perfection.

I remarked on this during my first week in the Reich capital, while Ernst Kaltenbrunner and I walked through a portion of the Tiergarten, Berlin's 520-acre central park, enroute to the headquarters of the Waffen-SS.

"Is this not a most gorgeous park, and in the very center of the city?" he remarked.

"Yes, Brigadeführer. Most impressive, but not quite natural. Every rose in the gardens is perfect in every way, as if gardeners come by evening and snip off any aging or dying flower. Same with the trees. Same with the greensward. Everything is just so. Things don't seem to age, things don't seem to wither. A garden maintained for the children of the gods."

"A bit cynical, Otto?"

"No. I'd say more realistic. Take that woman we just passed, tall, blonde, perfectly coiffed, not a hair out of place. Uncommonly beautiful – her face, her body …"

"The Northern European ideal. Like Renaissance paintings of Christ?"

"Pretty much." We stopped at a nearby kiosk where my friend and superior purchased a triple-cupped ice cream cone, vanilla, chocolate, and strawberry, for each of us. "I can't thank you enough for putting in a good word for me with the Waffen-SS. Now they want me to interview with them. I understand there are a hundred applicants in the cadet class and only ten will be accepted into the corps."

"It's an elite outfit. Getting you into the cadet class was not difficult. You're on your own from here."

"Anything I should know about the Waffen-SS, other than what I saw last year when the *Leibstandarte Adolf Hitler* marched by in Vienna?"

"The SS was originally formed to be Hitler's bodyguards at the end of 1924 after the SA was banned in most German provinces. By the early part of 1929, Hitler gave Himmler the task of organizing the SS into military-political fighters. They would fight beside the army, but they would not be part of the Army. The Army and the Waffen-SS were separate concepts. The Army was loyal to the German Reich; the Waffen-SS was loyal directly, and only, to Der Führer. The unit you saw last year, the *Leibstandarte Adolf Hitler*, was the first armed unit, the parade regiment."

"I remember how impressed I was, *Brigadeführer*. That was shortly before I met you."

"Today, there are two additional regiments, the Deutschland Regiment and the *Germania* Regiment. If we're ever forced to go to war, they'll be the top-of-the line corps, at least politically."

Two nights later, on what was to be my final evening in Berlin, I was invited to attend a dinner at the home of one of Hjalmar Schacht's industrial friends, whose name I forgot within a week thereafter. As was the custom in those days, single invitees to such soirees were paired, one man, one woman, and seated across from one another.

To my utter shock, I could have sworn the exquisite young woman sitting across the table from me was the same one I had seen two days before while I was walking with *Brigadeführer* Kaltenbrunner in the Tiergarten. I had no opening conversational gambit and I was damned if I'd resort to using the hackneyed and consummately stupid, "Haven't we met before?"

Before I'd even opened my mouth to introduce myself, the woman smiled self-confidently and said, "If you're thinking the same thing I'm thinking, the answer is 'Yes.' I saw you and that other large fellow, whose Schmiss is almost as ugly as yours, in the Tiergarten day-before-yesterday."

"I – "

"Emilie Linhart," she said, holding her hand out with the directness of a man reaching across the table to shake hands. "Or, if you prefer, Emmi."

"You - ?"

"You seem to be a master of economical conversation." She laughed, a charming, silvery sound, not at all what I would have expected from what I'd been told were stiff, humorless Germans. "Shall I fill in the blanks?"

"Do I have a choice?"

"Depends on how much time you have. I'm sure my friends, who think I'm a poor spinster halfway to grandmotherhood who'll end up in a convent if I don't find a man quickly, secured my invitation for tonight."

"You're Doktor Schacht's niece?"

"No relation, really. Hjalmar's known my parents since I was seven. He did tell me about you, though. I understood you met him at Ferd Porsche's quarters in 'Volkswagen city.' You're Otto Skorzeny, thirty-one and presently unmarried. I'm twenty-eight, if chronological numbers are important to you. And no, Herr Skorzeny, I am not a virgin if you must know. I will have a glass of white wine if you're offering."

I stood, walked over to a sideboard, and brought back two glasses, one for this most-direct-of-women and one for myself. "Am I not permitted to say anything?"

"Of course. God forbid I should monopolize the conversation."

During dinner, I became bemused and charmed by this young woman, so unlike anyone I'd met before. For flashes that passed far too quickly in the space of our two hours of animated conversation I found myself wondering what Lisbeth Hollander, my erstwhile but, occasionally still active lover, would think of Emilie Linhart.

At one point after dinner, when we'd adjourned to sitting on the sofa in an adjoining anteroom, I remarked, "Emmi, you've turned my impression of what German women are like on its head. I've always heard it's *küche, kinder, kirche*."

"Probably true," she responded. "But I wouldn't know. I'm a *Wienere*, bred and born."

"Seriously?"

"Well, certainly an Austrian. 'Uncle' Hjalmar's a stuffy old *Hochdeutsche*, born in Schleswig-Holstein province before it became part of Denmark. He bounced all over Germany before ending up here."

"That explains your *gemütlichkeit* charm."

"I thank you for that, Gallant Herr."

"And I'd thank *you* if we could see each other again."

"Well, Herr Skorzeny, that doesn't strike me as the most repulsive of ideas." She smiled and in that moment I knew with certainty that by no means would this be the last time I would see Emilie Linhart.

6

In the summer of 1939 I still believed there would be no war. The Munich Agreement seemed to me to be the prelude to a general agreement by the European powers for a revision of the postwar treaties. It seemed impossible to me that the Europeans, who together shared such a high level of culture and civilization, should not reach an understanding that was in everyone's best interests. The Czech problem was solved, Poland had recovered the Teschen region, and three-and-a-half million Sudeten Germans had again become citizens of the Reich. My father, whose family came from Lake Skorzenczin in Bohemia, had been deeply moved by their return.

The whole world knew that Danzig, which had been the capital of West Prussia until it had been taken from the Reich the year after the War ended, was undoubtedly German, something the Versailles Treaty could not change. Our scattered, torn-apart people could not continue to be held responsible forever for the mistakes made by its government from 1914 to 1918.

In August, I was spending my vacation with Ferry Porsche's family in Velden-am-Wörthersee. On August 23, Emmi and I took an hour's drive from Velden to *Burg Hochosterwitz,* one of the most impressive and romantic medieval castles I'd ever seen, perched as it was atop a 564-foot high Dolomite rock. Overlooking the valley below, it was easy to see the countryside for twenty miles or more in every direction. In the three months since that evening in Berlin, we'd become lovers, and thought it might be a pleasant diversion to spend the night alone in Sankt-Veit-an-der-Glan, the town adjacent to the castle. At day's end, however, we decided we could wait, since our holiday at the Porsches would only be for a week.

No sooner had we arrived back in Velden, we were surprised to see the senior Ferdinand Porsche standing out in the parking lot, awaiting us in a state of great agitation.

"Have you heard the news?"

"What news, Doktor?"

"Germany and Russia have signed a joint nonaggression pact."

"*What?*" I was shocked by this news. The entire family was deeply dismayed as we entered the house. In my life, I had never heard of such a sudden change of allegiances on such a monumental scale. I certainly wouldn't have believed such news if I'd heard it even a few days ago. That Der Führer would conclude a pact with Stalin, the arch-Communist, seemed impossible!

Yet the evening papers blared what must be the truth: The agreement provided a written guarantee of non-belligerence by each party towards the other and a commitment that neither government would ally itself to, or aid, an enemy of the other party. What none of us knew that night, and would not find out until years later, was that the Molotov-Ribbentrop Pact secretly divided parts of Poland, Lithuania, Latvia, Estonia, Finland, and Romania into German and Soviet spheres of influence, anticipating "territorial and political rearrangements" of those nations.

I was in for a greater, but not wholly unexpected, surprise when Emmi told me on the way back to Vienna she thought she might be pregnant. I was not disheartened by that news. At thirty-one it was time, as Lisbeth had reminded me some time before, to marry, this time for real.

Emmi was gratified at how well I took the news. "I expected you'd do what I've heard so many men do, deny everything and look for the quickest way to ditch a fallen woman."

"Emmi, neither of us is in the first blush of youth. You aren't my first love and I'm certain I'm not yours. Since we started as friends, I have no doubt we could continue in a more traditional relationship. What do you say to that, girl?"

She grinned. "I say let's find a romantic little hotel in Semmering, screw our brains out, and give our marriage a fighting start."

And so it came to pass.

On Thursday, August 31, Mussolini called for an emergency international conference for September 5 to review the clauses of the Versailles Treaty, which, he said, were the cause of the present crisis. Apparently no one listened to him.

Late that night, a small group of German operatives dressed in Polish uniforms, led by *SS-Sturmbannführer* Alfred Naujocks, seized the German radio station, *Sender Gleiwitz* in Upper Silesia, and broadcast a short anti-German message in Polish. The Germans' goal was to make the attack and the broadcast look like the work of anti-German Polish saboteurs. To make the attack more convincing, the Germans used human corpses and passed them off as Polish attackers. The Gestapo arrested Franciszek Honiok, a 43-year-old unmarried German Silesian Catholic farmer known for sympathizing with the Poles, dressed him to look like a saboteur, killed him by lethal injection, and left him dead at the scene, so that he appeared to have been killed while attacking the station. The Gestapo presented his body to the police and press as proof of the attack. In addition to Honiok, several prisoners from the

Dachau concentration camp were drugged, shot dead on the site, and their faces disfigured to make identification impossible. [1]

At 5:45 a.m. on September 1, the Wehrmacht marched into Poland "to protect the German people living in Poland." Great Britain declared war on Germany at noon the next day, followed by France at 5:00 p.m. "in order to defend the independence of Poland."

No German was pleased. I believe Göring expressed all our thoughts when he said to von Ribbentrop, "God help us if we should ever lose this war!"

Shortly after the war started, I was called up by the Luftwaffe. Since I had earlier been told I was too old and too tall to fly, I knew if I responded to the call, I'd be a mere office hack. I could not imagine anything worse.

Earlier, I'd applied to the Waffen-SS and been one of only ten out of a hundred applicants to be accepted. It was time for me to call on my friend, SS- *Brigadeführer* Kaltenbrunner, to transfer me from the Luftwaffe to the Waffen-SS. So powerful an ally was Ernst that my transfer went through in less than a week. I became a member of the legendary *Leibstandarte Adolf Hitler*.

The real father of the Waffen-SS was General Paul Hausser, whom we called "Papa Hausser" as a symbol of our affection. During my time in the Waffen-SS, no one I knew in any of the units confirmed

---

1   In oral testimony at the Nuremberg trials, Erwin von Lahousen stated that his division of the Abwehr was one of two that were given the task of providing Polish uniforms, equipment, and identification cards, and that he was later told by Wilhelm Canaris that people from concentration camps had been disguised in these uniforms and ordered to attack the radio stations, 20 *Nuremberg Trial Proceedings, Volume 2*; Friday, November 30, 1945.

Himmler's absurd "Theory of the Nordic Man" as superior to any other "subhuman *untermenschen*," to use his term.

In February 1940, I was assigned to the Second Company of the reserve battalion of SS-Leibstandarte Adolf Hitler in Berlin-Lichterfelde. Although I was an engineer-officer candidate, I had to endure six weeks of intensive training with18-year-olds. The other recruits who were my age, doctors, lawyers, pharmacists, and engineers, had to clench their teeth to avoid staying behind with this "moonlight company," so called because the company commander preferred to conduct exercises at night.

By May, after special training with the Waffen-SS *Germania* Regiment, I found myself on the roads of Holland, Belgium, and France, as a member of the artillery regiment *Das Reich* under Papa Hausser. To this day, I recall Hausser as the fairest and most moral of leaders. Two examples of this stand out in my mind.

On May 18, 1940, our regiment passed through a small village near Hirson in northeastern France, a stone's throw from the Belgian border. Bales of cloth lay scattered on the sidewalk, the sad remains of a shop which had been destroyed be a shell. A group of my artillery comrades took one of the bales of yellow material, cut it up, and made themselves yellow neckerchiefs from it. Next day a division order, applicable to all units, was read out at roll call:

"Soldiers of the division have been seen wearing neckerchiefs which apparently have been made from French materials. You are reminded that the appropriation of any item from the street, be it cloth or any other thing, is considered plundering. The division's officers are therefore advised to consider any soldier wearing such a neckerchief as a plunderer, to be arrested immediately and brought before a court-martial."

In February 1941, numerous French prisoners of war were released to return home as a result of the cease-fire agreement. One of the French soldiers arrived home unexpectedly, late one night, and surprised one of our comrades with his wife. The woman claimed she had been raped, hoping to escape her husband's wrath. One can't blame her for that. However, our countryman was arrested, brought before a court-martial, and sentenced to death. Several of us officers and non-commissioned officers asked our general for mercy, for we were convinced it was not a case of rape; rather that the affair had been going on for several weeks. But our pleadings were in vain. After he had listened to us, Papa Hausser said:

"Not a single member of the Waffen-SS, which is an elite force, may fall under even the suspicion of having committed an act which would shame a true solder. The sentence will be carried out."

And it was.

During the hard winter of 1940-41, while we were ensconced on the Langres Plateau, halfway between Paris and the Alsace-Lorraine, I became friends with a local French winegrower, Michel Dutarte. Our conversations, while not frequent, cut to the crux of nonpolitical human relations.

"Michel," I said one evening over a thick vegetable soup, baguettes, and, of course, some of his elegant burgundy, "What the hell am I doing here? I haven't seen outright hatred of the Germans here, and for damn sure I've only found warmth and charm among the French."

"That's because we manage to keep our shrewish old women indoors," he chortled. "But seriously, haven't both sides earned enough glory on the battlefield against each other to now start building a united Europe side by side?"

"Even at this early point in the war, I sure wish we had peace. I recently married a good and beautiful woman, we've started on our family already, and it would be nice to be back in Vienna when the little one comes. Do you think anything'll come out of the Montoire meeting?"

Both of us had learned only a day ago that Hitler and Marshall Petain had met secretly in a railroad car some eighty miles south of Paris.

"Truthfully, I'm not optimistic, Otto. This is not Verdun 1916. The *Marechal's* almost eighty-four and your Führer's got a lot more muscle than von Falkenhayn had twenty-three years ago. I fear he's going to announce collaboration with the Reich in a couple of days and that will set him as the great traitor if and when …"

We both left what might naturally follow unsaid and went on to less sensitive talk.

By the beginning of 1941, things were not turning out according to our expectations. Our allies, the Italians, were defeated in East Africa. The English had launched a successful counteroffensive against Marshall Graziani and occupied Tobruk and Benghazi. On February 26, Rommel's Afrika Korps intervened, but that pulled combat troops we could have used elsewhere.

Meanwhile, in Europe, the Duce invaded Greece with his badly-trained, poorly-provisioned, and indifferently-led army, without informing Hitler beforehand. Our allies were soon thrown back, then overrun in Albania, of all places. Then, a *coup d'état* overthrew Prince Regent Paul, our ally in Yugoslavia. Several days later, the new head of the Yugoslav government, General Simovich, signed a friendship pact with Stalin, guaranteeing mutual support. Although I didn't say anything, I had an uneasy feeling that the eternal marriage between the Soviet Union and the Reich might soon come to an unpleasant end.

✝

By spring of 1941, our division, retrained, rejuvenated, and renamed the SS-Division *Das Reich*, started checking our rolling stock, which was in really pitiable condition. At the beginning of June 1941, after several weeks of working extensively to put our machinery in working order, we received orders to load the entire division onto a long train. After we had rolled through Czecho-Slovakia, we continued east to Poland. Where were we going and why?

Talk among the junior officers – I had been promoted to *Obersturmführer* - first lieutenant - during the Balkan campaign was speculative and we gave our imaginations free reign.

"Unquestionably Russia will let us cross the Caucasus so we can occupy the Persian oil fields," Lieutenant Hochofer, a man my own age, said. "If this *verdammte* war continues, we won't be able to rely on Ploiești oil forever. Sooner or later the enemy may be able to penetrate Romania."

"I don't know," another young man, Langer, replied. "I've heard we're about to sign a friendship and assistance pact with Inönü in Turkey. That'll let us march through Atatürk's country, hit the Suez and Egypt, and attack the English from behind while Rommel and the Italians go on the offensive."

One believes what one hopes for. The idea of a campaign in Persia, Arabia, or Egypt seemed especially tempting to me. I had in my pack a copy of Colonel T.E. Lawrence's *The Seven Pillars of Wisdom*. Lawrence, a rather peculiar fellow, had been an adventurer, archaeologist, secret agent, and champion of Arab independence from the Turks. Could we not also achieve with the Arabs and Turks against England what he had started?

During our rail journey, I had time to think. I continued reading Lawrence of Arabia's fascinating account with mounting interest. I had just reached the part where, in 1918, Lawrence was preparing to blow up a Turkish military train, when our train pulled into Lvov station. From there, we continued on through the night into the area south of Brest-Litovsk, less than thirty-five miles from the Bug, the river which divided the Polish General Government, which was administered by the Reich, and the former Polish territory occupied by the Soviets.

At 10:00 p.m. at the summer solstice, June 21, 1941, our company commander read out an order from the Führer:

"Soldiers of the Eastern Front: Burdened by heavy concerns, sentenced to months of silence, the hour has now come when I can speak openly to you, my soldiers.

"Today there are 160 Russian divisions standing at our border. Violations of this border have been going on for weeks, not only against us, but against our allies in the far north and in Romania. At this moment, soldiers of the Eastern Front, an assembly of strength such as the world has never seen, is now complete....

"When this, the biggest front line in history, now begins its advance, it does so not just to provide the means for ending for all time this great war, or to defend those countries currently concerned, but the salvation of our entire European civilization and culture. German soldiers! You are entering on a harsh and demanding fight – because the fate of Europe, the future of the German Reich, and the very existence of our nation now rests on your hands alone. May the Lord God help us all in this struggle!"

Hitler was wrong and he was tricked. The armies he sent to the attack in Eastern Europe were not "the greatest in world history." The Soviet armies, superior in numbers, possessed armaments that were in some areas superior to ours. In 1941, we had three million men at the front, 3,580 tanks, and more than 1,800 aircraft. We immediately found ourselves confronted by 4,700,000 soldiers, 15,000 tanks, and, in Byelorussia alone, 6,000 aircraft.

At dawn on June 22, 1941, a Sunday, we went over to the attack in the east, just as Napoleon's Grand Army had done against the same enemy on June 22, 1812.

With a single order and a stroke of the pen, the Molotov-Ribbentrop pact was fractured.

Operation Barbarossa had begun.

7

From my diary, September 9, 1941

The battle ended yesterday.

Officially it was called a "planned withdrawal," but to me it was so much bullshit. The next day, we heard on the radio, in the 'news from the front' about the "successful front correction" in our Yelnya defensive lines and the enormous losses we inflicted on the enemy. But not a single word was heard about a retreat, about the hopelessness of the situation, about the mental and emotional numbness of the German soldiers. In short, it was again a "victory." But we on the front line were running back like rabbits in front of the fox. This metamorphosis of the truth from "all shit" to "it was a victory" baffled me and those of my comrades who dared to think.

We had been told the Russians were sub-humans. That did not correspond to the facts. From the first year on, I employed Russian prisoners as auto mechanics. I found them to be intelligent and inventive; for example, the Russians found out that a certain spring from a T-34 tank could be installed in our Horch cars, whose front and rear springs had all broken in a short time. Why should I treat these Russians like sub-humans? Even though I was, and still am, anti-Bolshevik, I was not and am not anti-Russian.

If Hitler underestimated the Russian soldiers in the beginning, he made a serious mistake. We had superior strategy; our generals were significantly better in dealing with the problems of mobile warfare and were more innovative than the Russians. But from common soldier to company commander, the Russian soldiers were our equals. Brave, tough, and with a sense for camouflage, they put up an astonishingly bitter resistance and walked *en masse* and with unbelievable fatalism into certain death.

In the hell of Yelnya, we had been led to believe we were fighting not only for Germany but for all of Europe. But the division was at the end of its strength. Like many others, I had contacted a severe case of dysentery. I refused to go to hospital and simply pitched my tent at the edge of camp. Fortunately, Das Reich Division was sent to rest position in the Roslavi sector. The men and vehicles were exhausted.

From my Diary entry – September 16, 1941

The Wehrmacht losses included 23,000 casualties of the XX Army Corp for the period from 8 August to 8 September. The Red Army losses for the period from 30 August to 8 September are estimated at 31,853 overall casualties. ... The newly-formed Soviet 24th Army lost 40% of its operational strength. ... Yelnya, a town of 15,000 was obliterated ... Nearly all able-bodied men and women had been formed into forced labor battalions and driven to the German rear. Only a few hundred old people and children were allowed to stay in the town. ... The countryside of the Yelnya salient, territory, which had been held by the Wehrmacht, was completely devastated. Every town was destroyed. ... The few surviving civilians lived in cellars.

Yet how in God's name had we *lost*? No matter how the War Office tried to "shine shit," no one at the front had any question but that the Yelnya Offensive was the first substantial reversal the Wehrmacht suffered since the beginning of Barbarossa.

$$\dagger$$

Diary entry – September 20, 1941

Received the first letter from Emmi in more than a month. It was dated 19 July, so it had been sent more than two months ago. Two pictures, both of Emmi and Waltraut. Hard to believe our daughter is more than a year old. When I last saw her, she was two months. Dressed in a traditional dirndl. She's almost big enough to wear one. Just looking at her brought tears to my eyes. Will she ever know her papa?

Emmi looks wonderful. Makes me realize I've been without a woman for four months. Much too long. I wonder if Emmi could be ...? But I can't torture myself with such thoughts. Still ....? If I let such things take over my mind I'll go crazy. Unable to concentrate. That would mean certain death or, at the very least, I'd lose a limb, an eye, whatever. Must force myself to think. I wonder whatever happened to *The Seven Pillars of Wisdom* I was reading when we left Poland for this godforsaken hellhole.

$$\dagger$$

That year winter came very early. The first snow fell during the night of October 6-7. When I saw this snow, which gave the countryside a monotonous but dangerous appearance, I felt a sense of foreboding, but my own optimism soon swept it away. After all, Moscow was less than a hundred miles away on the highway.

The word "highway" conjures up a broad road of concrete or asphalt, much like the new *autobahnen* back home. Not so in the Union of Soviet Socialist Republics. Here, it was nothing more than a wide raised wall of earth. To the south of us, the double battle of Vyasma-Briansk had ended with the destruction of nine Soviet armies. Our generals had taken 663,000 prisoners. Our objective was Borodino, Moscow's first defensive line, only 75 miles west of the Soviet capital.

But a very unpleasant surprise awaited Das Reich Division as we approached Borodino Field: for the first time, we had to fight Siberian troops. They were very well-equipped, strong and determined soldiers, with huge fur coats and caps, fur-lined boots, automatic rifles, and all manner of heavy weapons. It was the 32nd Light Infantry Division from Vladivostok, accompanied by two brigades of T-34 and KV tanks.

Of all the difficult battles in which I have ever engaged, I remember this as the most murderous. It lasted two days. Papa Hausser, positioned not far from me, was badly wounded, suffering the loss of an eye. But our massed artillery under Colonel Weidling opened a breach, through which our assault grenadiers forced their way. Moscow's first defensive line cracked. On October 19, we occupied Mozhaysk, only sixty-two miles from Moscow!

We were now convinced we'd take Moscow by the beginning of November. But then catastrophe struck: torrential rains fell on our area starting the evening of the 19th and continuing for three days. Our army literally sank into the morass. My job was to help with getting the trucks on the "highway" mobile again. But just how to go about this?

For many miles, thousands of vehicles in three rows sank in the mud, some up to their hoods. We had run out of fuel. Two hundred tons of supplies per day for each division had to be delivered by air. The complete stoppage of traffic extended several hundreds of miles to the west. We lost three precious weeks and an enormous quantity of material.

In a tremendous effort, Das Reich Division engineers built nine miles of corduroy road from trees felled by woodcutters while the fighting was going on. In spite of counterattacks by Siberian troops and

T-34 tanks, we crossed the Moskva River above Roussak. We wanted to be the first to arrive at Red Square.

A blessing! It froze during the night of November 6-7! Slowly, our supplies began to flow again: ammunition, fuel, food, even cigarettes. Finally, the wounded could be evacuated. We started preparing for the final offensive.

But on November 19, the temperature suddenly fell to minus 40 degrees. We had no cold-proof motor or gun oil. The engines were almost impossible to start. Nevertheless, we managed to take Istra on November 28. Ahead and to our left lay Khimki, Moscow's port, only five short miles to our goal! One of our motorcycle battalions entered Khimki without firing a shot. Unfortunately and inexplicably, the motorcycle infantry withdrew.

On December 2 we reached Nikolayev, nine miles from Moscow. I could see the spires of the Kremlin through my field glasses. Our battery fired on the suburbs and streetcars. But we had almost no tractors left for our howitzers. The temperature fell to minus 50 degrees. Six days later, after battling fresh Siberian divisions day and night, the Soviet forces broke through on our right wing. Our division's losses were more than 75%.

That day we learned that Germany and Italy had declared war on the United States after Pearl Harbor. The result was a precipitous fall in our morale. The most important thing for us was to learn what attitude our ally, Japan, would take against the Soviet Union. But the presence of the Siberian troops, most of whom came from the northern border of Korea, and whose numbers had been steadily growing for a month, gave us no cause for optimism.

Why were we unable to take Moscow? There are as many answers as there are excuses. My division was one of those which had to give up just short of the objective. We could have blamed the failure on poor planning, poor execution, poor leadership, any one of a number of things. But in my view, in spite of the morass, the ice, the lack of roads, in spite of betrayal by certain commanders, in spite of the confusion of our logistics and in spite of the bravery of the Russian soldiers, we would have taken Moscow at the beginning of December 1941 if the Siberian troops had not intervened.

In December, our Army Group did not receive a single division as reinforcement or replacement. In the same period, Stalin committed thirty light infantry divisions, 33 brigades, six tank divisions, and three cavalry divisions against us. From October 17 forward, Das Reich Division faced the Siberian 32nd Light Infantry Division near Borodino. Later, at the beginning of December, we faced the 78th Division. Our air force, which was already short of aircraft, failed to destroy the Trans-Siberian railroad net, as a result of which the Siberian troops were able to save the Soviet capital.

To get within 12 miles of Moscow, our division had had to fight an enemy that outnumbered us by 3-to-1 in soldiers and 5-to-1 in artillery in October. By the time we finally gave up the ghost in December, the ratio was 6-to-1 in men and 10-to-1 in materiel, munitions, and fuel.

"Was it that bad, darling?"

"From what I could see of the battle, it certainly *looked* bad. But I was really out of action after Mozhaysk, when I was caught by a stray salvo from a Stalin Organ. I considered myself damned lucky to escape with a head wound. And of course, there was the *scheiss harei*, the never-ending dysentery."

"Surely that didn't account for the six months' leave in Vienna," Emmi said. She added, "Thank God you're back in one piece, Otto. So many ..."

"It was the gallstones. They first hit during the retreat. I can't even remember them putting me on the hospital train back to Smolensk. I was told later that the only way they kept me on my feet was doping me up on injections, morphine I think. Here I am a big, strong, indestructible first lieutenant and they were this close to taking my gall bladder out when they transferred me to Karlsbad Hospital."

"Worse than the battle?"

"God, I wouldn't want anyone to go through that pain, not even the enemy. I still worry every night that I'll wake up with more stones. Waltraut's grown so tall. She looks twice her age."

"Well, neither Mama nor Papa is a dwarf," she said lightly.

I'd been home two weeks. As exhausted as I'd been when I was discharged from the hospital and reclassified "GvH," fit for garrison duty at home, we'd finally resumed our lovemaking a few nights ago. As fulfilling as it was, the excitement was muted by tenderness. I'd experienced the completely unexpected return of the unendurable pains, usually in the night, and my movements were – completely out of character for me – cautious and tentative.

"Is your father any better?"

"I wish I could say yes, Emmi, but I fear the end is very much in sight. And he knows it, too. When I saw him yesterday, it comforted both of us. He told me he was convinced that the European armies would defeat the Russians. He truly believes the world will only achieve a lasting peace when the West defeats the Bolsheviks."

"And you think?"

"He's deceiving himself. So many people are. But, as hard as it is for me to say about my Papa, he'll likely die before his illusion is shattered."

Emilie's hand flew to her mouth. "Surely you don't mean …?"

"I'm not talking about this war, darling. I just don't believe it's part of the human condition to accept any long-term universal peace."

"My husband's quite the pessimist."

"No, my angel. I prefer to consider myself a realist."

In June 1942, I was reassigned to Waffen-SS Division Leibstandarte Adolf Hitler as an engineering officer. The next six months were among the most boring of my life. Toward the end of the year, I volunteered for retraining with the panzer arm and, after passing several tests, I was transferred to the Waffen-SS Division *Totenkopf* (Death's Head), which was to be re-equipped as a fully motorized armored division.

Unfortunately, in the winter of 1942-43, I suffered a relapse of persistent dysentery. Reclassified "GvH" once again I was sent back to the Leibstandarte reserve unit in Berlin. Then came two events, almost simultaneously, that gave every German cause to think.

In January 1943 at Casablanca, Roosevelt and Winston Churchill decided that the allies would demand unconditional surrender from the Axis powers and especially from Germany. And on January 31, 1943, General Paulus and his staff surrendered Stalingrad to the enemy. The last soldiers of General Strecker's II Army Corps fought to the last round. Many officers took their own lives. Shortly before 9:00 a.m., the War Office received the final radio message: "II Army Corps and its 10 divisions have done their duty. Heil Hitler. General Strecker."

It was to be the turning point of the war.

8

———

By early spring 1943, I had the distinct feeling that we were no longer employing a revolutionary style of warfare that had led to the brilliant *blitzkrieg* victories of 1939/40, but instead we had been bogged down by a conventional war of attrition. More and more, I found myself convinced that if we wanted to return to those glory days, we must turn to daring methods and the element of surprise we'd had in those years. We had to consider the entire nature of the war, discover and produce new weapons which were especially useful for specific purposes, and, most important, we had to think of different, more effective, ways to engage the enemy

But how to get my ideas to anyone in authority who'd even listen? I was only an Obersturmführer, a First Lieutenant. If I had had an opportunity to present my unorthodox ideas to one of the staff officers wearing the red stripes of the general staff, he most likely would have smiled as dismissively as one would have treated a child.

My personnel files lay in the Operational Headquarters of the Waffen-SS, our general staff, commanded by Obergruppenführer Hans Jüttner, a former Reichswehr officer, who I thought was far superior to Himmler. I opened up to him and expressed my wish to serve in a combat unit in which I could show more initiative than in a Berlin barracks. Judging by his questions, it was obvious he had gone to the trouble of studying my military record.

Our conversation grew quite friendly. Gradually I told him of my unorthodox ideas for a more daring type of tactics. The general agreed heartily, and I suddenly got the feeling that General Jüttner had an ulterior motive. Jüttner revealed to me a few days later that he was looking for an officer who had experience at the front and good technical knowledge to organize and command a "special duties unit," a battalion at Friedenthal, near Berlin, and a *Seehof* school at The Hague in Holland.

"This is probably a new form of warfare for you, Skorzeny. During our last conversation I had the impression you are the man we need. Naturally you must consider the proposal. You are, of course, free to turn it down."

"I've already thought it over. I accept."

I stood up to take my leave and to thank the general.

He smiled. "You accepted immediately. Very good. However, I think you should have a look at Seehof and Friedenthal first. Certain difficulties may crop up that may cause you to reconsider. When you return and tell me what you think, only then will I consider your acceptance final."

†

Friedenthal, located eighteen miles north of Berlin, had been a Hohenzollern hunting lodge. In early 1943 a barracks camp had been erected around two pavilions in a large park. The barracks housed one more-or-less complete company, and a scattering of others. "Special Duties Unit Friedenthal" was commanded by a Dutch Waffen-SS officer, whose staff did not yet exist. He was friendly enough when I arrived. General Jüttner had apparently already briefed him about my role.

"So here you are, Hauptsturmführer Skorzeny," the commander said. "Welcome to whatever it is you want to call it."

"Good morning, Commander," I said, shaking his hand. "I suppose it would be best if I learn whatever I can about our troops and their records. Perhaps you might direct me to the records office?"

At that, the commander, who was more custodian than commanding officer, laughed ironically. "Captain, you surmise I was a bit ambiguous about what's here. The 'records office,' if you can call it that, is an 8-by-10 room, more of a large closet, perhaps a dozen boxes of records with no real arrangement to them. One telephone–*one* for the whole operation. No teletype, no radio station to communicate with the outside world."

I was beginning to see why General Jüttner had told me to look before I leaped. The custodial commandant continued, "On the positive side, we have about 300 men. Eighty-five percent German, the rest Dutch, Flemish, or Hungarian ethnic Germans. All volunteers, all Waffen-SS."

As I looked around this "base," and saw the spirit that seemed to infuse all of the men I interviewed, I became convinced that every unit must start somewhere, and the raw ingredients of this mix were indeed promising. The same could be said about *Seehof.* Hans Jüttner, the only SS officer other than Himmler who had the authority to create and organize units of the Waffen-SS, had ordered the *Sonderverband z.b.V. Friedenthal* into being shortly before he first broached the idea to me. In the beginning, Friedenthal was allowed to recruit from Waffen-SS volunteers only, but a few months into my time at Friedenthal, the general authorized me to "Pirate the ones you want from any of the German Armed Forces, the *Heer*, the *Luftwaffe*, the *Kriegsmarine*, the *Volkssturm*, provided they volunteer and that you can work it out with their commanders."

Like all the units subsequently formed on General Jüttner's orders, this one was ready for "special employment," which meant that any chief of an element of the armed services could call on them for special military operations. We were a unit within the armed forces and we received our orders from the commander of an army or army group. My staff or, subject to my approval, the general staff of the affected army, would work out the operational plans. From July 1943 forward, I always received my orders directly from the *Oberkommando der Wehrmacht*, the Supreme Command of the Armed Forces, or from Hitler personally.

When I took over the Friedenthal operation in April 1943, I determined that the training program was wholly inadequate. I don't mean this in a high-handed or patronizing way, but I felt changes needed to be made, and quickly.

For one thing, preparations for Operation Franz were already well under way. Although I was a rank beginner in commando strategy and tactics, it became immediately clear to me that I needed an entire battalion and first-class material if this idea had even a remote chance of succeeding. The scheme was for the Abwehr, the German intelligence arm, to bribe the dissident Qashqai tribesmen in Iran to sabotage British and American supplies bound for the Soviet Union.

I was supposed to completely reorganize everything as quickly as possible. Easier said than done. An incredible stroke of good luck occurred when I met the first two officers who sought to join the *Friedenthal Sonderverband*. Untersturmführer (Second Lieutenant) Werner Hunke came to me as a "China specialist." He had, in fact, been born in that faraway country, but had left at the age of two and didn't speak a single word of any of the Chinese languages. He knew no more about China than you could learn by reading a map. Naturally I nicknamed him "Chinaman."

But it was the second of the officers who became, quite literally, my "right arm," and who became and remained my adjutant and one of my closest comrades from the day he applied for special forces duty until the end of the war. Like me, Untersturmführer Karl Radl was Austrian. There was no way I could have done what I did without this incredibly bright, wildly good-humored man. Up that time, I'd been thoroughly dazed and demoralized by the grind-everything-to-a-halt obstinacy and bureaucratic nitpicking of the "higher echelons."

A most painful example of this took place very shortly after I'd assumed command of the Friedenthal operation, and I felt such an affinity for Karl Radl that I brought this subject up during our first conversation.

"God help me from ever having to deal with anyone like our intelligence chief, the great Admiral Canaris," I began. "I came in fully expecting to discuss my qualifications for this job and seeking his endorsement for our operations. Instead, he and I spent three hours wrangling over the transfer of two junior officers who wanted to join the Friedenthal group. In the end, he knew nothing about me, and I certainly walked away with a negative impression about that old fart. He said he'd think about it and let me know his decision 'at a later date.'"

"That is so typical," Radl replied, letting me know that while I would be his superior in command, he considered me very much his equal. "I've had a good deal of success with these admirals who've probably been around forever. Brigadeführer Walther Schellenberg, Canaris' underling, told me the secret of how he shot up the ladder so quickly:"

"The more absurd the harebrained idea put to you by a really important person, the more eagerly you should welcome it. Showy preparations should be started immediately. You must always give assurances that plans are advancing each day. Then gradually, drop by drop, the notion that certain outside factors may delay the glorious consummation of his brilliant idea may be allowed to seep through; until the author of the project finds himself wondering at his own earlier enthusiasm and begins discreetly to shelve the whole thing – if he hasn't forgotten about it already."

That answer cemented our relationship from the beginning. Time and time again, Karl was to prove his worth in so many ways. I could never have matched my bureaucratic adversaries, whose single-minded objective was to preserve the status quo and their place within that order. I'd found that officials were irked by my enthusiasm and objected to having their thinking stretched by my troublesome requests. When I continued to press for action beyond a point where my demands could be ignored, they knew many a trap which could be set for a brash, uppity, know-it-all puppy, and they'd enjoy a retributive triumph when the young upstart fell into such snares.

But Karl Radl was cut from a different piece of cloth. He'd taken the bar and had been marked out as a future judge when the war began. He found military regulations to be a fascinating child's game, compared to the Central European jurisprudence he'd studied. With that irreverence so typical of my Austrian compatriots, he indulged the "beautiful nonsense" of bumbledom. Instead of arguing with officials, he traveled alongside them on the road which led to total absurdity. Bureaucrats skilled in the art of evasion found themselves tripped up by their own red tape and badgered by Radl for more and more forms until they gave in, just to be rid of this nitpicker's nitpicker.

Karl and I started to refer to our opponents in GHQ as "the generals," or "the too-old Guard," comically mocking brass-bound complacency and the rebuking monocle in the Senior Officers' Mess. Radl was a master of securing letters signed by staff bureaucrats on behalf of General This or General That, which had given Radl his warrant. In the end, the generals themselves turned out to be the scapegoats when anything went wrong.

With Radl's bubbling good humor and his genius for squeezing out of dilemma after dilemma, my adjutant was never at a loss; soon he was mapping the whole field of bureaucratic strategy and advancing on many sectors of that vital front. Before Karl had joined me, all of my effort had been spent on this campaign of attrition. Now, with Radl on my side and at my side, I was able to finally spend more than half my time in considering the forgotten war against the Allies and to concentrate on the strategy and tactics to be employed in commando warfare.

On the one hand, the High Command demanded I create special forces for unprecedented tasks. On the other hand, they withheld the means for me to accomplish these tasks. The pretext I was given was that supplies were tight all around. What angered me was that the huge appetite of regular army formations was always met with as many tasty morsels as they wanted, while Friedenthal got cheese parings and candle ends. Thank God for Radl. Somehow, he always managed to cadge enough to keep us competently operational.

After I'd studied Operation Franz, I questioned the sanity, let alone the "expertise" of an exercise I felt was doomed to failure from the beginning. Of course, since it was not my project, and since it was a long way toward what the OKW staff thought was fruition by the time I become involved, I knew its success or failure would not impact me one way or the other.

Project Franz was designed to cut the Middle East supply route to the Soviet Union. A German officer had been smuggled into Tehran, where he was secretly dealing with the Iranians under British and Russian noses. Farsi-speaking Germans had been parachuted in to subvert the mountain tribes. If the plan had worked as intended, after the dissident leaders had been bribed and supplied with needed arms, the country would explode like a powder keg – or so they hoped.

Project Franz was delayed at the start, while those involved in the planning and implementation of the program ransacked Berlin's antique shops, grabbing off silver-handled pistols and inlaid fowling pieces as "gifts" for the tribal leaders. The fiasco ended when the powers-that-be, both military and political, refused to loan us a single long-range plane to drop reinforcements into Iran. Fortunately for my own future, I never became directly involved in this failed operation. Rather, I devoted the next period in my life to building up the commando unit and coming up with what I felt was a foolproof tactic in most situations.

I implemented strict security measures at Friedenthal. The park was surrounded by a 14-foot-high wall. Alarm units were soon installed. But the best protection was our trained dogs. Then I developed the "No shoot" strategy. After studying many situations that had resulted in success-by-surprise, I made up my mind to instruct my special unit forces to shoot only when it was absolutely necessary.

My men were all excellent shots, and we had every type of weapon we needed; but even more important, we had the discipline to attack without shooting in order to achieve total surprise. I found an effective, proven means of preventing my soldiers from firing: I would go in first and not fire, myself. This behavior, which steeled the nerves of the men behind me and instilled confidence, contributed greatly to two of our major successes. In neither action was there any general bloodletting. I led both operations and did not fire a single shot in either of them. The soldiers who came right behind me were under orders not to shoot until I opened fire. They followed orders and did not fire, to the great astonishment of those with whom we dealt.

Psychologically it is, of course, easier to fire while attacking. The training of our special units therefore focused on the massed and concentrated attack on the enemy. It would have been a mistake on my part to consider the Italians, and later the Hungarians, as enemies. Such behavior would not have been in keeping with the purpose of the missions entrusted to me. In reality, they were not our enemies but only our momentary opponents, who, for their part, had orders to shoot.

It is bewildering for the enemy when, surprised by the events, he sees an enemy, which all logic tells him shouldn't be there, suddenly appear and come towards him. He doesn't believe his eyes. In this way, the moment of surprise is extended, which is necessary for success.

Just one shot fired by the attackers is enough to awaken the self-preservation instinct of those being attacked, and they will automatically fire back. Nothing is more contagious than a shot. I have seen front-line units during the night suddenly open fire with everything they have, simply because a sentry fired at a shadow.

Don't shoot! The most difficult moment is when one comes upon the enemy. For this tactic demands the strongest nerves and a mutual, unshakable confidence in success. The disarming of the enemy is the actual objective of a martial action. I have found that one can also disarm the enemy by making use of the moment of surprise *without shooting*.

9

———

Until Monday, July 26, 1943, I had set eyes on Hitler twice in my life. The first time I'd seen him had been the 1936 Winter Olympic Games in Garmisch-Partenkirchen. The second time, I'd been standing with my workers on a scaffolding high above the Vienna Ring when he entered the city in triumph in 1938.

On that Monday, I had lunched with a friend from Vienna whom I had met in the Eden Hotel in Berlin. I felt relaxed to be in civilian clothes. We gossiped about all manner of things as we sipped ersatz coffee. Like so many things in Germany in those days, our scientists had invented, discovered, or fabricated things that were increasingly unavailable to us. They even produced synthetic food.

Ersatz – literally "substitute" – came to be a fact of life which we simply accepted. Through ersatz, we created modern homes for the workers, built the autobahns, and produced synthetic fibers. During the war, ersatz allowed us to hold out as long as we did. In Germany, we not only made fuel from hard coal, but we also came up with ersatz butter, sugar, and honey. Buna was an outstanding rubber. The cellulose processing industry, which grew considerably, gave us plexiglas, artificial silk, synthetic bronze, and brass. I won't clam that liverwurst made from cellulose byproducts could be compared to true goose liver pâté, but we were happy to satisfy our hunger with it.

Somehow, I felt uneasy. I understand people who are anything but clairvoyant somehow get dead-on accurate premonitions. I excused myself and telephoned Friedenthal to find out if anything was happening. I was put through immediately to my adjutant,

"Otto, where the hell have you been? We've been searching all over Berlin for you for two hours." I was not the least bit offended that Radl called me by my first name. Such was our relationship that even at this early stage we could comfortably say anything to one another, even things that a subordinate would never dream of saying to his superior.

"Something up, Karl?"

"Damn right. You're wanted at Hitler's headquarters."

"What??"

"You heard me, Captain. There's a special plane waiting for you at Tempelhof Airport. It must take off at five o'clock. I have no idea what it's all about."

"I'll take a taxi direct, Karl. Meet me at the airport, and could you bring me a uniform? I'm in civilian clothes."

When I met my adjutant, he gave me the war front bulletins and said there had been some change in the Government of Italy. He could not tell me more than that. Meanwhile, the plane's engines were ticking over. While I changed, I hurriedly promised Radl I'd call him as soon as I could. Meanwhile, I told him to stand the men to order; they might be needed at a moment's notice.

I settled down in a deep armchair in the plane. I was the only passenger. This must be some madcap mistake, someone's idea of a Teutonic joke. I saw a built-in rack of liqueurs, even French brandy. I poured myself a glass. May as well live it up. Me, Otto Skorzeny, with a Junkers JU-52 plane all to myself.

Karl Radl had most thoughtfully packed a map in my briefcase. As I followed the flight path, which was easy since it was still daylight and the plane was flying at an altitude of about 7,000 feet, we flew toward East Prussia, over plain and stream, to the town of Rastenburg. Then, in the gathering dusk, we touched down on an airstrip. The moment I stepped onto the ground, a Mercedes pulled up and a chauffeur held the rear door open for me.

The *Wolfsschanze*, Hitler's eastern front headquarters, was not a front-line dugout, but a sizable village in a forest, hidden from the air by camouflage nets and trees, protected by antiaircraft guns, bunker defenses, masses of barbed wire, and hundreds of guards.

When I reached the Wolf's Lair itself, an aide-de-camp led me at once to a comfortable anteroom, where I was introduced to five officers, all senior to me. They told me they, too, had been summoned to the Wolfsschanze from all parts of Europe, without any explanation.

After a seemingly long time, the aide-de-camp returned. "Gentlemen, you will now enter the leader's presence."

The six of us positioned ourselves along the wall. Since I had the lowest rank, I stood last in line. The room had indirect lighting, so there were no shadows. Before us was a long table with general staff situation maps and several colored pencils, a fireplace, a desk beside a large window, and, on the opposite wall, a small painting, Dürer's *Veilchen*, in a silver frame.

A door opened to my left. Hitler stepped into the room, walked past us slowly, and saluted us briefly with a raised hand. The Führer, perhaps 5 feet 8 inches tall, seemed shorter than he appeared at public events. He wore a white shirt with black tie under his field-grey jacket. The only medals he wore were the Iron Cross, First Class, from the First World War and the silver badge awarded for having been wounded three times.

His adjutant introduced the Oberstleutnant on the right end. Then the others followed. When Hitler stopped before me he shook my hand. His gaze did not leave me for an instant. I bowed briefly and gave a quick summary of my military career. Then he stepped back a few paces, sized us all up once again, and asked, "Which of you is familiar with Italy?"

There was silence. I was the only one to speak up. "I have traveled as far as Naples in two private trips by motorcycle, Mein Führer."

Again quiet. Then he addressed the second question to all of us. "What do you think of Italy?"

The Oberstleutnant answered that Italy was our military and ideological ally. The Luftwaffe officers mentioned the Rome-Berlin axis, and my immediate neighbor spoke of the anti-Comintern pact. When Hitler stood in front of me and nodded in my direction, I merely said, "I am Austrian, Mein Führer."

Hitler looked at me long and searchingly, waiting for me to say something else. I remained silent. I had said everything I had to say in three words. The silence continued. I sensed that something must happen now.

"I wish to speak further with Haupsturmführer Skorzeny," he said in a calm voice. "The other officers may withdraw."

They excused themselves and left the room. It was about 10:30 p.m. We were alone. Hitler informed me at that moment of the mission which he intended to entrust to me.

"Mussolini was betrayed yesterday. His king has had him arrested. The Duce is not only my ally, he is also my friend. I cannot abandon him. The new Italian government will surely desert us and deliver the Duce to the enemy. He will be betrayed and sold. I must prevent such a breach of faith from taking place!"

Both of us were still standing. He walked up and down the large room and appeared to be thinking. Then he stopped in front of me.

"We must find out where the Duce is being held and free him. This is your mission, Skorzeny. I have chosen you because I am convinced you will succeed with this operation. You must risk everything to carry out this action, which is now most important to the conduct of the war. This mission must be absolutely secret; otherwise it will fail. Only five other people know the details. I don't want Italy to become a trap for our soldiers. All false friends must be eliminated. I charge you personally with finding out where Mussolini is being held and rescuing him as quickly as possible. You will select your own people. But you must act quickly. The life of the Duce depends on it!"

"Jawohl, Mein Führer!"

"Most important, neither the German military headquarters in Italy nor our embassy in Rome will know of your mission. We will see one another again. Meanwhile, I wish you all the best." He shook my hand and left.

I felt hungry and was about to get something to eat in the tea house, when Hitler's adjutant, Otto Günsche informed me that General Student was waiting for me in an adjoining room. He was a jovial-looking, rotund man, who'd been badly wounded outside Rotterdam in 1940. He greeted me warmly. I told him of the mission I had just received from the Führer. Then, to my surprise, Reichsführer SS Himmler walked into the room.

I was not particularly impressed by Himmler. He had a weak handshake and his eyes shifted constantly behind his pince-nez.

"You must know there's more than Mussolini involved!" he exclaimed. "The conspiracy that has been planned for four months is not limited to Italy. Madrid, Ankara, and Lisbon are implicated as well." I had difficulty following and committing to memory all the names he parroted.

Himmler had plenty of illusions. He ignored the fact that the fascist military had recently been incorporated into the army and that the National Fascist Party was supposed to be abolished. "Do you know at least who the future foreign minister will be?"

"I'm sorry, Reichsführer, I do not."

"Guariglia, the former ambassador to Ankara. That's also clear."

It wasn't at all clear to me. Who was supposed to arrest the king and the crown prince? The Führer had given me very explicit instructions where the Duce was concerned. Himmler showered us with an avalanche of names: generals, admirals, ministers. Although I had a good memory, I pulled out my notebook to write down certain facts.

"*Have you lost your mind?*" the Reichsführer screamed at me. "Everything I'm saying here is strictly secret!"

He shrugged his shoulders again and pointed out that Student had witnessed this unpardonable behavior. As it was almost eleven, I asked for permission to telephone Berlin and let my unit know what was happening. Outside in the hall, I lit a cigarette as I waited for the long-distance call. Just then, Himmler came out of the room and started shouting again, "This is unbelievable! Don't you have enough willpower to stop smoking? Always these stinking cigarettes! I can see you're not the right man for this job!"

I said nothing. He walked away, furious.

"Don't take that too seriously," Günsche remarked. "You just can't talk to the Reichsführer when he's nervous." Hitler's adjutant kindly offered me a room to work in. I'd barely gotten started in sorting things out when General Student called for me again: I would act as his operations officer in Rome and fly with him to the Italian capital the following morning.

It was after midnight when I got Untersturmführer Radl on the phone.

"Karl, I'm afraid there will be no time to sleep much tonight. Get thirty volunteer soldiers and the best officers we have. Dress them in paratrooper uniforms and provide them with the necessary papers. They'll leave from Staaken Airfield at six o'clock this morning. Their destination is secret but it'll be given to the pilot during the flight. There'll be ten intelligence officers on board."

After breakfast, General Student and I set out for Italy in a plane flown by the general's personal pilot, Hauptmann Walter Gerlach. We took a new route over the Alps to avoid Allied planes, - an unpleasant reminder of the enemy's growing air superiority. On the way, we passed over my native Vienna. Since I was posing as Student's aide-de-camp, I wore a fur-lined air force suit over my army uniform.

When we landed at Rome at lunchtime on July 27, it was sweltering. Yet I had to keep my uncomfortably thick attire on until I could find something suitable to wear. This turned out not to be such an easy task. To avoid attention, I had to borrow uniforms which were too thick or too thin for the climate, and always too small because nothing could be found to fit my bulk. We drove 13 miles south to Generalfeldmarschall Kesselring's headquarters at Frascati. As General Student's operations officer, I accompanied him to dinner with Kesselring that evening.

In the course of the evening, I ascertained that Hitler was right. The Generalfeldmarschall, one of the most sympathetic commanders I ever met, was convinced that the new monarchist government would continue the war at our side. "Herr Hauptmann," he said positively, "I consider our Italian comrades to be honorable. The Italian armed forces are and will remain our loyal allies. They will fight with us until the end."

I did not respond to the field marshal, but he wasn't to hang on to his illusions much longer.

Radl and our soldiers arrived on July 29. I took Karl with me to Frascati. Only then did I explain what was involved: to find where the Duce was being held prisoner and free him as quickly as possible.

On September 3, 1943, in the course of an official conversation, Prime Minister Badoglio told our Ambassador Rahn, "I don't understand why the German Reich is so suspicious of me. They're trying to insult me, which hurts me deeply. Don't you think an old general like me knows what it means to give his word of honor to the Führer? Never, and you can be sure of that, never will we break our word."

At that very moment, his own chief-of-staff, General Castellano, was presenting Italy's declaration of surrender to General Bedell-Smith.

10

Thanks to a letter written by a lovesick carabinieri to his fiancée, we learned that the Duce was being held captive on the island of Ponza. Mussolini remained locked up in a small house near the sea for a week.

On August 11, we learned that Mussolini had left the penal island on a warship, destination unknown. General Student subsequently passed on to me a telegram from OKW, which said that Mussolini was a prisoner on the cruiser *Italia* in La Spezia harbor. Himmler sent a telegram ordering us to free Mussolini as quickly as possible. Trying to launch an attack against a military cruiser with the group we had seemed not only foolhardy but was a crackpot idea. In any event, we soon found that the OKW's information was false.

On August 15, I became aware of an interesting voyage north of the island of Sardinia. I learned from reliable sources that certain fascist sympathizers were being held prisoner on Isola del Porco and that a concentration camp was being prepared on the neighboring island of Caprera. On investigation, I learned that the Italian garrison on the island of Santa Maddalena off the northeast tip of Sardinia had suddenly been reinforced. Commander Hunäus, the German liaison to the Italian harbormaster of Santa Maddalena confirmed this news. General Student and I conferred and decided that our only officer who spoke perfect Italian, Untersturmführer Warger, should speak to the liaison officer personally.

I ordered Warger to make the rounds of the Santa Maddalena bars and act as if he was mildly drunk. The only problem: Warger was the only non-drinker among the Friedenthal volunteers, so I set to work teaching him to drink. In the beginning, he proved to be very averse to the effects of alcohol. But duty is duty, and in the end Warger played his role as a drunken sailor perfectly.

On August 18, Lieutenant Warger and I flew from Ciampino to Vieno Fiorita airfield on Sardinia in a Heinkel 111. Hunäus had sent his car for us and we drove 50 miles through the mountains to Palau in the north. The German commander there told me that Mussolini had been brought to the hospital at Santa Maria, a small village on the road we'd just traveled. Back at Vieno Fiorita I asked the pilot to fly us over Santa Maddalena to view the island and the coast from 10,000 feet and to take photos. I was lying in the nose by the aircraft's cannon and was about to end my observations when I heard the gunner's voice through the microphone.

"Attention! Two English fighters behind us!"

I waited for the attack with my finger on the trigger of the cannon. At that moment, the aircraft nosed down. The left engine had stopped. We hit the water with great force. I lost consciousness for a few seconds. Then the pilot, the copilot, and I clambered out through the upper escape hatch. I was able to retrieve the camera. We managed to rescue the other two members of the crew, then swam to a small, rocky island, where an Italian cruiser picked us up several hours later. I had injured my right arm and broken three ribs. By 11:00 that night, we reached Corsica, which was then occupied by Italian units.

I later learned that the engineers tested the Italian gasoline with which the pilot had refueled at Vieno Fiorita. The fuel contained thirty percent water!

Radl did not learn I had escaped the crash until August 20. Next day, I drove to Frascati, where our liaison advised me that Edda Ciano was back from Germany and had written her father in Santa Maddalena. Not three days later, Untersturmführer Warger, who'd remained on the island, sent news that he had seen Mussolini with his own eyes. Warger had made a wager with a fruit seller that Mussolini was dead. In order to win the bet, the fruit seller showed him the Duce, albeit from a distance, on the terrace of a villa.

Then a report reached us from the War Office: "Führer Headquarters has received word from the Abwehr, the German intelligence service, that Mussolini is being held prisoner on a small island near Elba. Hauptsturmführer Skorzeny is to prepare a parachute operation against the island immediately and report the earliest possible starting date. The OKW will select the date of the action."

After this puzzling telegram, I asked to be allowed to accompany General Student to Führer Headquarters on August 29, if possible, to explain to the Führer myself that the Duce was on Santa Maddalena and not somewhere else.

Once again, I found myself in the same room at Wolfsschanze where, two weeks earlier, Hitler had instructed me to find and free his friend. All the leading men of the Reich, Hitler, Keitel, Jodl, von Ribbentrop, Himmler, General Student, Grossadmiral Dönitz and Reichsmarschall Göring were seated around the table. General Student introduced me.

In the beginning, I had to overcome my shyness, but since I knew the material well, I described in simple and clear language how we had arrived at our conclusion that Mussolini was being held prisoner at the Villa Weber in Santa Maddalena. When I described the terrible adventure of teetotaler Warger, Göring and Dönitz smiled. Himmler's gaze remained ice-cold. Hitler stood up and shook my hand.

"Good! I believe you Skorzeny. The operation on the small island near Elba is cancelled. Now, please outline your plan for the action on Santa Maddalena." While I explained what I intended to do, Hitler,

Göring, and Jodl all interrupted me with questions. It was clear that I had won.

The action would begin in the morning. Surprise was critical. One day prior to the attack, a motor torpedo boat flotilla would anchor in Santa Maddalena harbor. A detachment from Friedenthal and a company of Waffen-SS soldiers under my command would land in close formation and our torpedo boats would cover us. We would appear to be a peaceful group of Germans on shore leave. It was vital that we reach the vicinity of the villa without hostilities breaking out. Afterward, we would act as dictated by circumstances.

Hitler took me aside and said quietly, "Something else, Hauptsturmführer Skorzeny. It's possible that at the time you carry out your operation, the new Italian government will still, officially at least, be our ally. Therefore, if the attack fails, or if Mussolini is not on Santa Maddalena, I might be forced to disapprove of your action publicly. In that case, you will have acted on your own and not informed your superiors. I hope you understand I will have to punish you against my will in the event of failure."

"I understand fully, Mein Führer."

After some further questions, I was about to take my leave when Hitler came up to me, shook my hand again, and gazed into my eyes. "You will do it, Skorzeny," he said. "I am convinced of it."

But I was not to do it on Santa Maddalena at the end of August and the action was never begun. We learned just in time – the evening before – that the Duce had been flown away in a Red Cross seaplane that morning.

Next day, I was to accompany General Student to Vigna del Valle on Lake Bracciano, north of Rome. There was a chance we'd come across the trail of the Red Cross seaplane that had flown out of Santa

Maddalena with the Duce on August 27. Numerous false trails led us to hospitals and to Perugia; but our investigations proved that Mussolini had been on a seaplane that landed at Vigna del Valle, and from there he'd been taken away in an ambulance.

Then the break we had been looking for jumped out at us! An intercepted radio message sent by one "General Cueli," gave us definite proof that the trail from Lake Bracciano to the Gran Sasso was the right one. Cueli, the inspector-general of the military police, reported to his superiors: "Security preparations around the Gran Sasso complete."

La Albergo Campo Imperatore, a mountain hotel at an elevation of 7,500 feet, seemed the safest prison in the world. The hotel could only be reached by cable car. What we needed – and immediately – were aerial photos of the area.

General Student instructed his intelligence officer to make a reconnaissance flight with an automatic camera installed in each wing. But the reconnaissance He-111 was in Nancy and could not make it to Rome before September 8.

All the pilot knew was that we wanted to overfly Rimini, Ancona, and Pescara, and return via the same route, which led over the Abruzzas and 9,554 foot-high Gran Sasso itself. Our pilot, Captain Langguth, advised us shortly after takeoff that the automatic cameras weren't working and there was no time to repair them. Radl and I looked at each other in amazement. Langguth casually showed us how to use a heavy, hand-held camera, on which the film had to be advanced by means of a hand crank. He had no intention of taking the photos himself.

So, for better or worse, I was tasked with taking the aerial shots. The aircraft flew at an altitude of 16,400 feet at 230 miles per hour. The outside air temperature was 17 degrees Fahrenheit, and I was in short sleeves. I stuck the upper half of my body in the opening through the dorsal turret's entry hatch. Radl sat on my legs to prevent me from falling out. The co-pilot had to give Radl a hand to pull me back into the aircraft. By journey's end, I felt completely frozen, but these photos gave us no idea of the slope of the mountain plains which formed whatever "landing strip" there might be adjacent to the mountain.

To make matters worse, the automatic large-format camera was also out of order. General Student would otherwise have noted that the slope on which we planned to land had about the same gradient as an average-difficulty ski slope and was full of boulders. Student would never have authorized the operation under those conditions.

On the evening of September 8, Radl and I outlined our plan of action. The ski hotel could only be reached by cable car from Assergi. The cable car stations had telephone communications with the hotel and were naturally watched from above and below. If the funicular railway was attacked, we would lose the vital element of surprise.

Parachute troops, who had jumped out onto the plateau, could have done this in front of the Italians' eyes. That meant we could neither carry out the operation successfully on foot, nor with the aid of a cable car. We also feared orders had been given to kill the Duce should a rescue attempt be made.

A parachute drop would have the same disadvantages. In the thin air and wind at this altitude, the rate of descent would have been too great and the paratroops would have come down widely scattered. Helicopters seemed the best solution, but the helicopter center in Erfurt couldn't spare any. The only option left open was a landing by glider. When Karl Radl and I discussed this with General Student's staff, they were all skeptical. Nevertheless, Hitler had given me the assignment and the directive to do what I thought was best.

That night, Karl and I discussed the tactics during a light dinner.

"We can get twelve DFS-230s," Radl began. "Each glider seats nine men and a pilot. That would give us 108 troops, at least in theory, if everything goes off perfectly. But given the altitude and the crazy tilt of the extremely tight area, Student's staff thinks we'd lose eighty percent."

I puffed nervously on my cigarette. As soon as it was down to the butt, I used what was left to light the next one. "Twenty of ours against ten times that many carabinieri probably armed with machine guns, automatic weapons, and mortars. We can certainly count on crash landings of at least half of the gliders," I said morosely.

The Führer had given me an order and I had given my word to carry out this order, but at the risk of eighty men, husbands, fathers, sons, brothers, many at the very beginning of their lives. Could I live with their deaths on my conscience? Eighty percent probable loss.

I announced to General Student's staff, "Gentlemen, I am ready to carry out any other plan as long as it is better than ours."

General Student finally authorized the operation on the express condition that the landing by the gliders on the terrain in front of the hotel would be as smooth as possible.

On the afternoon of September 11, I assembled all my people and said to them, "My dear friends: For six weeks you have waited without knowing why. Now I can tell you that tomorrow we will undertake an operation that the Führer has personally ordered. The task is not an easy one, and it may be that we will suffer heavy losses. But this operation must succeed under any circumstances. I will lead the action myself, and we will do our best. Anyone who wishes to volunteer, take one step forward."

Everyone stepped forward. I selected seventeen men, which wasn't exactly easy. A further dozen would accompany the Mors Battalion under the command of Untersturmführer Bramfeld. Their job was to occupy the crossroads from Aquila to Bazzano and Pescomaggiore to Paganica. This battalion was prepared to defend against an attack on the valley by Italian troops from Aquila.

It was bright and windless as the sun rose on the morning of the 12th over Practica di Mare airport just southwest of Rome. But one piece of bad news seemed to follow another. Radio Tunis reported that Italian warships from LaSpezia had arrived at Tunis. One of these ships bore Mussolini "who was now a prisoner on African soil." I knew this was a lie, since the ships had not left LaSpezia until yesterday. The large battle-cruiser *Roma* had been sunk by a remotely-controlled bomb and the Duce could not, at that moment, have been in Tunis.

The second piece of bad news was more serious: our gliders, which should already have arrived from the Riviera, would not be landing for another four or five hours. Last but not least, General Soleti, who was supposed to meet Radl and Warger in front of the Ministry of the Interior at 7:30 a.m. had not yet appeared and it was 8:30. Fortunately he showed up soon afterward.

Our twelve gliders finally landed just as my adjutant, Untersturmführer Radl was dining with the general.

To: Hauptsturmführer Skorzeny
From: Untersturmführer Radl
Subject: Memo for the Record, 12 September 1943

My Commander. Greetings and respects.

The following is my report on my meeting with General Soleti earlier this morning.

General Soleti watched as our twelve DFS 230s landed in front of us. "Very interesting, very ingenious these aircraft without motors, don't you think?"

"Yes, Herr General," I replied. The DFS 230 is an *excellentisima macchina!*"

"You are a paratrooper? Surely you have flown this machine often?"

I was neither a paratrooper nor were gliders my specialty. The general was not aware that he was going along; in fact, in the third glider with Hauptsturmführer Skorzeny. I had to reassure the general somehow or another. "Yes, very often, Herr General," I lied. "It makes an extremely comfortable impression, not only because there's no engine noise, which makes it difficult to talk, but also because one feels like a bird man, *uccello.*"

"What are these machines for?"

I looked at my watch. The moment of truth had now arrived.

"Simple, Herr General. Later we will take off in these gliders, land on the massif of Gran Sasso, and free the Duce."

General Soleti looked at me incredulously. "I hope you are saying that in jest. The Duce is being held prisoner at an elevation of nearly 7,500 feet in the high mountains. You really intend to land there? That is impossible, my friend. That would be an idiotic operation, a massacre, plain suicide. And you think that I, Soleti …?"

When Warger finally managed to convince him that he was part of this "idiotic operation," he actually became sick and we put out an urgent call for Dr. Brunner to come.

I understood General Soleti's behavior. He'd been an outstanding cavalryman, who'd proved himself magnificently while leading his cavalry regiment. Our operation seemed senseless and impossible to him. But after talking with General Student, he was forced to agree to come with us for better or for worse "in order to avoid a bloodbath." He had no other choice. Neither Radl nor Warger let him out of their sight.

Before General Student took leave of us, he assembled all of the pilots, officers, and group leaders taking part in the action and addressed us in the airport administrative offices.

"Gentlemen," he said, "very soon you will take off on an extraordinary mission. Each of you was selected from the best pilots and officers, accustomed to looking danger in the eye. This operation will go down as unique in military history, not only because of the enormous technical difficulties, but because this operation is of considerable political significance. Before you receive your final instructions from Hauptsturmführer Skorzeny, I would like to wish you all the best for a complete success. I am sure every one of you will do his duty for the glory of the Fatherland."

The expedition, twelve gliders with their towing planes, was to be led to the drop zone by Captain Langguth, the pilot who had taken Karl Radl and me on our numbing reconnaissance flight. Using a large-scale map of the Campo Imperatore, which was pinned on the wall, I explained to each pilot and each group leader his mission. I estimated that I and the people in my glider, number three, would have a little more than four minutes to reach the Duce before Italian troops on the ground would open fire at us. We would hopefully receive cover from the crews of gliders number one and two, while Karl Radl and the soldiers of glider number four would be only a minute behind us.

But one must always expect the unexpected. In our case, about fifteen minutes prior to our departure, a few English aircraft bombed the small Practica di Mare airfield from which we were to take off.

When I emerged from cover I saw that miraculously none of our gliders had been hit. The runway had been partially destroyed by bombs, leaving craters in parts of the tarmac. At 1:00 p.m., seven hours behind schedule, when the afternoon wind currents would play havoc with our aircraft, our gliders, towed by Henschel 126 glider tugs, set course to the northeast toward the mountain massif of the Gran Sasso.

11

One can see practically nothing of the landscape from the inside of a DFS230 glider. Its tubular steel frame is covered only with canvas. At 12,000 feet, glider number three emerged from a thick cloud bank and we broke out into brilliant sunshine coming through the tiny plastic windows. The first thing I noticed was that several of my people, who had already eaten their emergency rations, were now very ill. I looked at General Soleti. He'd been sitting in front of me between my knees, and his face had taken on the gray-green color of his uniform.

The tug aircraft's pilot kept our glider pilot leader informed of our progress. He, in turn, passed on to me the current position of our formation. In this way, I was able to follow our flight path with precision. I held a detailed map in my hands, which Radl and I had drawn using the photographs we'd taken on September 1.

"Hauptsturmführer Skorzeny?" Lieutenant Meier-Wehner's voice was tight.

"Speak."

"The tow pilot has just informed me that the lead aircraft and Glider Number One are no longer in sight."

"Shit!" I spat out the word involuntarily.

But more bad news was to come. "How many gliders are we supposed to have behind us, Hauptsturnführer?"

"Nine."

"Our pilot just got word from Practica di Mare that two aircraft ran into bomb holes on the runway and never left the ground."

I took a deep breath. That meant there was no one to lead us to the drop off point and no one to cover Radl's and my assault teams. Time for some ingenuity. I called out to Lieutenant Meier-Wehner, "Tell the tow pilot we're taking over the lead."

While he was doing this, I pulled out my paratrooper's knife and started cutting at the canvas deck and bulkheads. As the canvas ripped, we finally seized on some good luck. Cool air rushed into the overheated shell of the glider, crammed as it was with men and weapons, immediately bringing blessed relief from their torpor and airsickness. Concurrently, as I peered through the tears in the canvas I could see the granite mountains below. In this way, I was able to orient myself to some degree. I gave instructions to Meier-Wehner, who then passed those orders onto our "locomotive driver."

Shortly thereafter, I sighted the small city of Aquila and its airfield beneath us. Farther on, I saw the Mors column on the winding road to the cable car's valley station. It had just passed Assergi and was trailing a dense cloud of dust. They were on time. Everything was going according to plan. It was almost 2:00 p.m., X-hour.

"Fasten steel helmets," I shouted.

The hotel appeared beneath us. Lieutenant Meier-Wehner gave the order, "Release tow cable!" The tow rope parted and we swooped freely, with no sound but the *whoosh* of the wind on our wings. Meier-Wehner turned to me and then toward what he could see below, jabbing his finger in the direction the glider was flying.

I followed his gaze. I realized at that moment what it meant to have all those men dependent on me for their very lives. By no flight of imagination could the triangular space immediately below us be called a landing field: a sloping shelf, for all the world like a ski jump, studded with outcrop rock and boulders.

General Student had specifically laid down the law that unless we could make a smooth landing we must abandon the attack and glide to safety in the valley. There was no time for a second thought. In a spasm of defiance, I shouted to Lieutenant Meier-Wehner, "Dive! Crash land! As near the hotel as you can!"

Meier-Wehner looked at me for a flickering instant as if I were mad. Then, God Bless him, he carried out my orders.

We hurtled toward the mountains. In spite of our parachute brake whipping from the glider's tail, our machine landed much too fast. It bounced several times. We jolted and pitched over the boulders like a tiny dinghy in the midst of on ocean storm. A shuddering crash, then stillness and silence.

My first thought was, "I'm alive." My second thought was, "We have four minutes, no more."

The glider was almost completely destroyed. We'd landed twenty yards from the hotel.

From then on everything happened very quickly. I grabbed my weapon and ran as quickly as I could toward the hotel, followed by my seven Waffen-SS comrades and Meier-Wehner. An Italian carabinieri standing by the hotel's entrance stared speechless, apparently stupefied by this apparition which had just fallen out of a silent sky and landed virtually at his feet.

I forced my way through a door immediately to my right. A radio operator sat at a console preparing to transmit. I kicked the stool out from under him and he fell to the floor. A blow from my submachine gun destroyed the radio set. Later I learned that at that very moment the operator was trying to send a report to General Cueli that aircraft were approaching to land.

The room had no other doors, so my men dashed along the back side of the hotel, looking for an entrance. But there was none, just the terrace at the end of the wall. I climbed on the shoulders of Staff Sergeant Himmel, then climbed up a further wall and found myself standing at the front of the hotel. Suddenly I caught sight of Mussolini's profile in a window frame!

"Get back, Duce!" I shouted. "Get away from the window!" I dashed off around the terrace. At last the main entrance, flanked by two sentries. The guards looked amazed and stood still, with the same hypnotized stare as the carabinieri I'd encountered at the first door. They'd not recovered when my men booted their machine guns off their supports and scrambled through the door. My troops were followed by, of all people, General Soleti, who seemed to have become his old self again as soon as he was safely out of the glider.

A voice behind me shouted in Italian. "*Mani in alto!* Hands up!" I pushed against the carabinieri who were bunched up in front of the entrance and fought my way against the stream of soldiers trying to block my way. They were too close to shoot, even if they had known what had suddenly come upon them.

I had seen the Duce on the second floor to the right. I raced up a flight of stairs, taking three steps at a stride. I went down the hallway at the top of the stairs, shoved open a small door midway down the hall, and came upon the Duce, surrounded by two Italian bodyguards and a man in civilian clothes. One of my brawniest men, Untersturmführer Schwerdt, singlehandedly bundled them into the hall. Two more of my men, Sergeants Holzer and Benzer, who'd climbed the façade using the lightning conductor, climbed through the windows and surrounded the others.

Benito Mussolini was in our hands and under our protection! The entire action had taken barely four minutes, without a single shot being fired!

I had no time to say anything to the Duce. Radl's glider had made a tolerable landing. My adjutant and his men were bounding toward the hotel. Weapons in hand, they rushed to the entrance, where the carabinieri were just beginning to set up their machine guns again.

"Karl, we've got him here! Everything's in order! Secure below!"

Three more gliders crash landed and men poured out. The fourth, landing some distance away, was smashed to pieces. The ten men inside were immediately recovered by our medics and Italian soldiers, and were treated on the spot. None of those aboard the glider were seriously injured.

I heard a few shots fired in the distance. The Italian sentries had come to life. I turned toward the hall and shouted in bad Italian, "*Voglio il Commandante! Deve venire subito!* I want the Commander! He must come at once!"

Some bewildered shouting, and then an Italian colonel appeared.

"I ask your immediate surrender, Colonel," I said, switching to French. "Mussolini is already in our hands. We hold the building. If you want to avoid needless bloodshed, you must surrender now."

"I need time to think it over. I must speak with General Soleti."

"You have sixty seconds to do so."

Just then, Karl Radl walked into the room. He had been able to push his way through. I left two of our soldiers to guard the door and stepped into Mussolini's room. Schwerdt was still there. The Duce came forward: a stocky man who looked older than his portraits showed him, in a blue suit that was too large. He wore a stubble of beard and his pate sprouted gray bristle. But his eyes were ardent, and excited.

My first words to him were, "Duce, I have been sent by Order of the Führer to set you free."

He shook my hand and hugged me. Mussolini had always been, first and foremost, a politician through and through, He always considered his public, and now, as emotionally overridden as he was, he replied, no doubt for posterity, but sincerely nonetheless, "I knew that my friend Adolf Hitler would not abandon me. I embrace my liberator!"

The minute had elapsed and the colonel came back, carrying a goblet brimming with red wine. "To the gallant victor," he said, bowing graciously.

"Thank you," I replied lifting a glass of the wine which he had proffered. "*Al votre salute.* To your health, colonel."

We drank to one another. The colonel refilled my class immediately. I passed it over to my thirsty adjutant, who emptied it in one gulp. As a white sheet was flung from the second story window, cheers erupted from the Germans below.

At that moment, Lieutenant von Berlepsch, a young-old stereotypical Prussian officer, following my instructions to the letter, surrounded the hotel with his paratroopers. Through the open window I ordered him to disarm the numerous troops guarding the Duce, and added, "Gently, but as quickly as you can."

"*Jawohln Herr Hauptmann!*" He saluted smartly, clamped his monocle firmly in his eye, and marched off stiffly. There was no question that he understood precisely what had been asked of him, and preciseness was the bread-and-butter of his being.

At General Soleti's and Mussolini's request, I allowed the Italian soldiers to retain their side arms. The Duce told me that carabinieri captain Faviola, who'd been badly wounded at Tobruk, and the other officers had treated him well.

In minutes, I experienced another gratifying discovery. When I went to see the disarming of the Italian garrison I learned that the man we'd seen in the Duce's room, the one wearing civilian clothes, was none other than General Cueli, who was responsible for keeping Mussolini sealed up and shut away. Having been the one who'd unwittingly sent me on Mussolini's trail, he'd also picked the most unfortunate day possible to pay a visit to Gran Sasso. I was delighted to see him. Like almost every Italian I've ever met, the General was both gracious and graceful.

"*Ah, bene. È la vita, mio amico*" he purred. "Ah, well, that's life, my friend." He shook hands. "*Al vittoriano.*"

Later I heard that General Cueli was supposed to have spirited Mussolini away that very afternoon and hand him over to the allies. I decided that Soleti and Cueli should be taken back to Rome.

Meanwhile, there was a brief skirmish in the course of occupying the cable station and the Italians had suffered minor casualties. But both stations had fallen into our hands intact. We had undoubtedly been very lucky. We'd sustained nowhere near the 80 percent losses predicted by the regimental staff. About that time, Major Mors telephoned and asked if he might come up. Of course, I consented.

But now for a more urgent matter: How could we get the Duce to Rome? We'd planned for three possibilities. The first involved seizing the airfield at Aquila di Abruzzi. Three Heinkel 111s would land there. I would escort Mussolini to the airfield and accompany him in one of the aircraft. This plane would, in turn, be escorted by the others during the flight. Unfortunately, it proved impossible to reestablish contact with the parachute corps' radio station.

The second option: a Fieseler Storch aircraft would land near Assergi, site of the valley station. Unfortunately, the pilot of that aircraft, whose hard landing I had witnessed through my field glasses, radioed that his machine's undercarriage had been damaged.

Now, all that was left to us was the third solution. Hauptmann Gerlach, General Student's personal pilot, would land another Storch on the Campo Imperatore. Carabinieri and our parachute troops worked quickly to clear a narrow landing strip, for Gerlach was already circling overhead waiting for a green flare, the signal that he might land. Even though Gerlach was truly the best pilot I'd ever known, except perhaps for Hanna Reitsch, I was still amazed when he brought the Storch in for a perfect landing, with absolutely no margin for a single error.

But now the almost impossible reared its head: He had to take off again with the Duce and me aboard! I had received an order from Hitler himself. If I let Benito Mussolini fly away alone with Gerlach and he then, perhaps, crashed with the Duce, I'd have no alternative but to put a bullet through my head. It would have meant I was unwilling to risk the dangerous takeoff with Mussolini and Gerlach.

Since I was forced to opt for our third – and only – alternative, I informed the Duce that we would take off in the Storch in half an hour. Since Mussolini was a pilot himself, he knew what a takeoff at this elevation and without a proper runway involved. I was grateful that he didn't waste any words over the takeoff.

The Duce handed his luggage to Radl and stepped out of the hotel into the open. At that point, Hauptmann Gerlach recoiled. To weigh down his frail aircraft with the load we proposed – and Mussolini and I were each quite substantial – was sheer madness. He refused point blank to consider it. I took Gerlach aside and spoke very quietly to him. Rescuing Mussolini had been Hitler's direct order. If either of us failed, what would there be left for us?

Finally, he gave in and looked toward the sky. "Have it your own way. If it's neck or nothing, we'd better be on the move."

Squads hurriedly set to work again. Even Mussolini lent a hand in rolling one or two boulders. The three of us squashed into a plane built for a maximum of two. Mussolini was behind the pilot and I was behind Mussolini. With the single engine turning, twelve men clung to the Storch, digging in their heels for a tug-of-war. Gerlach held a hand aloft until the engine's pitch rose to a crescendo. Then he dropped his hand, the men let go, and the plane catapulted across the scree.

The aircraft glided down the sloping "runway." A large drainage ditch ran through the second third of the strip. Gerlach tried to miss it, but instinctively knew he couldn't. He tried to pull the aircraft up and then lift off. The Storch jumped over the obstacle, but then it tipped to the left and almost seemed to flip over. I grasped the steel spars on either side of me, throwing my weight from side to side against the swaying wheel as one wheel or the other was lifted by a rock. The Storch touched down again … the last few meters. Suddenly a crevasse yawned before us. The tiny plane shot over it and continued beyond, with the port wheel buckled. Then it went hurtling over the edge of the ravine. As I glanced back at the last moment, I saw there was a gap among the Germans standing on the Gran Sasso. Radl had fainted.

We had gone over the edge.

The aircraft side-slipped to the left and dived into the valley. I closed my eyes and waited for the impact. But amazingly, impossibly, I heard the sound of the little Storch's engine still pounding, still struggling, as Gerlach brought off his miracle. When I opened my eyes, I saw Gerlach slowly pulling back on the stick. With consummate skill, he lifted the Storch gently from its nosedive to flatten out a few hundred feet above the valley floor. I couldn't refrain from placing my hand on the Duce's shoulder. Although he was just as pale as Gerlach and me, he turned and smiled. He had been fully aware of the danger but hadn't wasted a word about it.

Only now did he begin to talk, and as we were flying quite low for safety reasons, he described the area for me and stirred old memories. It struck me that he spoke excellent German.

Soon the Eternal City passed by to our right. Gerlach landed artfully on the tailwheel and the right mainwheel, since the left had been damaged. As we landed, three of General Student's aides-de-camp stood stiffly at salute while we three crumpled figures stepped onto friendly soil.

But it might not be friendly very long. Fighting raged nearby with no time for ceremony. We were quickly escorted to the waiting Heinkel 111. Within the hour we took off for Vienna.

12

We arrived near Vienna in the middle of a storm. Our adventure wasn't over yet. We tried to make radio contact with Vienna in vain. Visibility was practically zero. I was sitting beside the pilot. We rechecked our course. It was night and we were getting low on fuel. We had to be close to Vienna and we descended cautiously. There was no question of trying a forced landing with the Duce on board. Suddenly I saw a large body of water shimmering through a gap in the cloud. I was sure it was Lake Neusiedler. When we dropped lower, my assumption proved to be correct. I told the pilot to fly north. We landed at Aspern airport in total darkness. There I learned from the control tower that we hadn't been able to make radio contact because it was Sunday and the radio center wasn't fully manned that day.

We rode to the Imperial Hotel where they had reserved a suite for Mussolini. He had no pajamas, but in any case he considered them a waste of time, which led to a lighthearted discussion. I was glad to see an entirely different man than the one I had met on Gran Sasso when I'd kicked open the door of his room at the Hotel Imperatore.

When I got to my own room I began to feel the fatigue that had accumulated in the last five days. But I was not to have any rest. The phone rang. It was Himmler. He seemed very friendly. After he had congratulated me, he said, "You are Viennese if I'm not mistaken? Your gracious lady isn't with you? Send a car for her. Of course, you'll stay with the Duce. You will accompany him to Munich tomorrow and from there to Führer Headquarters."

I gladly accepted the Reichsführer's suggestion. Just before midnight, General Quernet, who had escorted us to the hotel from the airport, informed me that the chief-of-staff of the Vienna Corps Headquarters wished to speak with me. Soon afterward, the Oberst introduced himself and declared, "Hauptsturmführer Skorzeny, I come on order of the Führer, the Supreme Commander of the Wehrmacht. It is my duty and privilege to present you with the Knight's Cross of the Iron Cross!"

He took off his own decoration and placed the band around my badly-shaved neck, over the jacket of my decidedly tattered paratrooper uniform. I regretted that my father was no longer alive. He would have been happier about this than I. In the confusion of congratulations, handshakes, and more questions, the telephone rang. I wasn't paying attention when General Quernet said, "The Führer himself wishes to speak to you!"

I took the receiver and heard Hitler's voice. "Herr Skorzeny, not only have you successfully concluded an act unique in military history, but you have also returned a friend to me. I knew that if anyone could do it, it was you. I have promoted you to Sturmbahnführer of the Waffen-SS and awarded you the Knight's Cross. I know you're wearing it already, for I gave the order that they were to present it to you immediately …"

Keitel and Göring came on the line and likewise congratulated me. I explained to them all that the Duce could not have been freed without the courage and imagination of everyone who had taken part in the action, particularly Untersturmführer Radl, Leutenant Meier-Wehner, the pilot of Glider Number 3, and Hauptmann Gerlach.

Next day I accompanied Mussolini from Vienna to Munich in a comfortable Junkers aircraft. The rejuvenated and ebullient Duce explained his grandiose plans to me during the flight. At Riem Airport near Munich, Mussolini tenderly took his wife Donna Rachele and his two children into his arms.

I remained at the Reich government's guest house in Munich until September 15. The Duce insisted I stay there as well and take my meals with him and his family. During that time, I was increasingly impressed by Mussolini's world view. Although he talked incessantly about the good of forming a European Union, which would embrace all the countries of Europe, and working together to manage the tremendous riches of the African continent for the benefit of the African and European peoples, I had no such illusions. I knew that the new republican-fascist state would have enormous difficulties to overcome. Chief among these difficulties was that the Allies, who, despite the tremendous propaganda boost that the Gran Sasso rescue had given the Führer, were very much on the ascendant. They considered the Duce's government, whose capital occupied Lake Garda, to be little more than a puppet propped up by what they viewed as the decaying Reich state.

We arrived at Führer Headquarters on the afternoon of the 15th. Hitler awaited the Duce at the airport and gave him a warm welcome. In my own mind, despite the promise of undying amity between the two states, I knew that the new fascist republic had no basis other than the friendship of these two men and perhaps fifty thousand staunch Italian followers. It seemed to me that Italy was more susceptible to communism than ever, for this time the communists came as allies of the great democracies.

In October 1943, my friend, the dictator of the Northern Italian fascist republic, was exceedingly generous, especially to me, but to my men as well. Mussolini's government inducted me into the Order of the Hundred Musketeers. Only one hundred Italian soldiers were admitted to membership, and I never learned whether a vacancy had been created just for me or someone had been pushed out or died to enable this to happen. That same month, the Duce presented gold wristwatches to all the paratroopers and my sixteen Waffen-SS men who had landed by glider on the Campo Imperatore. The watch faces were all engraved with the famous "M." Every officer received a gold stopwatch. But when it came to me, Mussolini outdid himself. He sent a wristwatch *and* a stopwatch, together with a gold pocket watch, whose "M" consisted of rubies and which bore the date September 9, 1943. Finally, as what the Americans call "the icing on the cake," the new government arranged to have a racy Lancia sports convertible shipped to me at Friedenthal.

When Benito Mussolini and I parted company at Führer Headquarters on September 16, he made me promise to visit him soon in Italy. But it wasn't until June 1944 that Radl, who'd received the Knight's Cross and been promoted to Hauptsturmführer at my instigation, and I finally went to Gargnano on the west bank of Lake Garda, Mussolini's new seat of government.

I found the Duce's capital guarded by First Panzer Corps of the Waffen-SS, under the command of my former chief, General Paul Hausser. While I was delighted to reunite with Papa Paul and with my friend the Duce, Radl and I were dismayed to see only a few Italian soldiers on guard outside Mussolini's residence, the Villa Feltinelli. Security was provided by a battalion of Waffen-SS, as if the former leader of millions of Italians couldn't have found thousands of his own countrymen to protect and defend him. Had we freed him from the Grand Sasso only to see him as a prisoner again? It was quite obvious that Mussolini was not a free man. Great sadness overcame me at this unexpected and sorry state of affairs.

It was even worse when he greeted us in his small office. He looked like a withered, defeated old man. He again accused the House of Savoy and regretted that Duke Aosta had died in captivity in Nairobi in 1942. "The traitors think they can save themselves, but they are wrong," he declared. "They believe our enemies will reward them for their betrayal. But they are already being treated like lackeys. Badoglio was forced to resign three times. The King abdicated in favor of his son. The House of Savoy is convinced they've saved the crown. But I can tell you one thing, Skorzeny: this crown is lost forever."

The enthusiasm and conviction he'd shown me only nine months earlier were gone. He seemed to convince only himself. Trying to make him feel that he was still worthy of honor, I asked him if he would do me the great favor of dedicating photographs of himself for all the participants of the Gran Sasso operation. He graciously and gladly did so. On the photo he presented to me he wrote, "To my friend Otto Skorzeny, who saved my life. We will fight for the same cause: for a united and free Europe." That photo was stolen from me by the Americans in 1945, as were other souvenirs that had been given to me by my friend, Benito Mussolini.

On April 28, 1945, I was on my command train in the vicinity of Salzburg. I had set up my command post in two special cars which had gotten out of Berlin with much difficulty. My mission was to organize an "Alpine Fortress," together with Field Marshall Schörner. I had an excellent communications system at my disposal: telex, telephones, and a dozen radios, so I was able to communicate with every front.

Shortly after noon, we received a report from Italian radio that Benito Mussolini had been captured and shot by partisans. I considered that impossible. If the Duce was no longer alive, it was because he'd taken his own life. I was firmly convinced of that. I knew that my friend was guarded at Gargnano by a battalion of Waffen-SS. It was totally inconceivable that even a large number of resistance fighters could successfully ambush a battalion of Waffen-SS in its quarters.

At that time, I knew nothing of the negotiations going on in Bern between General Wolff and Alan Dulles. The Duce had not been informed of this. But Himmler knew about it. When I was finally able to confer with Major Beck, the chief of my Commando Unit Italy, he confirmed that the Duce had left Gargnano on April 18 to go to Milan. Someone had withdrawn the Waffen-SS battalion assigned to guard him and had been sent to the front.

"What idiot gave that order?" I asked Major Beck.

"I have no idea," he replied. "All we heard was that the battalion was supposed to be replaced by a company of the Luftwaffe. I later learned that the Duce left Milan on the night of April 25-26 after speaking with Cardinal Schuster and one of the resistance leaders, General Cadorna. The Duce didn't want to surrender himself."

"So he was headed to Switzerland or Austria?"

"I don't know. I just learned that he stopped at the prefecture in Como awaiting a strong militia column and then put up a fight in the Valtini Mountains. There were no Waffen-SS soldiers with him. It was too late. There was nothing we could do …"

So it was that our Waffen-SS held Mussolini prisoner for a year-and-a-half and in the end did not even defend him. General Field Marshall Kesselring would never have allowed such a rotten trick, but he was in Bad Nauheim, acting as Commander-in-Chief of what was left of the Western Front.

The rest is all-too-well known. Benito Mussolini was abandoned by everyone. The hangman, Audisio-Valerio, a communist and former member of the loyalists during the Spanish Civil War, said, "Duce I have come to rescue you."

Mussolini is said to have asked, "You aren't armed, are you?"

Some have written that the Duce did not die bravely. But I learned later through an unimpeachable source that the Duce's last words were, "Aim directly for the heart."

Even today, I cringe as I recall seeing the horrible photographs from Loreto Square in Milan.

13

The Reich paraded the Gran Sasso rescue as proof that fortune had smiled on Germany despite the dark backdrop of increasingly bad news. The fact that the exploit had been carried out by an outsider in defiance of all the rules of conventional warfare irked the High Command. Worse, it gave Der Führer the opportunity to step into the limelight and regain his own prestige. It revalidated Hitler's intuition just when the High Command had hoped there might be some chance that sound judgment, *their* judgment, could take over again. Instead, the wildest chance of all had succeeded outrageously.

When I arrived at Wolf's Lair in mid-September 1943, I was received like a conquering hero. Photographs from that day show Hitler clasping my hand like a brother while the generals dutifully applaud. Marshal Göring adroitly timed his entrance by special train to present me with the Air Force Gold Medal. As the hero of the moment, I was bombarded with invitations: lunch with Hitler's deputy, Martin Bormann, tea with foreign minister Ribbentrop, dinner with Dr. Goebbels. When the latter told me malicious anecdotes about other Cabinet Ministers, there was no doubt in my mind that, socially at least, I had arrived.

But the greatest proof of how far I'd come occurred on September 17, when the Leader invited me to join the very intimate circle of those to whom he opened his heart at the end of each day, at midnight. Hitler sipped amber fluid from a glass perched on a silver saucer. A servant whispered in my ear, "If you don't like tea at this hour, I can always get you coffee." No mention of any alcoholic beverage, of course.

The talk, mostly from Der Führer, went on 'til nearly 3:00 a.m. I was later told this was pretty much *de rigeur*. During the meeting I attended, Hitler waxed eloquent about my "magnificent accomplishment," but truth to tell, I had had a stomach full of such accolades and I pictured myself petrifying into one of those stodgy sycophants who surrounded the Leader, one whose days of action would become limited to "overseeing" the acts of others rather than participating in those acts myself. After Hitler told those in attendance how he would rebuild and embellish his home town of Linz when the war was won, he asked me to return often and take part in these heart-to-heart talks. I smiled and nodded, but said nothing; and I never went back to any of his midnight meetings.

Before I left the Wolf's Lair, Hitler commanded me to give a lecture on commando strategy and tactics to a bunch of tight-lipped (and to me tight-arsed) generals. While the generals were prepared to accept me on their *own* terms – while they accepted my commando forces at Friedenthal as a necessary pain-in-the-neck, if for no other reason than to mollify Hitler, they did not see, and they did not *want* to see, the importance of commandos in modern warfare. This type of "dirty" fighting was beneath their station, beneath the dignity of the Junkers, the historical military guardians of the Prussian state.

Never mind. If I was by no means the generals' favorite, my time in the limelight of Hitler's favor gave me the one prize I wanted more than any other: a commando battalion of special troops for every front. Under his Leader's eye, General Jodl wholeheartedly agreed.

"But where would Major Skorzeny recruit these troops?" Der Führer asked rhetorically.

Jodl was quick to respond. "He can enlist four thousand immediately from the Brandenburg Division. There's absolutely wonderful material there, top notch men in every respect."

I needed no second invitation. If nothing else, Adrian Freiherr von Fölkersam who, with some other officers from the Brandenburg Division had requested transfer to Friedenthal some months before, had already given me a foretaste of the quality of Brandenburger troops.

Von Fölkersam, then 29, had been born in Riga, Latvia, the eldest son and heir of a Baltic German house. His grandfather had fought as an admiral in the Czar's navy during the Russo-Japanese War. He spoke fluent French, German, and English and had studied economics at the Universities of Berlin and Vienna. Like my right arm, Radl, Adrian was an absolutely tireless worker, and, in his few months at Friedenthal, he'd become my chief of staff, second only to Karl.

Like many others ready to take on the craziest risks if they could use their brains in doing so, Von Fölkersam had joined the Brandenburg unit when it was created in 1939 as a hush-hush battalion in which foreign language speakers might enroll. In the first few months, they were used on work of secrecy and danger. Then, as the battalion grew, first as a regiment and then to a division, the generals in their great "wisdom" began to employ the volunteers in everyday front-line work. Thus it was that Germany's best and brightest, men who had traveled abroad and spoke Western languages, were wasted in routine battles in the Balkans and on the Eastern front.

The more I found out about the Brandenburg Division, the more eager I was to take almost any of their volunteer transferees. By 1943, complaints about using the Brandenburg Division as cannon fodder and defections, such as Von Fölkersam's, had soured the High Command. What could they do about these independent-minded, unmilitary, versatile, and, most disturbingly, intelligent young men?

Their opportunity to rid themselves of this "pimple on the rear end" of established order came when General Jodl broached his suggestion to the Supreme Leader himself. Undoubtedly, they were as thrilled with the chance to dump these problem children into my lap as I was to grab onto these "misfits" at the earliest possible moment.

By all that was logical, Adrian Von Fölkersam and I should not have gotten along at all. He was a Junker, old-line, directly descended from highly traditional Prussian military nobility and I was the generals' worst nightmare. But Adrian regarded honor, duty, and leadership above everything else and I greatly respected those attributes, just as, for some completely inexplicable reason, he appeared to respect and genuinely like me.

Word spread from mouth to mouth. Within a month of Hitler's approval of the plan, more than four thousand men of the Brandenburg Division had put in for transfers to Friedenthal. After carefully interviewing every one of these volunteers myself, I happily accepted the vast majority of them.

"Gentlemen," I addressed them in a series of introductory remarks, "how many of you are glad to be here?"

To a man, their response was loud, boisterous, and affirmative.

"All right. You've signed up without even knowing what you're in for. I expect, and you can bet that if I don't receive it you will be out on your arse as quickly as I can make it happen, that each and every one of you will give me the moon and then some. Every commando in my unit will train like you've never trained before. By the time you're fully ready to be a commando, you'll be a parachutist, a swimmer, a linguist, and a saboteur. You already have shown you have brainpower and initiative. I can guarantee you you'll use every bit of that creativity. You'll be able to drive, and repair, anything from a steam roller to a locomotive to a tank. And don't think I'm one of those desk types who'll lord it over you from a plush office. I'll be out in the field with your units every day you're in training, and, even though I'm an old fart of thirty-five, I'll be pushing your arse every step of the way, and if you can't show me you're stronger, faster, tougher, and more resilient than me, you'd better have a damn good excuse. Understand?"

"Yes, SIR!" The roar was genuine, unanimous, and heartfelt.

During the next few months, the newest members of the commandos learned that I meant what I said. I did not hesitate to join, and even fraternize with, the men under our officers during a rigorous training program, which often ran to fourteen hours a day, six days a week. Imagine the look on the faces of our training officers, Obersturmführers, first lieutenants, when they found themselves shouting orders and commands not only to a Sturmbahnführer, a major, but to *the* Commander of the entire Friedenthal operation. But they soon learned that if there was to be the *esprit de corps* that was essential to the success of our missions, the leaders must *lead*, not follow, their men into the dragon's jaws. I had precious little time to get my commandos ready for the assignments which awaited them, and I drove all of my forces, officers and enlisted men, to the brink of exhaustion, but never even close to mutiny.

Friedenthal, the "valley of peace," eighteen miles north of Berlin, was a suburb of Oranienburg. In addition to the parklike setting of our commando training center, Oranienburg housed Sachsenhausen and the Auergesellschaft works. The first of these was a notorious concentration camp used for the detention of political prisoners and later Soviet prisoners of war. While not designated as a death camp, it served as the administrative center where SS functionaries were trained for reassignment to other camps throughout the Reich. During the period between 1936 and the end of the war, Sachsenhausen housed over 200,000 inmates, of which some thirty thousand perished.

The second, which was known to both Soviet and American intelligence, but otherwise top secret, housed an industrial-scale production plant for high purity uranium oxide, a major component of the German effort to produce nuclear weapons.

While our training program progressed with a vengeance, Karl, Adrian, and I faced a second set of problems which presented us with both a challenge and an opportunity to use all the creativity and ingenuity my two aides and I could muster.

Armed S.S. had told me to put in for all the equipment I needed. I sent an exhaustive list, well knowing that with materiel being gobbled up, particularly on the Eastern Front, what I needed was in precious short supply. I waited for weeks with no response. Finally, when the letter from Headquarters arrived, I eagerly tore it open and read the following terse message:

"Major Skorzeny:

Headquarters is pleased to inform you that your request has been processed. All of your requirements have been approved. However, we must also advise that since you now exercise the powers and authority of a divisional commander, you cannot look to Armed S.S. for these supplies. Rather, you are now designated independent, with license to secure these requirements from all sources at your independent disposal ..."

When I showed the letter to Karl Radl, he laughed at the mad "logic" of the headquarters mind. Then, with his own twist on the bureaucratic mind, he said, "Commander, read between the lines of the letter: this is a license to plunder every arsenal and supply depot in Europe. So we can use this letter as the key to the treasury. If desperate situations require desperate measures, by all means let's use them!"

I agreed with the letter and the spirit of what my adjutant said. I started seizing equipment using my Headquarters SS-supplied *passepartout*. I took weapons and left promissory notes. I "borrowed" stores of all manner of material with absolutely no intention of returning them. Radl joyfully played the bureaucratic game at which he was such a past master, sending reams of applications for supplies I had already taken or quoting nonexistent permits for requisitioning more.

We'd started by stealing equipment. Next, and I say this with no sense of guilt, Special Operations Friedenthal went on to steal men. My Gran Sasso venture and its aftermath seemed to ignite a flame that drew the "moths" of the adventurous. Since my command included elements of all three Services, Karl, Adrian, and I found ourselves besieged by volunteers, not only from the Wehrmacht, but from the Kriegsmarine and the Luftwaffe too. The fire-eaters, the knights-errant, and the ne'er-do-wells literally came out of the woodwork seeking to enlist under the new flag, all of them ready to march into the cannon's mouth instantly if only they could wangle a transfer to Friedenthal.

We were like those cattle rustlers in the American West as described in Karl May's *Winnetou* books, which had been so popular between the wars. Only instead of cattle, we rustled men. Once at Friedenthal, the toughest malcontents from other units became malleably docile in our hands, lest they be robbed of their once-in-a-lifetime chance. The legend of the Friedenthal Special Forces was by no means diminished by the fact that each of our latest recruits, particularly if they failed our unit, would more likely than not end up on the notorious Eastern Front.

Of course, those units who'd been robbed of their most creative and aggressive manpower complained to the War Office. But they lacked anyone to match Karl Radl. Karl continually eluded the pursuit of the envious losers in the same way he always had: he was absolutely scrupulous in paying the most eager and adhesive lip service to every word, sentence, and paragraph of every regulation, no matter how stupid, arcane, and contradictory. If the War Office demanded ten pages justifying every new Friedenthal recruit, Radl ensured they received one hundred pages, and in triplicate, and with at least three impressive, official-looking stamps "manufactured" by "Waffen S.S. Headquarters," answerable directly to the Führer himself. These units were hobbled from the start by ribbons of red tape which the generals had created.

If the Friedenthal Special Forces were eager to prove themselves the best of the best and the most imaginative of all the brave men I'd ever worked with when they joined the Special Forces, they were nearly apoplectic with excitement when I called the entire Friedenthal camp together on the parade ground two months after the Gran Sasso mission. My speech lasted less than two minutes.

"Gentlemen of the Friedenthal Special Forces. This meeting will be very brief. I have just received two encrypted telephone calls which have been combined into one recording. I will now play you that recording so you will have no doubt of their origin." I pressed a button and the unmistakable voice of the Supreme Leader himself came over the loudspeakers as clearly as if he'd been on the dais standing next to me.

"My Dear Major Skorzeny and your fantastically talented and crucial special forces at Friedenthal. I send each of you greetings from Wolfsschanze. Although every mission you undertake is critical to the War Effort, the next missions are of immediate importance. You are herewith charged with "rescuing" Marshal Pétain, the head of the Vichy government in France, and bringing him to me for "consultations," at the moment I give the word. Your second assignment is to bring in Marshal Tito, the leader of so-called 'partisan' forces in Yugoslavia – *dead or alive*. The way in which you handle these operations, except for the timing, which I will direct, will be entirely in the hands of Sturmbahnführer Skorzeny, whom I personally charge with strategy and tactics, from beginning to end. May God bless your efforts as you go forth with the hopes and dreams of the entire German people!"

14

The order for *Operation Der Wolf bellit* (The Wolf Howls), came the end of November 1943. OKW directed me to go to Vichy via Paris with the Friedenthal Battalion, there to await further instructions.

Once in Paris, I contacted the military commander who, like so many other officers from all branches of the Service, was staying at the Hotel Continental on Place de l'Opéra at Rue de Rivoli. Even more of the higher-ups stayed at the Hotel Majestic, the seat of the military commander of France.

It took me some time to find out why the order from the War Office came when and how it did. On November 9, General DeGaulle had kicked his superior, General Giraud, out of the National Committee for the Liberation of France, which was meeting in Algiers, and had named himself president of the committee. According to intelligence, which had to be taken relatively seriously, plans were being made to abduct Marshal Pétain by an English-Gaullist parachute commando.

Our forces in Paris were under the command of a general. I was a major. When I got word from OKW to go to Vichy, the general solved the problem of who should be in charge: he found an auberge on the outskirts of Pétain's capital which was renowned for its cooking. He disappeared into the bowels of this hostelry and I never saw him again during what was to be the entire operation.

Being tasked with authority to do what needed to be done, I surveyed the lay of the land. Six police companies of 150 men each, a battalion of my special forces, and a battalion of Hohenstaufen Waffen-SS, each battalion numbering about 700 troops, were at my disposal. I posted these troops around the city, at the airfield in the north, Cusset in the east, and Hauterive in the south. In all, I had about 2,300 soldiers, who could seal off the city in ten minutes' time. We would do this by forming a double cordon, blocking all highways into and out of town, but not close enough to put Pétain on his guard. I sent patrols to the outlying Randan Forest, but we didn't find a single enemy paratrooper in the course of an entire week.

No new reports arrived from either the Sicherheitsdienst or the Abwehr. While we were scouting around the city in civilian clothes, Adrian von Fölkersam and I received completely contradictory information. It became clear to me that Vichy was uneasy. We had now occupied France for three years. The tide of war was turning against us on all fronts. Resistance movements had sprung up, almost always led by the communists, the same group whose leaders had recommended that the local populace fraternize with our soldiers in 1940.

After I had made all the necessary preparations around Vichy, I drove back to Paris. I immediately telephoned Wolfsschanze, from which I was directed to return to the Auvergne and await the code words, "The Wolf Howls." I was to ensure that Marshal Pétain and the old man's physician, Dr. Ménétrel were safe and secure when the wolf howled.

Marshal Pétain lived on the fourth floor of the Hotel du Parc. My surreptitious observation of his bodyguard revealed that its members looked and acted in a disciplined and competent manner. A confrontation with that force could become serious. What worried me most was what time of the day the wolf would "howl." I hoped it wouldn't be at night. If two or three thousand enemy paratroops descended on Vichy at two in the morning, and if the Marshal was well-informed about the action and was waiting dressed in his uniform or civilian clothes, the enemy would surely be able to take him.

We waited a month for instructions that never came. At the end of it all, the wolf didn't howl. Just in time for Christmas leave, we received our departure orders, and left Vichy. At the invitation of the German submarine command, we spent the holiday in a rest and recovery home for U-boat crews on the Arlberg. It was to be my last leave of the war.

I am quite happy that of all these planned and prepared actions did not have to take place. I actually had great respect for the old warrior. He was eighty-six years old and still stood erect in his blue uniform. When I saw him, I couldn't help but recall Field Marshal von Hindenburg who, after the First World War, likewise had to bear the burden of loss on the battlefield. Philippe Pétain was eighty-nine years old when they sentenced him to death after the war. He died at ninety-five while a prisoner in the island fortress at d'Yeu.

In early 1944 I received orders from the OKW to locate Marshal Tito's headquarters, to destroy it, and to capture him. I hadn't the faintest idea where Tito was hiding. When I arrived in Belgrade, our "intelligence" was confusing and contradictory. Five different intelligence reports put the marshal in five different mountain areas. What I found in the Balkans was more Byzantine than anything I'd found in France. We were supposed to be fighting Tito's communists as well as General Mihailovich's royalists, while motley forces of Serb Chetniks and Croatian Ustachi changed sides and positions regularly. Italian garrisons, which had been marooned since Badoglio's surrender, had laid down their arms, which were immediately seized by their several enemies. Only one thing stood out in sharp relief: Tito's partisans had swelled to one hundred thousand full time guerillas, who held critical areas and who could strike anywhere at any time. Tito was the key to the entire puzzle.

Yugoslavia, with its mountainous, wooded terrain, was ideal for partisan guerilla warfare. The advance information which I received from the Abwehr and the SD was confusing enough, not to mention contradictory. Thus, as I had learned from my past experience to do, I drove to Zagreb and organized my own intelligence service. I entrusted the information gathering to three capable intelligence officers, each of whom worked independent of the others. I resolved not to take any action until I received three unanimous reports. This was all done in secrecy, of course, because the cunning enemy were able to hold half a dozen of our divisions, nearly 75,000 soldiers, in check.

I stationed one thousand of my men, a training battalion of my commando unit, in the Fruska Gora, a chain of mountains south of and parallel to the Danube Valley. We trained near the front, seeing action every day against Tito's forces.

Since a military convoy would have made the partisans suspicious, I drove from Belgrade to Zagreb in my civilian Mercedes, over land which had not seen a German car for months. I was quite aware that half the workers in the fields were ready to put down their spades and trade them for rifles at a moment's notice. I had no choice but to gamble I'd pass through the countryside safely before the moment was up.

Spring had come to the countryside. The area through which we were motoring, south of the main Alpine peaks and west of the Carpathians, was verdant with the fresh aroma of the most beautiful time of the year, and the lovely green of emergent rebirth had not yet been broiled by the oppressive summer Balkan heat. I did not, however, have time to enjoy the scenery because my eyes were on the lookout for signs of enemy presence.

After the Sava Valley and over poor roads, we reached Brcko, then Zagreb. The German garrison commander was extremely surprised to see us in one piece. It seems the roads we had used were all partisan-controlled. We had, in fact, encountered a group of bearded partisans, their rifles under their arms. We also had our machine pistols on our car's floor, invisible from outside, with the safety catches on "fire."

Soon afterward, I returned to Berlin where I learned from my three independent intelligence agents that Tito and his staff were, at the moment, staying in Dvar in western Bosnia. I dispatched my chief-of-staff, Adrian von Fölkersam, to the commanding general of Tenth Army Corps, which was stationed in the area, to inform him we would be carrying out Operation Knight's leap against Tito. Just as I was about to set off for the engagement, Adrian showed up.

"Something's not right, Commander," he said. "The general received me very coolly. I don't believe we can count on his support in this action." Shortly after, we received a radio message from our small detachment in Zagreb: "Tenth Corps preparing an operation against Tito's headquarters on June 2, 1944."

"How incredibly stupid!" I exclaimed when I showed my chief-of-staff the message. "I would gladly have placed myself under his command and left him the glory if the Operation were successful, or I would have accepted responsibility myself had it misfired. But if *I* know the plan is to be carried out on June 2, you may be sure Tito knows as well!"

I immediately advised Tenth Corps what I knew and sent another of my staff officers to Corps Headquarters in Banja Luka to try to convince the general to change the plan, or, at the very least, the date. To no avail. The general, unwilling to accept me as a subordinate, viewed me as a rival. The operation went forward as and when scheduled, and turned out to be a foreordained disaster.

In my opinion, the task called for a scalpel. Instead, the general brought a sledge hammer: full scale invasions of the Dvar Valley with bombers, paratroops, and gliders, and the partisans were more than ready. A battalion of Waffen-SS parachute troops were encircled. Reinforcements were flown in by glider. A battalion of the Brandenburg Division had to cover the withdrawal of our soldiers, who were attacked from all sides.

The sledge hammer missed, as I knew it would. All our troops found at Tito's headquarters were two British soldiers, who he probably wanted to get rid of, and a brand-new, empty uniform with marshal's stars on the shoulders. The marshal had escaped to Vis, an Adriatic island southeast of Split.

Meanwhile, although their leader had moved on, Tito's Partisans stayed behind and gave as good as they got. German infantry had to battle through the mountains to rescue the prideful and cantankerous Tenth Corps general.

Later, after the war, I chanced to meet one of the two English officers Tito had left behind. We became friends right away. My former enemy and new friend, later a Brigadier-General, told me that during his stay at Tito's headquarters he became aware that if Tito assumed power, communism would prevail in Yugoslavia. "The situation appeared serious to me," he said, "and so detrimental to British interests in the Balkans that I spoke with our prime minister by telephone. I gave him a very detailed report on what Tito had in mind for Yugoslavia. Churchill let me speak and then asked, 'What do you plan to do after the war?'

"Somewhat baffled, I replied that I intended to return to my estate in Scotland.

"'That means, if I understand you correctly, you don't want to stay and live in Yugoslavia?'

"'No, sir, of course not,' I replied.

"'Then why should you care a rat's arse what happens to Yugoslavia after the war?'"

15

═══

Although Germany was well advanced in developing an atomic bomb, Hitler summarily rejected this weapon as inhumane. Likewise, since, as a corporal, he had been gassed during the First World War, he always banned chemical warfare, even though our chemists had discovered a new gas against which, as we know today, there is no defense: the nerve gas *tabun*.

The V-1 and V-2 revenge weapons appeared more credible to us. The V-1 "flying bomb," officially the Fi-103, was a type of unmanned rocket aircraft. It flew at 400 miles per hour, had a range of 325 miles, and carried a 1-ton explosive charge in its nose. On takeoff, the V-1's flight path was controlled by automatic gyroscope. At the desired range, the engine was switched off and the bomb fell to earth. A wind could force the payload from its direction of flight, and nothing could be done about it. However, in 1944 its advantages were that it was cheap to manufacture and used very little fuel. It also projected an effective psychological effect on the enemy.

Preliminary tests had been carried out at Wernher von Braun's Peenemünde facility. The missile, which was mass-produced by Volkswagen, was fired from a simple launching ramp, usually three V-1's at once. One day, I had the opportunity to visit Peenemünde and witness the launching of a V-1 with a Luftwaffe colonel, an engineer like me, who was a specialist in these flying bombs. On our return flight, he and I explored the question of whether or not it would be possible for a pilot to fly a V-1. That evening, in June 1944, we set to work with Focke-Wulf and the Reich Air Ministry to come up with plans for such an "impossible" concept. The first thing was to find sufficient room in the V-1 to accommodate a pilot with ejection seat and parachute. Within two days, we had come up with the solution: all we had to do was build a prototype.

I approached Field Marshal Erhard Milch, state secretary for procurement. Milch was an enigma: first, he was openly Jewish. Hitler recognized this, although he had conveniently decreed that the Field Marshal, whose talents Der Führer quickly recognized, be officially classified as a *Mischling,* mixed race, thus fit to join the Party. Second, he'd been in the upper echelons of the Nazi hierarchy since well before the start of the War. Third, he was short and chunky, the very antithesis of the Aryan the Reich wanted to present as an example of German manhood. Finally, despite his high rank in the Wehrmacht, he had had absolutely no military experience in his entire career.

When I told the Field Marshal of my plan he gave me "clear road, provided that the German Air Ministry commission raised no objections." The chairman of the commission was a venerable admiral with a white seaman's goatee, who looked like he had been around since Noah's ark. After three meetings, we cleared the first hurdle, but then the commission raised an objection: "Where do you intend to get the workers, foremen, and engineers to build this prototype? We don't have enough labor as it is, especially in the aviation industry."

I replied that there was a Heinkel factory near Friedenthal that did not operate at full capacity and that Professor Heinkel had personally offered me three engineers, five mechanics, and three empty work barracks.

"Good," Noah replied. "But you can only carry out your work with already-built V-1s, and right now we have none."

"That's not what Professor Porsche told me. There are several hundred V-1s in his VW factory waiting to be picked up. I'm sure he would gladly let me have a dozen."

A short time later, I had two small workshops at Heinkel. I moved tables and beds into one of the shops. Everyone worked at full speed, sometimes more than fourteen hours a day, in order to bring *Operation Reichenberg* to fruition as soon as possible.

When I saw Field Marshal Milch again, he asked, "Are you satisfied, Skorzeny?"

"Naturally," I answered. "In spite of the two to three-week delay."

"Three weeks on such a project is nothing. If you can roll out your manned V-1 in four to five *months*, I'll congratulate you."

"Herr Feldmarschall, I hope that I can show you the prototype in four to five *weeks*!"

"You're making a joke, right?" Then he looked at me and saw by my expression that I was dead serious. "You're deluding yourself, my dear fellow. I wish you only good luck, but we'll talk about this machine in four or five months."

After fourteen days of round-the-clock work, I again contacted a flabbergasted Field Marshal Milch and informed him that we had both been wrong. I had three V-1s ready to fly.

He authorized me to undertake three takeoffs and landings at Gatow airfield in southwestern Berlin. After two test pilots were chosen, the manned V-1s were towed by a Heinkel 111 to a height of 6,500 feet, then released. Both machines made crash landings. However, both pilots escaped with only minor injuries. Field Marshal Milch told me he would appoint a commission to investigate the causes of the bad landings, but for the time being he forbade me to make any further attempts. I was speechless. Had we worked too carelessly and too quickly?

One day, shortly afterward, I was sitting somewhat despondently at my desk at Friedenthal when my Chief-of-Staff, Adrian von Fölkersam buzzed me on my intercom.

"Sturmbahnführer, Hanna Reitsch is on the line from Luftwaffe House."

Hanna Reitsch? I was stunned! Who had not heard of the legendary Hanna Reitsch? Before the war, she had amassed world records in every field of aviation. In 1941, she was the first woman to pilot a prototype rocket-propelled fighter, the Messerschmitt Me 163. She survived a disastrous crash of that aircraft, from which she recovered by her strength of will alone. As a result of her efforts, Reitsch became the first and only German woman to receive the Iron Cross First Class.

"Miss Reitsch?" I must have sounded as awed as I felt when I uttered that greeting.

"Sturmbahnführer Skorzeny? Now that we've crossed that bridge and I believe people in our position do not stand on ceremony, please call me Hanna."

"Fine by me, if I'm Otto to you."

"Otto it is, then. I hear you got your butt handed to you when your prototype V-1s crashed. I had the same idea as you, several months earlier. The V-1 can be flown as a manned aircraft. I tried to promote that idea to the higher-ups and I got shot down after the mishap at Gatow. Do you have any thoughts as to how the crashes happened?"

"I do, Miss … Hanna, and I don't need to wait for the results of the investigation to tell you my conclusions."

"I'm listening."

"Both pilots previously flew only propeller aircraft. Our prototype, which was much lighter than a standard V-1, reached a speed of 450 miles per hour and a landing speed of 115 miles per hour. This made both pilots uncertain when it came time to land, since the average fighter lands at 85 miles an hour."

"I understand exactly what you're saying. Otto, I have an idea. You're at Friedenthal, less than an hour's drive from where I'm staying. Suppose we meet at Gatow this afternoon for a chat?"

"You're kidding!"

"Never more serious. Remember, I've flown jet aircraft before. Within the last couple of months, I brought the ME 262 in safely."

"Absolutely not, Hanna. Don't forget, there's an official order that they won't make an HE 111 available to me at Gatow. I don't think there's any difference between a man and a woman when it comes to the ability to do just about anything, but I'm Viennese."

"And?"

"We may appear to coddle and treasure our women far more than Germans, but I would not only not want to risk your life, but you could get in trouble with the authorities for something that would be entirely my fault."

Hanna Reitsch was tiny. I was 6'4" tall and she was a slender 5'1", more than a foot shorter. Even though she shrugged her shoulders, her blue eyes blazed as she said, "I took you for a man who was willing to take a chance! One can always fly if only one wants to! My friends and I have visited your workshop and examined your first V-1s. I'm sure we're not fooling ourselves. They're outstanding aircraft. We'll talk more about this tomorrow."

She turned on her heel, fluffed her blonde hair saucily, and took her leave. In addition to her heroics, I found her to be a challengingly sexy woman, four years my junior. For more than the briefest moment,

I envied her lover, Luftwaffe Field Marshal Ritter von Greim, twenty years her senior.

This was not the first time in the past two years that I had thought about another woman. Emmi's and my marriage, while not in imminent danger, had cooled into less of a love match and more of an acquaintanceship, a "continental marriage." She continued to reside with our daughter Waltraut in Vienna, while my life had taken an entirely different direction, tied as it was to Friedenthal and beyond. We saw one another three or four times a year for a week at a time. Unquestionably she was a vibrant, sexually attractive woman. When we came together it was pleasurable, if not earth-shattering. I had no doubt she'd had brief affairs, just as I had had liaisons, but as increasingly sophisticated adults, these did not disturb either of us, so long as they remained discreet and did not become the stuff of parlor conversations. Besides, my work had become more important to me than dalliances.

I found it difficult to sleep that night, not because of prurient thoughts, but because a third accident involving the V-1 project would be unthinkable. Did I have the right to plunge Hanna Reitsch, this wonderful and courageous aviatrix, into such danger?

Next day, Hanna and her two companions were so convincing that I took it upon myself to dupe the airfield commander. I acted completely natural and told him I'd just received approval to continue Operation Reichenberg. I asked his opinion on numerous questions and assigned two of my officers to keep him in sight at all times, to accompany him to the mess, and, most important, to ensure that he did not telephone Field Marshal Milch's staff.

When I saw the V-1 flown by Hanna Reitsch separate from the HE 111, I felt my heart pounding. She had taken full responsibility for whatever happened. She knew her airspeed at landing would be well above flare-out speed for any other operational aircraft. Yet, as good as she was, I found myself praying that she could bring it off. And she did!

She then repeated the flight. When she landed safely a second time, I ran onto the tarmac and congratulated her. "This is a wonderful aircraft!" she exclaimed. "We'll be able to make it work!"

Afterward, the other two test pilots successfully flew the V-1 and landed without incident. When Field Marshal Milch learned of the missions, he gave us permission to build five more prototypes and to train 30 selected pilots. When word got out, several hundred Luftwaffe pilots applied for Friedenthal. We accepted sixty of them. I anticipated we'd not be able to engage in especially daring missions. Unfortunately, less than 15% of the fuel I'd ordered was delivered, as shortages became more acute after the Allies landed at Normandy. In the end, although a dozen V-1 pilots remained in my unit until the end of the war, the manned V-1 program was not destined to be a success.

The V-2 was not an aircraft but a rocket, which achieved a speed in excess of 3,300 miles per hour carrying one ton of explosives. It was the first craft ever to leave the earth's atmosphere, climbing to an altitude of 50 miles on its first successful test flight in October 1942. Its inventor, 30-year-old Wernher von Braun, the same age as Hanna Reitsch, was later "exported" to the United States and became an American citizen whose name is known throughout the world.

Von Braun worked in the army research center at Peenemünde under Walter Dornberger. Hitler took a personal interest in the tests at Peenemünde, promoted Dornberger to general, and had the younger engineer named a professor. I met Professor von Braun personally during the war and later exchanged letters with him.

Peenemünde is located on Usedom Island near the present border between Germany and Poland. Several weeks after Hitler met von

Braun, the island was bombed night and day by the Allies and was almost totally destroyed. Von Braun's concept of the multi-stage rocket was derived from the V-2. By March of 1945 the V-2 had evolved into a rocket capable of bombing New York or Moscow. It could have gone into production by July.

But the Russians came. General Dornberger and Professor von Braun, who were able to save some of their documents, fled to Bavaria and surrendered to the American 44th Division. Soon afterward, they signed a contract to work for the U.S. Army and in September they were spirited out of Germany and into the United States.

On the far side of the Atlantic the Americans assembled 127 German rocket specialists. Professor von Braun became head of the Army Ballistic Missile Agency and Deputy Chief of the National Aeronautics and Space Administration. As such, he became the leader of the Apollo Project, which, on July 21, 1969, placed the first men on the moon.

16

By autumn 1944, it had become clear to me that it was not so much a question *if* but *when.* Our enemies were at the Eastern frontier. Our cities were being bombed no longer just by night, but by day as well. The industrial base of the Reich had been shattered. Wolfsschanze was scarcely an hour's drive from the enemy's guns.

The Western scene looked bleak enough. Italy, for the most part, gone. France occupied by the Allies. England emergent and sensing German blood. On the Russian front, the position was catastrophic. In the North, Finland was gone. The Baltic states had crumbled. In the center, Poland was fractured, essentially lost. In the South, we had been pushed back more than a thousand miles into the Balkans. Romania with her oilfields was already lost. Bulgaria would go next. Tito's Partisans were now working in concert with the Soviet Army. Turkey had broken off diplomatic relations with the Reich.

On September 9, 1944, I received the following summons:

"Sturmbahnführer Skorzeny:

"At Der Führer's special request, you will please detach yourself from all other duties forthwith, to attend a series of discussions at Wolfsschanze on grand strategy. It is possible that the Führer will entrust you with an important mission on a fluid, uncertain, but highly critical front. Please come punctually to the noon briefing on September 10. – Jodl."

When I arrived at the Wolf's Lair, I was escorted to a large conference room which was located in a barracks, some 60 yards from the just-completed Führer bunker. Hitler was forced to live beneath 25 feet of iron-reinforced concrete. A complicated ventilation system provided fresh air. Nevertheless, the atmosphere was unhealthy as the concrete, which had not yet fully set, gave off a damp warmth.

In the situation room, a large map showing every front lay on a huge table, which received light from the windows along a 40-foot-long wall. Current troop strengths and their positions were entered in colored pencil. Two stenographers sat at the short ends of the table. Since 1942, Hitler had required that all situation briefings be recorded.

When I entered the briefing room on September 10, 1944, I introduced myself to the generals and the general staff officers who were already present, as I knew only a few of them. Many officers had been replaced after the failed July 20 attempt on Hitler's life. We all stood. A stool was provided for Hitler. The colored pencils, a magnifying glass, and the Führer's glasses lay on the map table.

At a curt announcement, Hitler entered. I was shocked when I saw him up close. I scarcely recognized him. He walked bent over and dragged one leg behind him. His left hand trembled so badly that he sometimes had to hold it with his right. His voice sounded veiled and brittle. He greeted a few generals.

As weary as he looked and sounded, the Leader's mind card-indexed every unit on the front. As each fresh gap occurred, he would call on reserves or switch forces from one front to another. I was stunned by the difference between what I saw and heard at the meeting and what I knew firsthand to be the true situation.

The generals' talk was all in terms of divisions and army corps. My heart fell as I heard them prattle in their Alice-in-Wonderland reasoning. I had seen the units coming out of line. I knew for a fact that what they were calling infantry divisions had actually been reduced to battalion strength. Whole armored "divisions" consisted of perhaps a dozen tanks, of which only half of those were in good repair. But here at headquarters no one spoke of such details. A division was a flag pinned to a situation map. So long as there were flags, all must be well. The Order of Battle was intact.

But truth to tell, many of the master cogs did not engage at all. Even the so-called High Command controlled only some areas of the battlefront. Something called Army Operations Staff had usurped others. Air Force and Naval liaison chiefs made little connection with the military. No department was ever sure what another might be doing, and if an inquiry was made it would, as often as not, invite reprisals.

When Hitler had gone off, leaving the situation map covered with angry whorls and arrows, the generals relaxed. "Not much to talk of, really, it's all pretty much the same."

I remember a day when Hitler threw one of what I had been told was one of his increasingly frequent tantrums. He strode to his place in the Situation Room, swept the color pencils to the floor, and gruffly raised his voice. He seemed incapable of actually shouting anymore.

"No situation maps will be marked today. Keitel, Jodl, you are both trying to pull the wool over my eyes. What in the hell is going on in Poland? The so-called underground army has turned Warsaw into a battlefield. None of the High Command has told me anything, *anything, do you hear?* You were hoping this mess would be cleaned up before I found out about it, yes? Well, your little game has been revealed and I found out this fraud you are trying to pull on me!"

I wished most fervently that I was away from this rat's nest and back at Friedenthal.

During my three days at Wolfsschanze, I continued to be amazed, not only by Hitler's extraordinary memory, which he certainly possessed, notwithstanding his terribly deteriorated condition, but by the intuitive sense he possessed for military and political situations. General Jodl knew how to present a military situation, but when Hitler spoke afterwards, everything was much simpler and clearer.

On my third day, after the evening briefing, which started at 10 at night, Hitler asked me to remain in the Situation Room after the rest had left. In addition to my presence, Hitler had ordered Keitel, Jodl, Ribbentrop, and Himmler for an extraordinary briefing. The Leader invited us to sit in armchairs. Our foreign minister, Ribbentrop, looked most uncomfortable. It seemed clear he would serve as scapegoat for the impending meeting.

Hitler started on a sarcastic note. "Our generals' stupidity has at last been surpassed. Our diplomats have gone one better. I am under no illusions here. The Admiral-Reich Administrator is in process not only of negotiating with the western allies, but very probably with Stalin as well, obviously without informing us.

"It has taken us great effort, but the front has been stabilized at the Hungarian border. If the Hungarian army goes over to the enemy, 400,000 soldiers will be trapped. And those fighters in Italy will also be hard-pressed if the Soviets mount an offensive from southern Hungary through Yugoslavia in the direction of Trieste."

He raised his voice as he continued, "That's out of the question! The Reich Administrator, Admiral Horthy, considers himself a great politician. He doesn't realize that he is opening the door, not only to our disaster but to his.

He turned to Ribbentrop. "Budapest really seems to have a short memory. They seem to conveniently forget that *you* made a certain arbitration award in Vienna on August 29, 1940 which gave Hungary back the greater part of Transylvania which had been taken from them by the Treaty of Trianon in 1920: 45,000 square kilometers of land and 2,380,000 people, who today are threatened by communism."

"My Leader," Ribbentrop replied, "the political situation in Budapest is becoming increasingly clouded. Two true friends of the Reich have been forced to step down: acting Minister President Raasch and Economics Minister von Imredy. A new cabinet under General Geza Lakatos has taken power."

"Power?" the Führer roared. "*Stalin* will take power in Budapest if we are forced to leave Hungary! The Reich Administrator spoke solemn words less than five months ago: 'We will fight at the side of the German Army until we have victoriously weathered this storm.' Now, he says to General Guderian, 'my dear comrade, in politics one must have several irons in the fire.' No loyal ally talks that way, only a man who intends to betray us and break his solemn promises. I won't tolerate that. Our soldiers are still defending Hungarian soil, too!"

"Skorzeny," he said, turning to face me. "You know I trust you almost beyond anyone else. I have asked you to take part in the briefings because you know Hungary, and especially Budapest. Under no circumstances will I accept a Badoglio in Hungary. If Admiral Horthy breaks his word, you are to take the Burgberg, Castle Hill, and seize all you can find in the Royal Palace and the ministries. Then, seal everything off and occupy the Burgberg militarily. Begin your preparations immediately, in cooperation with Generaloberst Jodl. We've talked about a parachute or airborne operation, but the final decision is up to you."

The Leader then handed me a signed document which was Hitler's blank check to me:

"SS-Sturmbannführer Otto Skorzeny is carrying out a personal, highly secret order of the utmost importance. I instruct all military and state offices to support Skorzeny in every way and comply with his wishes. s/Adolf Hitler."

Before acting rashly, I considered the entirety of the situation as I was formulating my plan. Hitler had said Hungary was the last ally; if Hungary were to fall, Germany would fall. There were no two ways about it. Hungary was now almost the Reich's only source of oil, of grain, and of bauxite for the jet plane program. But economics was not the only problem. Hungary's collapse would cut off seventy divisions from the main battlefront. Italy, Greece, and all that remained of Occupied Europe would be overrun in a week. The Soviets would pour across the Danube plain into neighboring Austria. Once Vienna was reached, there was no line to fall back on. The next stop in the Russian juggernaut would be Germany. The war would be over in a few weeks at most.

And yet, as I viewed matters, Hungary did not seem in such urgent danger. Our allies were fighting courageously in the Carpathians, aided by a million German troops. Together, we held a mountain chain which had shielded Southern Europe for centuries. Why should Hungary fall? Before I left Wolfsschanze, I looked at the map of Southern Europe in the Situation Room. Sixteen flags, each of them standing for a Russian army, was pinned beside the contours of Hungary's eastern frontier. That meant 120 enemy divisions, 1,500,000 troops, along the Carpathians. If the dams holding back these troops fell, the first to be engulfed would be a million German men for whom there could be no Dunkirk.

The task Der Führer demanded of me was both formidable and delicate. It began to sound like a replay of Gran Sasso, except this time we were not contemplating landing in some remote Alpine peak; my forces would be going into the heart of Budapest.

I'd been advised that Admiral Horthy was ready for the worst. Since Gran Sasso, he had taken every precaution against being kidnapped. In order to reach the Regent Admiral, we'd have to storm his castle.

The more I thought how to go about this, the more I was humbled by the enormity of what faced my Friedenthal men. Admiral Horthy had ruled Hungary since my boyhood. He was heir to an historic tradition, a link with Emperor Franz Joseph, who'd begun his rule nearly a century ago. Though Regent Admiral Horthy did not wear the Iron Crown of Hungary, he could credibly declare that he *was* Hungary. How could I expect to pull down the man and leave the state whole?

Then again, how could I reach Horthy? The Regent lived atop Castle Hill, attended by ministers and guards, fenced in by troops. It would be a Herculean task at best.

Under the cover name of Doctor Wolff from Cologne, and wearing civilian clothes, I drove to Vienna with Karl Radl. One of our true allies, a Hungarian German, placed his home, with servants and cook, at our disposal. In my entire life, I never lived as well as I did during those three weeks in the Hungarian capital. Our host, well-informed about everything going on in the court, provided me with invaluable information.

Horthy, an admiral with no fleet and a Regent with no king or queen, had resisted the return of the Hapsburgs to Hungary in 1920. On February 19, 1942 he named his eldest son Stefan to the post of vice regent with right of succession. This son, a wise and gifted young man, who had fought bravely against the Soviets as a fighter pilot, had been killed in action on the Eastern Front six months later. The character of Regent Admiral Horthy's younger son, Niklas, was quite different.

Nicky, a regular patron of Budapest's nightclubs, for want of a better word, lacked discretion. When we arrived in Budapest, our informers knew that Nicky had been in communication not only with London, but with Moscow and Tito's agents as well, all with his father's blessings. Our SS and police commander in Budapest, Winkelmann, knew of Nicky's dangerous associations. Fölkersam, who traveled with us, misheard the name "Nicky" and heard "Mickey." From then on, we knew Niklas Horthy as "Mickey Mouse."

The German police knew Nicky was supposed to meet one of Tito's agents for two conferences, the first on October 10, and the second five days later, both in an office building in the middle of Budapest. Winkelmann decided to catch Mickey Mouse "in the act," and set an appropriate trap. He asked me to provide military protection against possible intervention by the Hungarian army.

Horthy's son, who was suspicious, came to the meeting place by car at 10:00 a.m. on October 15. A few Hungarian army officers stayed hidden in a canvas-covered jeep parked behind Nicky's car, in front of the entrance to the office building.

I arrived by car, feigned engine trouble, and parked my automobile radiator to radiator with Nicky's car in order to prevent him from driving away. Suddenly, something moved in the jeep. Two Hungarian army officers were walking in the park opposite the building. I had one of my officers and two NCOs sitting on a park bench reading newspapers. At 10:10 a.m., two of Winkelmann's police officers appeared. They were about to enter the building when a burst of submachine gun fire rattled from the jeep and killed one of the men. The two Hungarian officers in the park also fired. I crouched behind my car until my soldiers came from the park to help.

Nicky was well-guarded. A strong Hungarian army occupied a nearby house. We set off an explosive charge, which destroyed the door to the house and prevented Nicky's guard detail from coming to his aid. Scarcely five minutes had passed.

The German police needed to go down only one flight of stairs to reach the room where the conspirators were meeting. To avoid passers-by from recognizing Nicky, we bound "Mickey Mouse" and rolled him up in a quite ordinary rug. The rug, together with Nicky's three co-conspirators, were put into a police truck which arrived on the scene just when it was supposed to. Fölkersam was in process of withdrawing our troops, in order to disappear as quickly as possible. On a hunch, I followed the police truck. Three Hungarian army companies converged on the truck as we approached the Elisabeth Bridge.

Fölkersam had not had time to escape. I had to bluff in order to gain a few minutes. I quickly climbed out of the car, approached an officer, and called out, "Halt! Where are you going? Let me speak to your major." When I found that the major was momentarily elsewhere, trying to deal with a wild mix-up in the square, I shouted to him in German, "We must avoid war between our peoples, which would have awful repercussions."

I gained six minutes, but that was enough. Adrian had time to load all our people into the truck. I took off, leaving the confused Hungarians behind. When I arrived at the airport, Nicky and his friends were already in a German military aircraft, which soon delivered them to Vienna.

Niklas Horthy wasn't very popular to begin with, and his kidnapping aroused little sympathy in Hungary. But Regent Admiral Horthy's reaction wasn't long in coming. At 2:00 p.m., Horthy announced over the Hungarian national radio, "Hungary has asked the Soviet Union for a separate peace." This was followed by a communiqué from the Hungarian Army's Chief of Staff that "Cease fire negotiations are under way."

I drove at once to our army corps' headquarters, where I met General Wenck, who'd come from Berlin several days earlier. Once there, we received a call from our embassy's military attaché, who was housed in a small palace on the Burgberg, advising us that Castle Hill was under a state of siege and that he had been turned back at every exit road. Shortly afterward, the telephone lines were cut.

That said it all. General Wenck and I agreed I must now implement Operation Panzerfaust, for which we had made preparations.

Shortly afterward, the Police-General of Warsaw brought in "Thor," a gigantic 650-millimeter howitzer, whose shells each weighed 4,540 pounds, capable of piercing any thickness of concrete known to exist. This monster had only been used twice before: against the fortress of Sevastopol, and in Warsaw. The Police-General suggested finishing off the Burgberg without a lot of fuss by using the monster to destroy the royal palace. There was no way I was going to destroy a magnificent piece of history such as the Burgberg. Much to his consternation, I told him so.

Just before midnight on October 15, an official of the Hungarian Defense Ministry reported to our corps command. He showed us a letter from the Minister of War authorizing him to negotiate with our German authorities. We gave him one simple answer: no negotiations until Admiral Horthy's cease-fire declaration was withdrawn. Furthermore, since our diplomats were virtual prisoners on Castle Hill, we countered by giving the Hungarian government an ultimatum: If the mines and roadblocks on the Vienna Road, which led to the German embassy, were not removed by 6:00 a.m. on the 16th, we would be forced to conclude that Hungary considered its German brothers the "enemy" and act accordingly.

There was a natural sense of fraternal camaraderie between Germany and Hungary: we had been fighting the common foe since June 1941, the same enemy which had devastated Hungary twenty years before. Szalassy's Arrow Cross party had gained a great deal of support as a result of the communist threat and had many supporters among the younger officers of the Hungarian army. From everything I had seen and heard, the mood in Hungary was not to surrender to the east; it was quite the contrary.

I must here note in passing that Admiral Horthy claimed to have been "protecting" Hungary's Jewish population from being deported to the General Gouvernement area of Poland. Because of this, Budapest's Jews felt grave concern about the deposition of Horthy and the accession of the Arrow Cross party. But was it not the leader of the Hungarian Jewish Rescue Committee, Reszo Kastner, who had suavely bargained with Adolf Eichmann that if we spared some 1,650 of his chosen favorites, he didn't really care what happened to the remainder of Hungary's Jewish population? I say this not by way of taking anyone's "side." To me the Jews were no different than any other human beings. I simply point out that at bedrock each individual has a natural tendency to save his own first and concern for others of his compatriots is only of secondary importance.

For my part, since we were outmanned and outgunned by a factor of three-to-one, I believed the only way to succeed in keeping Hungary within the German camp was to launch a surprise attack at 6:00 a.m. the following morning. Even then, the positioning of the Hungarian forces presented a formidable challenge. Castle hill was nearly two miles long and at least 1,800 feet wide. Its garrison, which towered above the Danube, had been reinforced. Regent-Admiral Horthy was guarded by 3,000 troops. The Hungarians' regimental barracks behind the Vienna Gate contained mortars and heavy machine guns, all of which had been arranged in battle position.

At the other end of the hill lay armed bunkers, machine gun nests, and tanks. A ten-foot high stone barricade in front of the citadel gate housed six anti-tank guns and a heavily-armed regiment of some 1,500 soldiers.

Those in Führer Headquarters had initially planned an airborne operation spearheaded by parachute assault. To attempt this exercise against the heavily guarded and fortified Hungarian forces was, in my opinion, suicidal madness. The only suitable landing place would have been Vérmező, a long, narrow park known as "Blood Field," where historic executions had taken place in 1795. Had our troops landed there, it would have earned its name all over again. I would have to find another solution.

At three in the morning, I had all my officers assemble on Blood Field and gave them final instructions. Castle Hill had to be assaulted from four sides simultaneously. Each group had its own tactics to confuse what was to us, at that moment, the opposition forces. I, myself, would drive through the Vienna Gate directly to the palace. Panther tanks and two companies of Commando units would protect my backside.

My entry was supposed to look like a peacetime buildup: the soldiers in the trucks were all to carry weapons with safety catches on and keep them out of sight beneath the side walls of the trucks. I gave directions that not a single shot was to be fired from our side. That included a strict ban on replying to single shots. At one minute to six, I gave the signal to begin the assault.

We drove past a few Hungarian soldiers, who were amazed when I saluted them cordially. Shockingly, no one attacked us enroute, and we made it to the fortress square in front of the palace. Once we reached that point, everything erupted at what seemed to me double-motion. I instructed my driver to pull over to the right and signaled the tank following me to head straight for the 10-foot-tall concrete barricade and ram it, forcing a large opening. We jumped from the car and ran through the opening into the fortress courtyard. The alarm went off. An officer appeared in front of us, aimed his pistol, and shouted something. My Chief-of-Staff, Adrian Fölkersam knocked the weapon from his hand.

Hungarian tanks and our tanks faced one another menacingly. Another Hungarian Army officer made as if to stop me. I shouted, "Take me to the fortress commander at once! We have no time to lose!"

He pointed to a marble stairway covered by a wonderful red carpet. We climbed the stairs at a run. We entered a hallway, then an anteroom. A table had been pushed against an open window. On it lay a man who opened fire on the courtyard with a machine gun. Feldwebel Holzer simply grabbed the machine gun and threw it out the window. The gunner was so surprised that he fell to the floor. To my right was a double door. I knocked and stepped in. A general sitting at a huge desk stood up.

"Are you the fortress commander?"

"Yes, but ..."

"I request that you surrender the fortress immediately. I'm sure you can hear the fighting outside. Do you want to be responsible for bloodshed between allies? We've surrounded all your positions. All resistance is now hopeless and could be very costly for you and your troops."

At that moment Obersturmführer Hunke – "Chinaman" – stepped in, saluted, and reported, "Courtyard and main entrances, radio station, and war ministry are occupied. Request further orders, Sturmbahnführer."

He saluted the general, who turned to me. "I will send liaison officers with you to have the firing stopped. Must I consider myself a prisoner?"

"If you wish, Herr General. But mind you, all your officers may keep their pistols."

It was agreed that the order to cease fire should be delivered by several officer patrols, each consisting of one Hungarian officer and one of my officers.

I left the general and came upon a group of excited, hostile-looking officers. I picked out two Hungarian Army captains who looked especially nervous to me, took them with me as liaison officers, and with Fölkersam and a few of my Friedenthal colleagues, set out to look for the Reich Administrator, Regent Admiral Horthy.

Ultimately, I had to face the fact that Horthy was not in the palace. He had fled his residence at 5:45 that morning and was lodged in the home of Graf Karl von Pfeffer-Wildenbruch, a good friend of Kaiser Wilhelm II, the last German Emperor and King of Prussia, who'd been forced to abdicate in 1918, and who'd died a little over three years ago. Horthy had left the commanding general no orders of any kind for the defense of the Burgberg,

By 6:30 a.m., it was all over. We had lost sixteen men – four dead and twelve wounded. Losses were equally light on the Hungarian side, three dead and fifteen injured.

At 9:30 that morning, I assembled all the Hungarian officers, about 400, and gave them a short speech: "At this historic site, I would like you to remember above all that the Germans have not fought the Hungarians in centuries and that I, as a Viennese, can never forget our common liberation of 1718. The situation at the moment is so serious that European soldiers, whatever their faith or their political views, must stand together, especially the Hungarians and the Germans. As of tomorrow, any of you who wants may once again command his regiment, his battalion, or his company. For no one has the right to force a man to fight against his will and his convictions. We must fight voluntarily. Therefore, I would like to ask those of you who wish to continue the struggle at our side, take on step forward."

Every Hungarian officer stepped forward. I shook hands with each of them.

On October 16, Szalassy's Arrow Cross Party took power. There was no opposition.

17

On October 20, 1944, I was summoned to Wolfsschanze and told that Hitler wanted me to brief him in person on Operation Panzerfaust. When I arrived, I found vast changes had occurred since the short time before, when I'd been requested to keep Hungary on our side. For one thing, it seemed clear that Wolfsschanze was about to be moved. The Wolf's Lair was in danger of becoming a "front headquarters" in fact as well as in name. The High Command was being shifted before it could come under the Soviet Army's guns. No sooner had I walked into the adjutant's office than Major General Jodl advised me that Der Führer wanted to speak to me alone. The Leader's warm welcome calmed me.

"From now on, you are an Obersturmbahnführer of the Waffen-SS, Lieutenant Colonel Skorzeny, and I am personally awarding you the German Cross in Gold. No, you don't need to thank me for it. I approve in advance all the decorations you propose for your soldiers. Take your proposals to Günsche, my adjutant. And now, tell me how it was in Budapest."

We sat in a small room in his bunker. The air was poor, but he seemed calmer than the last time I saw him. His left hand didn't tremble so much. He listened without interrupting me. I was about to take my leave, when he held me back. Then he told me in every detail the plan for what is now known as the Ardennes offensive, what the Allied history books call the Battle of the Bulge.

"Skorzeny, the world thinks Germany is finished and that only the day and the hour of the funeral remains to be announced. I am going to show them how mistaken they are. The corpse will rise and hurl itself in fury at the West. Then we shall see."

Hitler bade me follow him to a wall map. He pointed out how Germany's armies had been driven back to where they'd stood in 1940, before starting the blitzkrieg, which had shattered France and driven the British off the Continent in three weeks. Now, the last thing anyone could foresee was a second attack on the same sector: to strike a sledgehammer blow that would split the Allied front in the Ardennes.

He put a finger on the Belgian supply port of Antwerp, the target, to be reached in a week. The enemy in North Belgium and the Netherlands would be cut off and would be driven into the sea. The rest of the American armies south of Antwerp would be strung out nearly five hundred miles from the North Sea to Switzerland. With their northern wing chopped off, they would have more appetite for a negotiated peace than for fighting.

Such was the picture Der Führer laid out for me on October 20. Looking back, I can see that this grandiose scheme was, in reality, impossible. The place, the time, even the concept of a German counteroffensive, was unthinkable to so-called "experts" on both sides. Any suggestion that the quarry would leap at the throat of its hunters was absurd. What the Allies could not guess was that Hitler had abandoned military logic and was now consumed by political intuition.

The Leader continued, "I mean to exploit the Allies' uneasiness over the Russian advances, which are bringing the communists so deeply into Western Europe. I believe many British and American leaders will welcome any chance to stop the Russian Bear, but right now they can do nothing in the face of the peoples' admiration for their "heroic

Soviet allies." A violent shock might bring the masses to reason. If they're confronted with a second Dunkirk, they might be willing to call it quits. If that happens, we could sign a truce with the West and throw our whole weight against Russia."

I must say that as Hitler continued to expand and expound on his ideas, I concluded that our grand Leader might be losing touch with reality.

"I've been waiting for this opportunity ever since the Americans and British landed at Normandy. The Allies' supply lines are stretched, their equipment has been worn down by continuous fighting, and their armies overconfident, while, at the same time, they're overstrained.

"On the other hand," he said, his left arm starting to shake once again, while his eyes took on an overly bright gleam which hinted he might actually be becoming a bit unhinged, "we expect thousands of new tanks, guns, and jet planes from our factories. The roads from the Fatherland to the front are short. New divisions will be freed to operate in the West once we plug the southeast front."

I was deliberately noncommittal, but did not want to risk Hitler's ever-darkening temper. "That sounds promising, My Führer."

"It is, my dear Colonel Skorzeny. I will very likely entrust you with the most important mission in your career as a soldier. In the course of this offensive, whose basic concepts I have just explained, and which is obviously top secret – I probably don't have to tell you that – you and your special commandos will occupy one or another of the Meuse bridges between Lüttich and Namur before they can be blown up.

"You must raise an armored brigade in the image of the enemy. Your people will make their way behind enemy lines in English or American uniforms and drive their vehicles. They will mingle with the enemy and do everything to demoralize and confuse them."

"But *Mein* Führer," I ventured tentatively, "Every man who joins such a venture will immediately face a firing squad if they are captured."

"When they finally fight, it will be in German uniforms," Hitler responded. "I know the Americans used the same tactic at Aachen. We will give these people a dose of their own medicine. I know you have only a little time to organize such a large operation of this kind, but I also know you will do your best. Generaloberst Jodl will answer your detailed questions.

"One more thing: I do not want you to cross the front line personally under any circumstances. You must be at the front in the course of the offensive. But it would be a catastrophe if you were wounded or captured now. I have complete faith in you, my dear Skorzeny," he said, grabbing my forearm with his right hand. "We will see each other again soon."

And thus it was that I was tasked with Operation *Greif:* Griffin, the mythical animal, half eagle and half lion.

If I had had all the cooperation and assistance in the world, I might have gotten my forces into shape in six months, maybe even five if I stretched things to their limit. But soon enough I saw I would have to fight tooth and nail for any help at all. Hardly any of the Army chiefs outside Hitler's personal staff had even been informed of what was coming. The one commander who did know everything, and whose support was most essential, Field Marshal von Rundstedt, was bitterly against the whole idea.

Sixty-nine-year-old Karl Rudolf Gerd von Rundstedt was the ultimate picture of the military officer of a century before. Born into a family with a long military tradition, he'd entered the Prussian Army in 1892, sixteen years before I was born. During World War I, he served mainly as a staff officer. In the inter-war years, he continued his military career, reaching the rank of *Generaloberst* before he retired in 1938.

He'd been recalled at the beginning of World War II as commander of Army Group South in the invasion of Poland. He commanded Army Group A during the Battle of France, and was promoted to the rank of Field Marshal in 1940. In the invasion of the Soviet Union, he had commanded Army Group South, in which he was responsible for the largest encirclement in history, the Battle of Kiev, as well as the largest mass killing of the Holocaust to that date, at Babi Yar. He was relieved of command in December 1941, but was recalled in 1942 and appointed Commander-in-Chief in the West.

In July 1944, von Rundstedt had been fired after a stand-up argument with Hitler, but he'd again been recalled as Commander-in-Chief in the West in September, when he returned to take charge of the Ardennes attack. But that didn't mean he was by any means "on board." Privately, he called the plan "stupid and nonsensical." He had no faith in it at all. Why, then, did he agree to lead it? Because, as he later complained, "As commander-in-chief, I found Hitler's pressure behind me was always far worse than the pressure of the Allies in front. I had only enough independence to change the guard at my gate."

Von Rundstedt's pride was further abused when the Leader gave me a direct briefing. It became clear that my new brigade would be born in spite of him.

I was to form a special unit for the purpose Hitler had given me: the 150th Panzer Brigade.

With the full agreement of Generaloberst Jodl, the 150th was to consist of two tank companies, each equipped with 10 Sherman tanks; 3 armored reconnaissance companies, 10 American armored cars; 2 anti-tank companies; 3 battalions of motorized infantry with American trucks, reconnaissance units, and a screening company; 1

special mission company; 1 light flak company; 1 signals company; and 1 regimental headquarters for brigade and command sections for each battalion. This was to give me a total strength of 3,300 men, all volunteers. Theoretically, they were all supposed to wear American uniforms over their German uniforms.

The High Command had promised me twenty Sherman tanks for Operation *Greif.* In all, I received *two*, only one of which was in working order. As an interim measure, we modified 12 of our Panthers to look like Shermans, so that we might, perhaps, be able to fool the young enemy soldiers from a distance and in conditions of poor visibility. We encountered similar difficulties with the 23 machine guns, 247 jeeps, 32 armored tracked vehicles, and 193 trucks I had requested. We had to improvise everything.

And then, the High Command itself committed one of the worst blunders of the war, which left me completely in the lurch where the 3,300 English-speaking volunteers were concerned. Field Marshal Keitel signed a circular to all units in Germany:

"VERY SECRET: To Divisional and Army Commands only.

"All units of the Western Front are to report before the 10th of October the names of those officers, NCOs, and enlisted men who are willing to volunteer for a special mission in the western theater. The volunteers must be in good health, have experience in hand-to-hand combat, and speak fluent English. They are to be sent to Friedenthal, where they will be placed under the command of Lieutenant Colonel Skorzeny."

I am certain that this order was copied by the division headquarters and sent to every regiment, battalion, and company. It turns out that this Order was in the hands of the American intelligence service eight days after it was disseminated.

I almost choked with rage. At first, such stupidity seemed unbelievable and I suspected sabotage. Today, I think it was stupidity of such a magnitude that it was worse than treason. It now seemed to me that Operation *Greif* was doomed to failure, and I believed it advisable that Hitler know exactly why.

But fate was to deal me a bitter hand of cards. General der Waffen-SS Fegelein, Himmler's liaison man to Hitler, intercepted my report and declared that under no circumstances could this "annoying incident" be brought to the Führer's attention. Generaloberst Jodl, who was as shocked as I, told me it must be passed on. Himmler, who at that time wanted to bombard New York with V-1's, shared Fegelein's view, and so Hitler never received what I felt was a vital message.

But things were to get far worse. The experts sent 600 volunteers for testing. Ten spoke fluent English; 40 spoke it fairly well; 150 could make themselves understood; 200 spoke broken English; and 200 could answer yes or no. *Fifty out of 3,300. A disaster in the making.* It was therefore impossible to form an "English-speaking brigade." The OKW acknowledged this, and agreed that the brigade was only to advance in enemy uniform if the enemy was in full retreat. This, at least, enabled me to retain the soldiers with the best knowledge of English for the commando company, which was to carry out the function of infiltrating behind the enemy lines, reconnoitering there, cutting telephone lines, issuing false orders, and causing general confusion. They were to use their weapons only in extreme emergency and to do so exclusively when they were in German uniform. As long as my commandos acted according to these principles, they were not breaking international law. But if they engaged in combat in the enemy uniform or even opened fire, they would be deemed guilty of war crimes and sentenced accordingly.

I asked High Command for additional units for Operation *Greif,* which, together with the two battalions of my commando units and the rest of the 600 volunteers, made a total force of 2,000 men, about 60% of the promised strength. One-hundred-twenty volunteers were subsequently designated as talkers. All others were emphatically instructed to keep their mouths shut. If forced to join in a conversation, they were to murmur or speak in single syllables.

None of the volunteers and none of the officers or men of my own units were told the objectives of Operation *Greif* until a day or two before we went into action. One can just imagine the fantastic rumors that surrounded the unit's mission. One of the most outrageous, and one that spread the fastest and farthest, was that we were going to kidnap General Eisenhower.

The brightest of our candidates were sent off to interpreters' school, but when they returned new problems surfaced. We were told we'd be used almost exclusively against the American sector of the front, so all our men must pass as Americans. A few volunteers were sent into prison cages to "wise up" on the idiom. The real prisoners usually "got wised up" first, and at least one impostor was badly beaten up at one of these "finishing schools." In the end, I had to advise most of the men to rush past the enemy with teeth clenched, acting as though they were shell-shocked.

But there were bound to be circumstances where, silent or not, our masqueraders would be exposed to close observation. We'd have to teach our men "G.I. behavior," and that did not mean the bark of a Prussian drill sergeant. Whenever I came on a group they would stiffen to attention. "Relax," I would say. They would immediately stamp their boots militarily as they assumed an "at ease" position. No good.

Hour by endless hour I would try to instill in them to *stroll* by, hands in pockets; to chew gum, to flick a cigarette out of a "pack." I drilled them in learning how to be "American," to acquire the arts that were so effortless to the enemy: eyes that "failed to see," and hence failed to salute, one's officer off duty. The Germans simply could not accept the democratic way of life so casually demonstrated by real Americans.

Ultimately, I sorted out my men, nearly 3,500 of them, placed them in a special training camp near Nuremberg, made section leaders of the best young men, and waited for the American equipment to arrive. General Jodl had promised there would be plenty for all, "just ask for what you want." By that time, I'd had experience in whittling down my needs to the bone. I decided to sacrifice all extras, even field kitchens, in favor of firepower. We had already dealt with the horrible muck-up when it came to Sherman tanks. We'd used pieces of tin to alter the outlines of the Panthers we ended up using.

Karl Radl, with his usual sardonic humor, said, "The farther you stand away from them, the better they look. With great good luck they *might* be mistaken for Shermans a mile away in the dusk."

Six American armored cars arrived. Our protests brought four more vehicles, but they were British. How could their appearance in an American sector be explained? Our discussion came to an abrupt end when all four broke down on trial. Obviously they had been left for junk. We camouflaged German cars with khaki paint and white stars on the hood and hoped for the best.

Next came the jeeps. Every other officer I met seemed to have captured a jeep for his private use, but on the day Jodl's order called them in, every jeep in Germany vanished, So much for requisitioning. Our foragers, led by the indomitable Karl Radl, found fifteen jeeps hidden in barns and warehouses. We painted a few German Fords, some Czech cars, and what we could find of French vehicles in the same khaki and white star pattern.

The guns arrived: half as many as we wanted, but still more than we hoped for. Several railway wagons full of American shells arrived, but most of them exploded the next day, thanks to inept unloading by newly-arrived men. In the end, only the special commando company could be outfitted with American weapons.

The High Command's answer was singularly stupid and unpromising: "Why worry? There will be plenty for the taking when the Americans begin to run."

The first load of uniforms had to be sent back: they were British. Then we received a variety of American greatcoats. Since the troops opposing us were wearing field jackets, these were useless. At last field jackets appeared, alas, covered with prisoner-of-war triangles, which had to be inartfully torn off. "Never mind," OKW told me once again. "You can pick up all you want after the breakthrough." Since I could not find so much as one American uniform that fit me, I had to wear a khaki sweater.

But for all these problems, I experienced much greater concerns during the High Command meetings at the Chancellery in Berlin. Hitler had abandoned Wolfsschanze to the Russians. The gloomy howl of air raid sirens matched the feel of malaise and depression that accompanied the meetings. At each of the three gatherings, the promised number of men and materials for the main offensive dwindled.

When Hitler had first confided in me, he had talked of six thousand guns smashing the Allied front line; of a thousand tanks spearheading the way to Antwerp; of three thousand jet planes, which Göring was building to challenge the Allied mastery of the sky. Now it became obvious that we could never hope for anything near these totals. Thanks to incessant bombing, new armaments were not coming off the production lines in time. We couldn't find more men and we couldn't find more materials. Every commander, especially in the East, clung to what little he had. Not a single man, not a single weapon could be spared. It was as simple as that.

The final meeting at the Reich Chancellery was macabre. The offensive, which was supposed to have begun on November 1, then December 1, was postponed until December 16, due to lack of materiel and anticipated bad weather. On the eve of the start of the Ardennes Offensive, I learned to my astonishment that instead of the 3,000 promised aircraft, we had 250.

18

I established my command post in Schmidtheim on December 15. No one slept that night. Our artillery went into action at five in the morning on Saturday, December 16, 1944. Groups X, Y, and Z were in position, together with Waffen-SS I Panzer Corps in the Losheim-Graben sector. My radio operator signaled there was heavy fighting. Then catastrophe struck. Obersturmbahnführer Hardiek, the same rank as me, commander of Group Z, was killed. Fölkersam took over command of Group Z. When I drove to Losheim that afternoon to survey the situation firsthand, I realized that our offensive was bogged down. The narrow roads were clogged with every type of vehicle and I had to cover more than over six miles on foot to get to Losheim.

Next day was even worse. It was obvious that our groups couldn't advance. I decided to wait until the following day. We could not reach the Meuse until our panzers had crossed the High Venn, the plateau near the German-Belgian border.

Meanwhile, I sent thirty men from the special commando to infiltrate between the lines in the southern sector of the front. When the first American prisoners arrived, I struck up a conversation with a lieutenant. His unit had been taken completely by surprise. The Americans had believed they were in a quiet sector. The bad weather and the fog had prevented their air force from intervening.

Towards midnight, I learned that the 1st Panzer Regiment of the Leibstandarte Adolf Hitler, commanded by Jochen Peiper, had gone over to the offensive and smashed open a breach for our battle groups.

On the morning of the 17th, I made my way to the front to inspect the commando units. The roads were now completely clogged. It was impossible to get to I SS-Panzer Corps at the front. We began to suffer from a shortage of fuel on the morning of the 18th. There was no more talk of reaching the Meuse bridges. Therefore, I radioed General Jodl that I was placing my brigade at the disposal of I Panzer Corps.

On Wednesday, December 20, I elected to attack Malmédy with a dozen tanks the following morning. Since there was fighting, no one wore American uniforms. Heavy barrage artillery fire by the enemy and a tremendous counter-offensive by American tanks caused our plan to fail. The skies cleared on the 23rd and the U.S. Army Air Corps carried out massive attacks on Malmédy, which was held by American troops.

Contrary to my belief, the town hadn't been evacuated. Still, my commando unit, unaware that it was behind enemy lines, conducted itself with cool competence. But our attack on Malmédy resulted in heavy casualties, among them Fölkersam, who barely managed to withdraw, and we were forced to remain on the defensive. A short time later, I was hit. I suffered a minor leg wound, which did not concern me, and a more serious one above my right eye. At first, I feared I might lose the eye. The doctors at the division command post wanted to send me to the rear, but I refused to go.

What we lacked was heavy weapons. On December 24, we finally received a battery of eight mortars. It was too little, too late. With the addition of the reinforcements, we now had 20 mortars. By then, most of our tanks had been destroyed, so a new attack was impossible. By the next day, I sought out Adrian Fölkersam, who had set up his command post only four hundred yards from the main line of resistance.

While there, we met an American patrol of half a dozen captured GI's, who seemed friendly enough. The American NCO in charge allowed us to listen over his walkie-talkie as one of our English speakers, masquerading as a Yankee, began a conversation with the American unit. This was quite amusing until our man "lost it" by his increasingly outrageous and largely incredible tales. When he finally declared that a formation of flying submarines would soon attack the American lines, the American officer shouted, "You're drunk! Get back here immediately, soldier! That's an order!"

I turned to the NCO, smiled, and said, "Don't feel embarrassed. We've got 'em in our outfits, too."

The sergeant, shocked, asked, "Where'd you learn that lingo?"

"We're not all dumb-ass Germans, you know. One day, when this war's over, you may find that not all of us are bad."

"D'you mind if I ask …?"

"Where I got the scar? Dueling. That *is* one of our German traditions. My name's Otto Skorzeny, by the way."

"Jimmy Larsen."

"Swede?"

"I guess. A long way back, anyway."

On December 28, we were relieved by an infantry unit which was covering the northern flank of I SS-Panzer Corps. Our attack, and with it *Greif*, had failed. We had not reached the Meuse bridges. Only eight squads, each consisting of four phony Americans, had gone behind enemy lines, a total of 32 men. Twenty-four returned. Eight were declared missing on December 29, 1944. That day, the rest of the

150th Panzer Brigade was sent to Schlierbach, east of St. Vith, to rest. The brigade was disbanded a short time later.

On December 30, I took time to walk around the area between the two towns. The snow, which was ankle-deep in the center of Schlierbach, had increased to knee-high by the time I reached the outskirts. The landscape was a mix of bombed-out land and untouched half-timbered country cottages between the two areas. As the sun gave way to a cold twilight, a sudden gust of wind, followed by a brief, knifelike rain, caused me to seek shelter until the brief gale had blown over. I approached a partially-ruined structure which still appeared to have four walls intact.

As I reached the entrance, I found myself deeply moved by the sound of a few men's voices singing *Lili Marleen*, a love song which Goebbels had banned, but which had spread throughout the ranks of the ordinary German soldiers as they recalled home and a particular loved-one, now, perhaps, gone forever:

> *Vor der Kaserne, vor dem großen Tor*
> *Stand eine Laterne und steht sie noch davor*
> *So woll'n wir da uns wiedersehn*
> *Bei der Laterne woll'n wir steh'n*
> *Wie einst, Lili Marleen*
> *Wie einst, Lili Marleen*

Even more moving, their voices were joined by other men singing in English. Since the song had been introduced in the West by German-born Marlene Dietrich a year or two before, it had become a worldwide phenomenon, which, despite its origins, tore through differences of race, nation, and politics, uniting human beings on both sides of the war with the common thread of the love of a man and a woman.

Outside the barracks, by the corner light
I'll always stand and wait for you at night
We will create a world for two
I'll wait for you the whole night through
For you, Lili Marleen
For you, Lili Marleen

Bugler tonight don't play the call to arms
I want another evening with her charms
Then we will say goodbye and part
I'll always keep you in my heart
With me, Lili Marleen
With me, Lili Marleen

Give me a rose to show how much you care
Tie to the stem a lock of golden hair
Surely tomorrow, you'll feel blue
But then will come a love that's new
For you, Lili Marleen
For you, Lili Marleen

I entered the building to find myself in the midst of six young soldiers. Half wore German army tunics; the others wore American field jackets. By their insignia, I guessed they were all enlisted men, none of them over twenty-five. They sat around a makeshift campfire, companionably sharing army rations and two bottles of cheap local wine. An atmosphere of bittersweet nostalgia permeated the room. Tomorrow, these men would be on opposite sides of the lines, trying to kill one another, and for what? Tonight, they were brothers, children of the same God, someone's lover, husband, son, father.

No one seemed to notice I was wearing the epaulets of a Schutzstaffel Obersturmbahnführer, or, if they did, they didn't appear to care. I was neither more nor less than they and the men welcomed me into their circle, pressed a bottle into my hands, and passed me a paper plate of some kind of food which would never have seen its way into the Officers' Mess.

Since I knew both the English lyrics and the much darker German lyrics, I joined in each chorus, feeling something I hadn't felt for more than a decade, the warmth, and the all-enveloping softness of Lisbeth Hollander, who'd passed away far too early from cancer in 1942, and who, despite the differences in our ages and the accident of circumstance which eventually led to our parting, was, and would always be, my only love.

I don't know how long I remained in that warm cocoon of camaraderie, but I know that as I trudged the few miles back to my headquarters it wasn't the darkness that made it so hard for me to find my way back. It was the tears.

†

At sunset the following evening, New Year's Eve, hoping to once again regain what I had lost and re-found the night before, I walked back toward the house where I'd been, As I neared the structure, something seemed amiss. A thin wisp of black smoke curled from the top of the building. As I came closer, I saw, to my horror, that the smoke did not come from a fire; rather, what had been the roof of the house was no more. A bomb, a mortar shell, *something* large and deadly had destroyed what had been.

I had no idea when this had happened, but when I entered what was left of the house and saw the commingled remains of bodies, the mix of American and German uniforms, the unity of enemies in the finality of death, I surmised it must have happened last night. *God, I thought, this could have happened within minutes of my leaving the convivial group. A few minutes later and one of those bodies could have been mine.*

I walked very slowly back toward my quarters. I slept little, if at all, as 1944 turned to 1945.

In retrospect, *Unternehmen Wacht am Rhein* ("Operation Watch on the Rhine"), the Ardennes Offensive, which lasted from December 16, 1944 to January 25, 1945 was our last major offensive campaign in the western theater during World War II. It was launched through the densely forested Ardennes region of Wallonia in Belgium, France, and Luxembourg. The surprise attack caught the Allied forces completely off guard. American forces bore the brunt of the attack and incurred their highest casualties of any operation during the war. The battle also severely depleted our armored forces, and we were largely unable to replace them.

The German offensive was intended to stop Allied use of the Belgian port of Antwerp and to split the Allied lines, allowing us to encircle and destroy four Allied armies and force the Western Allies to negotiate a peace treaty in our favor. Once that was accomplished, we could fully concentrate on the Soviets on the Eastern Front.

Indeed, we achieved total surprise on the morning of 16 December 1944, due to a combination of Allied overconfidence, preoccupation with Allied offensive plans, and poor aerial reconnaissance. We attacked a weakly defended section of the Allied line, taking advantage of heavily overcast weather conditions that grounded the Allies' overwhelmingly superior air forces.

While the Siege of Bastogne is often credited as the central point where the German offensive was stopped, the battle for Elsenborn Ridge was actually the decisive component of the battle, since it stopped the advance of our best equipped armored units, forcing them to reroute these troops to unfavorable alternative routes that considerably slowed their advance.

Fierce resistance around Elsenborn Ridge, and, in the south, around Bastogne, blocked our access to key roads to the northwest and west that we counted on for success. Columns of armor and infantry that were supposed to advance along parallel routes found themselves on the same roads. This, and terrain that favored the defenders, threw our advance behind schedule and allowed the Allies to reinforce their thinly placed troops. Improved weather conditions permitted air attacks on our forces and supply lines, which sealed the failure of the offensive. In the wake of the defeat, many experienced units were left severely depleted of men and equipment, as survivors retreated to the defenses of the Siegfried Line.

Our initial attack involved 406,000 men, 1,214 tanks, tank destroyers and assault guns, and 4,224 artillery pieces. These were reinforced a couple of weeks later, bringing the offensive's total strength to around 450,000 troops, and 1,500 tanks and assault guns. Between 67,200 and 125,000 of our troops were killed, missing, or wounded in action. For the Americans, out of 610,000 troops involved in the battle, there were 89,000 casualties. It was the largest and bloodiest battle fought by the United States in World War II.

Our task, minuscule as it seemed in the scope of what became known as "The Battle of the Bulge," was to go behind American lines and change signposts, misdirect traffic, generally cause disruption, and seize bridges across the Meuse River. Although ultimately less than 24 troops were directly involved in Operation *Greif,* with the exception of taking the Meuse bridges, we were surprisingly successful.

I returned to Hitler's headquarters at Ziegenberg on the second of January. When Der Führer saw me with a bandaged head, he insisted that his doctors examine me before I told him anything about our operation. My wound had become infected and I now received proper treatment, courtesy of Dr. Stumpfegger. Hitler expressed his pleasure that I hadn't lost my eye and we talked for half an hour.

He regretted that the offensive hadn't reached its objective. Our panzers, which had been bogged down on the first two days while the enemy's air forces were grounded by bad weather, could not advance quickly enough over the impossible roads. Infantry divisions on foot had advanced as fast as our panzer divisions. Nevertheless, the enemy had been forced to take heavy losses, and, in any case, our offensive had struck a heavy blow to American and British morale.

"The most important thing," he said, "is that the American or British soldier believed it was going to be a military cakewalk. Their commanders had led them to believe that. But then, the mortally wounded stood up and attacked. We couldn't wait for them to wring our neck. The only solution for Germany is victory."

Unfortunately, I was of the opinion that neither of *Greif's* two objectives had been achieved. When I told this to the Leader, he replied, "I have no complaints with you, Skorzeny. You had to improvise everything with limited means and your panzer brigade couldn't play its role in cooperation with Sixth Army. You would have been successful if I had placed you at the head of the Fifth. You might, perhaps, have reached Brabant, and who knows what might have developed from that? Where your commando unit is concerned, I have the impression that its psychological effect was much greater than you might think. We shall see later."

19

By the end of January 1945, it was clear to everyone with eyes, ears, or a shred of intelligence, save perhaps those who dreamed the most optimistic of fantasies, and those unrealistically toadying sycophants who surrounded and advised the Leader, that the end was imminent. Examples of the idiocy surrounding this never-never land of gossamer were the unflagging and unbelievable belief that we still had ample divisions where none existed, nonexistent jet aircraft, tanks, fuel, and weapons, and the appointment of none other than Reichsführer Himmler as field commander of Army Group Vistula.

By the time even the Führer realized that the Ardennes Counteroffensive had failed, the Soviet Armies had come to within sixty air miles of Berlin. I was tasked with the thankless and impossible assignment of establishing a bridgehead east of Schwedt-on-the-Oder. Of course, that meant squandering a substantial portion of what puny and pathetic resources we had left.

On the evening of March 29, 1945, I was summoned to Führer Headquarters in Berlin. Friedenthal had been heavily bombed and the BBC had reported that, "the headquarters of Mussolini kidnapper Skorzeny has been completely destroyed." However, my most important offices had already been transferred to Hof on the Czechoslovakian frontier in Northeast Bavaria.

The monitoring service informed me of a further BBC report, according to which Hitler had promoted me to Major General, given me an important post in the defense of Berlin, and that I had already begun a purge. In fact, the Leader decorated me with the Knight's Cross with Oak Leaves for the defense of Schwedt and congratulated me personally.

I had just come down the stairs of the Reich Chancellery when he left the situation room. I was shocked by his appearance. Bent, with gray hair, he was a picture of misery. The date was March 30, 1945.

"Skorzeny," he said. "I want to thank you again for your accomplishments on the Oder."

The bridgehead had been abandoned on March 3, nearly a month earlier.

"We will see each other again, soon," he said. But I was never to see Hitler alive again.

I had often driven to the Reich Chancellery on official business during that terrible month. My eye injury hurt and Dr. Stumpfegger wanted to look at it. The examination took place in Hitler's secretary's office. On one of my visits, I'd been introduced to Eva Braun, who, shortly before she died, was to become Hitler's wife. She was a young, very simple, and extremely likeable woman, whom I'd never previously met. We had a long talk, during which she invited me to have dinner another day. I never took her up on her invitation because Dr. Stumpfegger informed me that Fegelein, who was married to Eva Braun's sister, and with whom I'd had difficult relations during the Ardennes Offensive, was always present at such functions. I had no desire to know him any better.

I spent three nightmarish weeks in devastated Berlin, a shadow of the city I had known, and which Hitler had planned to completely rebuild in 1940. Writers and survivors of what was to come have written reams about the final days of the war in Germany's capital, and I have no need to add to their accounts of unmitigated misery.

One evening, an air raid warning had been issued. When the 4,400-pound bombs began falling, I fled to the large bunker near the Zoological Gardens. While there, I visited two of my Friedenthal men who'd been wounded at Schwedt. I also found Hanna Reitsch, who was in a poor state of mind, and my comrade and friend, Luftwaffe Colonel Hans-Ulrich Rudel, the famous Stuka pilot, who'd just had a leg amputated. Rudel had flown more than 2,530 combat missions, destroyed 519 tanks, and had sunk the 23,000-ton battleship *Marat* in Leningrad's Kronstadt harbor. Hitler created a special decoration for Rudel: the Knight's Cross in Gold with Oak Leaves, Swords, and Diamonds In spite of his injuries and a strict ban from the Führer, Rudel continued flying until May 8, 1945.

On that day, Rudel and what was left of his squadron voluntarily surrendered to the U.S. Army Air Corps at Kitzingen airfield in Bavaria. The pilots destroyed their aircraft after landing. They were led into the officers' mess and Rudel was taken to the hospital, where they bandaged his bleeding stump. When he returned to the mess, his men stood up and greeted him with the Hitler salute. An interpreter told Rudel that the American commander wanted no further demonstration of this kind and that he didn't care for this salute. Colonel Rudel responded, "We have been ordered to salute this way, and, as we are soldiers, we will obey this order whether you like it or not. We have landed here on German territory, because we don't want to stay in the Soviet zone. We are prisoners and don't want any further discussion. We would like to wash, if that's possible." The American commander subsequently had a very cordial relationship with Rudel.

In 1948, I assisted Rudel in moving to Argentina. In return, he helped me get a position with President Juan Péron. Some years later, after assisting Stroessner in Paraguay and Pinochet in Chile, my friend moved back to West Germany, where he unsuccessfully ran for the Bundestag.

†

The area in which we fought shrank day by day on both fronts. Shortly after my meeting with Hitler, OKW ordered me to transfer my headquarters to the Alpine Fortress, where the principal Führer Headquarters was scheduled to be set up. The last battles of the war were supposed to take place in this redoubt. I was told that the "Fortress" was fully ready to mount a defense.

Radl and I found the mountains, the glaciers, the forests, and the wild streams all in their place, but there was not a trace of military preparation or fortification. Once again, we'd have to improvise everything. However, my units were decimated, for the most part destroyed. In all, I was able to assemble 350 soldiers.

On the morning of April 10, I learned that the remnants of Battle Group Danube had been forced to leave Vienna to defend the so-called Alpine Fortress. Vienna was my birthplace. My mother, my wife, and my daughter must still be there. Perhaps I could get them out of the battle zone. I set off in the direction of the old Imperial City with my adjutant, my driver, and a radio operator who'd been sent by OKW.

Before we drove across the Florisdorfer Bridge, we witnessed something that proved to me that the end really had come. We had just passed a tank obstacle. Wounded people sat in the ditches to the right and the left of the bridge. We came upon a convoy of wagons drawn by teams of six horses. A fat Sergeant in the company of a young girl sat on the first wagon. The six wagons were overflowing with furniture and linen. I tried not to lose my composure and asked the Sergeant to take along some of the wounded.

"Can't do it," he replied. "All full."

Everything happened very quickly after that. We disarmed the portly NCO and the other drivers. I passed out weapons to those with minor injuries. We unloaded the wagons and lifted the wounded into them. The others took the places of the furniture movers. I directed another noncommissioned officer who was wounded in the arm, "Drive in a westerly direction to the nearest hospital and take as many wounded with you as you can."

Then I addressed the fat Feldwebel who wanted to rescue the furniture, "You filthy pig, get yourself and your people out of here. If you don't intend to fight, at least try to be less greedy and more charitable in the future."

We arrived in Vienna as darkness was falling. We heard the sound of cannon firing and saw houses burned here and there. The city seemed to be dead. We drove to the Stubenring, past the former war ministry, which was empty. A sentry told us that the command post had been moved to the Hofburg, the palace in the city center, where the Kaiser had lived when I was born.

Where were our troops? Who was defending Vienna? Finally I reached headquarters Commando Unit Southeast. The remnants of the unit had withdrawn into the area north of Krems that afternoon. Commando Unit Danube had likewise evacuated its quarters in the Diana Baths. When I found these soldiers on my way back to the Alpine Fortress, I ordered them to Salzburg.

In the cellar of the former Kaiser's palace, an officer reported to me that the Russians had already infiltrated the city and were being engaged everywhere. The answer to the question, "By whom?" was a mystery. I wanted to know precisely and continued on my way.

When I reached the Matzleindorf district, it was already after midnight. I heard the sound of battle coming from my left and soon came to a barricade. When I got out of the car, two elderly Vienna policemen appeared. They declared to me, "We are manning the barricade. If the Russians show up here, we will surround them and they'll have to give themselves up." They had always had a sense of humor in Vienna, even if it was only gallows humor.

I drove through the dead streets, back to the Hofburg, and spoke briefly with the adjutant to Gauleiter and former Nazi Youth Leader Baldur von Schirach. My reports left the adjutant unnerved but skeptical. "The reports we have prove to the contrary," he said. "The front has been stabilized. Why don't you speak to the Gauleiter yourself?"

When I was shown to von Schirach's "headquarters," it turned out to be a single, candle-lit room. On the floor lay magnificent carpets. Paintings of battles and portraits of Eighteenth Century generals hung on the walls. The ante-room was used for eating, drinking, and partying. I explained to the Gauleiter that I hadn't seen a single German soldier in the city and that the barricades were unmanned. I invited him to come with me on an inspection of the city.

He declined the invitation and, as he bent over a map, he explained to me how they would save Vienna: two elite divisions were ready to attack, one from the north and the other from the west. The enemy would certainly capitulate. "Prince Starhemberg used a similar maneuver to lift the siege of Vienna by the Turks in 1683."

Any further discussion was pointless. I took my leave. Schirach looked at me. "Skorzeny, my duty is expressed in three words: 'prevail or die.'" He undoubtedly meant to say, "prevail or retreat," because five hours later the defense commissar of Vienna district left the city as fast as he could.

I found my mother's house half in ruins. However, a neighbor, who crawled out from his cellar, assured me that my mother had left Vienna with my wife and daughter the day before. I drove to my home in

Döbling. The house was untouched. I quickly collected several huntng rifles and took a last look at the home I was about to leave ready for the occupancy by the enemy or by looters.

I left the city by the Florisdorfer Bridge and turned around once more. "*Auf Wiedersehen, Wien.*" Then we took the Waldviertler Road to Upper Austria. In carrying out the mission given me by Generaloberst Jodl, I sent the following radio message: "All indications are that Vienna will fall today, 11 April 1945."

20

During the last days of the war, Hitler dismissed Hermann Göring as head of the Luftwaffe and appointed Generaloberst Robert Ritter von Greim to replace him. On April 26, Greim and his lover, my friend Hanna Reitsch, flew from Gatow Airport to Berlin in a tiny Fieseler Storch, the same type of aircraft that had safely carried Mussolini, Hauptmann Gerlach, and me off the Grand Sasso. As the Red Army troops were already in central Berlin, Reitsch landed on an improvised airstrip in the Tiergarten near the Brandenburg Gate. While I was in the Alpine redoubt at the time, I later learned that when they met with our leader in the Führerbunker the following day, Hitler gave Reitsch two vials of poison, one for herself and one for von Greim.

The following evening, Reitsch flew von Greim out of Berlin in an Arado Ar 96 from the same improvised airstrip. Troops of the Soviet 3rd Shock Army, which was fighting its way through the Tiergarten from the north, tried to shoot the plane down fearing that Hitler was escaping in the plane, but it took off successfully. This was the last plane out of Berlin.

I heard that Hitler had died on April 30. After the initial shock, I considered that this news was unlikely, for Der Führer was supposed to go to the Alpine Fortress where there were still troops ready to fight. It was impossible that he was dead.

Yet the next day, when we heard Anton Bruckner's 7th Symphony on the German radio, we knew what had happened. On May 1, Grossadmiral Karl Dönitz, whom Hitler had named head of state before his death, addressed the German people.

"Our leader, Adolf Hitler, has fallen. His life was service to Germany. His actions in the struggle against bolshevism, were also for the benefit of Europe and the entire cultured world. The Führer chose me as his successor. My first task is to save the German people from destruction by the advancing Bolshevik enemy. As far and as long as the achieving if this objective is hindered by the British and Americans, we will also have to defend ourselves against them and fight on. Maintain order and discipline in the cities and in the country. Each must do his duty in his place."

In spite of a lack of preparation, the Alpine Fortress had to, and could, afford sanctuary to many people. The economics minister and the president of the Reichsbank sent me two of their adjutants and asked me to look after the Reichsbank's treasure. I politely declined. I was a soldier, not a safe watcher. Theoretically, the Alpine Fortress should have been made into a fortified area 220 miles long and 50 miles wide, from Bregenz in the west to Bad Aussee in the east, and from Füssen-Salzburg in the north, to Bolzano, Lienz, and Cortina d'Ampezzo in the south, However, the southern frontier was pulled back to the Brenner Pass following the surrender of the German armed forces in Italy.

After a few days, I realized this fortress had never existed and never would exist. On May 1, 1945, I received my last order from High Command South: organize the defense of the South Tyrolean passes so that our remaining forces in Italy could withdraw. Seeing the mass confusion on the Italian border, my forces were smart enough to return to me instead.

On May 6, Grossadmiral Dönitz ordered us to lay down our arms on all fronts at midnight on May 8. Germany had lost the Second World War, in spite of the courage of its soldiers.

I could have committed suicide. Many of our comrades sought death in the final battles or took their own lives. I could, for that matter, quite easily have flown to a neutral country in a Ju-88, which had a range in excess of 1,400 miles. But I refused to abandon my country, my family, and my friends in their hour of need. Besides, I had nothing to hide. I hadn't attempted, done, or ordered anything that would shame a true soldier.

I decided to surrender voluntarily and sent two messages to the American division headquarters in Salzburg, proposing that the soldiers of the Alpine Guard Corps go into captivity together. I received no answer. What I did not know was that I was being eagerly sought and that the allied press and radio were calling me "the most devilishly intelligent man in Germany." I really had no idea of the legend that already surrounded my name.

On May 20, 1945, Radl, "Chinaman" Hunke, an interpreter, and I requested that the Americans send a jeep to pick us up at a bridge near Annaberg. The jeep was there to drive us to Salzburg when we reached the bridge. Our driver, a man from Texas, showed a great deal of interest in us. Along the road, he stopped at an inn. I got out with him. He ordered a good bottle of wine, for which I paid. After we resumed our journey, he turned to me and asked, "Bullshit aside, are you really Skorzeny?"

"Of course."

"Well, then, have a drink with your boys 'cause they'll surely hang you tonight."

I drank, "To our health." Toward midday, when we arrived in Salzburg, our driver dropped us off in front of a hotel, saluted cordially, and disappeared. Several German liaison officers looked at us in amazement. We were still carrying weapons.

An American major finally took the trouble to listen to us. He sent us back to St. Johann-im-Pongau in another jeep. There, we were told to pick up trucks and other vehicles with which to transport the Alpine Guard Corps from the German office to the prisoner of war camp. A German general then sent us to a U.S. battalion stationed at Werfen. I instructed Hunke to stay in St. Johann; if we weren't back in three hours it meant we were prisoners and everyone would have to take care of himself.

When we arrived at Werfen, I found myself surrounded by American troops bearing a dozen submachine guns. I was strip-searched and my Mussolini watch was stolen. Radl, the interpreter, and I were put into three jeeps and driven to Salzburg that night. When we alighted from the jeep, MPs grabbed us from behind and handcuffed us behind the back. I was shoved into a room where a fifteen people, among them reporters and photographers, were present.

When an officer began interrogating me, I calmly responded that I wouldn't speak a word until my handcuffs and those of my associates were removed. Then I sat down in front of the major and said, "I am now prepared to answer your questions."

"You had a plan to murder General Eisenhower, didn't you?"

"No."

"If you didn't intend to kill him, did you plan to kidnap him?"

"No."

The questions got more absurd and repetitive. "Why didn't the Italian forces on Gran Sasso fire on you? What were you doing in Berlin at the end of April 1945? Where did you take Hitler? We know from a reliable source that you flew away with Hitler in an aircraft early in the morning of April 30. You know how to fly, don't you? You flew the aircraft and Hitler sat beside you in the cockpit. Where is he hiding? How do you know that Hitler killed himself in Berlin if you weren't there?" And so on.

After several days, I managed to convince American intelligence that if I had taken Hitler to a safe place, why wouldn't I have stayed there instead of turning myself and my troops in to the Americans? But the press wasn't buying what I said. They needed a super-bad-man, a mythological character capable of anything, and I appeared to be the perfect candidate.

But as time went on, the Americans and the British concluded there never had been a serious plot to kidnap or kill Eisenhower, Montgomery, or any of the top allied generals, and that they had been fooled by German propaganda.

Thereafter, I was taken from one prison to another. On May 29, 1945, I was placed in a wooden hut with my first mentor and sponsor, Ernst Kaltenbrunner. The shack was equipped with microphones throughout, something we discovered within minutes of being left alone there. We talked about our student days and trivial matters of no consequence. The listening service must have been very disappointed.

In one of the camps, I was allowed to share a cell with my adjutant and friend Karl Radl. But on September 10, 1945, I was once again handcuffed, put on an aircraft with Grossadmiral Dönitz, Field Marshal Keitel, Major General Jodl, Colonel General Guderian, Dr. Ley, and Baldur von Schirach, the Gauleiter of Vienna, and flown to Nuremberg.

When we arrived at Nuremberg Prison, I met the commander in charge, American Colonel Andrus, a Lithuanian by birth, who bore a striking resemblance to Heinrich Himmler, even down to the pretentious pince-nez. This prissy functionary almost had an apoplectic stroke when he found that Admiral Dönitz and I were still wearing full uniform and badges of rank. Andrus declared that the uniforms were not permissible and that our wearing them was a willful provocation. But when he came to formally discipline us, he found we'd each removed he other's badges of rank so he had no charges he could level against us.

Nuremberg Prison was a large building, shaped like a five-pointed star. We were guarded by a large number of black soldiers. Our jailer, Colonel Andrus, thought to degrade us in this way. But I always got along well with the blacks, who proved to be much more humane and considerate than the whites. One huge young man, a black sergeant, became my friend and more than once slipped me a few cigarettes and chocolate.

We were quite well-fed during the first weeks. Older German prisoners, soldiers assigned to kitchen duty, did their best for us, which annoyed Colonel Andrus no end. Having become an American citizen only recently, he hated everything German. One day, he said to us, "They call you 'Krauts' because you like sauerkraut so much. Therefore you will get some to eat every day." He saw to it that the food was bland and of very poor quality. But the kitchen staff continued to see to that I received dumplings and tasty German treats.

At the beginning, I was assigned to the "accused" wing. Just before Christmas 1945, I was transferred to the "witness" wing. Our cells were locked at night and open all day. Then, Andrus issued a maliciously motivated, absurd decree: whenever he appeared, every prisoner had to stand in the doorway of his cell and salute Andrus fifteen paces before he passed and twelve paces after he passed. I managed to duck into the nearest cell every time this "illustrious" person came by. Andrus noted this and called out, "So, Skorzeny, you refuse to salute me?"

I responded, "My name is *Colonel* Skorzeny. I will salute you when we are treated like soldiers who are prisoners of war. I refuse to salute you in a subservient way. I am an officer with the same rank as you and not your lackey."

"I can have you punished for disobeying orders with a month in solitary confinement!"

"You can do whatever the hell you like."

I believe the American officers under Andrus hated him more than he hated us. I had occasion to meet one of these officers a few years later. He recognized me and told me that my behavior toward Andrus had been a source of admiration to him and his associates.

The most demoralizing thing for me was the prison's oppressive atmosphere: the constant spying, the deals they tried to make with the most cowardly and malleable prisoners, the use of informants, the denunciations, the false accusations, the servile behavior of certain of the accused and witnesses, who hoped to come out of the entire affair with enhanced reputations - all of the things I found inimical to the fundamental German character.

Meanwhile, the journalists were hungry for sensational news. Some of them asked me for "ready to print" text, for which they would pay me munificent sums. I refused. Many prisoners, however, spent whole days typing, either for the press or for the prosecution, often for both. The autograph trade was in full swing. Without embarrassing myself, I demanded a package of cigarettes for each autograph. The more "dangerous" one was, the higher the fee. I knew more than one prisoner who made himself out to be a very dangerous criminal in order to make his stay more profitable.

I was incarcerated in Nuremberg Prison three times, from October 1945 to May 1946, in July and August 1946, and in February and March 1948. I must admit that a real solidarity existed between us and the black guards, the pariahs. The authorities made a big mistake when they had us guarded by blacks, who refused to treat us like animals and, in so doing, gave Colonel Andrus a lesson in humanitarian behavior.

In May 1946, I was transferred to the old Dachau concentration camp. Soon afterward, I found myself in a camp in Darmstadt, then back in Nuremberg, then in Dachau again, where I went on a hunger strike to protest against my solitary confinement and against the treatment of German prisoners in general.

The tribunal assigned three officers from the American army as my defense attorneys: Lieutenant-Colonel Robert Durst from Springfield, Missouri; Lieutenant-Colonel Donald McClure, from Oakland, California; and Major Lewis I. Horowitz from New York. The latter, I wish to emphasize, was of the Jewish faith. In addition, half a dozen German lawyers, who had no chance of ever hoping to get paid, volunteered to represent my interests. On August 5, 1947, trial proceedings against me, which lasted more than a month, commenced in Dachau.

⸸

Before the trial commenced, I was questioned by Lt. Col. Durst, who was armed with files provided by the prosecutor, Lt. Col. Rosenfeld, for three solid days. "I would like to point out to you that I will only take over your defense if I know every detail about your life before and during the war."

I had nothing to hide and at the end of the third day he offered me his hand for the first time and said, "I am now convinced that you are completely innocent, and will defend you like my own brother. However, I cannot guarantee you a favorable outcome if the leadership of the defense is not given to a team leader, but to a single defender, namely me. It seems important that you alone speak for the defense, in your own name and in the names of your associates."

I had little choice but to agree with him. He was an American lawyer, dealing with American law in an American court.

The Chief presiding judge, Colonel Gardner, was called "the hanging Gardner," since, up to that time, he had only handed out death sentences by hanging. However, Colonel Durst was able to have five of the nine members of the military court, who were all colonels, replaced by five other officers, all proven front-line soldiers.

Halfway through the trial, prosecutor Rosenfeld had to withdraw his charge of murder against us. He was left with only one charge: wearing the uniform of the enemy during actual combat. Lieutenant-Colonel Durst presented no evidence that the English and Americans had used German uniforms. But it was already common knowledge that the commander of the Polish uprising had worn a German uniform. They knew that the Americans had fought in Aachen while wearing German uniforms. General Bradley wrote the court a letter in which he assured the judges that he never had knowledge of these events, but the facts could not be denied.

Then came the turning point of the trial. RAF Wing Commander Forest Yeo-Thomas, one of Britain's most brilliant and credible intelligence agents, took the witness stand. He did not need to be introduced to the court. The French resistance fighters knew him as "the white rabbit."

Colonel Rosenfeld was completely bewildered by the appearance of Yeo-Thomas. Eugen Kogon, who wrote *The SS State*, had claimed that Yeo-Thomas had been killed by the Germans in Buchenwald. As Lieutenant-Colonel Durst began his questioning, Wing Commander Yeo-Thomas, sitting ramrod straight and looking every inch the English officer portrayed by Sir Alec Guinness in the movie *Bridge on the River Kwai* several years after the trial, answered the questions in a clipped, no-nonsense manner.

"Did members of your own commando unit use German uniforms?"

"Yes, Sir."

"Did your unit use German vehicles?"

"Affirmative."

"Were there conditions under which your commandos would 'take no prisoners?'"

"Yes, Sir."

"Were your forces sometimes forced to take and use the papers of German prisoners of war?"

"Of course, Colonel Durst. A prisoner is not supposed to have any papers on him, and if he does, all the worse for him."

"Are you familiar with Colonel Skorzeny's actions?"

"Yes, Colonel Durst. As leader of the English commando units, I thoroughly studied the actions of Colonel Skorzeny and his units. I can, without reservation, assure this court that the colonel, his officers, and his soldiers acted entirely properly and like real gentlemen on all occasions."

For a moment, it appeared as though prosecutor Rosenfeld was having a heart attack or a stroke. Of course, I was not allowed to shake Yeo-Thomas' hand, but when he stood up to leave the witness stand, my comrades stood at attention as one, in salute to this truthful and noble man. After Yeo-Thomas' statement, Lieutenant-Colonel Durst said he had no need to question the three American officers who had placed themselves at the defense's disposal; their testimony would be cumulative and superfluous.

The presiding judge asked me to explain what happened. Using a map, I explained as simply as possible the entire story, including the actions during the course of Operation *Greif*. Colonel Rosenfeld asked me a few more questions in his role as prosecutor, but he was far more courteous than he had been at the commencement of the trial. This did not stop him from arguing for the death penalty in his closing statements, even though he was unable to prove our guilt.

Lieutenant-Colonel Durst gave a well-documented, thorough, and convincing closing argument, expressing surprise that the prosecution was still asking for *any* punishment after its failure to present any convincing proof of our guilt.

On September 9, 1947, the court announced its decision in front of a room filled to capacity: Not Guilty.

As I was about to thank my defenders, Colonel Rosenfeld came toward me, his hand outstretched. Although I was not resentful and would gladly have shaken my accuser's hand, I didn't believe in his goodwill. He knew very well that we had neither beaten nor murdered Americans or other soldiers, and that we had no plans to attack Eisenhower's headquarters and liquidate him or any other general. Nevertheless, he had tried to implicate the 150th Panzer Brigade's actions as part of the "proven massacre" at Malmédy. He had also produced false statements concerning my unit's alleged use of cyanide bullets during the Ardennes offensive. The prosecution had even called Karl Radl and "Chinaman" Hunke as witnesses for the prosecution. The court allowed them to testify over Lieutenant-Colonel Durst's vigorous objection. Fortunately, Radl was uncooperative and gave monosyllabic answers and Hunke persistently remained silent.

But without the Herculean efforts of our defense attorneys, without the generous and honorable statements by Wing Commander Yeo-Thomas, we would have been sentenced to death.

We were acquitted, but we were not yet free. We of the Waffen-SS were subject to the enemy's "automatic arrest" decree. On September 11, 1947, two days after our acquittal, the world press published a statement by prosecutor Rosenfeld: "Skorzeny is the most dangerous man in Europe." The next day, I learned that Denmark and Czechoslovakia had demanded my extradition. After two weeks, they conceded that this was a mistake. However, I was sent back to Nuremberg, then to Darmstadt for "denazification."

Although the court never permitted me a few words with Colonel Yeo-Thomas in order that I might thank him, I did so in a letter. I received a note from him: "You did a jolly good job during the war. If you are looking for a place to stay, I have a home in Paris ... Escape!"

That was my intention, too. Three years and two months was long enough. I warned the American commander of the Darmstadt camp that I had decided to get away. He didn't believe me. But two hours later, on July 27, 1948, I stuffed myself, with difficulty, into the trunk of his car. The German driver, who was going shopping for the camp commander, unwittingly drove me through all the checkpoints. When he stopped outside the first merchandise depot and went in the front door, I popped the trunk with a wire I had installed, got out of the car, closed the trunk slowly and quietly, and walked away – to freedom at last.

PART TWO

21

Over the years, the most outrageous legends were fabricated about me by so many people who "knew firsthand," that I lost count. It is impossible to quote even a fraction of these figments of the imagination which have been printed about my alleged activities. I devoted some attention to this sort of journalism in the Sixties. I even kept several thousand newspaper and magazine clippings devoted to my fictitious adventures. By that time, these fairy tales had become boring.

Still, as I look back, it is entertaining for me to explore my supposed activities since 1950, five years after the war had ended.

Two years before I ever visited Argentina, I was the "commander-in-chief of the army of the republic," while General Galland and Oberst Rudel commanded the air forces there. After my two-week stay in Cairo in 1954, I was accused by the *Daily Sketch* of having, for years, instructed Egyptian special commandos in the art of killing British officers and soldiers. This was a little too much even for me to stomach. I filed suit against the *Daily Sketch* in London and was awarded £10,000 plus costs. I turned £5,000 over to the Red Cross for the seriously war disabled of Britain and donated the remainder to the fund for the German war-disabled.

In 1950, the weekly *Wochenend* claimed that since 1944 I had a double, who was almost as tall as I, and whose real or fictitious name was Vohwinkel. A doctor had made the scars on his cheek, so it was impossible to tell us apart. The author of this article wanted to locate a photo of "Vohwinkel" and me together. Unfortunately, he was unable to find one. The stupid thing was that *Wochenend* no longer knew which of the two of us was traveling about the world.

In time, the world press became aware that I "prepared a few revolutions here and there," and that I also organized the "Nazi International," a mysterious mafia always involved in criminal and subversive activities. At the end of 1950, *Reynolds News* and *Münchener Illustrierte* wrote that the heads of the "Spider" (for that's what they called the organization) were none other than Serrano Suner in Spain, Prince Junio-Valero Borghese in Italy, the Grand Mufti of Jerusalem, Strasser in Canada, Sir Oswald Mosley in Great Britain, Oberst Rudel in Argentina, General de Gaulle in France, Martin Bormann, and myself. Only in 1972 did the West German Ministry of the Interior conclude that "the Spider" never existed.

Not only had I sunk the "SS Treasure," but I had fished it out again several times, from Lake Wahl, Lake Tirpitz, Lake Hinter, or even from Lake Constance, the Neusiedler See. And the journalists even claimed they saw it. I also found the secret correspondence between Mussolini and British Prime Minister Winston Churchill, since the Duce had "confided in me." Regrettably, I don't know on which matter he confided in me.

In August 1953, the French government deposed the Sultan of Morocco, Mohammed Ben Jussuf, and deported him and his family to Corsica. Soon, the French authorities learned that he wasn't safe there. Numerous French and Swiss newspapers claimed I had been hired by the Arab League to kidnap the sultan and his family. Their reliable sources informed them that I had been paid one million dollars for this operation. So they took the monarch first to Fort Lamy and then to Madagascar, The government went on the highest alert. There was no cause for these screaming headlines, for not only did I never harbor any intention of freeing this noble prisoner, but I would not even have had the time to do so. Mohammed V returned to Rabat in triumph in 1955. Two years later, he was proclaimed King of Morocco.

I also deny, of course, that I ever intended to kidnap Ben Bella of Algeria or Fidel Castro of Cuba. However, before the head of the "27th of July" Revolutionary Movement seized power in February, certain American newspapers proclaimed to the public that I was Castro's advisor in the guerilla war against Batista.

During the 1950s, the *Sunday Graphic* did not make the same mistakes as the *Daily Sketch*. That journal had me followed by two alleged officers of the intelligence service, Major Stanley Moss and Captain Michael Luke. Their mission was to find me, which was not easy because I "moved like lightning," and subsequently interview me about my adventures. Moss and Luke had an aircraft at their disposal. They "came across my tracks" in Sweden, Bavaria, France, Italy, Egypt, Baghdad, and so on, but on each occasion I learned "through dumb luck" that they were coming, several hours before their arrival at the place in question. This was attributed to my being warned in time by the infamous "Spider."

I followed my supposed adventures from my desk in Madrid with great interest, and I am sure that Ian Fleming read them too. I lived in the most extraordinary palaces in the world, surrounded by nubile, always-willing blondes or by mysterious, ever-passionate dark-haired women, who used their charms in the service of my dangerous activities.

At one point, I heard that I was the commander-in-chief of a secret army headquartered "near Mursuk" in the Libyan desert, "five thousand miles from any civilization," on a rocky plateau "where many peaks were over 10,000 feet high." On October 13, 1956, the weekly magazine *Samstag* published the account of an old Jesuit Missionary, Monseigneur Jean Baptiste de la Gravaires. As he knew the Sahara "like his own vest pocket," in the course of his explorations, the Good Father was a guest in a mysterious city in the desert. The city was the capital of a military empire and I was its leader.

"Monsieur de la Gravaires" admitted that I had treated him well. I had placed leftover units of the Afrika Corps under my command, about ten thousand troops in all. I had tanks and aircraft which dove out of the sky and could land in the smallest surface in this rugged area. My capital city was protected by the most sophisticated alarm system. The only reason it remained unknown was that women were strictly forbidden to enter.

In 1959, several newspapers disclosed that I was supposed to have kidnapped the Duke and Duchess of Windsor, who were in Portugal, in July 1940. When the papers were looking for more information, they discovered that in 1940 we in the *Das Reich* Division were planning the occupation of the British Isles. Alas, this "invasion" never took place, except in some overactive imaginations.

Apparently, I was in constant communication with Martin Bormann. I met him in a forest on the Czechoslovak-Bavarian border, or perhaps it was in the Amazon, or maybe even in Israel, which is, at least, more original. Naturally, I lived in grand style, owning various castles, a villa on the Riviera, a yacht, and fast cars.

Unfortunately, they were only castles on the moon. When the telephone rang in my Madrid office, my customers, as always, asked for spiral-welded pipes, sheet metal, cement, a cost estimate for a machine tool, and the like.

Still, in 1962, it was obvious to the *American Weekly* that I intended to storm Spandau Prison and free Rudolf Hess. In the following year, the "holdup of the century" took place on August 8. The Glasgow-London train was stopped. The mail car was robbed and the thieves got away with more than £2,500,000. The affair was prepared down to the smallest detail by a "brilliant mind" and was executed perfectly. "Who else could this mind be?" asked the French weekly *Noir et Blanc*, "if not Otto Skorzeny." It was perfectly clear! I must admit that this magazine published all the letters of protest I sent,

From 1957 to 1960, I simultaneously organized an army in India and another in the Congo, supplied and advised the Algerian FLN, the French OAS, and, in Ireland, the IRA. But the most bizarre and exaggerated information of all was published by the Polish newspaper *Glos Robotniczy* and the story was immediately picked up by an East German newspaper: Israeli General Moshe Dayan and Otto Skorzeny were, in reality, one and the same person.

These "news stories," which I swear were actually published, since I kept clippings of them all, only prove that human stupidity knows no bounds.

Occasionally, a few – very few - people came into my life for brief moments, who seemed content to learn "the real truth" about me, from me. One I remember in particular was Charles Foley, an Indian-born Englishman, who'd been born a year after me, and who had had a respectable career with the *New York Herald Tribune* before moving to the English *Daily Express* as its foreign editor in 1940. He "tracked me down" in Madrid in 1954, which was not at all difficult to do, since most of the expatriate German community knew I could be found at Horcher's Restaurant with my long-time friend and later uncle-in-law, Dr. Hjalmar Schacht on any given day.

I was impressed by Foley's apparent sincerity and charmed by his directness when he introduced himself by saying, "I want to know about you, but I don't want to know everything there is to know. Some things are best left to one's privacy. I can assure you I'm not interested in anything you don't want to say. Anyone can speculate and I'm not looking to do that."

"So you don't consider yourself an 'investigative reporter?'" I replied.

"No," he said. "I don't consider myself a rumormonger like the *Daily Sketch*. If you want to investigate my credentials before you talk to me, be my guest. I have nothing to hide."

"Nor do I. I have no problem looking anyone, friend or former enemy, in the eye."

That was our introduction to one another. Over the next several days we met, usually at my apartment or in Foley's room at a nearby high-rise hotel. I talked, he listened. He never poked nor prodded. I opened up to him to the degree I thought prudent, and provided him with a fairly accurate recollection of my early life, omitting some private matters, such as my relationship with Lisbeth Hollander, up to the time of my escape from the authorities after my trial at Dachau. He never asked for anything beyond that timeframe and I didn't volunteer anything after then.

When his book, *Commando Extraordinary*, was published by an English publishing house, Longman-Green, a short time later, I was pleased, although a little embarrassed by the extent of its laudatory tone. The following year, he moved to Cyprus and took over the *Cyprus Times* newspaper. We remained in touch, albeit infrequently, since both of us had moved on in our lives. I feel we respected one another, including each other's privacy.

Twenty years later, at a time when I was quite ill, I was approached by the venerable French publisher *Editions Albin Michel* and asked to write an autobiography about my Commando adventures. Once again, I chose to write because the Paris house agreed to my conditions – nothing solid after my escape in 1948. I alluded to wild speculation that had been made about my many perceived "careers," but post-1948 facts remained hidden until now.

At this point in my life, however, it is time for me to disclose my *true* postwar life, shorn of sanctimonious pretense or coverup, so that the one or two people who will even remember my name may know that there lived an unrepentant German patriot who was loyal to the end, and who recognized that soldiers, regardless of what government they might serve, are, on the whole, the most honorable of men.

22

Friends outside the camp had arranged for a suitcase and tickets to be waiting at a tiny stop, not even a station, ten miles from Darmstadt. I discarded my prison coveralls and changed in a nearby wood, then took the train to Stuttgart. By next day, I arrived at Berchtesgaden, in the high mountains that would have been Hitler's last redoubt.

For some time, I wondered how my escape would be taken. I'm sure the German authorities were relieved that I was out of their hair and that they would not be required to weigh in on my future. While they had nothing against me, the release of "the most dangerous man in Europe" might adversely impact the flow of Allied goods to the Federal Republic of Germany. I elected to remain "out of sight" until the fuss was over and my countrymen were relieved of their obligation to rearrest me.

Still, I refused to go into hiding. A bottle of hydrogen peroxide was the answer. Snapshots taken of me at that time show a blond-haired giant hugging his daughter, who'd come to Berchtesgaden to visit. I spent months sunbathing, climbing in the Alps, boating, and felling trees. I was relaxed and content, recuperating from stresses to which I'd refused to admit.

By March 1949, I was ready to broaden my horizons, since, by then, my escape had largely been forgotten. I drove openly throughout West Germany, seeking out my wartime comrades. The prewar magic between Emmi and me had evaporated, and while we still respected one another and concentrated on being the best parents to Waltraut we could be, the specter of continuing to live together as husband and wife did not appeal to either of us. We parted amicably in May.

While much has been made in the press about *Das Organization der Ehemaligen SS-Angehörigen*, ODESSA, the so-called Organization of former SS Members, an alleged international Nazi underground organization which facilitated secret escape routes, "ratlines," to allow the SS members to escape to Argentina, Brazil, or the Middle East under false names, no one has ever been able to furnish concrete evidence such a network ever existed. Although I can verify that such an organization did, in fact, exist, it never realistically functioned under that name. Just as every organized crime organization was collectively known as "the mafia" - it was never known to the families who were loosely organized within its umbrella as such – the name "ODESSA" was a code word used to mask the true identity and functioning elements of those that helped our former comrades escape to new lives.

Another widely-used pseudonym for an organization I helped found, and in which I remained active for several years, was *Die Spinne* – The Spider, whose real name is now irrelevant. This group, which operated independent of, but within the umbrella organization, actually gave over 600 former Waffen-SS members a second chance after the collapse of the Third Reich.

On June 15, 1949, I met with Reinhard Gehlen, Hitler's former chief intelligence officer, at Gmunden, a hypnotically beautiful health resort in Upper Austria, halfway between Salzburg and Linz. Each of us boarded the Traunsee ferry separately, nodded to each other perfunctorily, and moved to the inside seats, since it was windy and rather chilly on the large lake. There were no more than half a dozen passengers headed toward Ebensee on the southern end of the lake.

After ascertaining that none of the passengers were in hearing distance, Gehlen, who was wearing an Alpine hat and *kniebundhosen*, knee-length *lederhosen*, approached me. On anyone else, such an outfit would have looked laughable. But Reinhard Gehlen looked so *average*, so unobtrusive that he could have been wearing the most outrageous outfit and ten seconds after you met him, you'd forget him. He truly could have "disappeared into the wall."

"Excuse me," he said. "Are you by some chance Otto Steinbauer?"

"No, sir, I fear you are mistaken. My name is Steinbacher, Robert Steinbacher," I replied, noncommittally. Gehlen well knew I used those two names interchangeably when I was about my current business.

"Since there are so few of us on this delightful journey, do you mind if I seat myself next to you? The journey is long and I could use someone to talk to."

"Suit yourself." I added, more quietly, "Quite a career move you've made, my friend. How're things going between you and your new employers?"

"They can't believe their good fortune. Now that the bear and the eagle are combatants in the cold war, the Americans feel they've plucked a real plum when I gave them access to my anti-bolshevik network. Beats the hell out of prison," he added.

I lit up an American Phillip Morris cigarette, offered him one, which he accepted, and gazed out the window at the incredibly blue lake. "I don't blame them. You've always thought two moves ahead. It was your idea to convene the meeting and invite me to attend."

"Ah, yes, almost five years ago," the spymaster said. "August 10, 1944, the *Maison Rouge* hotel in Strasbourg. Emil Kirdorf, the coal tycoon, Georg von Schnitzler of I.G. Farben, Gustav Krupp von Bohlen und Halbach, Fritz Thyssen, Kurt von Schroeder, you and I. It was no secret to me that Germany's assets would fall into the hands of the enemy if they weren't transferred and hidden. I'd filled you in on the idea a few days before, when I enlisted you in the *Deutsche Hilfsverein*."

"Which has gone through many changes of name since then. I can't say I wasn't intrigued by the idea, since I thought the collapse was, at most, a few months away. How did you come up with the idea that I would be the one who "loaned" big money to German industrialists so they could set up secret post-war operations abroad?"

"Simple, Otto. You were so high-profile, what with the Gran Sasso operation, Friedenthal, Horthy, and all, that the last person anyone would suspect of doing quiet work would be you."

"And in exchange, the powers-that-be demanded that the 'collateral' for such loans be made available overseas to fund former Party members and Waffen-SS soldiers in their quest for a new life."

Gehlen abruptly changed the subject. "How many did you help escape?"

"Three hundred eighty-seven, more or less. From Memmingen, Bavaria, through Austria and Switzerland, and into Italy, from where they dispersed to Spain, Argentina, Paraguay, Chile, and the Arab Middle East."

"Do you mind telling me how you organized it, not that the details matter at this late date?"

"Not at all. We used German drivers who'd had been hired to drive U.S. Army trucks on the autobahn between Munich and Salzburg for the *Stars and Stripes*, the American Army newspaper. They'd applied for their jobs under false names, and the Americans in Munich didn't check them carefully, 'cause they satisfied the two most important needs: cheap and efficient. We set up ports of call, along the entire Austro-German border, and an export-import company in Lindau, with representatives in Cairo and Damascus."

The water grew choppy and the sound of the ferry's engines increased as the boat struggled to break free of the momentary rough waters.

"Interesting choice of headquarters, Gmunden, Ebensee…"

"Actually, quite logical, *Generalmajor*," I replied, using his former Reich military rank. "Little did the Allies know that inmates of the concentration camp, who were being killed off by overwork, were building tunnels for storing armaments, V-2 parts, and … other things."

"Eight hundred million dollars, which have since been exported elsewhere," the former intelligence chief said. "Which, by the way, is the reason I wanted to meet with you."

"I'm listening," I said, with interest.

"You've pretty well finished the major part of moving our friends to their new homes. It's time you were getting on to other ventures in a new venue. How well do you know Ilse Lühtje?"

"The Countess von Finckenstein? Another of Hjalmar Schacht's 'nieces.' I just parted from another one of those ladies. I've met her once or twice at events Emmi and I attended."

"Nice woman. Bright," Gehlen responded. "Thirty-two, a decade younger than you, previously married to Graf Adolf Finck von Finckenstein, and certainly attractive enough. It might be a wise, not to mention pleasurable, interlude to stay at her villa for a couple of months."

"While you're planning my next move?"

"Yes. The Finckenstein and Schacht families are close with Alfried Krupp, whose company controlled 138 private concentration camps under the Third Reich. We believe it would be a wise move for Krupp A.G. to name you as its representative in industrial business ventures in Argentina. It should take no more than sixty days to arrange things. While you're relaxing, you might want to bone up on the Péróns."

At that moment, the ferry's horn hooted that we were approaching the dock at Ebensee. "Ah, I fear I must leave you here, Herr Steinbacher. It was a pleasure making your acquaintance. Perhaps one day we shall meet again. *Auf Wiedersehen.*"

Indeed, Ilse Lühtje, Countess von Finckenstein, was a charming and gracious hostess. Ilse's first husband, the Graf Adolf, had been several years her senior and, as she amply and convincingly demonstrated during our time together, she relished the idea of being with a man she considered to be in his prime. She certainly made me feel that way. For my own purposes, while my memories of Lisbeth Hollander never quite faded, and the last years with Emmi had been far from passionate, as Reinhard Gehlen had presciently stated, Ilse provided a most pleasurable diversion from my prior postwar activities.

23

On February 14, 1950, Emmi and I filed for an uncontested, amicable divorce. Next day, I flew from Munich to Madrid. It took five more days and four stops, Nouakchott, Monrovia, Natal, and Rio Di Janeiro, before I reached Ministro Pistarini International Airport in Buenos Aires after 32 uncomfortable hours in unpressurized Iberia and Aerolineas Argentinas DC-4 airliners.

Johann Mehrholz, Krupp's representative, greeted me at the airport. Noticing my post-flight pallor and my obvious exhaustion, he'd thoughtfully commissioned a limousine to take me straightaway to the Alvear Palace Hotel in the upscale Recoleta District. I spent the next twelve hours in well-deserved and much-needed sleep. After a marvelous buffet breakfast with my host of the previous evening, I felt fit and ready to assume my duties as Krupp's Argentine agent.

"Precisely what will my duties be?" I asked Krupp's man, who was a touch older than me, fit, with thinning hair. "No call for weapons nowadays, I take it?"

My host looked at me sidewise. "There'll always be a market throughout the world for Krupp arms. They're as necessary as food, clothing, and shelter. You've never been briefed on the real reason you're here, Herr Skorzeny?"

"Exactly why I asked, Doktor Mehrholz." We'd left the hotel and entered a two-tone tan and black Chevrolet Styleline, impressive but nothing that would stand out on the wide street abutting my lodgings.

"It has nothing to do with steel," he replied.

"So I gathered."

"You're aware Perón is holding eight-hundred million U.S. dollars as 'security' for the ten thousand blank Argentine passports he issued to our people in Barcelona and Madrid?"

"*Our* people? I trust you're ODESSA and your name's not Mchrholz."

"*Natürlich*. But it's sufficient for our purposes."

"Which are?"

"To retrieve the money that Krupp and others have 'loaned' General Perón to assist him in his wonderfully progressive programs."

"Re-election," I remarked sardonically.

At that moment my eyes widened as we turned onto the broadest road I'd ever seen.

"Avenida 9 de Julio," Mehrholz said. "The widest road in the world. Twice the width of the largest autobahn." Moments later, he pointed out a huge tower I estimated to be over two hundred feet tall. "The *Obelisco de Buenos Aires,* built by a good German conglomerate, Siemens Bauunion - Grün & Bilfinger. Something you as an engineer might appreciate."

"You've familiarized yourself with me."

"Who hasn't? It's a little bit hard to conceal you. I noticed your *schmiss* has softened since the war."

"Just age and," I said, patting my stomach, "good, solid German food."

"You won't get a chance to miss such fare here, Obersturmbahnführer."

"Gehlen told me there are a hundred German restaurants in Buenos Aires."

"More than that, Herr Skorzeny. But we've got a different destination in mind. Ten days from now, we're supposed to meet El Présidente in Bariloche, over a thousand miles southwest of here. I think you'll find the town very much to your liking."

Mehrholz's claim that I'd like Bariloche turned out to be an understatement. Situated in the foothills of the Andes in the midst of a chain of lakes stretching 75 miles to the Chilean border, it was so reminiscent of the Salzkammergut that I could swear the place had been bodily transplanted from Austria. With its Alpine-style architecture, the mid-sized city, with its nearby skiing, trekking, and mountaineering facilities, reminded me so much of Salzburg that I became momentarily certain I was back home.

Doktor Mehrholz told me he had arrangements to make for our meeting with President Péron tomorrow morning and that I should use the next couple of hour to familiarize myself with the town before meeting him at Villa Huinid Lodge.

"Avenida Gral San Martin's probably as good a shopping street as any, and it's close enough to the hotel that it's an easy walk. Plus, you'll be close enough to Rio Negro to enjoy a fine breeze off the lake."

I've never been much enthused by shopping. By the time I'd been walking twenty minutes, having passed shop after shop seeing an endless stream of storefront windows filled with chocolate or peculiar gnomes of all sizes, which were sold in nearly every shop downtown, I'd become bored. Flying into San Carlos de Bariloche Airport, I'd been amazed at the sheer beauty of the lakes and the not-so-distant Andes. I thought it might be more interesting to escape the rabbit warren of shopping streets perhaps find a quayside café to pass the time.

I'd not walked long or far when I felt, rather than saw, a presence beside me. My commando experiences had taught me to stay cool and alert to visual and other nuances. Thus, without turning my head or making eye contact of any kind, I was able to see enough of the man beside me through storefront windows to surmise with some accuracy who was walking beside me. He was about ten years older and four inches shorter than me.

"Do I detect the American bandleader, Louis Prima?" I said offhandedly, neither changing my pace nor looking to my right.

The other man surprised me with his own shrewd response. In perfect German he said, "At least I didn't gain such an ugly *schmiss* when I tried my hand at *mensur.*"

We continued feeling one another out without once looking at each other.

"You may have been the fencing champion of your infantry unit, but I doubt you ever engaged in *mensur, Coronel*," I said, referring to him by his military rank rather than his position."

"Perhaps not," he rejoined, "but I'll pay for coffee in far more conducive surroundings than Gran Sasso or Belgium if you'd care to join me where we can sit at a table and meet each other face to face."

"*Touché*, Señor Presidente."

"Juan."

"Otto."

"Feliz de conocerte, Otto."

"Mi privilegio, Señor Presidente."

And that was how I met President Juan Domingo Péron.

For the next hour or so, we cautiously, but optimistically, spoke of many things, from Péron's admiration for Fascism and the National Socialist policies of Der Führer to his conscious harboring of the largest Jewish community in South America. He felt Argentina would best survive and prosper by walking a middle road between socialism and capitalism, without becoming embroiled in any nation's politics.

"But won't that line of reasoning alienate everyone?" I asked at one point.

"It might, but for the present, my country enjoys the strongest economy in the region, perhaps only second in the Americas to the United States. Three years ago, we instituted universal health care for all our citizens. Since last year every working class Argentinian has been covered by social security."

"All well and good, Presidente, but the United States is not that happy with you, and they have a reputation for interfering in what they call 'banana republic' politics. You obviously know how United Fruit made Central America its puppet for years."

It was then that our talk veered toward security.

"I'm not unfamiliar with your Friedenthal methods, Obersturmbahnfüher. I'm told you once advised Hitler himself how any dedicated operation could break through the security at the Wolf's Lair."

"Anyone whose motivation is strong enough can crack the security of any facility."

"Which is one of the reasons I wanted to meet you in person, and, quite frankly, before our formal meeting tomorrow with Rheingold and our present security chief."

"Rheingold?"

"Ah, I forgot. You probably know him as Mehrholz and he's ostensibly working for your great steel company, Krupp."

"Seems you're one step ahead of me, Mister President."

"I'm not saying our own security agencies are lacking, Colonel Skorzeny. I am saying that in politics, as in many aspects of life, there is always a *quid pro quo*."

I seized upon what the cagey Péron was saying immediately.

"Shall we cut through the political doubletalk, Presidente?"

"I'd be happy to listen your theories, Otto Skorzeny, although you know that I won't necessarily show my cards."

"Very well. You have something we want – eight hundred million dollars of our seed money, in bank deposits, 2500 kilograms of gold, 90 kilograms of platinum, and 4600 carats of diamonds and other precious stones, which you've sequestered in banks around Buenos Aires in your wife's name. We have something you want. Like any Latin American dictator – and I'm happy to call a spade a 'shit shovel' – you know that the continuation of your own position is a function of the best *security* your government can offer. You know my background, I know yours. Eight hundred million is not a particularly steep price to pay for 'insurance,' particularly when the Bormann treasure was ours to begin with."

The man fingered his chin reflectively for a few moments, savoring what I'd said. Finally he spoke. "*Cojones*," he said, "I'll certainly give that to you."

"Thank you," I responded good-humoredly. "But I already have two of my own."

He grinned. Wolfishly, I thought.

"You're forgetting, Herr Skorzeny, the ten thousand blank passports. Putting the treasure in our safekeeping for a little while is certainly a bargain to save the lives of ten thousand Waffen-SS fugitives on the run from American, English, and French, not to mention Soviet Russian 'justice.'"

"So, Juan Domingo, do you think we can cut a deal?"

"I think so, my friend. And now it's time for you to be getting back to 'Doktor Mehrholz,' in time for both of us to be fresh when we meet for the first time tomorrow.

And that is how I came to work for the Pérons for the next year.

During my tenure with the Pérons, I attended several meetings with Austrian and German compatriots, now resident in the Argentine capital. Generally hosted by sympathetic clergymen, Bishops Caggiano and Barrére, several Roman Catholic noteworthies, most notably Cardinal Tisserant, Father Krunoslav Draganović, who had organized the earliest ratlines while the Ustaše were still in power in Croatia, and the inimitable Bishop Alois Hudal, National Socialism's greatest champion in Germany and Austria, often flew to Buenos Aires to discuss the status of my countrymen, who had discovered new lives in the South American safe havens. On one such occasion, I went to a top-secret meeting in a tiny German Bierstube in the remote hills ten miles beyond the city limits, with Juan Péron's intelligence chief, Ludwig Freude,

I was amazed to see how many SS luminaries were openly in attendance: Adolf Eichmann, who'd changed his name to Ricardo Klement by that time; Erich Priebke, Eduard Roschmann, and Ante Pavelić, who'd moved to Patagonia and retained their original names; and Josef Mengele, who'd obtained a passport from the International Committee of the Red Cross identifying him as Helmut Gregor.

After a spectacular repast of *Rouladen, Sauerbraten,* red cabbage, and home-friend potatoes, accompanied by several light Rieslings, we finished off the festive meal with Black Forest cherry-torte, before breaking into serious pilsners and boisterous singing.

As the evening wore on, lips loosened. Freude and I, who were nursing our huge steins rather than refilling them, were able to surreptitiously make notes or commit to memory much news concerning our "expatriate" communities in Argentina, Chile, Paraguay, and Brazil.

"The ratlines are fraying," Ludwig said quietly, referring to the exit routes that had been used by our *landsmen* to escape the dragnets of the allied authorities during the immediate postwar years. "So far nine thousand have escaped."

"No need to escape anymore," I said. "Lots of National Socialists have become respected members of West German society, now that Americans, Brits, and even Frenchmen have finally learned the communists are the real enemy. If only they'd realized that before ..."

"A lot of us have become quite comfortable here. Look how high we've climbed the ladder in such a short time, Skorzeny. You intending to make it permanent?"

"Don't know yet," I replied noncommittally. "Depends on how firmly entrenched our present employer remains – and how firmly he remains committed to his present love for things German."

"Lots of Jews in this burg," my associate remarked.

"Moths are always attracted to the flame. Don't forget, until the National Socialist administration no country in Europe gave its Jews such a good life. Who knows how long they'll want to remain here now that they've got a place of their own."

"I don't know how to answer that, Otto. For now, I'm the guy in charge of knowing everything that's going on, and you're the 'independent contractor' who makes sure El Presidente sits firmly on the seat of power and his head sits firmly on his shoulders."

As we drove home in the wee hours of the morning, far less inebriated than most of the other attendees, we compared mental notes about the latest safe settlements for our brethren: Bariloche and Buenos Aires, of course. More than half of the newest South American arrivals resided in Péron's territory. A thousand each had made it to Brazil and Chile; the rest claimed safety in the wealthiest South American nation, Uruguay, in the poorest, Alfredo Stroessner's Paraguay, and in Bolivia.

"What amazes me most, Ludwig, is how many of our people don't bother to hide or look over their shoulders when there've got to be spies, diplomats, even strongarm types everywhere who undoubtedly would like to bring them to a bad end."

"Why should that surprise you?" my companion said. "It's the same everywhere, in every generation. The latest scandal is delicious and exciting for sixty, maybe ninety days at most, and then we wait for a new scandal to erupt and titillate us. Face it, Otto, every man is really only interested on what impacts his own life. They say millions of Jews were killed during the Regime, and the English and the Americans made a big deal about it at the time. But after the War, exactly how much did the Brits do to let as many Jews as were left into Israel?"

"Not many. Britain did its best to cozy up to the oil sheikhs, and once the survivors of the camps kicked the living shit out of the ragheads who'd lived on that land for centuries, they suddenly became 'our poor, oppressed Arab brothers.'"

Freude lit up two cigarettes and handed one to me. "What percentage of emigres from the fallen Reich do you think still use their real names?"

I puffed contentedly for a few moments before hazarding a guess. "Ten, maybe twenty percent?"

"Closer to seventy," he said. "Don't forget, I'm the intelligence chief. I'm paid to know this stuff. By the way, the same percentages apply in Deutschland, at least in the FRG."

"Not in the DDR?"

"I don't know the figures there."

"Come on, Ludwig, you intelligence types are all brothers in the trade."

"Maybe, but the Stasi's very much under Uncle Joe's thumb."

As we pulled into the driveway adjacent to my residence, Freude added, "As long as our *kameraden* do as well as they seem to be doing, that's all that really matters, isn't it?"

24

Juan Péron and I got on famously from the start, I suppose because under the skin we were two of a kind: opportunists, risk-takers, and adventurers. Once I'd broached the subject of the Bormann treasure, neither of us mentioned anything about that very substantial cache again. Presidente Peron readily accepted my offer to help maintain order in the country. One result of my assistance was my opening of a private "academy" on the outskirts of the capital, a sort of specialized Friedenthal operation, where my trainees, an elite corps of Argentine police, security, and intelligence officers, became quite versed in National Socialist methods of "persuasion" and interrogation. It was not long before most of the unruly mobs and boisterous dissidents of Buenos Aires became quite docile and law-abiding.

The First Lady, María Eva Duarte, twenty-four years younger than her husband, was a different kettle of fish, who'd escaped the dreary life of Los Toldos, a village in the Pampas. The youngest of five children, she'd moved to B.A. in 1934, when she was fifteen, to become an actress. She met her widower lover, then an Army Colonel, ten years later. From the start, he wanted to make her more than his mistress. Péron married her a year later and the following year, 1946, while I was in a German prison awaiting a trial which, it seemed, was never going to take place, he ascended to the presidency.

Despite her pretensions to be the champion of the poor, the angel of mercy, my first impression of Evita was that she was a social-climbing vixen, albeit, at 30, a very sexy one. Despite her husband's *bonhomie*, I surmised she was the brains of the family. While she'd never been anything but courteous to me, I was aware I'd have to earn her trust, since hers were the hands that held the keys to the treasure my countrymen so coveted.

In July 1949, my opportunity presented itself. I received word from one of my well-placed informers in the Ministry of Defense that two recently cashiered Argentine naval officers were planning to kidnap and murder the first lady.

Although this informant had never failed me, I was loath to take the word of a single source. My "Argentine Friedenthalers" included experts in surveillance and the latest bugging techniques, as well as interrogators and criminal psychologists. Over the next two weeks, my minuscule army of experts confirmed the truth of what my man in the Ministry had told me. A few evenings later, I led an unpublicized police raid on the men's apartment, where I found guns, ammunition, and details of the hit.

Early the following morning, I secured an audience with the President's wife, who was no less popular in Argentina than the near-sanctified Eleanor Roosevelt was in the United States.

"Madame Péron, thank you for seeing me this early. As your husband's security adviser I would not have bothered you with trivial matters while the Presidente is away on business, but this concerns you directly."

"Would you like coffee? Tea?"

"Coffee, if you please."

A few moments later, no doubt accomplished by her pressing a buzzer I knew had been installed under the top of her desk, a middle-aged woman in spotless, pressed white uniform wheeled in a cart bearing two Meissen pots, a creamer, cups and saucers, plates, and an assortment of pastries. The woman poured coffee for each of us,

"You may proceed, Herr Skorzeny," she said coolly, and, I thought, a bit haughtily.

I ignored her superciliousness and continued respectfully. "Madame, my … associates …have learned of a serous plot to kidnap you and to do you great bodily harm."

"I'm listening."

I went on to detail what I'd unearthed and how I'd found out about the proposed crime.

"Did you arrest the perpetrators?" she asked, raising perfectly-shaped eyebrows slightly.

"Our police inspectors are in process of searching for them, even as we speak, Madame Presidente. Unfortunately, they must have seen my law enforcement agents surrounding their apartment house and never returned to their residence. But I'm certain it's only a matter of hours before we find them."

"I see." She reached for a cigarette in a glass case on her desktop. I snapped my lighter and reached out to assist her. "You know, of course, that my husband and I hear of such plots several times a month?"

"I do, My Lady. As your husband's security adviser, it's my job to hear of such things and to be prepared to combat them."

"How tall are you, Mister Skorzeny."

"Six-foot-four."

I felt no discomfort at this question. I'd been asked about my height since I was seventeen. Although Eva Duarte Péron was a very attractive woman, there was none of the electricity I'd felt twenty years before, when Lisbeth Hollander and I had begun our relationship. I didn't view the President's wife as a higher being, to be placed on a pedestal. The fact that she had succeeded in marrying my employer, who happened to be in a position to influence the lives of several million people, among whom were thousands who'd served with me under Adolf Hitler, made her no better nor worse than me.

"But I digress, Señor Skorzeny," she continued. I noticed she had addressed me first as Herr, then as Mister, then in the more familiar Spanish, never once acknowledging my military rank, which was similar to that of her husband. "You believe you're close to capturing these … people?"

"I do."

"Then what caused you to seek me out this morning? Why not simply capture then and be done with?"

I looked at her levelly. "Simply because your safety is important to your husband and thus to me. And because these men, who I assume are both intelligent and dangerous, are still at large."

"All right, I accept what you say. While I don't perceive I am in significantly more immediate danger than any other day in my life, I'm scheduled to visit the Little Sisters of Charity Home for the Aged within the hour. Perhaps we might both feel safer if you'd care to accompany me?"

"As you wish, Madame Péron."

Shortly thereafter, an official-looking factotum knocked sharply on the door to her office, to announce that the limousine was waiting downstairs. Within ten minutes, we were on our way into a poorer *barrio.*

As we approached our destination, I saw three police cruisers approaching a nondescript three-story building. As our limousine came closer to the building, I directed the chauffeur to slow down, then to stop.

"Something wrong?" the passenger asked.

"Probably not, Madame," I responded. "But I've been a commando in many situations and sometimes I get a third sense of ..."

At that moment, the unmistakable sound of gunfire erupted. I pushed open the right rear door of the limousine, jumped out of the car, and said, in a tone of voice I'd used many times in the past to calm my troops, "Madame Presidente, I'm going to close this door. Please lock it immediately, then lie down and cover yourself so no one will see you."

"Herr Skorzeny, is this some sort of a joke?" she asked calmly. "Because if it is ..."

A much closer, louder noise interrupted her in mid-sentence as a bullet pierced the right front fender, followed by a *hisss* as another punctured the rear tire. As Evita Péron quickly obeyed my instructions to her, I ran toward the police cruisers, exposing my own sidearm, then entered the building.

It was over in a matter of seconds. I emerged from the building moments later, holding two men at gunpoint. At a signal from me, the police surrounded my captives, manhandled them into a squad car, and left the area, sirens blaring. I was not even breathing hard. I returned to the limousine, knocked lightly on the window, and gave no indication that I knew the wide-eyed First Lady had been watching the entire scene as it unfolded.

After a phalanx of the President's staff arrived, escorting a replacement limousine, we continued on our way. The visit to the First Lady's charity went off without further hitch, and she thereafter asked her husband to invest me with the additional duty as her personal bodyguard.

I thought it only prudent not to mention that the entire event had been staged. The two assailants had been captured and placed in the building several hours earlier by former SS comrades, the "police," whom I had quietly dispatched after the "raid." But the payoff for the charade was worth it, for I had now irreversibly gained her trust.

"Face it, you might be a big fellow, but you're by no means the best looking stud in the stable."

"As if that matters to you. The saintliest woman in the world and you need to screw as much as any fishwife." I slapped her gently, playfully across her voluptuous bottom.

"You'd say such a thing to the First Lady of Argentina?"

"Hell yes, and you know you love it."

The nicest thing about the relationship after we'd become lovers was that we'd become *friends*. There was no talk of eternal faithfulness, no protestations of love, no need to possess or control one another, and no outward change in our lives. Her marriage to Juan Péron, contrary to the overt sense of affection shown to their adoring public, was political, the power of one augmenting the influence of the other.

"How long do you think you'll stay in Argentina?" she asked seriously.

"Ludwig Freude asked me the same question some months back. Do I look like the kind who'd become impatient staying in one place?"

"Hell, yes. You know the answer as well as I do. I'll miss you, you know."

"It goes without saying I'll feel the same way if and when that happens. You're one hell of a woman, Eva, and I'm sure you've been told that many times before. You'll never want for anyone, whether it be a man or an entire country, to adore you. You're far more than a good lay, and I mean that sincerely. If we're together one more day or twenty more years, we'll never know. Chances are you'll be around far longer than I will, but only God knows the answer to that."

"You're quite the philosopher, Obersturmbahnführer Shorzeny," she said, ruffling the hair on my chest.

"Have you considered what I asked you last week?"

"Ahh, now we get down to business. Surely you're not after me for my money," she said, laughing.

"As a matter of fact ..."

"I know, I know. Your people are claiming it's *their* money, but I'm sure in today's topsy-turvy political world the present government in FRG, and certainly those in the worker's paradise would differ sharply. Don't look at me like that, lover, I have no intention of turning any part of it over to either of them, but my husband and I need to live, too. Not to say our adoring people would ever think of a time when Juan would not be the Father of his Country, but just in case ..."

"Fifty-fifty, Evita? Four hundred million now, the rest in ten years?"

"I was thinking more along the lines of a hundred million now and three over the next twenty years. Call the other four hundred *quid-pro-quo* for a boatload, you should pardon the pun, of Argentine and Spanish passports or call it a long-term tax deductible donation to the Eva Péron Foundation. I really don't care what you call it, but you've seen as well as I how well your fellow Germans are doing, and you're not a stupid man, Otto. You know exactly why."

I did. My countrymen were highly placed in positions of power and influence. When the United States turned cool toward Argentine exports, German companies had taken up the slack, and trade was remarkably brisk between the Federal Republic and what was then the wealthiest country in South America. Still ...

"Two now, the rest in 1955, with no interest – you keep whatever interest the bank will pay you, for yourselves."

"Fair enough," she said. She squeezed her magnificent breasts, splayed her long, shapely legs and reached down lustfully toward me. "Shall we seal the deal?"

"I see no reason why not," I said, hardening to her touch.

And we did.

Within two weeks, I was able to report to Gehlen that two hundred million dollars had been transferred to a numbered account in the Union Bank of Switzerland, which, at that time, still scrupulously honored Swiss secrecy laws, much to the confidence placed in it by its depositors, and even more to the benefit of its shareholders.

During the next nine months, "Robert Steinbacher" or "Otto Steinbauer," traveling on Spanish "Nansen passports" issued by Franco's government to "stateless persons" who had been "Denazified," shuttled between Madrid and Buenos Aires several times, tending to the international business interests of Krupp, I.G. Farben, and similar German companies, and to the security of the Péron government.

Alas, my offhand statement to her that she'd be around far longer than me turned out to be tragically wrong. Less than four months after we'd made love for the last time, Evita fainted in public and underwent surgery three days later. Although it was reported that she had undergone an appendectomy, she was diagnosed with advanced cervical cancer. To my horror, I experienced that her fainting continued through 1950. She confided in me that she felt extremely weak and was suffering severe vaginal bleeding. By 1951, it had become evident to me that her health was rapidly deteriorating. Although Juan and I withheld from her what we knew to be her true condition, she was no fool and knew she was not well.

Early in 1952, Evita underwent a secret radical hysterectomy performed by an American surgeon, in an attempt to eradicate her advanced cervical cancer. Unfortunately, it had metastasized and returned rapidly. She was the first Argentine to undergo an experimental new treatment, chemotherapy, but despite all available treatment, when I saw her for the last time on June 4, 1952 as she rode with her husband in a parade celebrating his re-election as President of Argentina, Evita weighed only seventy-nine pounds. I know, because I had helped dress her for the celebration. By that point, she was so ill she was unable to stand without support. Underneath her oversized fur coat her dresser and I had installed a frame made of plaster and wire that allowed her to stand. I administered a triple dose of the strongest pain medication short of morphine to her, before the parade, and gave her another two doses when she returned home.

On July 26, 1952, two months and nineteen days after her thirty-third birthday, Eva Duarte de Péron, the eternal First Lady of Argentina, who had been, for however short a time, my lover and my friend, died at 8:25 in the evening. Radio broadcasts throughout the country were interrupted with the announcement that "The Press Secretary's Office of the Presidency of the Nation fulfills its very sad duty to inform the people of the Republic that Mrs. Eva Péron, Spiritual Leader of the Nation, has died."

Over three million mourners attended her funeral, congesting the streets for ten blocks in each direction. During the time we'd spent together, I found her to be everything – good and not so good – that could make up an incredible human being. Yes, she was the ultimate social climber, and once she had risen from the gutter to the stars she assumed airs and graces consonant to her position. She was shrewd, immensely cunning, and self-possessed. But conversely, she was one of the kindest and greatest women I've ever known – and, yes, she was sexy as hell. And I missed her for the times we had, good and bad, from that day forward.

25

On Thursday. July 2, 1952, Reinhard Gehlen asked me to join him at Gmunden. It was the kind of day the Austrian Department of Tourism loves to photograph for travel posters: a sky so blue it challenged the Traunsee, gentle whitecaps that reflected the small, puffy clouds scudding toward the Alps, and that quality of sunlight that can be found only in the Salzkammergut on a midsummer's day.

There was no need for us to use assumed names any longer. Memories of World War II were rapidly fading as the Cold War had taken center stage in world politics. Former Head of Reich Intelligence, Major General Gehlen was now highly-placed in the American CIA and the Gehlen Organization, known simply as the "Org," constituted the eyes and ears of the United States in Eastern Europe.

"Thank you for coming on such short notice," he began. "I don't need to tell you how much I appreciated your retrieving $200 million from Eva Péron. It not only helped our emigrés, but now that our comrades are making their fortunes in Latin American it is no longer necessary to fund them. We can actually start paying back our sponsors, increasing our credibility for ... other projects."

"She's dying, Reinhard."

"I know. I'm sorry. I didn't want to mention that at this time. Did you love her?"

"Love is a very elastic word in our kind of lives, Generalmajor. Let's just say that to the extent people of our stripe can, I cared about her a great deal. But I'm sure you didn't summon me here to commiserate with me about Evita or to enhance your own reputation as a money man. You mentioned 'other projects.'"

"I did, Otto. What do you know about Farouk bin Fuad, by the grace of God, King of Egypt and the Sudan, Sovereign of Nubia, of Kordofan and of Darfur?"

"He's managed to survive on the throne for sixteen years, but I don't know how long that'll last, particularly with his smart-mouthed comment last year, 'The whole world is in revolt. Soon there will be only five Kings left — the King of England, the King of Spades, the King of Clubs, the King of Hearts, and the King of Diamonds.'"

"Bit of a shit as a ruler," Gehlen responded.

"You know something. Otherwise you wouldn't have invited me to a lovely peaceful voyage on the Traunsee. How long will it be before … ?"

"Three weeks."

"Naguib, Nasser, and the Free Officers?"

"Uh-huh,"

As the wind was blowing off the port side of the ferry, I cupped the lighter in my hand and shielded it from the breeze as I lit a cigarette.

"So you want me to funnel part of the two-hundred million down to them?"

"No. We need you in a different role."

"We?"

"The Federal Government."

"*Which* Federal Government?"

"Both. The Brits are unpopular in Egypt, which gives some cache to the Germans. The Egyptians suspect the Americans of being in Israel's pocket, so there's no love generated there. You're a bit of legend, but no one sees you as having loyalty to any players. In fact, the word is you're a whore."

"Nice," I said.

"Think of yourself as a *Rechtsanwalt*."

"A lawyer? I'd rather be a woman who spread my legs."

"Oh, come off it, Skorzeny. You think your shit doesn't stink? You think our *kameraden* in the East don't think I've sold out to our former enemies? They pay me well and I haven't spent a single day in some armpit jail or camp waiting for my number to come up."

"Okay. Let's say I buy into your story, Reinhard. By the way, you look quite natural in your new wardrobe. American civvies are certainly preferable to *lederhosen*."

He guffawed at that.

"For whom do I spread my legs, when do you want me to go, and do I screw or get screwed?"

"Six months, maybe a little more. Naguib. You do what you're best at."

"Training?"

"As the American comic Groucho Marx would say, 'Give the man a cigar.' Do you know anything about the Free Officers?"

"Can't say I do."

"Young middle-class workers, government officials, junior officers. As far as trained soldiers, not worth a sack of *dreck* in their present state. Mohammed Naguib, the figurehead president of the Committee, trained as a lawyer, but stayed in the military and rose through the ranks, becoming a Major General and a bit of a hero, even though the Arabs somehow failed to push the so-called Jew state into the sea."

"Sort of like the Reich Major General who defected to the other side?" I remarked, humorously, though not without its snide side.

"Hey, both of us survived," Gehlen remarked, deflecting my comment. "Like I said, Naguib's at least a general, but they're way short of trained combat troops. The best they can do is two Light-Colonels, Nasser, who's the real leader, and a guy named Anwar Sadat, who's pretty much in Nasser's shadow."

"And my job's to shape them up?"

"Exactly. You'll be Naguib's military adviser and our man on the ground in the land of the Pharaohs."

My first job was to recruit officers I knew and trusted from my days in the Waffen-SS. My initial staff choices for the third incarnation of Friedenthal included Wehrmacht General Wilhelm Fahrmbacher, a highly decorated Artillery General who'd commanded several corps and been awarded the Knight's Cross of the Iron Cross; Wehrmacht Major General Oskar Munzel, whom I had met while we were both being held for trial in Dachau, and with whom I'd established a close relationship; former SS Standartenführer Colonel Leopold Gleim, head of the Gestapo Department for Jewish Affairs in Poland; and Joachim Daemling, former chief of the Gestapo in Düsseldorf, who'd became a Consultant for the Egyptian penitentiary system and was an active member of Radio Cairo.

Although my top choices would, of course, have been Radl, von Fölkersam, and Hunke, they were either dead or no longer available to me. While there may have been better choices than the four with whom I ended up, I considered the old adage, "When in Rome ..."

The world, even the Soviets and especially the West Germans, had come to accept, and even promote, the State of Israel. But the

Egyptians, on whom the Arab world depended to a large degree, had been humiliated during the 1948 War that secured Israel's existence. Hatred for Jews in general and for the "nonexistent" state of Israel was so rampant under Naguib and Nasser, that the new leadership insured that ample copies of *Mein Kampf* and *The Protocols of the Elders of Zion* were virtually required reading.

Thus, for public relations purposes with my new employers, I found it necessary to recruit those with experience in dealing with Jews during the Second World War. Gleim fit the bill perfectly. After the war, he'd converted to Islam, taking the name of Ali al-Nahar. By the time I started looking for appropriate staff, Gleim had already been serving with the Egyptian state services for three years.

Munzel had been a highly decorated Generalmajor in the Wehrmacht during World War II, who had commanded several divisions. Like Fahrmbacher, he'd received the Knight's Cross of the Iron Cross in recognition of his extreme battlefield bravery and successful military leadership. Oskar Munzel was by no means as virulent as Gleim. Like me, he had served on the Russian front in 1941, on the Western Front toward the end of the war; and he'd been incarcerated until 1947. What made him most valuable to me, he'd already served in Egypt for a year, so he was familiar with the culture which I was about to enter.

My next task was to study the 1948 war in exhaustive detail: its strategy, tactics, and the degree to which commando warfare had been effective.

On November 29, 1947, the United Nations General Assembly had adopted a Partition Plan which would take effect at the conclusion of the British Mandate the following May: Palestine would be divided into three areas: an Arab state, a Jewish state, and the Special International Regime for the cities of Jerusalem and Bethlehem.

The General Assembly resolution on Partition was greeted with overwhelming joy in Jewish communities and widespread outrage in the Arab world. In Palestine, violence erupted almost immediately, feeding into a spiral of reprisals and counter-reprisals. The British refrained from intervening as tensions boiled over into a low-level conflict that quickly escalated into a full-scale civil war.

The British Mandate ended on May 14, 1948. Prime Minister Ben-Gurion declared the establishment of the Jewish State on that day. The following day, a combined invasion by Egypt, Jordan and Syria, together with expeditionary forces from Iraq, entered Palestine. The invading forces took control of the Arab areas and immediately attacked Israeli forces and Jewish settlements.

On the date the War started, Egypt had a population of 19,500,000. The Jews in Israel numbered slightly over 800,000. There were nearly twenty-five Egyptians to every Jew. With those odds, it made absolutely no sense to me that the Israelis had "won" the war. Over the next two weeks, two questions, "Why?" and "How?" occupied my mind. Even my commandos could not have surmounted those odds, which was why we operated as guerilla forces. But the Jewish experience in 1948 was not without a precedent. That had occurred two thousand years earlier, when the Maccabean force of 7,000 defeated 60,000 Persian troops.

Search as I might, I could find not a single Egyptian, nor, for that matter, a single Arab combatant, who fit the mold as a commando fighter. I approached Munzel on one of my pre-assignment trips to Cairo.

"*Generalmajor,*" I began. "What do you know of commando warfare during *al-Nakba?*"

"Ah, Otto, I see you've already learned the lingo. Of course, our employers use the words 'the catastrophe' only in referring to the previous administration or in private. The Egyptians have thousands of years of pride behind them, and they would never admit to being other than the children of the pharaohs. The plain and simple truth was the Israelis used their brains, their ability to call on the world's guilt over the War, and 'Skorzeny tactics' to squeeze every last ounce of toothpaste out of the tube."

"'Skorzeny tactics?'" I said, grinning. "I'm flattered."

"They tried many of the same tactics you used in Operation *Greif.*

"Seems they've got quite a few Otto Skorzneys," General Munzel said. "One in particular comes to mind."

"Who's that?"

"Guy by the name of Moshe Dayan."

"Never heard of him."

"There a lot of men like him you've never heard of. But from the way he operated, he sounds very much like you. Seems to like the long odds. Like you, he seems to believe it's not the size of the dog in the fight, but the size of the fight in the dog."

I grinned at that comment. "Can you give me an example?"

"Man, you are one ugly monster when you smile like that," Munzel remarked, but it was obvious to me he did not mean it as insult. "The best example I can give you is the battle for a city called Hebron."

"That's in Jordan," I replied.

"Today it is, after the armistice. It's was held sometimes by the Egyptians and sometimes by the Israelis during the Arab-Israeli war. But that's not the point. In the battle I'm talking about, back in '48, the Jews had five tanks and a few hundred men. The Arabs had ten times that many. A large hill stood between the Israeli forces and the city.

"Moshe Dayan, who's about ten years younger than you, by the way, sent the five tanks toward the city, but very widely spaced, so that one tank disappeared around the south side of the hill just as another tank was coming by way of a different road around the north side of the hill. The tanks never went directly into the city, but continued going around and around the hill. The Arabs assumed the Jews were massing a large number of tanks on the south side and they'd make an all-out attack on Hebron.

"Several supporters of the Jewish cause spoke the local Arab dialect fluently. They spread word throughout the marketplace: the Jews had sent hundreds of tanks and ten thousand troops to attack Hebron. The Arabs never thought to climb the hill and look, not that they had much of a chance to climb the hill, since the entire force of a few hundred Jews had set up a chain from one end of the summit to the other. So the Egyptians and their allies just watched as the Israeli tanks kept coming for two hours. The Arab forces surrendered without a shot ever being fired."

"Is this some kind of bullshit story?"

"Absolutely not," Munzel said. "Sound familiar?"

"Like you said, Operation *Greif.* But you've been working for the Egyptians, not the Israelis. How'd you find out about this Dayan fellow?"

"A lot of our *kameraden* have moved smoothly into FRG military. Your friend Gehlen works hand-in-hand with the American CIA, We Germans have always been smart enough to play both sides at the gaming table of international politics by keeping our eyes and ears open."

"But why would any Jew trust a single German after what happened in …?"

"Same old story," General Munzel replied. "The enemy of my enemy is my friend, when and if need be. And in pretty much universal language, 'Money talks, bullshit walks.' Who do you think are Israel's biggest supporters?"

"America, of course," I said.

"West Germany's not far behind. Our compatriots have acknowledged what happened and the Federal Bundestag has voted what will probably turn out to be billions of marks in 'reparations.' So, we share intelligence with all of today's bedfellows, and if we can make it look good, that doesn't harm us in the eyes of the world. Don't forget how the Reich used your Gran Sasso operation and milked it for headlines around the globe at a time when the Allies thought we were dead and awaiting our burial."

"Are these guys truly better than the ones we're supposed to train?"

"Truthfully, yes. From what I've seen of the Egyptian military, it's 'You go fight the battle and I'll sit back and support you,' whereas in Israel, the officers lead the charge and you'd better be right there fighting alongside of them – not because you'll be court-martialed or anything, but because there's a sense of 'We're all we've got.' In Egypt, a thousand men will die and it's an unfortunately large number. In the new Israeli state, every soldier is a precious human being, someone's father, son, husband, brother, family. Those Jews believe if you lose one man, you lose the universe; if you save one man, you save the universe."

"General, you sound like you support *them*."

"Frankly, Otto, we can train the Egyptian forces with everything we've learned, and I'd still wager that if it came down to war, the Israelis would find a way to win it."

"If they're as good as you say, why did so many of them … you know …"

"Different time, different conditions, maybe even a different kind of Jew. These survived and they're already spouting the slogan, 'Never Again!'"

"So, what are we doing working with the guys on this side?"

"Simple, Obersturnbahnführer. The Israelis will take all the money our West German government is willing to give them, but when it comes down to manpower, they'll accept no help from anyone. And, if you hadn't noticed, Egypt's not only a safe haven for our type of Germans, but they pay very well indeed for what we have to offer."

26

Once I had solidified my familiarity with the current political situation in Egypt, I started to design my training academy and what I felt was necessary to bring the regime's eager young military forces into the mid-twentieth century. To do this, I realized I would be dealing with troops whose history was one of lethargy in the heat of the Egyptian desert.

General Naguib had afforded me free rein as to where I wanted to set up my academy. My choice was not difficult. Friedenthal, my most successful operation to date, had been located in a suburb of Berlin, close to road and air facilities. But the political climate differed between National Socialist Germany and the Revolutionary Government of Naguib and Gamal Abdel Nasser. I envisioned a small cadre of highly-trained special forces, completely divorced from the bloated army that had guarded King Farouk. The locale would have to be far enough from Cairo and Alexandria so I could exercise my own independence.

When I'd been growing up, I'd read ancient plays and stories set in Thebes, which I'd always thought was some imaginary locale. I was surprised to find there was a real Thebes, modern-day Luxor, which served my purposes perfectly. Although it is one of the hottest and driest places on earth, it sits astride both banks of the Nile River, which allows it to support well over 150,000 people. It was over four hundred miles south of Cairo, far enough from the capital to give me the freedom of movement I needed, and it had enough historical sites to appeal to antiquities-addicted Germans, who'd flocked there for more than a century. This would be quite valuable to me, because I counted on Germans, particularly National Socialists, to help me maintain the discipline and orderliness so much a part of the German character. It was not long before many former soldiers of the Reich flocked to *Friedenthal III Marfiq Altadrib Aleaskarii*, my imaginatively-named military training facility.

On the opening day, I addressed my fifty hand-selected recruits as follows: "Gentlemen, soldiers, welcome to Hell!" There was mildly sarcastic laughter from half a dozen troops. I had serious second thoughts about my new engagement when I glanced up and down the five rows of ten men each. These had been handed off to me as "the best of the best." It was going to be a long haul, and I harked back to General Munzel's assessment of these fellows when measured against the forces to the north and east. Nevertheless, I plowed on.

"I don't just mean the weather, men. I mean the training you're going to get here. My name is Otto Skorzeny, *Colonel* Skorzeny to you, and you'd better not forget it. I am forty-four years old and I don't look like I'm in condition to take on any of you. Don't be deceived by my looks. If any one of you – *any of you* – steps out of line or misbehaves in any way, or fails to obey a single order from me or any of my staff, or fails to call me *Sir* in any conversation we have, there will be no second chance. You and I will go to the courtyard in view of everyone else in this unit. You get to choose whether we fight with bare hands or swords or knives. It will be *mensur*, which means you stand where you are and neither one of us can run away because every man at *Friedenthal III Marfiq Altadrib Aleaskarii* will form a human wall, and if any of them allow either of us to escape, that man will be the next one in the arena. Is that understood?"

"Yes," spoken desultorily by perhaps half of the recruits.

"I beg your pardon?" I snarled.

"Yes, *Sir!*"

"I can't hear you, *ras alqarf.*"

"YES, *SIR!*" The last was much more emphatic, since a dozen of my associates encouraged the troops by whacking them on their buttocks with billy clubs.

"Now, then, gentlemen, a few words of what we're doing here at *Friedenthal III*. The Israelis kicked the living shit out of you during the last war. I trust none of you served in that conflict?"

Two hands raised.

"It's not because you were cowardly or less courageous or less resourceful than the enemy. You were simply not trained in modern commando warfare. You were used to the way wars have been fought since the days of the pharaohs, uniformed regiments of soldiers fighting each other on a well-defined battlefield. That doesn't work anymore. Even though we Germans did not win the last big War, and you know about that War since you hosted both Montgomery and Rommel, we did pretty well until we were simply overwhelmed.

"The course at *Friedenthal III Marfiq Altadrib Aleaskarii* will last six months. If you make the grade, you will be the best-trained troops in the entire Arab world, and you may expect promotions and women more than you ever dreamed possible. If you fail, you may count on being reassigned as a prison guard in the worst place we can find. Understood?"

"YES, SIR!"

"What you'll learn here is absolute reliance on your mates and absolute reliance on yourselves. Instead of organized armies, we'll have small, roving bands of guerilla fighters, sporadically attacking different priority targets and then disappearing into the background. This kind of warfare is almost impossible to guard against, because you won't be in either a traditional military uniform or mindset. No structured environment."

At that moment, General Gehlen's words popped into my head. *You, Otto Skorzeny, are a whore! Not so*, my mind countered. I'm simply a guerilla warfare consultant for hire, to whoever wants to learn my tactical and creative ideas, including the United States Special Forces.

My reverie was broken by a very short, extremely scruffy-looking young man some twenty years my junior. "*SIR!*" he barked in a sharp military manner. "A question, SIR?"

"Proceed, Mister …"

"Abu Ammar, SIR!"

"You're not Egyptian?"

"Palestinian, SIR!"

"Proceed, Ammar."

"What is our focus, *Colonel*? Our tactics?"

"Good question. The basic focus of commando warfare is a small, well-organized unit or cell inflicting as much damage and chaos as it can, and then, slipping back into society. It's not focused on traditional military skills, but rather flexibility, adaptability, creativity, and technological skills in order to acquire a target, plan a well-coordinated attack, and demoralize the enemy. Small units can inflict huge damage. Commando warfare s not about establishing an attack pattern, but just the opposite. A well-planned attack does not mean moving regiments and coordinating hundreds of vehicles. It might be as little as coordinating two or three individuals, creating one event or a sequence of events which play off one another. The goal is to develop multiple target strategies that flow into the next target to maximize the impact of a small insurgency unit on a single mission. Many times, there may be only one target selected."

"Example, SIR?" Ammar pressed.

"A commando bombs a downtown building. This creates havoc and pushes survivors to leave the area. As they flow into the train station to leave the area, the train station becomes the next target. Blowing up a portion of the train station takes out more victims. Or take a truck loaded with explosives that runs down a series of pedestrians on a crowded city sidewalk. When it stops, the driver escapes into a nearby crowd. The police surround the truck. As they start to search it, the truck explodes, injuring another twenty people. Panic ensues. The devastation and residual impact is not because of a large strike force. One motivated person can accomplish a lot."

I watched carefully as my students' looks turned from slack disinterest to fear, and from there to respect. Throughout the next several days, I noticed the vestigial beginnings of what I most wanted to see: cohesion. But there was still the disunity that Munzel had mentioned. This Abu Ammar fellow showed greater initiative than the others, but it was obvious that the Egyptian recruits kept their distance from him to the point of disdaining him.

Ammar didn't seem to care. There were seven or eight of his own fellow Palestinians, and they seemed to afford him all the respect he needed. During training, although he was far from the largest, strongest, or most athletic enrollee, there was no question in my mind that he worked harder and exhibited greater initiative than anyone else.

I found myself facing a dilemma. Part of my job was to pick out those I saw with leadership potential candidates and move them into positions of increased responsibility. While Abu Ammar, who was almost a foot-and-a-half shorter than me and always portrayed as something of an "unmade bed," was unquestionably as ideal a candidate as I found among this bunch, it was equally obvious that no Egyptian *Friedenthaler* would give him the time of day, let alone submit to his orders.

One day, two months into his time at the training facility, I asked him to join me in my offices for a light lunch and a chat. When he entered he was properly deferential, given our respective stations within the complex, but he was by no means obsequious.

"You requested I join you, Sir?"

"I did, Cadet Ammar. You need not stand at rigid attention. You may sit down, young man."

"Thank you, Sir. But given your position at this academy, you must sit first."

I did. Within moments, a Filipino waiter brought a well-prepared, though hardly overwhelming, lunch, accompanied by sweet mint tea.

"Your *kunya* is Abu Ammar. May I ask your given name?"

"Of course, Sir. Mohammed Yasser Abdel Rahman Abdel Raouf Arafat al-Qudwa at your service."

"Would you care to give me a shortened version?" I asked, unconsciously breaking into a grin. "Or would you prefer your *nom de guerre?*"

"As you wish. I notice you speak French, Sir?" he remarked in fluent French.

"Am I to presume you're more educated than you make out to be?"

"If you mean, am I more than a dirty little Palestinian raghead, the answer is yes," he said, without rancor or bitterness. "You and I are both trained civil engineers," he continued. "And Obersturmbahnführer Skorzeny, you needn't stare at me as if I'd somehow ascended from an ape to an educated man. I've obviously studied your dossier as I'm sure you're familiar with mine."

"Not really," I remarked, flabbergasted as the apparent intellectual breadth of the man.

"More's the pity, then. I was born in Egypt, grew up in Cairo, graduated King Fuad University, and I was one of the two men who held up his hand when you asked which of us had participated in *al-Nakba*. However, I wasn't in the Palestinian fedayeen. Although I fought alongside the Muslim Brotherhood, I never joined any organized army. I was in Gaza, a rogue, sort of like you, Colonel Skorzeny. Is there anything else you'd like to know, Sir?"

"Your common name? Short form?"

"Among my friends, I'm known as Yasser Arafat."

I have always been drawn to intelligence and sensitivity. I have always felt I could spot signs of leadership, whether in myself or in others, and, given the chasm that separated young Arafat from the rest of the trainees, I found myself frequently conversing with him, mostly outside the camp, in Luxor itself.

I was hardly surprised when Arafat advised me that, as a boy, he'd frequently visited the Jewish quarter in Cairo and attended religious services. "My mother died when I was four years old. My sister Inam and I lived with our father for some years. Whether it was because there were seven children in the family or because he was frustrated that as a Palestinian from Gaza he was never successful in Egypt, he took it out on us. When he found out I was going to the synagogue, he beat me black and blue. When our father moved back to Gaza, the seven of us went to live with our mother's family in the Moroccan quarter, adjacent to where the Jews lived. I still attended Jewish services,"

"Why?" I asked.

"Why did the Jews move to South America after the War when they knew there were so many Nazis who'd as soon kill them as look at them?

Why is the moth drawn to the flame? In my case, I wanted to study the Jewish mentality. How was this small remnant of a people, a third of whom had been killed in Hitler's ovens, somehow able to occupy land – *our* land – and defeat the Arabs against such overwhelming odds?"

"I notice you didn't say 'our' Arabs. You were born in Egypt, and that's about as Arab as you can get."

"Very true, Colonel Skorzeny. But the Jews who lived in Germany weren't considered 'real' Germans by the *Germans*, any more than most white people in the United States don't consider Negroes as 'real' *Americans*. Whether I was born in Egypt really makes no difference. I'm a Palestinian in their minds. Whether anyone wants to admit it or not, the Palestinians are the *Niggers* of the Arab world. Does that shock you, Obersturmbahnführer?"

"Not really, Yasser. You and I seem to see things through the same pair of glasses. We've both seen how most of the Egyptians at Friedenthal III seem to ignore you. Your few friends are Palestinians."

"Mark my words, Colonel," he said. "We're destined to be at war with the Israelis for ten, fifty, a hundred, maybe a thousand years. The rest of the Arab world will cheer us on, calling us their poor, downtrodden, brave brothers. They will give us millions of dollars and they will use us to promote their own agenda in the United Nations. But the one thing I can guarantee you is that they will not send so much as a single one of their soldiers into Palestine to help us retrieve *our* land. They will try to tear off little pieces of Palestine and annex them to Egypt, Jordan, Syria, and Lebanon. But they're no more willing to carve out a country for *us* than the Israelis."

As we stopped at a nearby kiosk and ordered falafel wrapped in pita bread, my young acquaintance continued, his tone more sanguine than bitter. "The Israelis will win every war against the Arabs, including the Palestinians. But because the Muslims of the world will command a majority in the United Nations by sheer force of numbers, and because the Israelis and their 'Never again' paranoia will never give an inch in negotiations, the Jews will lose the peace every time."

"Do you think you'll ever get a state of your own, Abu Ammar?"

Arafat smiled sardonically. "Only if we're able to negotiate for one with the Jews," he said. "Peace among the Palestinians and the State of Israel is the last thing the Arabs want. It's just like in Nazi Germany. Who could the Nazis blame for their troubles if every Jew in Europe had been annihilated?"

"You still spoke to Jews after you graduated King Fuad University?" It was two weeks later and we'd decided to go out on the town for a Middle Eastern feast. He insisted we split the bill.

"Of course, Colonel. Debated with them, went to concerts when the Soviets sent Oistrakh, Piatigorsky, and Horowitz. Read books by all the prominent Zionists, Theodor Herzl, Ze'ev Jabotinsky, Babel, Schneerson, Trotsky ..."

"You know my politics?"

"Ah, yes, I almost forgot. You're the antithesis of the Bolsheviki. Allah forbid I should be poisoned by any of their ideas, eh? Of course, Stalin's people took Trotsky out with an ice axe. Godawful way to die, if you ask me. Mint tea? That meal's sitting pretty heavy on me."

"You're not going to stay in Egypt when you're finished here?"

"How would you know that?"

"Call it anything you want. Intuition. Seeing a pretty good slice of the world. You're a bit like me: an opportunist waiting for the right opportunity to come along."

"O.K., German prophet. What do you see?"

"Sooner or later there'll be another war with the Arabs and the Israelis. Looking at these guys I've been training for the past few months …"

"The best of the best …?"

"Bunch of fucking raghead goatherds who'll run at the first sign of danger."

"Such talk from a man who's paid very well to train them," Arafat said, grinning.

"Yeah. Back in Germany we have a saying: 'You can't shine shit.' Anyway, the fact that they are what they are could take a good bounce for you, Yasser."

"Meaning?"

"Next time around, the Israelis'll kick the shit out of the Arabs. This time harder. Then there might be another war, and just about that time the rest of the Arabs will start saying, 'Who the fuck needs this shit? Why don't we just give the land to the Niggers of the Arab world and let them deal with the Hebes?' About that time, you'll be well into your thirties, maybe close to forty, a perfect time to become a national leader."

"You're kidding me, right?"

"Stranger things have happened, my friend."

By the Fall of 1953, I felt what usefulness I had coming to an end. In addition to training the army, I'd trained Arab volunteers in commando tactics for possible use against British troops stationed in the Suez Canal zone. Although I'd continue to be a paid adviser to Nasser after Naguib retired, there was no need for me to remain in the Land of the Pharaohs any longer. Besides, it might just be time to settle down into a "respectable" European life for a while.

27

Some years before, Ilse Lühtje, the Countess von Finckenstein, had shown her generous nature, both by providing a roof over my head and a matrimonial bed in which we enjoyed other elements of one another's company. When we met again, I was living in an upscale villa in the heart of Madrid and deriving a quite substantial income from what appeared to be my successful engineering firm, despite the fact that I had never worked on a single construction project for *El Caudillo's* government. President and Dictator Franco was, however, aware of the real source of my ample lifestyle and happily turned a blind eye toward my doings, since I provided his numbered account in the Union Bank of Switzerland with three percent of the net profits on the first day of each month.

These were the days when revolutions were changing the face of much of the known world: the Mau Mau revolt against Colonial Britain; the unrest in Haiti and the rise of François "Papa Doc" Duvalier; the Independence Movement in Algeria; and the rise of Revolutionaries throughout Asia, Africa, Latin America, and Ireland. Very fortunately for my stock in trade, these upheavals were not fought with sticks and stones.

Some of my former employers, such as Krupp, were eager to obtain much-needed hard currency and were not too proud to manufacture small arms and not-so-small arms without an identifying nameplate, never mind they were knockoffs of guns patented by other manufacturers. Others, including my most recent friends in Egypt, were more than willing to part with hard currency in exchange for the most successful means of keeping themselves in power. But, of course, direct dealings between the parties in such situations was simply "not done." Each side needed a middleman, and I offered a very discreet private service, often to both sides of a conflict at the same time, and to purveyors who had no scruples providing both sides with many of the same weapons. As a result, by mid-1953, my own personal fortune was worth hundreds of thousands – of dollars, not Deutschmarks.

Ilse was thirty-five that year, only a couple years younger than Lisbeth had been when we'd first come together. When I saw her in Madrid, I realized for the first time that her resemblance to my great Viennese love was so striking that I felt a sharp pang the took me back almost a quarter of a century. My God, I was already forty-five at a time when the average European had only twenty more years to live! Yet I certainly did not consider myself "middle-aged" by any stretch of the imagination.

Once we'd renewed our sexual acquaintance that evening, we shared what had happened during the preceding half-decade. When Ilse spoke with such worldy-wise knowledge and sophistication, I was assailed by a sharp memory of what Herr Schreiber, my first employer, had said the day I'd first interviewed with him, "The Hollanders spoke highly of you. I respect Friedrich's judgment. *I assure you that Frau Hollander is far brighter than most women in Vienna. Indeed, although you'd never think so now, Lisbeth Rausch was one of Vienna's great beauties in her day...*"

"Otto, darling boy, I'm certain you've been quite naughty during your time away from this old woman. Perhaps the time has come for you to find a suitable wife." *Almost the precise words Lisbeth had used nineteen years before.* I had to convince myself this was not Lisbeth Hollander, who'd been eighteen years my senior. Although by no means in the first blush of youth, and certainly not the seductive siren Emilie Linhart had been when I first met her, Ilse Lühtje, the Countess von Finckenstein, possessed a far different kind of allure. She possessed much the same quiet sensuality as the late Frau Hollander, but she was very much a woman with whom one would feel comfortable *talking* or sitting in a car, or a living room, *after* the lovemaking. In short, a perfect wife.

"Why would you suggest such a thing, Ilse? You know my history."

"I know your *marital* history, Otto. Gretl was a simple country girl, barely out of girlhood, and Emmi and you were forced by events to live separate and apart for months at a time, so you never really got a chance to meet and know one another. Kind of like Adolf and me." She sighed. "He was eighteen years my senior. Since we divorced, the old goat married Judith Trömer, who's three years younger than me, would you believe?" Ilse did not sound the least bit bitter when she said this.

"Are you proposing to me?" I asked, only half in jest.

"You could do worse, Otto. For that matter, so could I. We're both more-or-less of an age. We're certainly compatible in *that* department. And once that's done, we have similar things we can talk about. Call it a loving friendship. I've never had that before, have you?"

Somehow, I felt enough at ease with Ilse to open up, *really* open up to her. "There was a woman once. Like you and the Count, only she was eighteen years *my* senior and married ..."

It was Ilse who suggested we take a driving holiday together to see if we were really as compatible as she thought. "You've nothing better to do for three weeks and neither do I. That way you can experience me at my worst, during that time of the month, when I haven't bathed for two days, when my dirty stockings are hanging over the sink. Likewise, I'll see how it is to live with you when you do those things men do which are not so attractive."

"But didn't we do that five years ago?"

"Different time, different circumstances," she replied. "Times change, people's attitudes and habits may change as well."

That did not sound like a bad idea to me. If the trip was unsuccessful, we'd have lost three weeks of our lives, and if it was as we hoped it would be ...

When Ilse told me where she thought we should go, it sounded enticing enough to me, particularly after my postwar years in Dachau, the Argentine, and most recently the hot desert of Southern Egypt.

"The Fatherland has a way of capitalizing on just about everything," she said. "After the War, Germany, which had become a pariah, wanted desperately to rebuild a tourism industry, and not only for the cash it would bring in. The Ministry of Tourism came up with the idea of 'the Romantic Road' in 1950, just after military occupation ended."

"Never heard of it," I responded genially.

"You wouldn't have, darling boy. You were gallivanting around the world, while I remained in the neighborhood. Of course, you're free to suggest any other place you want to go."

"No, no, this was your idea. Let's see where it leads us."

†

We flew to Rhein-Main Flughaven, Frankfurt's international airport, hired a Mercedes 220 convertible, and motored two hours to Würzburg before checking in to the Würzburger Hof, where the

Countess had reserved a commodious suite for us. It did not take me more than a day to realize that Ilse was a clever seductress who, like all women since Eve, knew exactly how to manipulate a man to fall in love with her.

During the next days, the stresses of my life of the past two years receded. I luxuriated in the relaxed state of spending time in the company of a beautiful, intelligent woman, and virtually no one else, from the moment we awoke in the morning until the end of each evening, sometimes after passionate lovemaking, but more often after simply talking 'til we fell asleep.

And talk we did, about anything and everything, as we drove south, through the lush countryside of the Tauber Valley. From time to time, when the mood overtook us, we'd find a hidden glade in a remote place off the road, where we'd kiss and fondle one another for several moments before resuming our drive.

Sometimes, Ilse would handle the driving chores and I was content to lie back on the headrest and doze for an hour or two. Her threat about my experiencing her at her worst, turned out to be largely a fiction. Our friendship deepened, as we walked hand-in-hand along the made-for-loving streets and alleys, and, afterward, atop the wall enclosing Rothenburg-ob-der-Tauber. I'd heard of this most renowned and romantic of German medieval towns – who hasn't? – but I'd never been there before.

Two hours south of Rothenburg, Ilse suggested we turn off the Romantic Road and travel west toward Ulm. When I asked her why, she said, "There's a certain castle I want you to see."

"Neuschwanstein, of course," I said. Far be it from me to betray my ignorance of the area, since few, if any, Germans were unaware of Bavaria's most famous landmark, which had appeared on travel posters even during the National Socialist days.

"No, not exactly," Ilse responded.

"What then?"

"Different castle. I've used every one of my connections as the former wife of Graf Adolf Fincke von Finckenstein, who's still entitled to use the title Countess, to reserve space in this castle for a single night.

"Aha! You want to further seduce me in an ancient medieval castle," I said, playfully pinching her arm.

"I'd hardly call it that," she said. "This one's less than a hundred years old."

"Didn't you and the Count have an ancestral castle of your own?"

"I'd hardly call the ruin of Schloss Finckenstein in Carinthia a castle."

"Carinthia, as in Austria?"

"That's right."

"But I thought …"

"Adolf may have been Austrian, but I, my dear, am East Prussian. The less noble German end of the spectrum."

Three more hours and I saw why Ilse had planned this surprise for me. Hohenzollern Castle in Baden-Württemberg province, 30 miles south of Stuttgart, sits atop a small promontory, 2,800 feet above the surrounding valley. To my eyes, more spectacular by far than its more famous cousin, Neuschwanstein, this was the third castle built on the site.

I was jolted out of my astonished reverie when my friend and bedmate said, "This castle was actually built as a memorial. No member of the Hohenzollern family ever lived for any substantial amount of time in this *schloss*. Crown Prince Wilhelm, the son of the last Hohenzollern monarch, stayed in the castle very briefly in 1945. And tonight, Dear Boy, it's all ours. So imagine yourself sleeping with a queen!"

"That takes no imagination, Darling. I've been sleeping with one for the past two weeks."

"Have you given any thought to making that arrangement permanent?" she asked seriously.

"I'm not at all sure that would be a bad idea."

And I meant it.

†

My resolve to marry this incredible woman solidified during the remainder of our trip. Even more so during the next six months that she occupied my villa in Madrid.

Ilse made certain I understood we would marry as equals, each of us being independently wealthy and wealthily independent. "I will not attempt to hold you captive or deny you the freedom to do anything you want, with whom, whenever, and wherever you want. And I take it as a given that you have no intention of similarly shackling me."

Although this meant what today is called an "open marriage," I felt that given my extensive business and military dealings, Ilse's friendship and guiding wisdom, and my attraction to her in so many other ways, it was not likely I would have the need to stray that often.

†

In February 1954, atop Berg Hohenzollern, the Countess Finck von Finkenstein changed her name to Frau Otto Skorzeny. And I became a husband for the third and final time.

28

As early as 1953, it had become obvious to me that Gamal Abdel Nasser had created a rift with General Naguib and would attempt to unseat him. I viewed this with suspicion because whatever else he may have been Muhammad Naguib was a legitimate general, whereas Nasser struck me as ready to smile with jovial camaraderie at everyone, while secretly plotting to stab anyone who stood in his way in the back. I attended rallies that year where I saw him say one thing with obvious sincerity to one faction, then say its exact opposite to an opposing crowd the very next day.

By February 25, 1954, Naguib announced his resignation. Within twenty-four hours, Nasser accepted the resignation, put Naguib under house arrest, and the Revolutionary Command Council proclaimed Nasser as both RCC chairman and prime minister. As Naguib intended, a mutiny immediately followed, demanding Naguib's reinstatement and the RCC's dissolution. While visiting the striking officers at Military Headquarters to call for the mutiny's end, Nasser was initially intimidated into accepting their demands. However, on February 27, Nasser's supporters in the army launched a raid on the General Headquarters, ending the mutiny. Later that day, hundreds of thousands of protesters, mainly belonging to the Muslim Brotherhood, called for Naguib's return and Nasser's imprisonment. A sizable group within the RCC demanded Naguib's release and return to the presidency. During the next several months, the power struggle between the two men continued until October of that year, when Naguib was effectively neutralized and Nasser succeeded to full power in Egypt.

During that period, both Naguib and Nasser sought out my advice, but I was so involved with Ilse and with my "import-expert" trade, that I could gracefully stay out of their dispute by honestly claiming press of business.

This did not stop me from relying on Generalmajor Gehlen, who seemed to have inside information from all the players. It was through Reinhard that I learned, in late 1954, that Nasser had made secret contacts with Israel. Gehlen told me these feelers were bound to fail, since the Israelis, not without good reason, did not trust the Arabs as far as they could see them.

On the last day of February the following year, Israeli troops attacked the Egyptian-held Gaza Strip with the stated aim of eliminating Palestinian fedayeen raids. At my urging, Nasser, who agreed with me that the Egyptian Army was not ready for a confrontation, did not retaliate. Instead, half a year later, Egypt's strongman ordered the tightening of the blockade on Israeli shipping through the Straits of Tiran and restricted Israeli use of airspace over the Gulf of Aqaba.

Meanwhile, Nasser had bigger fish to fry than pestiferous little Israel. When Britain's Middle East regional allies formed the Baghdad Pact, Nasser considered it a threat to his efforts to eliminate British military influence in the Middle East, as well as his aim to become the *primer inter pares* in that neighborhood. Concurrent with the formation of that Pact, Nasser felt that if he was to maintain Egypt's regional leadership position he needed to acquire modern weaponry to arm his military. When it became apparent to him that the West would not supply Egypt, Nasser turned to the Soviet Bloc and concluded a

$320,000,000 armament agreement with Czechoslovakia. The balance of power between Egypt and Israel was now more or less equal, and Nasser looked much stronger to his base.

As profligate as the regime had been in paying me regularly and well, Egypt was much poorer than Nasser led his minions to believe. Although he was not always a wise man, in fact, quite the contrary, he was an extremely proud one. His dream was to build the Aswan Dam, a project which would make his country not only self-sufficient in the production of food, but also the dominant power in the region. He could not go it alone, so in December 1955, during the period when he was playing the East against the West in his quest for advanced arms, he convinced the United States and the United Kingdom to pledge $70 million to help Egypt finance the massive project.

Seven months later, the ink was hardly dry on the arms deal between Egypt and Czechoslovakia when, on July 19, 1956, the American Secretary of State, John Foster Dulles, announced that "due to U.S. concerns that the scope of the project would overwhelm the Egyptian economy," the United States and Great Britain were regretfully withdrawing their offer to finance the construction of the Aswan Dam.

Although I have never considered myself a strategic thinker, it didn't take anyone with more than a modicum of intelligence to fathom that a huge disaster on all sides was brewing, and that the only ones who'd come out of this catastrophe "smelling like a rose" would be the Soviets and their allies. Thus it was that on Wednesday, July 25, I telephoned President Nasser, to whom I felt I owed loyalty, to prevail on him in the strongest possible terms not to take any steps that might further deepen the impending crisis.

Instead of getting through to my erstwhile employer, I was told by some minister of this or that, that the President was in private conversations with Arab leaders throughout the region and could not be disturbed. Perhaps if I were to call back tomorrow …? Furious at this rebuff, I held my temper in check and politely said I'd try back the following day.

My next call was to Reinhard Gehlen at his private number at the American CIA. I could tell from the tenor of his voice that Gehlen was deeply disturbed. He asked if he could telephone me back on a secure line within the hour, which he did as promised.

"Something is up, Generalmajor?"

"I'll say. The proverbial shit is about to hit the fan, Otto. As they say in American slang, the U.S. may really have its tit in a wringer on this one. The Brits are royally pissed, France feels America has driven Egypt into the arms of the Commies. Nasser's about to make an announcement that will throw the gauntlet down. The Israelis are sucking up to the Frogs and the Limeys, and the Russian Bear is licking his chops."

"I tried to get through to Nasser, but that door was closed."

"Not surprising. He doesn't know which way the FRG is going to swing on this one. He's risking his position in the Arab world, and if he doesn't show he's got a pair of balls as big as his mouth, he could be knocked off his perch in a matter of hours."

"Do you think …?"

"The big powers have always speculated that a nuclear war would start in the Middle East. But I think it's best to just see where the train takes us."

On April 1, 1956, the U.S. Government and the CIA formally transferred the Gehlen Organization to the authority of the Federal Republic of Germany, under Chancellor Konrad Adenauer. By virtue of that event, my friend Reinard Gehlen left the CIA and his

Organization became the nucleus of the *Bundesnachrichtendienst*, the German Federal Intelligence Service, which, like so many Cold War spy operations, became known by its acronym, in this case, the BND. As spymaster of the Gehlen Organization, Gehlen became president of the BND, where he remained until 1968.

On July 26, 1956, during a broadcast address delivered from Alexandria, Nasser announced he had signed into law a presidential decree nationalizing the Suez Canal Company, effective immediately, and that while he spoke, Egyptian officials were taking over the administration and management of the Company. Nasser led up to this announcement by giving a long review of "imperialistic efforts to thwart Egyptian independence." He particularly condemned past British actions and the United States' refusal to finance the Aswan High Dam. He exclaimed that the revenue gained from the nationalization would enable Egypt to build the High Dam without American aid.

Since I was in no position to influence what eventuated, I could do nothing but sit by and speculate on what would happen when the Arab world and Western Europe collided. But while Western Europe relied on the 120-mile long Suez Canal for more than two-thirds of its oil flowing through the strategically vital waterway connecting the Mediterranean and Red Seas, this was not my immediate concern.

My "engineering / import-export" business was booming, since the European powers had started to leave the African Continent. While the French were preparing their Colonies for a relatively smooth transition to independence, except, of course, for Algeria, the same could not be said for Belgium, England, Portugal, which retained its iron grip on Mozambique and Angola, and even Germany, which by that time retained only a vestigial toehold in German East Africa, German West Africa, and German Southwest Africa.

Because my Swiss bank account had, by that time, amassed seven figures, I was constantly reminded of the Helvetii, the Swiss, who had, in ancient days, been a warlike people until they discovered, about the time that the ancient Romans came to power, that it was much more profitable to sit on the sidelines, provide comestibles to both combatants, and reap the munificent benefits. To this day, the Swiss have made an art of remaining neutral. I know, for sure, that several *billions* in Reichsmarks or today's functional equivalent in Swiss francs, remains on deposit in numbered accounts in a dozen paragons of virtue under the watchful eyes of the gnomes of Zurich.

But I digress. France, which objected to Nasser's support of rebels in its colony of Algeria as well as the seizure of the canal, and Israel, which had engaged in sporadic battles with Egypt along their shared border, joined Great Britain in a tripartite invasion that began on October 29, 1956, when Israeli armed forces attacked the Sinai Peninsula. Two days later, under the guise of protecting the canal, Anglo-French forces began bombing Egyptian targets. On November 5, British and French paratroopers and marines began to occupy strategic positions in the canal zone.

The United Nations quickly passed a resolution calling for a cease-fire. Both the United States and the Soviet Union pressured Great Britain, France, and Israel to withdraw. The Soviet Union, which had supplied arms and money to Egypt, made ambiguous—and ominous—threats about using nuclear weapons to aid its ally, while the United States wielded its economic power. Furious at not being informed of the attack in advance and fearful of a wider war in the Middle East, President Eisenhower threatened America's NATO allies and Israel with sanctions if they did not draw back their forces. British and French troops left Egypt in December 1956. A few weeks later, English Prime Minister Anthony Eden, humiliated by the apparent fiasco, resigned.

Only Israel remained in the Sinai Peninsula until March 1957, when, in accordance with the cease-fire agreement, Israel withdrew and Egypt reopened the canal to commercial shipping, including ingress and egress by the Zionist State. The Suez Crisis made clear that the old colonial powers, Great Britain and France, had been supplanted as the world's preeminent geopolitical forces by the United States and the Soviet Union.

In June 1957, I'd visited Ireland for the first time as a guest of the Portmarnock Country Club hotel in County Dublin. I had known that during World War II, the Irish – certainly those living in Eire – had remained determinedly neutral, both because of a love of things German, and because of a stormy history between Britain and the Irish Republic. At that time, I still relished my notoriety and basked in the adulation I received from a ballroom packed with representatives of various societies, professional men, and several representatives of the Dáil Éireann, the Irish Parliament. I was particularly attracted to a bluff, somewhat blustery young Irishman, Charles Haughey, who'd recently been elected to that governing body after three unsuccessful campaigns.

When we engaged in conversation that evening, Haughey told me he'd first heard of my Gran Sasso operation when he was eighteen, two years after he'd joined the Local Defense Force. "We weren't exactly England's best friends back then, any more than we are now. Although the Brits more or less forced us to go along with their ride, me and my mates gave a bit of a cheer when we heard you'd given Winnie a good, swift kick in the bum."

"I didn't know I had admirers west of the Rhine back then, Mister Haughey."

"Charles, please, and yes, you did indeed. It's also not common knowledge that on VE-day a bunch of us University College Dublin students burned the Union Jack on College Green outside Trinity College, because the Brits ignored the Irish flag when we tried to put it up to celebrate the Allied victory. Moving into today, I know you've lived in many parts of the world, mostly in Franco's Spain, but have you ever given any thought to moving into our beautiful little corner of the world?"

"Can't say as I have, Mister ... Charles."

"Outside the North, very peaceful, very restful. Although I understand you're quite a wealthy fellow, it's also very cheap. You could live like a king, you could."

"Really?" I said, only partially feigning interest.

"Yessir," my young friend responded. "There's some lovely land nearby in County Kildare, southwest of Dublin. Mostly raised bog wetlands. Perfect for potato farming, raising horses, and such. Bit of a change from your past lifestyle I'm sure, but give it a thought, why don't you?"

†

I did, and for the next two years I visited Ireland more and more frequently. Haughey was right. Glendalough in the Wicklow Mountains was a magnetically lovely slice of Irish history. My sole reluctance to consider settling down in Ireland was that the government would not extend me permanent residence, but only allowed me to stay in the Republic six weeks at a time, and never allowed me to set foot in Great Britain itself. I felt insulted, since the War had ended more than twelve years before. I came to believe that what passed for English justice was little more than long-term vengeance.

Still, by 1959, Haughey encouraged me to buy Martinstown House, a 160-acre parcel and mansion in Ballysax, the Curragh, County

Kildare. The main house was a converted 1830s hunting lodge. The Strawberry Gothic style cottage nestled in a peaceful setting in its own park, with many fine old trees and a beautiful walled garden. Looking over the property for the first time, I felt, "Who could ask for more?"

My needs were simple. Although I'd always considered myself in good shape, I was surprised to learn that my weight had crawled up over the years until I now weighed 265 pounds. During the next couple of years, I kept my bulk in check by working the potato farm by hand, and caring for the eight horses and four donkeys on the premises.

Alas, all was not peace and light. While my neighbors, the closest of whom lived more than a mile away, were generally friendly in a reserved fashion, I was never invited, nor did I invite anyone, to my home. I preferred to drive the narrow country lanes of the district in my large, distinctive Mercedes saloon. Just because I wanted quiet and simplicity did not mean I had to deprive myself of accoutrements symbolic of my station.

It was not long before I became embroiled in controversy and dispute between the Irish Department of Justice and the Department of Foreign Affairs. The Justice Department was, at the time, almost paranoid about the incursion of communism, the "Red Menace." On the other hand, Foreign Affairs believed that by letting former Nazis into the country, virtually unchecked, the cure was worse than the disease. That seemed to explain why the government gave me continual temporary visas, but insisted that only my Nansen Passport, given to "stateless persons," provided me with legitimate passage between countries.

Charles Haughey did everything in his power to help, but the Dáil refused to issue me Irish citizenship papers. Thus it was that I maintained my permanent residence in Madrid, even though Franco, as accommodating as he was to my countrymen, could not – or would not – grant me Spanish citizenship.

The Dáil was somehow convinced that I had been involved in the ratlines, the means by which Nazis were funneled to South America, to the Middle East, and to Spain. While I confess that their belief was convincingly founded on fact, their accusation that I was anti-Semitic and had been involved in the wholesale destruction of Jews was not true.

During the next several years, I would return to my manor in County Kildare periodically. I felt no need for confrontation, so I never pressed the issue for Irish citizenship and used the time to engage in hard physical work and solitary contemplation.

29

At 7:30 a.m. on May 22, 1960, I received an urgent call from my friend, Generalmajor Reinhard Gehlen. "Otto, I need to see you, this morning. Yes, it is that urgent. I will pick you up at your villa in one hour. This impacts our efforts in South America and it impacts you. All I can tell you by phone is it will hit every newspaper in the world by this evening."

Reinhard Gehlen was by no means an alarmist, so when I heard the tone of his voice, I expected something momentous, but I was completely taken aback during the next two hours, as he poured out a story that left me nervous, concerned, and not a little bit frightened.

He started without preamble. "The Israelis have captured Adolf Eichmann."

"It's not the first National Socialist they've caught," I said. "I'll admit he's a pretty big fish, but we've fought this out in the courts of Argentina before. Usually, we've been able to put money in the hands of the right people or keep things tied up for years while our countrymen endure very comfortable and very loose 'house arrest.'"

"Not this time, my friend. They've kidnapped him and my informants tell me that even as we speak he's on board a special El Al flight, a turbo-prop Bristol Brittania, enroute from Buenos Aires to Lod Airport."

"But there are no flights scheduled between Israel and Argentina," I said, not quite so robustly.

"True, but Argentina scheduled an international celebration to commemorate the 150th anniversary of its independence on May 19, and Israel was invited to send its representatives to the big event. The Mossad arranged through the Foreign Ministry that the delegation fly to Buenos Aires in a specially chartered El Al plane."

"You've got my attention, Reinhard. Go ahead."

"One of the great myths of the postwar era was that Israeli agents were constantly scouring hideouts all over the world, relentlessly tracking down Nazi war criminals. Nothing could be farther from the truth. The Mossad was up to its neck monitoring the Jews arriving from Eastern Europe and the Soviet Union.

"The Kremlin had firmly aligned itself with the Arabs against Israel. When the KGB or their affiliates behind the Iron Curtain received reports from their planted agents in Israel, they would promptly share that information with Israel's Arab neighbors. The new state desperately needed more settlers, but it also needed to identify those who were serving different masters. The first priority was checking for spies, not capturing Nazis."

I lit up a cigarette and offered one to Gehlen, as he continued.

"Rafi Eitan, the coordinator of relations between the *Mossad* and Israel's *Shin Bet,* headed up the Eichmann operation. In the early days of Israel's existence, there was simply not enough time, energy, or desire to hunt Nazis. The struggle for Israel's survival in a region filled with enemies trumped everything else. By the late '50s, however, Prime Minister David Ben-Gurion started thinking seriously about a major operation to seize a notorious Nazi war criminal.

"In 1957, Fritz Bauer, attorney general of Hesse, arranged a secret meeting with Felix Shinar, the head of Israel's reparations mission in

West Germany. According to Isser Harel, the Mossad director, Bauer told Shinar that Eichmann had been traced to Argentina, but he did not trust the German judiciary, let alone the German embassy staff in Buenos Aires."

"That's certainly understandable," I said. "You and I know that from our own experience."

"Shinar filed a detailed report with the foreign ministry. When Walter Eytan, the ministry's director general, met Isser Harel to relay the news, Harel promised he'd investigate fully. When he did, he concluded that Eichmann pulled the strings controlling most everything that had to do with the extermination of Jews by the Reich. However, it took more than two years before he put Operation Eichmann into play.

"Harel detailed Shaul Darom to make contact with Bauer in Cologne. Darom and Bauer met there on November 6, 1957. Bauer explained that his source was a half-Jewish German in Argentina, who had written to the German authorities after he had read in the newspapers that Eichmann had disappeared. Bauer told Darom that Eichmann's wife Vera and three sons had left Germany, supposedly to live with a second husband. Bauer's informant provided an address for the man he presumed to be Eichmann: 4261 Chacabuco Street in Olivos, a suburb of Buenos Aires.

"Bauer was open about why he had turned to the Israelis instead of going to the German authorities. 'Extradition proceedings could tip off Eichmann and allow him to escape again. I won't reject the idea of your getting him to Israel in your own way.' Those words left little room for ambiguity. As a representative of the law in West Germany, Bauer was, in effect, urging the Israelis to come up with a practical solution that ignored normal legal procedures."

Yet Harel's initial attempts to check out Bauer's leads resulted in apparent failure. In January 1958, he sent Yael Goren, an agent who had spent considerable time in South America, to Buenos Aires, with strict instructions not to take any actions that might attract attention. Accompanied by an Israeli who was doing research in Argentina, Goren checked out the address Bauer had provided and the neighborhood. They immediately concluded that something was off. It was an impoverished area, the street was unpaved and, as Harel put it, "the wretched little house could in no way be reconciled with our picture of the life of an SS officer of Eichmann's rank." At the time, the common assumption was that prominent Nazi fugitives had managed to smuggle out vast wealth, most of it seized from their wartime victims.

The two men were also thrown off by the slovenly looking European woman they spotted in the yard. Eichmann was known as a womanizer, and they couldn't believe she could be his wife. Their obvious conclusion was that the information passed on by Bauer was unfounded. But Harel dissented.

Thus, he took the logical next step: he asked Darom to meet with Bauer again, this time insisting they had to learn the name of his source, so they could check his story further. On January 21, 1958, they met in Frankfurt. Bauer provided Darom with the name of Lothar Hermann and an address in Coronel Suárez, a city more than 300 miles from Buenos Aires. Bauer also provided a letter of introduction for whoever Harel would decide to send to confront Hermann.

That someone was Efraim Hofstäter, a top police investigator, who was on his way to South America on a different case. Harel asked him to check out Hermann once he had completed his other business, supplying him with Bauer's letter of introduction. When Hermann rebuffed the investigator's request that they meet in Buenos Aires, Hofstäter traveled on an overnight train to Coronel Suárez. When the traveler knocked on Hermann's door, Hermann invited him in, but immediately asked for assurances that he really represented the German authorities, which was the cover story Hofstäter and Harel had agreed on. "How do I know you are telling the truth?" he asked.

Hofstäter explained about the letter of introduction from Bauer, holding it out for Hermann. But his host ignored his extended hand. At that moment, Hermann called his wife and asked her to read the letter aloud. It was only then that Hofstäter realized that Hermann was blind. The wife read the letter and said, "The signature is Dr. Bauer's."

Hermann visibly relaxed and began telling his story. His parents had died at the hands of the Nazis, and he had spent time in the concentration camps. "I have Jewish blood in my veins, but my wife is German and our daughter has been brought up according to her mother's traditions." His only motivation for tracking Eichmann was "to even the score with the Nazi criminals who caused me and my family so much agony and suffering."

The Hermanns had lived in Olivos, the Buenos Aires suburb, until 18 months earlier, where they were "accepted as German in every way." Sylvia, their daughter, began dating a young man named Nicholas Eichmann, who had no idea she was partly Jewish. He visited their house on several occasions, and once remarked that it would have been better if the Germans had completed the extermination of the Jews. He explained that he did not have a distinct regional accent because his father had served in many different places during the war.

Prompted by a news report about a war crimes trial where Eichmann was mentioned, Hermann concluded that Nicholas was Eichmann's son. In those days, many Nazis felt so much at home in Argentina that they took only minimal precautions. While Adolf had been living under an assumed last name, his sons never bothered to change theirs. But Nicholas did take one precaution when he started seeing Sylvia: he made a point of never revealing his home address. When Nicholas and Sylvia wrote to each other after she moved, he instructed her to mail her letters to a friend's address. But that only strengthened Hermann's suspicions, and soon he was corresponding with Bauer.

At that point, Sylvia, an attractive woman of twenty, entered the room. It was clear that, whatever she had once felt for Nicholas, she had decided to help her father in his quest to confirm his theory. When Bauer asked Hermann to go to Buenos Aires to investigate further, the blind man took his daughter along, not just to serve as his eyes but also to exploit her ties with Nicholas. With the help of a friend, she located his house and simply knocked on the door.

When a woman opened the door, Sylvia asked if this was the home of the Eichmann family. "Her reply did not come immediately. During the pause, a middle-aged man wearing glasses came and stood beside her. When she asked him if Nick was home, he told her Nick was working overtime. She then asked if he was Mr. Eichmann. When he hesitated to answer, Sylvia asked if he was Nick's father. He said he was.

Sylvia related to the investigator that the family had five children: three had been born in Germany and two in Argentina, Although the ages of the sons born in Germany tallied with what Bauer already knew about Eichmann, Inspector Hofstäter remained cautious. "What you say seems pretty convincing but it isn't conclusive identification," he said. He added that Vera may have remarried but allowed her first three children to keep her first husband's name.

Lothar Hermann insisted there was no doubt that the man she was living with was Eichmann. Promising to cover his expenses, the Israeli told Hermann he needed him to get more information about the suspect: what name he was using, where he worked, any official photograph or personal document, and fingerprints. Returning to Tel Aviv, he reported to Mossad Director Harel that he had found

Hermann to be "impetuous and overconfident," indicating he had doubts about his story. But he was favorably impressed by Sylvia, and recommended following up quickly, since she was planning to travel abroad soon.

Harel approved additional funds for Hermann's expenses so he could conduct further research in Buenos Aires, but he did not get the results he was hoping for. Lothar and Sylvia Hermann learned from a property registry that the owner of the house on Chacabuco Street was an Austrian named Francisco Schmidt, and that the residence had two apartments with separate electric meters, one for someone named Dagoto and the other for someone named Klement. Hermann concluded that Schmidt must be Eichmann, and that he had undergone plastic surgery to change his appearance.

But when the Israeli researcher in Argentina who had worked on the case earlier followed up, he discovered that Schmidt could not be Eichmann: his family situation was different, and he did not even live in the house he owned. These findings damaged Hermann's trustworthiness. By August 1958, Harel gave instructions to allow the contact with Hermann to lapse gradually.

"That was the year West Germany opened the Central Office for the Investigation of Nazi Crimes in Ludwigsburg," Gehlen continued. "In August 1959, Tuvia Friedman, a Nazi hunter who had collaborated with Simon Wiesenthal, claimed to have received a letter from Erwin Schüle head of the Ludwigsburg office, mentioning that Eichmann was possibly in Kuwait. Friedman turned to Asher Ben-Natan, his old Israeli contact from Vienna, who was now serving in the Defense Ministry. Ben-Natan brushed him off, so Friedman concluded that those officials were no longer interested in hunting Eichmann, and he turned to the Israeli press to publicize the fugitive's purported presence in Kuwait."

✝

For Bauer, the Mossad's lack of follow-up with Hermann, combined with the sudden publicity about Kuwait, was intensely frustrating; he was increasingly worried that Eichmann would learn of the efforts to track him and run again. In December 1959, Bauer went to Israel with more information. He reported to Harel that according to a new source Eichmann had traveled to Argentina under the name of Ricardo Klement. This corresponded to the name on one of the electric meters of the house on Chacabuco Street, which Hermann had been talking about all along.

As Harel pointed out, Hermann had mistakenly assumed that Eichmann was the owner of the house, not one of its tenants. Realizing what had happened, the Mossad chief assigned a new man, Zvi Aharoni, to follow up. Suddenly, Hermann's lead looked promising again, but no one knew whether Eichmann was still there.

When Bauer met with Harel, Aharoni, and Israel's Attorney General, Chaim Cohen, in Jerusalem, he did not disguise his anger. "This is simply unbelievable!" he declared, pointing out that the name Klement had been mentioned much earlier by Hermann and now again by the new source. "Any second-class policeman would be able to follow such a lead. Just go and ask the nearest butcher or greengrocer and you will learn all there is to know about Klement."

Harel informed Ben-Gurion of the possible breakthrough. The prime minister told him that, if the lead panned out, he wanted Eichmann brought back for trial in Israel. He believed such a trial would be an achievement of tremendous moral and historical consequence.

This time, Harel sent Aharoni to Argentina to check whether they could identify and locate Eichmann at the original address Hermann had given them. The Mossad chief considered Aharoni to be one of the best investigators in Israel; born in Germany, he had escaped to Palestine in 1938 and later served in the British Army, interrogating German POWs.

Aharoni had to finish up another assignment first, which meant an additional delay of two months, but during that time Aharoni prepared for his mission by learning the background of the case and meeting with Bauer. On March 1, 1960, he finally landed in Buenos Aires, armed with an Israeli diplomatic passport under a false name. His cover was that he worked for the Foreign Ministry's accounts department.

Accompanied by a local student who had agreed to help out, Aharoni drove in a rented car to Chacabuco Street in Olivos on March 3. But when they reached the two-family house they were looking for and the student walked up to it, pretending to be looking for someone else, it turned out there were no tenants in either of the two apartments. Instead, the windows were empty, and painters were at work inside. Aharoni realized that Eichmann and his family, if they had been there earlier, must have moved.

Next day Aharoni improvised a plan to learn more. Remembering from the Eichmann file that Klaus, the eldest Eichmann son, had a birthday on March 3, he instructed a local young volunteer named Juan to drive back to the empty house carrying a gift and card for him. The cover story was that a friend, who worked as a bellboy in one of the large hotels in Buenos Aires, had asked him to deliver the package, which came from a young woman. If pressed, he could maintain that he knew nothing more about its origins.

Not finding anyone at the front of the house, Juan went around to the back. There, he saw a man talking to a woman, who was cleaning something near a hut. "Excuse me please, but do you know whether Mr. Klement lives here?" he asked. Both of them immediately confirmed the name, and the man responded, "You mean the Germans?"

To avoid arousing suspicion, Juan claimed to have no knowledge of their nationality. The man added: "Do you mean the one with the three grown sons and the little son?"

Again, Juan pleaded ignorance, saying he was there only to deliver a small package to him. The man volunteered that the family had moved out two or three weeks earlier, but he didn't know where they had gone.

This could have been devastating news, suggesting that if Aharoni had arrived just a bit earlier he would have found them at the house. But the man clearly accepted Juan's cover story and took him to one of the painters who was working in a back room. The painter was equally forthcoming. He said the Klements had moved to San Fernando, another suburb of Buenos Aires. He didn't know the address, but suggested they could talk to one of Klement's sons, who worked in an auto repair shop nearby.

Dressed like a mechanic, the young German confirmed he was one of Klement's sons. Juan heard others calling him something that sounded like Tito or Dito. Aharoni concluded this must have been Dieter, Eichmann's third son. Dieter was more suspicious than the Argentine workers. He questioned Juan about his story and asked who had sent the package. When Juan repeated his story, Dieter said the street where the family now lived had no name or numbers. Realizing he wouldn't learn anything more directly, and to avoid further questioning, Juan handed the small package to Dieter, and asked him to give it to his brother.

Staking out the auto repair shop, Aharoni and his small team decided to track Dieter's movements after work. The first night they never spotted him leaving. Later, they saw two people on a moped, and assumed that the passenger on the back was Dieter. The moped traveled in the direction of San Fernando, and the driver dropped off the passenger near a kiosk. This turned out to be about one hundred yards from a newly built, small house on Garibaldi Street, which they would soon learn was where the Eichmann family had just moved.

Aharoni was convinced that "Klement" was really Eichmann, but he kept looking for additional confirmation. He had Juan return to see Dieter at the auto repair shop and tell Eichmann's son that the sender of the package had complained to him that it never was delivered. Dieter insisted he had passed along the package and also revealed that it should have been addressed to Nicholas "Aitchmann," not "Klement." Juan believed this was bad news, indicating they had not found their man. But Aharoni, who didn't want to let him in on who they were really looking for, assured him he had done "a fantastic job."

Aharoni made repeated trips to San Fernando, initially talking to neighbors, using a variety of pretexts. He confirmed that the German family had moved in recently. An architect obtained the document showing the plot 14 on Garibaldi Street, where the new house was situated, was registered under the name of Veronica Catarina Liebl de Eichmann, listing both her maiden and married name. After repeated passes to observe the house, Aharoni caught his first glimpse of a man of medium size and build, about 50 years old, with a high forehead and partially bald, on March 19. The man collected the wash from the clothesline and went back into the house.

Aharoni cabled his superiors that he had spotted a man at Vera Eichmann's house who definitely resembled Eichmann, and there was no longer any doubt about his identity. He also recommended that he return to Israel right away to help plan an operation to kidnap him. Before he did so, however, he was intent on getting a photo of their quarry.

Sitting in the back of a small truck covered with a tarpaulin, Aharoni had the driver park next to the kiosk and get something to eat. Meanwhile, he observed the house and pointed a camera through a hole in the tarp. He photographed the house and the surroundings. But he had to delegate the job of photographing Eichmann with a camera hidden in a briefcase to another local helper with native Spanish. Intercepting Eichmann and his son Dieter when they were outside, the helper engaged them briefly in conversation, just long enough to trigger his camera.

Aharoni left Argentina on April 9. Harel joined him on the flight from Paris to Tel Aviv. "Are you absolutely sure he is our man?" he asked. Aharoni showed him the photo that had been taken with the briefcase camera. "I have not the slightest doubt," he replied.

"It wasn't just Vera Eichmann's use of her real name on the property registration that indicated the family's increasingly relaxed attitude," Gehlen said. "Simon Wiesenthal, who kept monitoring the rest of the Eichmann family back in Austria, had spotted other telltale evidence that the purported widow was living with her infamous fugitive husband. Eichmann's stepmother had died, and a death notice in the *Oberösterreichische Nachtrichten*, the Linz daily, was signed by Vera Eichmann, using her married name. She also signed a similar notice in the same newspaper when Eichmann's father died in February 1960. The Eichmanns' family loyalty evidently made them blind to danger."

Wiesenthal also reported to Mossad operatives that he had hired two photographers, equipped with telephoto lenses, to snap pictures of the mourners at the father's funeral. They included Eichmann's brothers. One of them, Otto, bore a striking resemblance to Adolf. Wiesenthal claimed this explained the repeated alleged sightings of Adolf in Europe over the years. He gave the photos to two Israeli agents and told them, "Anyone with Otto Eichmann's photograph in his hands would be able to identify Adolf Eichmann, even if he now called himself Ricardo Klement."

There was now no doubt that the Israelis were on the right trail and closing in on their target. But Harel and Rafi Eitan, the man Harel had designated to lead the operation on the ground, knew they had to work out what they would do with Eichmann to get him out of the country, before they could kidnap him. That meant arranging a safe house to hold the prisoner, and then the transport to Israel.

Harel took charge of making arrangements for the preferred option, flying Eichmann out. But El Al, the Israeli airline, had no flights to Argentina at that time, so they needed to find a pretext to send a special plane. Fortuitously, Argentina was planning to commemorate the 150th anniversary of its independence in late May, and Israel was invited to send its representatives to the celebrations. Harel suggested to the Foreign Ministry that the delegation should fly to Buenos Aires in a special plane. He worked directly with El Al's executives to ensure that he had the airline's full cooperation. They even allowed the Mossad chief to approve the crew that would be selected for the flight.

While Harel handled the flight arrangements, Eitan looked into a back-up plan: the much less desirable option of a lengthy journey by sea. He got in touch with the chairman of Zim, the Israeli shipping line. Zim had two refrigerated ships at the time, which were used to transport kosher beef from Argentina to Israel. Working with the captain of one of those ships, Eitan arranged for the preparation of a special compartment that would have served as Eichmann's floating temporary prison if the flight had not worked out for any reason. He would have been smuggled out with a regular shipment of kosher beef.

After two weeks in Israel, while Harel prepared the team members who would soon make their way to Argentina using a variety of passports and cover stories, Aharoni landed back in Buenos Aires on April 24. He was no longer posing as an Israeli diplomat but as a German businessman, with a new passport, a new moustache, and new clothes. One of the first to follow Aharoni was Avraham Shalom, Eitan's deputy for the operation. Harel told Shalom he wanted him to meet up with Aharoni, check out everything about the purported sightings of Eichmann and his family on Garibaldi Street, and send a coded signal if he felt certain they had the right man in their sights.

Shalom was an experienced agent, but he nearly blew his cover a couple of times. After reaching Paris on the first leg of his journey, he picked up a German passport with new identity papers. In transit in Lisbon, he and other passengers were required to hand in their passports and then to ask for them back when they were ready to board their next flight, in Shalom's case, the flight to Buenos Aires. Shalom forgot his fake name and had to reach behind a startled airport official to point to the passport which he recognized only by its color. When he finally reached his hotel in Buenos Aires and had to register at the desk of his hotel, his mind went blank again. No matter; ultimately Shalom was safely in Argentina.

When Aharoni took Shalom to see Garibaldi Street, Shalom discovered it was not a real street, but rather a footpath for cars: an ideal place for an operation—no electricity, few people. The only lights came from the occasional passing car. By then, the Israelis were no longer startled by the notion that the once powerful Eichmann lived in such humble surroundings. By the time more members of the team arrived, Aharoni confirmed they were tracking the right man. They also observed his daily routine from a safe distance. They watched him walk to a bus stop, travel to a Mercedes factory every morning, and return by bus to the stop right at the corner of his street at the same time every evening. From there, Eichmann had a very short walk to his house.

Zvi "Peter" Malkin, an especially strong member of the team, was assigned to grab Eichmann first. Eitan, one of the last to arrive, concurred with Shalom that the conditions were promising. He knew, however, there was always the possibility of something going wrong. Good cars were hard to get in Buenos Aires, and the beat-up vehicles the team had rented broke down often. There was also the chance that some slip by one of the Israelis could arouse suspicion.

Harel, who also flew to Argentina but stayed in downtown Buenos Aires to monitor the action from a short distance, had given Eitan a pair of open handcuffs, keeping the key for himself. If the Argentine police should catch up with them after they seized Eichmann, Eitan was to handcuff his hand to Eichmann's. Then he would tell the police to bring both of them to the Israeli ambassador.

On the evening of May 10, the day before the scheduled operation, Harel gathered the whole team for a final briefing. At this point, everyone knew their assignments. A total of seven safe houses and apartments were prepared, primarily to provide alternatives for where to hold the captive until he could be smuggled out of the country, but also for members of the team. Some of those who had been staying in hotels had already checked out and moved to one of the safe houses, but the Mossad chief did not want everyone checking out from hotels on the day of the kidnapping, which could tip off the police about their identities. Harel then sounded the inevitable cautionary note: if they were caught, they should admit they were Israelis, but they should also assert that they undertook this action on their own initiative. They were not to admit that this was an official Israeli action.

When one of the agents asked bluntly, "How long do you think we'll have to sit in prison if we're caught?" the Mossad chief answered, "A good few years."

The team deployed two cars for the operation, which was timed to intercept Eichmann when he normally got off the bus from work, 7:40

in the evening. Aharoni drove the first car. Eitan and Malkin drove with him. Harel had specifically warned Malkin that Eichmann must not be bodily harmed. "Not a scratch."

Shalom, Eitan's deputy, was in the second car with other agents. They were parked about 30 yards away, with the hood up as if they were doing some repairs. As soon as they spotted Eichmann, they were supposed to turn on their bright lights, blinding Eichmann so he wouldn't see the first car just up ahead.

Eichmann normally followed the same routine every day, but on that evening he did not get off the 7:40 bus. By eight, when he still hadn't arrived, Aharoni whispered to Eitan: "Do we leave or continue to wait?" Eitan replied they should wait, but he, too, was calculating they could not do so much longer. Although it was dark, the two parked cars risked attracting attention.

At 8:03, Shalom spotted Eichmann in the evening darkness. He rushed back to the car. Another agent quickly slammed the hood down, and Shalom flashed the headlights. In the first car, Aharoni saw Eichmann clearly through his binoculars. Leaning out the window, he warned the waiting Malkin, "He has a hand in his pocket. Watch out for a weapon."

As Eichmann turned the corner from the bus stop and walked directly by their car, Malkin turned around and blocked his path. *"Un momentito, Señor,"* he said, using the phrase he had been practicing for weeks. Eichmann stopped abruptly. Malkin took advantage of that instant to lunge for him. The problem was that, because of Aharoni's warning, he grabbed for his right hand instead of his throat and the two men tumbled into a ditch.

Eichmann began screaming. This turned a well-planned and carefully exercised operation into an unholy mess. Aharoni gunned the engine to drown out the screams, while Eitan and another agent jumped out of the car to help. Malkin grabbed Eichmann by his legs while the two others took him by his arms, quickly pulling him into the car through the back door. They put him on the floor between the front and the back seats, where they had placed blankets, both so that he would not be injured, and to cover him. Eichmann's head was pressed against Eitan's knees, and Malkin sat on the other side. Their captive had no weapon.

Aharoni delivered a sharp order to Eichmann in German, "If you don't keep still, you'll be shot." Malkin still had his hand on his mouth beneath the blanket, but when Eichmann nodded, signaling he understood, he took it off. They then drove in silence. Eitan and Malkin shook hands. Eichmann, who was now outfitted in thick goggles so he could not see anything, lay completely still.

On their way to the main safe house, they stopped to switch license plates. They briefly lost the second car that was supposed to be with them, but it soon reappeared and followed them to the designated villa, where other members of the team were anxiously waiting. The Israelis walked Eichmann to the small second floor room prepared for him, and put him on an iron bed, shackling one of his legs to its heavy frame. They undressed him and a member of the team, who was a doctor, examined his mouth to make sure he did not have any poison. The prisoner protested that after all this time as a free man he was not taking such precautions, but the doctor still removed his false teeth to be sure, and then inspected the rest of his body.

Eitan, Shalom, Malkin and Aharoni were all in the room, watching while the doctor checked his armpit, where normally SS officers had a tattoo with their blood type. Instead, Eichmann only had a small scar, which he later admitted was the result of his efforts to burn away the tattoo with a cigarette when he had been detained by the Americans at the end of the war. His captors had failed to realize his true identity at that time.

Given his experience as an interrogator in the British Army, Aharoni was tasked with getting the prisoner to admit his true identity this time. Aharoni had studied Eichmann's file, which Fritz Bauer had shared with the Israelis, and he was ready to keep asking as many questions as needed to force a confession. His normal style was to ask them slowly and repeatedly.

As it turned out, Eichmann broke down much sooner than anyone expected, making that procedure unnecessary. When Aharoni asked for his name, he replied, "Ricardo Klement." But when he asked him his height, shoe size, and clothing size, each of his answers matched those in his file. Then Aharoni asked him his Nazi Party membership number, and he provided the correct answer. The same thing happened when he asked him for his SS numbers. He also provided his correct date and place of birth, March 19, 1906 in Solingen, Germany.

"Under which name were you born?" Aharoni then asked.

"Adolf Eichmann," he replied.

At that point, the tensions of a long and difficult operation dissolved.

The special El Al flight landed in Buenos Aires just before 6 p.m. on May 19. The delegation was headed by Abba Eban, a minister without portfolio, who had already served as Israel's ambassador to the United States and the United Nations. Prime Minister Ben-Gurion had told him earlier that the flight's real mission was to bring Eichmann back to Israel. That information was shared with only a small number of the others on board. But the presence of three unfamiliar men in El Al uniforms, who did not even pretend to be carrying out any flight duties, tipped off most of the crew that something was afoot.

Back at the safe house, Aharoni and Malkin kept questioning Eichmann during the wait for the plane. Eichmann claimed he was never anti-Semitic. "You must believe me, I had nothing against the Jews," he insisted. But Hitler was "infallible," and he had sworn an oath as an SS officer, which meant he had no choice but to follow orders. "There was a job to do and I did it."

As a prisoner, Eichmann was more than obedient. Initially, the prisoner was terrified that his captors would execute him or poison his food. He seemed almost relieved to hear that they planned to have him stand trial. He tried to convince his captors that he should stand trial in Germany, Argentina, or Austria, but when Aharoni told him this was not even a remote possibility, he agreed to sign a statement declaring his willingness to be tried in Israel.

During this whole period, the Israeli team kept monitoring the newspapers, fearful of any indications that the Argentine authorities had learned of Eichmann's kidnapping. The Israeli team's main task was to get Eichmann on board the El Al flight. Earlier, Shalom had repeatedly driven to the airport to familiarize himself with the route and make himself known to the guards.

When the plane was parked in the maintenance area, he could come in and out without being stopped. On May 20, the scheduled departure day, Shalom made a final inspection of the aircraft and sent a courier to Harel, informing him it was open and safe. Earlier in the day, another member of his team had told key crew members that the plane would be carrying a passenger wearing an El Al uniform who would appear to be sick. They were not told his identity, but the nature of the mission was now clear.

Back at the safe house, Eichmann was completely cooperative as he was bathed, shaved and dressed in the airline's uniform. When the team doctor brought out an injection to sedate him, the prisoner assured him this was not necessary since he would remain quiet. But the Israelis were not about to take that risk. Seeing that they were determined to stick with the plan, Eichmann once again cooperated fully. By the time the agents were ready to take him out of the house, the drug was already beginning to work, but Eichmann was still alert enough to point out that they had left off his jacket, asking them to put it on so he would look exactly like the other crew members.

Eichmann dozed as he was driven in a three-car convoy to the airport. Seeing that all the passengers of the first car were in El Al uniforms, the guard opened the gate and allowed everyone through. Once they reached the plane, the agents kept Eichmann surrounded tightly and supported him as he was maneuvered up the steps. Deposited in the first-class cabin, he was near other "crew" members who also pretended to sleep. The cover story was that they were all part of the relief crew that needed to rest up before they would take over later. Just after midnight, officially May 21, the plane took off. When the plane left Argentine airspace, the "crew" in the first-class cabin got up to embrace each other and celebrate their success. The rest of the real crew finally learned the identity of their mystery passenger.

Harel was on board, but most of the other agents who had carried out the operation, including Eitan, Shalom, and Malkin, were not on the flight. They would have to make their way out of Argentina separately, arriving back in Israel days later.

†

"Frightening, *nicht wahr?*" Gehlen concluded.

"Not the kind of thing to make one sleep peacefully each night," I responded. "But why would you tell me these things now?"

"Because, my friend, from things I've learned through my Israeli connections, you could be the next target. How would you like to be sitting in the dock next to Eichmann?"

30

Eichmann's trial opened in the Jerusalem District Court on April 11, 1961. The trial adjourned on August 14. The verdict was read on December 12, 1961. Eichmann was found guilty of crimes against humanity, war crimes, and crimes against Poles, Slovenes, and Gypsies.. He was also found guilty of membership in three organizations that had been deemed criminal at the Nuremberg trials: the Gestapo, the SD, and the SS. When considering the sentence, the judges concluded that Eichmann had not merely been following orders, but that he believed in the Nazi cause wholeheartedly and had been a key perpetrator of the genocide. On December 15, 1961, Eichmann was sentenced to death by hanging.

His lawyer immediately appealed the verdict, mostly relying on legal arguments about Israel's jurisdiction and the legality of the laws under which Eichmann was charged. On May 29, the Israeli Supreme Court rejected the appeal and upheld the District Court's judgment on all counts. At 8:00 p.m. on May 31, Eichmann was informed that his final appeal had been denied. His last meal was the usual prison fare: cheese, bread, olives, and tea, along with half a bottle of wine.

Hours later, Eichmann was hanged at a prison in Ramla. The execution was attended by a small group of officials, four journalists, and the Canadian clergyman who had been his spiritual counselor while in prison. His last words were, "Long live Germany! Long live Argentina! Long live Austria! These are the three countries I will not forget. I greet my wife, my family and my friends. I am ready. We'll meet again soon, as is the fate of all men. I die believing in God."

Within hours Eichmann's body had been cremated, and his ashes scattered in the Mediterranean Sea, outside of Israeli territorial waters, by an Israeli Navy patrol boat.

By the beginning of August 1962, I was seriously concerned for my own well-being. Although I was still providing periodic information to my former Egyptian employers, I found that quietly, and with no sudden flash of an epiphany, my views on the Jewish people in general, and the State of Israel in particular, had undergone a radical change.

Although I was, and would, to my dying day, be a diehard National Socialist – indeed I still remained loyal to the precept of the now-dormant ODESSA, whose sole remaining area of concern was to provide what protection it could from the ever-more-successful efforts of Nazi-hunters like Simon Wiesenthal, Tuvia Friedman, and the Israeli intelligence agencies, I harbored an occasional, but nagging, sense of guilt over my actions with respect to the *Juden* during the Hitler years.

I may not have been *directly* involved in the operation of the camps, particularly those in "the East," since my job had been that of a soldier-of-the-line rather than an administrator, but my conscience would never let me forget that I *knew* what was going on, and not once had I raised so much as a weak protest. After the Gran Sasso operation of 1943, my stock with the Führer had risen to the degree that I might have been able to make a small difference. Why, then, had I not uttered a word?

Sometimes, when I woke in the middle of the night, the galling truth cut through my sanctimonious pretense: I had not said a word *because I relished Hitler's adoration of me; because I, in turn worshiped Der Führer; and because I was fêted and celebrated and drunk with the aura of power showered on me.*

Six million had perished under the Nazis. While, to my knowledge, I hadn't directly killed a single Jew, neither had I *saved* one. And there *were* a few in high places who had risked their lives and their wealth to do so. Although few even remember today, Reichsmarschall Göring's own brother, Albert, saved hundreds, perhaps thousands, of Jews, and managed to gum up military production in Czechoslovakia, even as his brother saved him from prosecution by the Gestapo. After the War, Albert couldn't find work, simply because of his last name and because of his relationship to the disgraced number two man in the Reich.

Wilhelm Furtwängler, one of the two greatest conductors in the world, saved as many of his Jewish compatriots as Albert Göring, but because he had the courage to remain in *Deutschland* conducting the Berlin Philharmonic, to show the world that German civilization still flowered during the Hitler years, he was vilified and denied the opportunity to conduct in the United States until the day he died.

There were others, of course, but I was not one of them. And after the War, my loyalty to my *kameraden* somehow transcended my conscience at what we – my adopted homeland – had done in the name of saving Western Civilization from the communists – the *Jewish* communists.

I had never feared retribution, whether by the Soviets, Americans, British, or French. But now, for the first time, I felt the cold breath of mortality creeping up on me in the person of a tiny state and a basketful of Jewish survivors who had adopted the phrase, "Never Again."

31

On Thursday evening, April 12, 1962, I had been seated at my favorite table in *Horcher's Restaurant-Bar* for ten minutes, when Ilse joined me. We'd been sitting at the table, casually conversing, when the bartender approached us, accompanied by a remarkably pretty woman in her late 20s, and her escort, a well-dressed man of about forty.

"Herr und Frau Skorzeny," the bartender said. "Permit me to introduce you to two of your countrymen, who are in Madrid for a brief visit. They seem to have had a most unfortunate incident. They were robbed at gunpoint a few minutes ago and someone told them this place was a haven for Germans."

"I'm so sorry," I said sympathetically. "Perhaps you might join us for a drink to calm your nerves. Waiter?" I called. "Drinks for our new friends."

"Thank you," the man said, after he'd ordered for himself and his companion. "I am Hans-Dieter Dielmann. This is my fiancée Anke." I noticed immediately that he spoke with a Viennese accent.

"Otto Skorzeny," I said, holding my hand out and shaking his. "This is my wife, Ilse. You are not originally from Germany?"

"*Wien,*" Dielmann replied. "But how did you guess?"

"I recognize *Wienere Deutsch.* I was born in Vienna. One never loses the accent."

"*Grüss Gott!*" The four of us held our drinks aloft and clinked glasses.

For the next half hour, we engaged in pleasant small talk. Hans-Dieter's fiancée, Anke, was quite sensual, and it was obvious she found me attractive as well. For her part, Ilse relished the attention she was getting from Hans-Dieter Dielmann. From the beginning, our marriage had been founded on candor. We were mature, sophisticated adults, and neither of us held the other accountable for the occasional dalliance.

There were more drinks, then somewhat flamboyant flirting, and soon Ilse invited the young couple, who had lost everything — money, passports and luggage — to stay the night at our villa. There was something irresistible about the newcomers. I felt an air of sexual anticipation between the four of us.

After we had entered the house, at a crucial moment when playful flirting reached the point where it seemed time to pair off, an inner sense warned me that something was very much amiss. I had not survived in the jungles of my existence without an always-present alertness to danger. I reached into my inner breast pocket and pulled a gun on the young couple. "I know who you are, and I know why you're here. You're Mossad, and you've come to kill me."

The young couple did not even flinch. The man said: "You are half-right. We are from Mossad, but if we had come to kill you, you would have been dead weeks ago."

"Or maybe," I rejoined, "I should just kill you now."

Anke spoke up. "If you kill us, the ones who come next won't bother to have a drink with you. You won't even see their faces before they blow out your brains. We want you to help us."

After a long minute, I did not lower my gun, but asked, "What kind of help?"

"Israel needs information and the type of action for which you are well-known. We'll pay you handsomely," the man who had presented as Hans-Dieter Dielmann said.

"Money doesn't interest me. I have quite enough, thank you," I responded.

"Name something you want, then."

"I want Wiesenthal to remove my name from his list."

"That can and will be done. We'll take care of that."

I lowered my weapon, and the two of us shook hands.

"Herr Skorzeny, my name is Yosef Raanan. 'Joe,' if you prefer. Like you, I was born in Vienna, where I was called Kurt Weisman. Unlike you, I lost most of my family in the Holocaust. I'm now employed by The Institute for Intelligence and Special Missions – the Mossad - in my adopted country, Israel."

"Go on," I said calmly.

"As Anke told you, you could have killed them in your residence a few nights ago. Had you done so, parts of your corpse would have been found in a ditch outside the city within the next week."

"I trust you're not simply a small cog in your organization?"

"Would I have been assigned as your contact if I were?" he said. "Would you like another shot of whisky?"

"As long as you're serving Johnnie Walker Blue, why not?"

"You have discerning taste, Herr Skorzeny. Not that I would have expected less."

"But you're not drinking, Mister Raanan."

"'Joe,' if it makes you more comfortable. And you're right. Some central European Jews cannot consume alcohol without serious side effects. So my not drinking is not based on any moral superiority, but for gastric comfort. To answer your question, my 'official' position, if you want to call it that, is Mossad's senior officer in the Federal Republic. We needn't waste words or stand on ceremony. You're as aware of your reputation and standing as I am."

"If you don't mind my asking, since you look rather young to be Mossad's top dog in Germany, how old are you?"

"Forty. Fourteen years your junior."

"So you're to be my handler? Don't look surprised that I know the term."

"I'm not surprised. We're men who've 'been around the block.'"

"Would you mind if I asked your background?"

The younger man grinned. "Are you trying to play the game of who's handling whom? But no, I don't mind. If we're going to be working together it's the kind of thing you're entitled to know. After the Nazis took over in 1938, when I was 16, I was sent to British-ruled Palestine. My mother and my younger brother stayed in Europe and perished."

I remained impassive as he continued. "Like many Jews in Palestine, I joined the British military looking for a chance to strike back at Germany. I served in the Royal Air Force. After the creation of Israel in 1948, I took on my Hebrew name." He laughed and said, "If you guys couldn't kill me one way, you tried to do it another way."

"What do you mean?" I was more curious than offended.

"I was one of the first pilots in Israel's air force. Germany built one of the best fighter planes ever designed, the Messerschmitt Bf-109. Your people built almost 34,000 of them during the war and they were superb. But at the end of the war, they left a bunch of parts in Czechoslovakia, and the Czechs used these parts to build a piece-of-shit copy which they called the Avia S-99. Guess whose first 25 fighter planes were S-99s?"

"Problems?"

"The Czechs ran out of the 109's Daimler-Benz DB 605 engines. They needed a replacement engine if they didn't want to sell those babies as paperweights. Of all the harebrained ideas, they decided to use the same engine and propeller as that of the Heinkel He-111 bomber. Once it got into the air, it was great. The problem was getting it up or down. The engine lacked the responsiveness of the Daimler-Benz unit, and the torque created by the huge propeller made control almost impossible. When you combined the substitute engine and the oversized propeller with the 109's narrow-track undercarriage, it became a flying coffin. It was only by God's grace that any of them made it back safely. We didn't lose a single one of them to enemy fire, but we lost more than half of those S-99s and several pilots when they tried to land."

"You weren't one of those casualties," I remarked.

"Not after they switched me into *legitimate* Spitfires. Then I became an air base commander and worked my way up to be the Air Force's intelligence chief. Isser Harel recruited me for the Mossad five years ago and sent me to Germany as Director of Operations."

I nursed the shot of 21-year-old Johnnie Walker and gazed steadily at my new associate. "What about the operation to snare me?"

"Pretty direct, aren't you?"

"False posturing doesn't suit our kind."

"About four months ago, we assembled a team that traveled to Spain for pre-action intelligence. Our members observed you, your home, your workplace, and your daily routines."

"Hans-Dieter? Anke?"

"Hans-Dieter's not his real name, of course."

"I thought not."

"He's Mossad. Anke's not a trained, full-time Mossad agent but a "helper," a "*saayanit*." She was like an extra, playing whatever role might be required. Pretty …"

"I'll say."

"A *saayanit* often poses as the girlfriend of an undercover Mossad agent. You ever hear of the "badger game," Otto?"

"Can't say I have."

"Some variation of it has been used throughout history. Nowadays, it's called the honey trap."

"The fisherman's lure," I said. Now he was talking about a game I knew. "Gets the guy in a compromising position and while he's staring at what he thinks is going to be the nicest snatch ever, he's 'snatched' all right, when the 'husband,' or 'fiancé,' or spymaster, shows up."

"It worked with you, didn't it?"

"It *almost* worked. Fortunately, my gun was out before my …"

"True. Answer me one question, though."

"Go ahead."

"Why did you agree to cross over? It's not the first time someone has threatened you. Your whole career has been based on security."

"If you know all about me, you know I told Hitler there was no such thing as 100% foolproof security."

"Now you're playing games, Otto. I don't believe for one moment you were frightened by Anke and Hans-Dieter. Cut to the chase, why did you change sides?"

I looked around, unable to formulate an answer, buying time. "Let me think about that for awhile," I finally said.

"By all means, take as much time as you want. Meanwhile, I'd like you to take a brief trip to Israel with me next week. Five, six days at most."

The Fokker F-27, which the Israeli government had leased on a short-term basis from Turkey's *Türk Hava Yolları* Airlines approached Lod Airport from the Eastern Mediterranean, landing gently on Runway 3. I had a mental flashback of the time I'd been the only passenger on a Ju-52 flying from Berlin to the Wolf's Lair in 1943. Joe Raanan had given me plenty of room and plenty of space during the flight from Munich to Tel Aviv. I'd dozed for part of the time, but as we came closer to the Jewish State, I found myself searching for the answer to my contact's question: exactly *why* had I switched sides?

Was it simply the adrenalin high of a new adventure with new employers and a new opportunity? Or could it be something much deeper than that? I had told Hans-Dieter, which wasn't his real name, and Anke, who was a startlingly attractive young woman – but there were hundreds of young women as good-looking, or better-looking, whom I could easily have charmed into my bed, that I wasn't interested in money, which was true, but that I wanted to be off Simon Wiesenthal's list.

Why was *that* of even remote interest to me? Adolf Eichmann had been responsible for the death of thousands of Jews, and he was a high-profile nemesis of that people, so he was clearly a prime target. On the other hand, Adolf Eichmann had been an SS Obersturmbahnführer, my rank as well. I was as high profile as Eichmann, even though my job was substantially different than his.

Why should I fear Simon Wiesenthal? Despite his claims about how instrumental he was in hunting down and capturing Eichmann, I knew much of that was empty bragging, and that his true role was much smaller than he made it out to be. Why, he was fifty-four years old. All one had to do was look at a photograph of him in any newspaper or magazine to see that he was an *old man*. What did I have to fear from an old man who functioned out of a small, shabby office in Vienna?

Fifty-four.

The same age as me!

Fifty-four.

My God, where did the time go?

Der Führer was only two years older than my present age when he died. My first mentor, Ernst Kaltenbrunner, was forty-three when he was hanged. He would have been 59, five years my senior, had he survived. Eichmann was two years older than me when he was executed earlier in the year. Generalmajor Gehlen, truly an "old man," was sixty. Granted, my wife Ilse was only forty-four, and a damned attractive forty-four at that, but still …

As flirtatious as young Anke had been with me, it was clear she had thought of me as … as what? … as an *old man*? An old fool who would so easily succumb to her honey trap?

As we deplaned, I could not help but notice that, contrary to most airports I'd seen in Europe, South America, and even Egypt, Lod Airport was bristling with security guards in virtually every corner. At one point, I saw that someone had left an unattended briefcase near a row of seats abutting one of the entry gates. Less than sixty seconds later, two guards approached with submachine guns and obliterated the briefcase with two bursts of lethal fire. They waited another two minutes before summoning a third man to dispose of the charred mass of metal and leather. Joe Raanan seemed to accept this as an everyday occurrence.

After a deplorable meal, followed by a restful night in a high-rise hotel adjacent to a long, lovely sugar-sand beach on Tel Aviv's Mediterranean waterfront, I felt ready for action when Joe picked me up at eight the next morning.

"Time to meet the boss man," he said.

While I'd never met Isser Harel, I certainly had heard of him. The Director of Mossad had been instrumental in the kidnap-capture of Adolf Eichmann the year before.

I was genuinely surprised when I met him to see how absolutely *ordinary* he looked: thinning hair, almost bald in front, large, protuberant ears, and a face which didn't look particularly intelligent. The type one would forget within moments of meeting him. The kind who would disappear into a wall if he was standing in a room amid a crowd of people.

Yet I'd done my homework on the man and I knew that appearances could be, and usually were, deceptive. This fifty-year-old man, four years *younger* than me, born Isser Halperin to a wealthy vinegar concessionaire to the czar, whose property had been confiscated when the Soviets came to power, left his native Vitebsk in White Russia, emigrated to Latvia, and subsequently to British Palestine in 1930 when he was eighteen. When Israel declared independence, Harel founded and became the first director of *shin bet*, Israel's internal security agency. Three years later, he added the directorship of Mossad to his résumé.

"Not that impressive-looking a man," I whispered to Raanan, just before I was introduced to Harel.

"Don't let looks fool you, Otto. One of the secrets of his success is that so many people, including Israelis, mistake him for a minor bureaucrat. Less than one in ten thousand can identify him by sight. Good morning, Isser."

"Joe," the Director acknowledged with a nod. Turning to me, he said, "Otto Skorzeny, I trust? The most dangerous man in Europe? You certainly look the part." He stuck out his hand. When I shook it, I found his handshake firm and strong. He smiled. "I was frankly astonished that you came over to the bright side, given your history.

I won't pretend I don't know your background, just as I'm sure you've studied mine."

"Correct," I said, with what I thought was an equally disarming smile.

"If you don't mind my saying so, that is one ugly *schmiss*. You must have been a helluva swordsman. At the very least a very courageous one."

"I suppose I should say 'thank you.' By the way, what should I call you? Director? Boss? Mister Harel?"

"Isser'll do just fine. We don't stand on ceremony or rank around here. Everyone's as worthwhile as anyone else. If we lose even one, we lose a universe. Unlike your former Muslim employers, that includes women."

"You're aware I trained Arafat?"

"Of course. I can give you the same line we give everyone publicly. Privately I've met him. That dirty, slovenly raghead appearance is the perfect disguise in this part of the world for a damned good mind, not to mention a good man. I see you're shocked to hear me say that."

"I won't say I'm not."

"I'm equally sure you've been waiting for me to ask you why you switched sides. Another surprise, Otto, if I may call you that."

"Of course."

"I try not to pry into a man's innermost thoughts. You could *tell* me anything you want. It might be true or it might not, and it wouldn't make a bit of difference to me. Who you are or what you are is your own business."

Harel was right. I was astonished. This mild-mannered little man, so ordinary in his appearance and speech, was someone who should be watched carefully. Perhaps emulated. *Emulated*? A Jew? Why should I be surprised at that? Hadn't Erhard Milch, a Jew, been a Field Marshal in National Socialist Germany? Had he not been the *real* brains behind the Luftwaffe when Göring had been a pompous, posturing blowhard? There was something unique and special about these people. *We don't stand on ceremony or rank around here. Everyone's as worthwhile as anyone else. If we lose even one, we lose a universe.* That turned the German philosophy on its head.

†

"Gentlemen, I suggest we go for a short drive so our newest recruit might see a little bit of *Eretz Israel,*" Raanan said, barging through the door without knocking, after Harel and I had spent the better part of an hour engaging in small talk which, to me, was far more meaningful than "small talk."

"Welcome to Israel!" the Director remarked sardonically. "The bravest, most caring people in the world, but without a doubt the rudest."

I was to hear, and most pointedly *see,* this attitude displayed throughout my sojourn in the Holy Land. No wonder Arafat had confided in me that the Jewish state would win every war but lose every peace. Special they might be, but dreadful they certainly were.

"Where to?" Harel replied patiently.

"Probably the place where our guest will learn the most about *why* we are what we are. I'll meet you out front in five minutes."

If I'd been surprised before, I was truly dumbfounded when Raanan pulled up in a relatively new Mercedes 220.

Raanan answered my unspoken question smoothly. "Don't look so surprised, Otto. We do a lot of trade with the Federal Republic. I'm sure you've heard that after what happened in World War II no Jew would be caught dead driving a 'Hitler car.' You'd probably crap your pants if you knew that the largest Mercedes dealership in the world is in Tel Aviv."

With Joe driving, me sitting in the front passenger seat, and Isser Harel sitting in back, the large car accelerated smoothly as the road climbed from coastal Tel Aviv toward the hills of Jerusalem. West of the Holy City, we ascended the slope of Mount Herzl, which, at 2,638 feet above sea level, hardly qualified as a "mountain." Despite the fact that it was midsummer, which I'd been told was brutal in Israel, the weather up here was remarkably tolerable. A mild breeze ruffled the thin trees which inhabited this sparse "forest." Raanan stopped the car just outside the entrance.

"Herr Skorzeny," Harel said. It was the first time he'd addressed me formally. "This journey is best experienced alone," he continued gently. "Would you mind terribly if we allow you to proceed at your own pace, in your own time?"

I shrugged. "Do I have a choice?"

"Of course, my friend," he replied. "We all have choices. Life is dynamic. In God's eyes, we all make mistakes. Life is a journey in which we all learn at our own pace. This is not a place to make judgments. Rather it is a place to remember, and by remembering, to grow beyond what we once were."

That was my introduction to *Yad Vashem*, Israel's memorial to the victims of the Holocaust, and not just the Jews.

At the entryway, I read a small sandstone plaque: "This place is dedicated to preserving the memory of the dead; honoring those of every race or religion who fought against their oppressors; recognizing Gentiles who selflessly aided Jews in need; and researching the Holocaust in particular and genocide in general, so that no one should ever forget."

I don't know why my new associates suggested I explore *Yad Vashem* alone, any more than when, after nearly two hours walking, stopping, stooping, sitting, and, yes, crying, in the horrifying, uplifting simplicity of the place, I had no idea of whether I'd changed, whether I'd learned anything or not.

When, finally, I left *Yad Vashem*, and crossed a small field to where the Mercedes was parked, I was accosted by a man in his mid-sixties. He pointed at me and shouted, "I know you! You are Obersturmbahnführer Skorzeny, a war criminal. You must be brought to justice now!"

Without batting an eye, Joe Raanan got out of the driver's seat, crossed the field, and said softly, but sternly, to the man, "No, you are mistaken, my friend. He's my relative, and he, himself, is a Holocaust survivor." He said nothing more about the incident during the return trip to Tel Aviv.

32

During the following days, I was exhaustively briefed on why the Israelis wanted my help and what they hoped I would do.

The Mossad's playbook for protecting Israel and the Jewish people had no preordained rules or limits. The agency's spies had evaded the legal systems in a host of countries for the purpose of liquidating Israel's enemies: To get to unexpected places on these improbable missions, the Mossad sometimes found itself working with unsavory partners. When short-term alliances could help, the Israelis were willing to dance with the devil, if necessary.

During my briefing, Joe Raanan told me, "Six months ago, Nasser announced four successful tests of missiles capable of striking anywhere 'south of Beirut'. That meant anywhere in Israel. Israeli officials panicked. The Mossad had never guessed that Nasser was developing the means to destroy 'the Zionist entity,' as he had repeatedly promised.

"We quickly learned that Egypt had built a secret facility in the desert, known as Factory 333, staffed by German scientists, builders of the V-1 and V-2 rockets that had devastated London. Even the project's security chief was a veteran of Hitler's SS. The Egyptians' plan was to build 900 missiles, all of them aimed at Israel."

"Early on, a Mossad planning team started to work on where it could be best to find and kill you. Isser had a bolder plan: instead of killing you, turn you. We'd known for some time that to catch the German scientists, we needed an inside man. We needed a Nazi."

"But how could you trust me?" I asked.

"Don't kid yourself, Otto, we knew we would never find a Nazi we could trust, but we saw in you someone we could count on, someone with a record of success in executing innovative plans, and skilled at keeping secrets."

"You know, of course, my original reason for coming over?"

"Of course. Life insurance."

"You think I couldn't have been protected by my former employers?"

Raanan arched his eyebrows for a long moment before he answered. "No, and you don't think so either."

"Assuming that to be the case, why do *you* think I agreed to work for the Israelis?"

"Don't ask me, Otto. During World War II, I was engaged in psychological warfare for the Brits, but that doesn't mean I'm a trained psychologist, or even an amateur at that kind of hocus pocus bullus shittus. That's for you to ask yourself."

"Point taken. Joe, you've been fair and honest with me. Turnabout's fair play. Despite Isser's 'We're all equal in the eyes of God' lecture, you're one of the higher-ups in the Organization. I very much doubt you've been detailed to be my prime contact. Face it, you've got bigger fish to fry. You're in strategic planning. I'm a tactician."

"You're right, of course. I'll continue to be project manager for the whole German scientist operation. But you're wrong when you say you're a mere tactician. You, my friend, are the lynchpin, absolutely critical to the entire operation. That's why, for the most part, you'll be an independent contractor, running your operation the same way you ran Friedenthal. But when you need contact points, and we all need contact points, I'm assigning you two of the best Mossad agents we've got: Rafi Eitan and Avraham Ahituv."

Eitan was one of the most amazing characters in Israeli intelligence. He'd earned the nickname "Mr. Kidnap" for his role in abducting Eichmann and other men wanted by Israeli security agencies. Eitan had also helped Israel acquire materials for its secret nuclear program.

Ahituv, who'd been born in Germany in 1930, had been similarly involved in a wide array of Israeli clandestine operations all around the globe.

Later, I found out that the Mossad agents had tried to persuade Wiesenthal to remove me from his list of war criminals, but the Nazi hunter refused. The Mossad, with typical chutzpah, forged a letter, supposedly to me from Wiesenthal, declaring that my name had been cleared.

The key to understanding the story is that the Mossad had made stopping German scientists then working on Egypt's rocket program one of its top priorities. After Nasser's galvanizing disclosure about Egypt's successful rocket launches, Mossad agents started sending threatening messages to the German engineers employed in Egypt's weapons program. When they traveled home to Germany, they got phone calls in the middle of the night, telling them to quit the Egyptian program. When they were in Egypt, some were sent letter bombs. Several people were injured by the explosions.

Heinz Krug, the 49-year-old manager of Munich Intra Trading Company, a principal supplier of rocket parts for the Egyptian program, was near the very top of the Mossad's target list. When the war had ended 17 years earlier, Krug was part of a team of stars at Peenemünde, where top German scientists had worked in the service of the Third

Reich. The team, led by Wernher von Braun, had engineered the rockets for the Blitz that nearly defeated England. Its wider ambitions included missiles that could fly a lot farther, with greater accuracy and more destructive power.

According to Mossad research, a decade after the war ended, von Braun invited Krug and other former colleagues to join him in America. Von Braun was, at that time, leading a missile development program for the United States. Krug opted for another, seemingly more lucrative option: joining other scientists from Peenemünde, led by professor Wolfgang Pilz, in Egypt, where they set up a secret strategic missile program for that country.

In the Israelis' view, Krug had to know that Israel, the country where so many Holocaust survivors had found refuge, was the intended target of his new masters' military capabilities. A committed Nazi would see this as an opportunity to continue the mission of exterminating the Jewish people.

Meanwhile, I proved not only to be consummately reliable, but I used the same initiative that had ingratiated me to my Nazi overlords nineteen years before. I flew to Egypt on my own recognizance and compiled a detailed list of German scientists and their addresses. I also provided the names of many "front" companies in Europe that were procuring and shipping components to Egypt for its military projects. During another trip to Egypt, I mailed exploding packages. One Israeli-made bomb killed five Egyptians in the military rocket site, Factory 333, where German scientists worked. I then procured critical information on Heinz Krug's company, Munich Intra Trading Company.

The threatening notes and phone calls, were driving Krug crazy. He and his colleagues knew the threats were from Israelis, that much was obvious. It was reasonable for Krug to feel that a Mossad noose might be tightening around his neck, too. That was why he summoned help: a Nazi hero who was considered the best of the best in Hitler's heyday.

One evening, at the beginning of September, while I was attending to my arms shipment business in Madrid, I received a telephone call from Munich. When I answered the phone, a man with a Bavarian accent, whose voice conveyed fear even over the phone line, asked, "Obersturmbahnführer Skorzeny?"

"*Wer ist das?* Who is this?" I asked.

"Heinz Krug." Although I had been well-briefed on Krug's identity and had exhaustively researched both his activities in Egypt and his affiliation with Munich Intra, I pretended ignorance.

"I'm sorry, Herr Krug, the name means nothing to me."

"We met once at Peenemünde." He spoke hurriedly, the tone of his voice nervous. "I understand you were instrumental in helping many of our *kameraden* start new lives in South America."

"Yes?" I replied, my own voice neutral.

"They say you worked in Egypt some years back, training Colonel Nasser's legions at Luxor."

"True, Herr Krug."

"I have great need of your services, *Obersturmbahnführer*. My life is in imminent danger. Money is no object. Is there a place we can meet?"

Although my heart was beating quite excitedly, since one of Israel's prime targets was literally landing in my lap, I said nothing.

The man continued, "One hundred thousand marks, or Swiss francs if you prefer."

"I'm listening, Herr Krug. Where do you propose we meet?"

"Would Munich be convenient for you?"

"Not inconvenient," I replied, catching the urgency in his voice. "There's a Lufthansa flight leaving Barrajas at 7:35 tomorrow morning. It gets into Munich-Riem Airport 2½ hours later. How long will we need?"

"An hour, two at the most. You could be on the 15:20 flight back and be home in time for dinner." I could hear the hopeful relief in his voice. "I'll have a chauffeur from Intra pick you up at the airport."

"Very good, Herr Krug. I'll see you tomorrow morning."

My next call was to a private number in Frankfurt.

"Skorzeny here. ... Fine, thank you, as is Ilse. Are you still looking for large jugs of well-priced Rioja tempranillo?" Although I was confident Raanan's line was encrypted, there was no need to take unnecessary chances. We'd agreed on "jug," the English translation of Krug.

The Mossad's senior man in Germany was quick on the uptake. "I'll have to check with our wine distributors, Malkin & Sons. How large a case lot, and when would you need to know?"

"I'm traveling to Munich tomorrow. I have an appointment to intraview a prospective customer tomorrow at ten-thirty."

"*Intraview*? Are you certain your English is as good as you seem to think, *Amigo*? Even Germans like me know the term is *inte_r_view*."

"Did I say that? All this international traveling must be rattling my brain. If you've got the time, I could meet you and the Malkin representative for lunch about one o'clock. My flight home doesn't leave until 15:20."

"I see no reason to make you late for your flight. There's a very convivial, quiet restaurant, Café Icarus, in Maria-Montessori Strasse, quite close to the airport."

"Very good. I'll see you then."

"You're certain this threat is real, Herr Krug? There are all kinds of crank letters in this day and age. It's postmarked Würzburg. Nothing suspicious about that."

The manager's office was commodious but essentially utilitarian. The only touch of elegance was the Meissen chinaware and Bruckmann & Söhne silverware on which we were served coffee and pastries.

"I am, Herr Skorzeny. These letters and phone calls started three months after I became involved with the project. The letter I've shown you is only the latest. This one's postmarked Würzburg. There've been a dozen others – Basel, Hallstatt, Znojmo, all over Europe. Then there've been phone calls. Sometimes three in the morning. Always unexpected, always terrifying. A sentence or two and then the telephone disconnects. They know my home number."

"You're certain you're not the only one who's been receiving these threats."

"Absolutely. My associates at Factory 333 have received letter bombs. Five were killed two weeks ago."

"Have you any suspicions as to who would do this and why?"

"Of course. There's only one possible suspect. The Zionist entity. I'm sure you'll agree, we should have eradicated them all during the last war. If you don't get rid of all the nits, you'll have a houseful of lice."

"It seems to me you'd be safe in Egypt or certainly here."

"You don't understand, or perhaps you do, *Obersturmbahnführer*, since you lived through those times. These *Juden* are everywhere. They know no borders. I'm told that nowadays it's become the fashion for them to undergo surgery to get rid of the large hook noses."

I was shocked to realize that only a few months ago that could have been me speaking. Now, for some reason, such talk left me cold. Nevertheless, it behooved me to encourage this man's confidence.

"I can well understand your fear, Herr Krug. What would you have me do?"

"I need security. Because of my position, I can afford the best and I want only the best. You must know of your reputation?"

"I do."

"Then you know why I came to you before anyone else. The regime for which I work had nothing but good things to say about your work in Upper Egypt."

"You know my fee?"

"I do. That's why I offered it to you without bothering to bargain. If I save a few marks but lose my life, what is the money worth to me?"

We spent the next thirty minutes discussing details and strategies. I told him this seemed like a job that could be accomplished with a minimum of fuss, using known experts who'd worked with one another before. I'd had great success in Argentina using such tactics to protect Péron.

"We should assign six agents as bodyguards. Because such work calls for maximum alertness, they should ideally work no more than a four-hour shifts. They should tail you in different vehicles and wear different styles of clothing, everything from military gear to *lederhosen*. We'll put a tap on your phones, both here and at home. You're married, I trust?"

"Yes," he said, proudly turning a photograph of his wife, a plain-looking woman in nondescript clothing, toward me.

"Of course, you should have a local phone number which you can dial any time of the day or night, which will connect you to whichever of your guards is on duty at that time."

"Good, good," he said, smiling and relaxing for the first time that morning. "I feel safer already. When would you want to initiate this protection?"

"It will take me a short time to get everything arranged. Let's say I meet you back here on Tuesday morning the 11th at the same time. We can arrange to drive to a more private place where you can meet with the guards I select for you."

"That sounds wonderful, *Obersturmbahnführer*. I'll be waiting impatiently."

"Not to unduly concern you, Herr Krug, but starting tomorrow, there'll be at least one of my agents observing you each day until we meet. While you will not see him, you will have the security of knowing he'll be watching over you."

"Thank you again, Herr Skorzeny. Now about the money …?"

"I'm prepared to trust your word as a National Socialist, Herr Krug. We'll discuss that on September 11th as well.

When we met at Café Icarus, Raanan was accompanied by two men, "Peter" Malkin, whom I'd met in Tel Aviv, and a very short, pugnacious-looking man, whom I judged to be around fifty, Malchiel Shemer. Malkin was a large, powerful man, who nonetheless gave the appearance of a mild-mannered Teddy-bear. Shemer, on the other hand, reminded me of a very small, very vicious dog whom you would not approach without a large stick, or, better yet, a handgun to protect yourself.

"These will be your two watchdogs," Joe said.

"What about Rafi and Avraham?"

"They'll be watching the watchdogs. The four of them will be in direct contact with you at all times."

"And you?"

"Otto, I'm a busy man," he said, mock-arrogantly. "You think I have time to waste on small fish like you?" He winked to let me know there was a humorous side to this deadly game. "I'll be at least a quarter of a mile away. The eleventh, you say?"

"Yes."

"Peter and Malchiel will be following you in a white Mercedes."

"How will they know to intercept me?"

"Who said anything about intercept? They'll be waiting across the street from Intra's front door. If there's any problem, one of ours will be sitting at the security desk, just inside the door. He'll be in radio contact with the Mercedes."

As the waiter came by to take their orders, Raanan said, smoothly, "Ah, yes, I'm quite hungry this afternoon. I do believe I'll have the jugged hare."

33

"I'm so relieved you came right on time," Herr Skorzeny.

"I was fortunate, Herr Krug," I replied. "The plane left ten minutes early and we had a favorable tailwind. For security reasons, I rented a car under the name of Ron Pren, a citizen of the Netherlands, resident in Rotterdam. Have you had any more calls or letters in the time since we met?"

"Thankfully, no. You were correct, I never saw the guards you hired on my behalf, although, to be honest, I had Intra's internal security search for them."

"I'm glad you did because it would prove to you how safe you'll be when the entire program kicks into action. I suggest we wait until we get into the car before we talk more."

As we entered Intra's underground parking garage, Krug walked toward his company car, a late model white Mercedes Benz.

"I think it might be better to travel to our destination in my rental car. I'm certain if someone knows enough to make anonymous telephone calls and send you mail they must have surveilled your daily movements and they most likely know your car. We should take my rental, which is far less conspicuous."

"Yes, *Obersturmbahnführer*," he said. "That was wise thinking."

As he followed me to my car, he seemed pleased that the auto I'd rented, a beige Opel Rekord, looked so ordinary. "No sense in being obvious," I remarked. "When we leave the garage, we'll be joined by a white Mercedes, the same model as yours, which will follow us to our destination. Even if the Israelis believe it's your vehicle, they'll change their minds when they see two men in that car. Keep an eye out for them."

"Thank you for telling me that, Herr Skorzeny. That makes me feel more secure."

As we pulled out of the garage, I switched the headlights on and off three times, the prearranged signal, then turned left. I nodded with satisfaction as I looked in my rearview mirror and found the Mercedes had pulled into traffic immediately behind me.

We headed north on Highway 301 in the direction of Mainburg. When we reached provincial road 2049, we turned right and drove into a heavily forested area west of Landshut.

Krug seemed nervous when we turned onto a dirt path that ended in a clearing.

"Not to worry," I said. "Our tail car is right behind us. This is as good a place as any to ensure no one is around to hear our plans. Remember, these fellows don't know my real name. As a way of double-blind protection, they know me only as Ron Pren."

The man looked unsure, but replied, "Ah, yes, the Dutch fellow who rented the car. You're my protector. I'm sure you know what you're doing."

Malkin emerged from the Mercedes and came toward us. Krug and I, in turn, got out of the Opel.

"Good morning, Herr Krug," Malkin said, his huge hand outstretched in friendly greeting. "I'm sure Mr. Pren has told you we will be in charge of the operation. I'm Peter. My associate, the big fellow with me is Herr Shemer. As you can see, he's the brute strength of our team."

Krug smiled at the heavy Germanic humor when he saw the diminutive Shemer exit the passenger door of the Mercedes. The small man turned toward the back of the car, grimaced, and approached us.

"Problem, Dietrich?" Malkin called out.

"Unfortunately, when we reached the end of this so-called road, the right rear tire of our car must have hit a sharp rock and it's flat. I'll join you gentlemen as soon as I open the boot and get the spare out."

As the three of us approached the larger automobile, it became apparent Shemer had the spare tire and the jack out of the trunk. He'd just removed the tire iron when he turned to us. "I'm Dietrich Shemer," he said to our passenger. "You must be Heinz Krug, the famous scientist."

Suddenly, Shemer bent over, as if in pain and started to moan. Krug, who was closest to him, reached over to assist the smaller man.

"Are you all right?" Krug asked solicitously.

Those were the last words he ever uttered. Shemer rose to his full, if not very impressive, height and struck Krug a blow on the head with the tire iron. Intra's manager fell to the ground, unconscious. A moment later, I unholstered a sidearm I was carrying and shot Krug between the eyes, ending his life in an instant.

Afterward, Shemer reached into the Mercedes' boot for a large bottle of acid, while Malkin and I went back to the Opel, took out two spades, and dug a shallow trench thirty feet from where the dirt road dead-ended. The three of us grabbed hold of Krug's body, carried it to the makeshift grave, and poured acid over it. We waited awhile as the acid burned away his facial features, then buried what was left in the hole. We covered the makeshift grave with lime, so that neither search dogs nor wild animals would ever pick up the scent of human remains.

While we were still standing around, a nondescript older-model Auto Union 1000 drove up and parked behind the Mercedes.

"A little too late for the action, Joe," I said, as the man approached. "Heavy sonofabitch. We could have used a little help."

"Surely you didn't expect a man in my position to dirty my hands in such a deed," Raanan replied. "Besides, I was less than a quarter mile away, so I could rescue you guys, if need be. By the way, Malchiel, that was a very nice touch you added."

"I thought you'd like it," Shemer said.

I looked questioningly at the three men.

Malkin explained to me, "Call it a ritual slaughter. A Kosher killing. Jewish law provides that in order for food, such as beef or lamb, to be Kosher, it must be killed in the most humane way. Historically, when a steer is slaughtered, the butcher will hit the animal on the head, rendering it unconscious before he kills it. That way, all the beast knows is that one moment he is standing, the next he is sleeping. He doesn't feel a thing and doesn't even know he's dead."

"That's what happened here. Mister Krug was so fearful coming to meet us that the last thing he expected, once we'd put him at his ease, was to be knocked out. He died without fear and without pain, and Israel is the safer for it."

"What happens when the rental agency finds out their car and its renter have gone missing?"

"We took care of that as well," Raanan added. "We'd arranged early on with the rental agency, which is owned by a friend, to allow us the use of space and a clerk, who was one of ours, when 'Ron Pren' showed up. We own the Opel. By tonight, it will be in some small town in Moravia, complete with totally valid Czechoslovak plates, as will 'Ron Pren's' rental contract. And you, Mister Pren, will be on a flight to Barcelona, continuing on to Madrid on a second flight."

The campaign of intimidation was largely successful. By the following month, only a very few low-ranking Germans remained in Egypt. Israel stopped the violence and threats, however, when one team was arrested in Switzerland while putting verbal pressure on a scientist's family. A Mossad man and an Austrian scientist, who were working for Israel, were put on trial. Luckily, the Swiss judge sympathized with Israel's fear of Egypt's rocket program. The two men were convicted of making threats, but they were immediately set free.

Prime Minister Ben-Gurion, however, concluded that all of this being out in public was disastrous to Israel's image, and might very well upset a deal he had arranged with West Germany to sell weapons to Israel. Isser Harel submitted a letter of resignation, and to his shock, Ben-Gurion accepted it. The new Mossad director, commander of military intelligence General Meir Amit, moved the agency away from chasing or intimidating Nazis.

By the end of 1962, I'd had my fill of excitement living the "legend" I had become. Like so many "celebrities" whose fame has faded after a few years, I craved the sort of anonymity that most mature adults desire unless they are politicians or addicted to that sort of life. One ultimately comes to realize that proving oneself is necessary at a young age, but peace becomes more important as we grow older.

I continued to advise various "clients" about military training and tactics, but I did little traveling and handled all of my business interests from Madrid. In the middle of 1966, I received a short letter postmarked Usingen, a small town 20 miles north of Frankfurt-am-Main. On opening the envelope, I was surprised and delighted to find it was from my closest associate during the War years, Karl Radl.

"My Dear Commander:

"Can it be that almost fifteen years have passed since we last saw one another? There is so much to catch up on and so much to reminisce about. The last I heard, you escaped in '48 and became a close associate of Generalmajor Gehlen.

"In my own case, I, too was acquitted by U.S. authorities but was retried by the German Government in 1949 and sentenced to two years in labor camp. After my release in 1952, I met and married Trude Ochsner. We have two lovely youngsters. By God's grace, I became a successful tradesman. I still commute to Frankfurt on the RB-15 line each day.

"From time to time our destinations may have coincided. How is it we've always missed each other? Hoping you will write back and we can spend an evening or two together talking about old times. Fondly, Karl"

I was quick to respond to the letter, and within a week I joined my dear friend in Usingen.

His home, while by no means sumptuous, was ample, as was his girth. His wife was a short, somewhat stout, woman, but then Karl was not a tall man. Their children, Hans and Eva, eight and six, were apple-cheeked urchins right out of a woodcut from a Grimm Brother's fairy tale, flaxen-haired, blue-eyed, and conspicuously German.

The three days we spent together seemed like three hours as we relived times past, singing the old war songs as well as Viennese lieder. Although I could never relate that I envied my former adjutant, I celebrated his life, which had taken a different turn from mine after the War. Karl had married in his late thirties – *one* wife, and they seemed quite content with one another. Trude Ochsner Radl was no one's idea of a beautiful or glamorous woman, but does one's happiness truly depend on what the world thinks of one's mate? I'd been married three times, the first time to a mere girl who knew nothing of life; the second to a beauty, when she announced her pregnancy with a child I'd seen twice in the past ten years; and the third to an attractive ex-countess. The marriage to Ilse was peaceful enough, but it was more a marriage of convenience to both of us than a true love-match.

I was a millionaire. Like it or not, my services were still in demand for goods by which one man could kill another. I had been called, "the most dangerous man in Europe," more times than I cared to remember, but with that appellation came the knowledge that my own life was always at risk. On the other hand, Karl Radl, whose fortune was a twentieth of mine's, biggest worry was that he'd miss the RB-15 rail line to or from Frankfurt-am-Main and be delayed coming from or going to his home for an extra hour or two. I drove a large, late-model Mercedes wherever I traveled, be it in Madrid, Dublin, Buenos Aires, or Vienna. Karl Radl didn't even have a car. Yet, I found myself wondering, whose life was the happier, which of us was more content?

In early April 1967, I received a call from Joe Raanan asking me to meet him in Munich. Since we'd remained friends and since I'd continued to do occasional advisory work for the Mossad, I had no difficulty in agreeing to his request. We met two days later at the Café Icarus, where we'd last seen one another more than four years earlier.

Raanan, as blunt as ever, stated his business immediately. "Otto, we've got a very sensitive problem, a diplomatic one, not a hit-man operation."

"I'm listening."

"Nasser is threatening to close the Straits of Tiran. He's demanded that the United Nations Emergency Force clear out of Sharm el-Sheikh."

"Didn't they learn their lesson back in '56?"

"Obviously they've been spoiling for Round Three since 1948."

"Do they have any idea that Israel has increased its strength and preparedness since that time?"

"They must have, Otto, but Nasser doesn't seem to care."

I was not unaware that Israel's only Red Sea seaport, Eilat, was at the head of the Gulf of Aqaba. The Straits of Tiran connected the Gulf of Aqaba to the Red Sea. Ninety percent of Israel's oil passed through the Straits, making them strategic for both Israel and Egypt.

"What does U Thant say about this?"

"The U.N. Secretary-General says it's all or nothing. UNEF stays at Sharm el-Sheikh or they're out of the entire region. U Thant and Nasser are at loggerheads."

"If you mean for me to mediate the dispute between President Nasser and Secretary General Thant, it sounds like a bigger job than I'm capable of handling."

"I don't know," my Mossad superior said, smiling. "Sometimes it's the little guys, the one-on-ones, who can make a difference."

"Meaning?"

"You and Yasser Arafat go back a long way," he said. "You know him and he trusts you. He and General Dayan have held peripheral talks over the years. We've approached both men, indirectly of course. Even though he's a Palestinian, and our sworn enemy, he may have some influence on Nasser. Regardless of his public persona, he's nobody's fool. He realizes that if he could be seen as a peacemaker, or even a war-avoider, his standing in the Arab world would be significantly higher, and he might just get a slice of land for the Palestinians."

"Have your people approached Abu Ammar about this?"

"Through an intermediary."

"And?"

"He doesn't hold out much hope, but he's willing to talk."

"Where?"

"I would have suggested Turkey, since it's a Muslim country, but it has relations with Israel and, despite their protestations about eternal brotherhood, there's no love lost between Cairo and Ankara. The Turks aren't Arabs, but they picture themselves as the power player in the region. Time might be very tight."

"What about Cyprus?"

"Probably the safest place, Otto."

Although Cyprus is nominally aligned with Greece, there have been deep-seated problems between its Greek and Turkish populations since before independence in 1960. Kyrenia, which the Turkish Cypriots call Girne, is situated in the north. The dry rises of the Troodos grudgingly give way to a deeply indented, dramatic Mediterranean coast. At a high point overlooking the sea, there is a largely-hidden villa. It was there that I reconnected with my friend, Abu Ammar, better known to the world as Yasser Arafat. After an emotional greeting between us, sweetened by mint tea and baklava, we approached the problem facing both sides.

"What've we got to gain, Otto?" he began. "If the Israelis win, we're treated like shit, and if the Arabs prevail, we're still the 'Niggers' of the Arab world. Either way, the Palestinians lose."

I thought long and hard about his trenchant remark before I responded.

"You're right when you say either way you lose. But exactly what do you have now?"

"Nothing."

"Isn't anything better than nothing?"

"Better the devil you know than the one you don't?"

"Exactly what devil are you're now dancing with? Gaza's a cage. Rather a large cage, but a cage nonetheless."

"What does Moshe have to offer?"

"The potential for peace. The potential for economic development."

"Yes, but within the Zionist state. No one has said a word about a Palestinian homeland."

"At least we can ask these questions of him."

"When is my 'sworn enemy' arriving?"

"Tomorrow morning. Overland from Nicosia rather than by sea from Girne, so it won't look conspicuous to anyone who might be spying, meaning every country in the region, plus the United States and the Soviet Union thrown in for good measure."

The greeting between Moshe Dayan and Yasser Arafat was not nearly as tense as I thought it would be. The two men engaged in the traditional hugs and kisses of this part of the world without preamble. My participation was mostly listening to their dialogue, which, although candid, was not promising.

For his part, Dayan could only offer that a tense truce was better for the Gazans than an all-out war, which could only result in mass destruction within the Palestinians' tiny enclave.

"Yes, but we get no territory of our own. At least if the Arabs win, even if they don't give us something, we get recognition and a voice at the United Nations."

"I wish I had something different to tell you, Abu," Dayan said. "But the Palestinians and the Arabs know I've always been truthful. Perhaps in years to come, under a different administration, things might happen. For our part, could your people even think of recognition of Israel as a state?"

"I'm like you, Moshe with one difference. If you say anything positive about us, you lose your seat in the Knesset, but you preserve your manhood. If I say anything positive about the Zionist presence, I don't retain my leadership role *or* my testicles."

"Gentlemen," I suggested mildly, "could either of you talk with Nasser or his foreign minister? Perhaps the Palestinian representative to the Arab League? Moshe, I know Israel's got open lines of communication to the Saudis and Hussein bin Talal is dependent on the U.S. for a lot of things."

"Unfortunately, Jordan's a weak, follow-along state," Dayan replied. "Egypt views Saudi Arabia as a wallet. As for Nasser's ability to keep a secret, it's akin to the stale old joke: How do you make sure word gets out to everyone in the world? Telephone, telegraph, and tell-a-Nasser."

"What if Jordan and Israel could work out a deal with the Palestine Liberation Front?" I persisted. "Say, Jordan and Israel give the Palestinians a chunk of the West Bank of the Jordan River twice as large as Gaza, Palestine trades the Gaza Strip to Israel for the West Bank territory?"

"In theory that sounds good," Arafat replied, "but then my country has no access to the Sea."

"A customs union irrevocably giving Palestine a seaport and access to it?"

"Israel would never accept that unless the Palestinians acknowledged the legitimacy of Israel."

"Otto, Moshe, unfortunately while the three of us are in lockstep, in the chess game of the Middle East, we're less than pawns," Arafat said sadly. "The only thing worthwhile about this meeting is that I got to visit with two old friends again."

"Anyone willing to take bets on who wins if the Arabs and Israelis fight Round Three?" I asked.

No one was willing to comment.

In May 1967, Israeli Prime Minister Levi Eshkol declared that closing the Straits of Tiran would be an act of war. Egypt immediately picked up the gauntlet and blockaded the straits on May 22, 1967. Oil tankers due to pass through the straits were required to submit documents ensuring their cargo was not destined for an Israeli port. At that time, Israel viewed the Straits of Tiran as vital, since it was from there that Israel received essential vital imports, mainly oil from Iran. A blockade threatened Israel's ability to develop the Negev. With the withdrawal of the UNEF forces, the stage was set for the third war since the creation of the Israeli state.

On June 5, 1967, Israel launched a series of preemptive airstrikes against Egyptian airfields. The Egyptians were caught by surprise. Nearly the entire Egyptian air force was destroyed with few Israeli losses, giving the Israelis air superiority. Simultaneously, the Israelis launched a ground offensive into the Gaza Strip and the Sinai, which again caught the Egyptians off guard. After initial resistance, Nasser ordered the evacuation of the Sinai. Israeli forces rushed westward in pursuit of the Egyptians, inflicted heavy losses, and conquered the Sinai Peninsula.

Nasser initially claimed Egypt had defeated the Israeli air strike. Israeli counterattacks resulted in the seizure of East Jerusalem as well as the West Bank from the Jordanians, while Israel's retaliation against Syria resulted in its occupation of the Golan Heights.

On June 11, a ceasefire was signed. Arab casualties were far heavier than those of Israel: fewer than a thousand Israelis had been killed compared to over 20,000 from the Arab forces. Israel's military success was attributed to the element of surprise, an innovative and well-executed battle plan, and the poor quality and leadership of the Arab forces.

Israel seized control of the Gaza Strip and the Sinai Peninsula from Egypt, the West Bank and East Jerusalem from Jordan, and the Golan Heights from Syria. Israeli morale and international prestige were greatly increased by the outcome of the war. The area under Israeli control tripled. 300,000 Palestinians fled the West Bank and 100,000 Syrians left the Golan to become refugees. Across the Arab world, Jewish minority communities were expelled, with refugees going to Israel or Europe.

34

During the rest of the 1960s, I concentrated on setting up the Paladin Group in Albufera, near Alicante, Spain. The organization specialized in arming and training guerrillas. I originally conceived the Paladin Group as the military arm of the anti-Communist struggle during the Cold War. Under the guise of being a legitimate security consultant office, our real purpose was to recruit and operate mercenaries for conservative regimes worldwide.

In addition to recruiting many former SS members, the Group also recruited from the French Nationalist OAS, the SAC, and the 'Légion étrangère,' somewhat romanticized as the French Foreign Legion. I hired Dr. Gerhard Hartmut von Schubert, formerly of Josef Goebbels' Propaganda Ministry, who had trained security personnel in Argentina and Egypt after the war. to serve as my hands-on manager. Under his guidance, Paladin provided support to the PFLP, led by Wadie Haddad; the South African Bureau of State Security; Colonel Muammar al-Gaddafi of Libya; the Greek military junta of 1967; and the Spanish Dirección General de Seguridad, who recruited Paladin operatives to wage clandestine war against the Basque separatist ETA. We assisted Salazar in his later years as dictator in Portugal.

This was the fourth incarnation of my Friedenthal operations. But, as I looked in the mirror, it was hard to deny that I was aging, and not so gracefully. I was more exhausted each day than I'd been the day before.

Ilse and I continued to see one another sporadically. We'd always remained on the friendliest of terms. Sadly, I was not even invited to my daughter's wedding in Vienna, but then I'd never concentrated on being the father to her that I should have been.

As 1969 gave way to 1970, the constant physical stress of my trips to Ireland, coupled with the continued obstinacy of the British government and the Irish themselves in refusing to grant me citizenship, wearied me to the extent that, as lovely as my retreat in County Kildare was, I decided to sell my estate, albeit at a most handsome profit, and left the lovely green Isle for the last time. I was now nearing sixty-two years of age, and there wasn't a day I didn't awaken with the aches and pains caused by the phenomenal physical stresses of my earlier life.

†

As the year progressed, I noticed changes in my body. The lower part of my back had gotten progressively stiffer, particularly when I lay down at night and after I had sat for more than half an hour at a time. These did not overly trouble me. During my occasional visits to Karl Radl, he told me he experienced many of the same symptoms. I also suffered from the urinary problems I'm told are so common as men age. Frequent attempts at urination at night, were often only partially successful, which meant my sleeping patterns were tied to these difficulties.

Still, I managed to stave off the worst of these symptoms through a rigorous regimen of long walks and exercises in the tepid water pool I'd had installed in a covered shed adjacent to my Madrid villa. At my doctor's direction, I managed to lose ten pounds, not very much, but the physician said this would put less strain on my skeleton.

As my sixty-second birthday approached, I attended my annual physical examination. It seemed to me that the doctor spent significantly more time with me than he had the previous year, and that he paid far more attention than normal to the lower part of my back. I noticed that when he touched certain parts of my spine I felt an increased, although not necessarily sharp, discomfort.

When we sat down after the examination, the doctor asked me numerous questions: Had I experienced increased cramps in my extremities? Did this occur more often during the night or during the daytime? Had I noticed any difficulty in bowel movements? As I answered these, and several other queries, he nodded gravely and wrote notes on a pad.

At the end of the session, I stated, lightly, "Well, Doctor, am I aging more quickly than usual?"

"I don't know that I could say that, Mister Skorzeny, but I would like you to undergo a few more tests."

His words alarmed me, as I'm certain they frighten everyone who hears them. I'd found throughout my life that the greatest fear is fear of the unknown. Although we pretend to stoicism and courage throughout our lives, I, for one, have never gone for a physical examination when, although I somehow knew I was "normal," I was one hundred percent certain there was "nothing wrong." We humans are put on earth for a finite period. All of us know that, but we know it as something that affects *other people*. No matter how old we are, and no matter how much we're told by priests, pastors, and clergymen in general of a much better life beyond our human existence, we cling to life stubbornly, unreasonably, even when pain, disease, and age makes life as we know it almost unbearable.

But why was I suddenly harboring these dark thoughts? The doctor hadn't said anything was particularly *wrong* with me. His answer was one I've since learned is the cautious way physicians usually deal with a question they don't know how to – or maybe don't *want* to – answer. *I don't know if I can say that you're aging more quickly than usual. I would like you to undergo a few more tests.*

"What kind of tests, Doctor? Blood tests? Stress tests?"

"No, Herr Skorzeny. You've been through those routine tests already. I would like to examine your spine by way of an extremely recent experimental diagnostic tool called positive-emission tomography, or, in shorthand, a PET Scan. Unfortunately, we don't have such a machine available in Spain. The closest of these scanners is in Hamburg."

"So you're saying you don't know if anything is seriously wrong, but you're suggesting I travel to Hamburg?"

"Yes. The University Medical Center Hamburg-Eppendorf is one of the world's great oncology institutions."

Now the fear became palpable. I felt myself breathing shallowly, rapidly. I asked for a chair and barely managed to sit without passing out. The doctor, a kindly man to whom I had gone for the past six years, quickly reached for a vial of ammonia smelling salts. It took me the better part of ten minutes to regain my equilibrium.

"You mean a cancer hospital?"

"Yes."

"Tell me, Doctor, have I just been given a death sentence?"

"I think that question is a bit premature, Mister Skorzeny. Unquestionably, with few exceptions, cancer is the most fearsome disease known to man. We've been able to recognize it for hundreds, maybe a couple thousand, years. There are an almost incalculable number of such conditions, and none of them work precisely the same."

"Doctor, you know my history."

"That I do."

"I ask you tell me what you think is my condition, as directly as you can."

"Very well," he said, lighting up a cigarette. "Would you like one?" he asked, handing the pack to me.

"Isn't that one of the major causes of cancer?"

"Some types. Lung cancer, certainly. But your lungs seem clear for your age, and I don't think at sixty-two one cigarette will cause irretrievable damage. Why don't you come into my office and we'll go over what I think I found?"

When we sat down, across his desk from one another, he pressed a buzzer on his desk phone. "Mariela, would you please bring me the x-rays we took of Mister Skorzeny's lower spine earlier today? Thank you."

When the large, black, plastic slides were brought in, the doctor hung them on a white-backlit visual screen. He pointed out certain bright points on the x-ray.

"There appears to be a fairly good-sized tumor just to the left of the center of your spine," he said, "and a smaller one above that and to the right. I have no idea whether or not they're cancerous. It might very well be a benign cyst, but with the diagnostic tools I have here, the only way to be certain is by opening you up and performing surgery. If these growths are cancerous, I believe we have a much better chance of treating whatever they are aggressively if we can better pinpoint an early diagnosis."

"You mentioned something about positron emission tomography?"

"Yes. Although this may sound like science fiction to the ordinary man, your own experiences in Germany during the last war demonstrated the tremendous scientific advancements made in Europe and the United States. It seems the more we discover, the faster science seems to move. We've already viewed your spine by x-ray. The next step would be the CT Scan, which uses computer-processed combinations of many x-ray measurements taken from different angles to produce cross-sectional images of specific areas of a scanned object, allowing the user to see inside the object without cutting. Are you following me?"

"I think so. This is all very new – and very scary to me."

"That's a natural reaction, Mister Skorzeny. The PET scan operates differently from the magnetic imagery and x-ray overlap of the CT scan. The simplest way of explaining it is that a radioactive substance is injected into your body. It's not dangerous and it flushes out quickly. The substance 'lights up' cancer cells so we can more accurately assess where they are, where they've grown, things like that."

"What then?" I was not feeling any more comfortable, but the survival instinct had taken over, and now I wanted to learn whatever I could about the foreign element – at least I thought it was a foreign element – that had invaded my body.

The doctor proceeded to explain the numerous procedures if – and he emphasized the word *if* – the growths in my body were cancerous. I also learned that anytime there was even a suspicion of cancer, the reaction in the medical world was akin to an entire battery of air raid sirens during the waning days of World War II. Whereas one might wait a week or longer if a hip was broken or tonsils needed to be removed, once the word "Cancer" was uttered, a patient could rely on instantaneous diagnosis, and, if worse came to worst, treatment. Cancer patients were treated as if every moment was vital to saving a life.

Thus it was that I found myself in UKE, the Hamburg University Hospital, within three days of my doctor's announced suspicions. And this speed was just as well, for the oncological specialists determined that the two tumors which had developed on my spine were, in fact, malignant.

Within two days after that, I underwent surgery to remove these lesions. When I awoke, I saw from the calendar that I had been in a state of unconsciousness or semi-consciousness for three days. Oddly enough, I did not feel pain. Indeed, I felt *nothing*, and that truly frightened me. But I was still alive, and now I was fully conscious.

"The good news, Herr Skorzeny," the surgeon, a competent-looking, handsome man in young middle-age, announced, "is that we seem to have eradicated the tumors. They don't appear to have spread, and they're what we call primary. There is, however, unfortunate news."

"But I *am* alive? And might I expect to remain alive for the time being?"

"The answers to those questions is affirmative. That does come with bad news, however." I looked directly at the name stitched on the chest of his blue surgical outfit, "Michael Stuntz, M.D."

"And what is that, Doctor Stuntz?"

"It is most likely you will be paralyzed from the waist down for the rest of your life."

The news was so stunning, so frightening, that I seriously contemplated suicide. There were a number of ways to accomplish this. The quickest, most painless way, of course, was the way in which so many National Socialists had chosen to take their lives when Hitler's reign ended in the fiery inferno of Berlin. During World War II, I had been given such a pill during Operation Greif. It was an oval capsule, approximately the size of a pea, consisting of a thin-walled glass ampoule covered in brown rubber to protect against accidental breakage and filled with a concentrated solution of potassium cyanide. It could be carried in the mouth, shaped as a false tooth; if it was accidentally swallowed it would pass harmlessly through the body.

I'd been instructed to bite down on the pill, crushing the ampoule to release the fast-acting poison. Since the end of the War, potassium cyanide was a means of avoiding physical torture, which would result in confessions that could be extremely damaging to one's cause.

However, as days passed and I more-or-less regained my mental and emotional equilibrium, I came to the conclusion that as long as I was still alive, and as long as my mind was functioning as strongly as ever, I would plan and plot, scheme and work tirelessly, to address this impediment in any way possible.

Within the first ten weeks after my surgery, I endured radiation therapy, wherein highly-concentrated radioactive particles bombarded specific portions of my body in the vicinity of the operation. I was surprised, perhaps even astonished, that the radiation treatments were not horrendously painful during the first half of my treatment. During the second half, I suffered radiation burns, which were tolerable, provided the attendant providers ensured that my skin was deeply moistened after each such treatment. The pain was no more than a very severe sunburn, and God knows I'd experienced worse during my days on the Russian front, and later at Luxor.

It was the realization that I was surviving these treatments that gave me the first hope – the impossible dream – that somehow I might one day find myself walking once again, even if I was propelled by a cane.

It was my decision to endure six months of sheer hell – pain the likes of which I had never known any time during my life. Constant falls at unexpected times. Knees buckling, ankles slipping sideway, crashing falls on both sides of my back and my front. Hours and countless more hours strengthening my arms to carry my weight when – if – I would ever advance to using crutches.

Weeks of daily sitzbaths, hot and cold, to encourage the regrowth of almost totally pinched, starved nerves. Endless massages, which felt good until they were followed by bending and stretching movements, which were so painful I passed out several times rather than enduring them.

Exhilarating successes, and, more frequently, agonizing, debilitating setbacks.

I remained in hospital or on the hospital grounds during the entire six months of physical therapy which made my entire career in the four Friedenthals seem like child's play. But for Doctor Stuntz, there was no way I would have, or could have, emotionally survived.

"Why am I even doing this?" I asked him on so many occasions he must certainly have become more than impatient at this endlessly complaining husk surrounding what had once been a Herculean body. "You told me I would never walk again, so why even bother putting me through this insane effort."

"I did *not* tell you that you would never walk again," he responded with endless patience, never raising his voice, never losing what appeared to be his incessant smile and his contagious good humor. I said to you, "It is *most likely* you will be paralyzed from the waist down for the rest of your life. *Most likely* does *not* mean absolutely, positively, certain. And I'm encouraged by what I see. You must have been a helluva man in your time."

"*In my time*, you insolent puppy?" For the first time since I'd been diagnosed with the dread disease, I found myself strong enough mentally and emotionally to give a smart-mouthed retort. "I'll have you know that less than five years ago I was teaching commandos who could have sliced off your balls with a snap of their fingers."

"Oh, yeah, big shot," he retorted, getting into the mood of the game. "Then prove me wrong. Stop bitching about how hard it is, how painful it is, how impossible it is, and get your fat arse back into the gym and prove me wrong. And while you're at it, if you can make it on crutches over to that table, there's a pack of Gauloises and a liter of Mouton Cadet waiting for you."

On April 4, 1971, I walked out of the UKE Hospital under my own power, into the waiting car of my adjutant and closest friend, Karl Radl, and, surprise of surprises, my lovely daughter Waltraut, now a grown, married woman of thirty-one. Doctor Stuntz had arranged for some of my old *kameraden*, most of them now successful pillars of West German society, to be present at my "graduation." Not that I could necessarily hop, skip, jump, or even walk *completely* on my own, without the aid of a sturdy cane. But once again I had beaten the odds, and whether I was in a lot of pain or less pain, because of modern medicine and an old-fashioned, humane surgeon, who never allowed me to quit, I walked straight and tall into the morning sun of springtime Hamburg.

35

In 1938, the German-Jewish composer, Kurt Weill, who'd fled Germany with the coming of the National Socialists in 1933, composed a song for a Broadway Musical, which remains popular to this day. The American singer, Frank Sinatra, recorded the work, *September Song* three times, most recently in 1965. As 1974 became 1975, the cancer had returned. This time, it was not spine cancer, but lung cancer. With this cancer, I did not suffer the impossible, debilitating pain. Nor was I crippled so that I would never walk again. But the immutability of the Angel of Death hovered about my shoulders.

More and more I was content to simply sit on a soft rocking chair that had been specially built for me, or, even more frequently, to lie in my bed, propped as comfortably as my condition would allow, and listen to the music of times past, *The Emperors' Waltz*, *Die Fledermaus*, even *Lili Marleen*.

And the lyrics of *September Song* held a richer, deeper meaning for me, now that I understood their meaning with greater clarity.

"Oh, it's a long, long while from May to December
But the days grow short when you reach September
When the autumn weather turns the leaves to flame
One hasn't got time for the waiting game.

Oh, the days dwindle down to a precious few
September, November
And these few precious days I'll spend with you
These precious days I'll spend with you."

EPILOGUE

Otto Skorzeny died peacefully in his bed of lung cancer on July 5, 1975 in Madrid. He was 67 years old. At no point in his life did Skorzeny ever denounce Nazism.

He was given a Roman Catholic funeral Mass in Madrid on August 7, 1975. His coffin was draped in the Nazi colors. His body was cremated afterwards, and his ashes were later brought to Vienna to be interred in the Skorzeny family plot at Döblinger Friedhof. His funeral was attended by dozens of German military veterans and wives, who did not hesitate to give the one-armed Nazi salute.

One man who attended the funeral, and stayed conspicuously in the background, was none other than Yosef Raanan, a fellow Austrian who had lost most of his family to the Holocaust. He flew in from Israel at his own expense to pay his respects to his former agent, SS Colonel Otto Skorzeny.

THE END